MW01106124

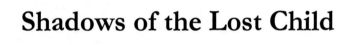

Shadows of the Lost Child

Also by Ellie Stevenson

Ship of Haunts: the other Titanic Story (novel)
Watching Charlotte Brontë Die and other surreal stories

For more information on Ellie Stevenson and her work see:

http://elliestevenson.wordpress.com
http://www.facebook.com/Stevensonauthor
http://twitter.com/Stevensonauthor

Shadows of the Lost Child

Ellie Stevenson

Rosegate Publications

First published in 2014 by Rosegate Publications
Copyright © Ellie Stevenson 2014

ISBN 978-0-9572165-5-6

Image © Shutterstock
Cover design by James Allwright

For Cass, Leonie and Amber

Always loved and always remembered

About Shadows of the Lost Child

The Present

Aleph Jones is running away but the house he ends up in turns out to be haunted. Or is it just him? For Aleph has a terrible secret that's changed his life.

Cressida Sewell's daughter won't speak and she sets up a meeting to get Aleph's help. But Cressida has a hidden agenda and Alice, the daughter, knows more than she's saying.

About Aleph.

Guinevere James is not what she seems. Disguised as Aleph's business client, she wants to solve an age old murder and learn about the children who vanished.

Aleph and Alice can hear them scream.

The Past

Miranda and Thomas live in the slums. Miranda's mother runs a pub but in their attempts to protect her from slander, they set on a path to even more trouble.

Then Tom meets Alice and the past and the present begin to collide, with dangerous consequences.

1

Now – Aleph

I've always lived in the shadow of churches. Now, when I see one, I walk the other way.

It was Thursday morning, the beginning of spring. I walked down Narrowboat Lane to the arch, and under the archway onto the street. I saw the house, it was over to the left; it looked quite something. Then I raised my eyes above the windows and saw what was towering high above it. An enormous church. A single word sprang to my lips. Or maybe two.

'Hell,' I said. 'Hell and damnation.'

Not just a church behind the house, but a great big giant, a monster of a thing, all gables and parapets, much more like a cathedral really. My heart sank, for I knew what it meant, another place I'd have to turn down.

'Curdizan Abbey,' said the voice beside me, 'and don't say no to the house just yet. It has some truly *amazing* features.' I shook my head and looked to the right and there was Gemma, from Cloud House Properties. The word *amazing* wasn't strictly accurate. I imagined the house had draughty rooms and uneven floors, and doors that didn't quite fit properly. But, what did I think the woman would say? She was an estate agent after all. Gemma Pearce held out her hand.

'Good to meet you, Mr Jones.'

'Good to meet *you*,' I said, smiling, and grasped her hand which was small and neat. She was blonde, beautiful, tall and thin with china doll features and perfect straight hair. I could feel the benefits of the house already.

We moved a bit closer and she jangled her keys, and a flash of the sun caught the edge of the steel. A sharp strip of light fell down from the sky, splitting the steps up ahead in two. There was light and dark and I knew which side of the steps were mine. I raised my head and there was the abbey, all of a shimmer. It almost felt like some kind of welcome.

'It seems to me it's yours already,' said Gemma coyly, as she pushed on the door, which was old and warped. I followed her in.

No, I thought, as we entered the hall, *it's not my house*. But it was, really.

Later that day I was standing inside the estate agent's office. The lovely Gemma had long since gone, leaving me there with somebody different. Exceedingly different. Her eyes were cold and her face disapproving.

'You're *self-employed*?' she said, frowning. 'We'll have to see your accounts, I'm afraid.'

'But I don't have any accounts,' I said. 'I don't earn enough to be VAT registered.' I could feel the palms of my hands sweating. This wasn't going the way I'd hoped.

'Well, what about your tax returns? We do need to see you can cover the rent.'

The way she was making me feel right now, I doubted I could. I said nothing.

'Do you have any other assets? A house, perhaps, or maybe some savings?' I shook my head. *Nothing*, I thought, *that's what I've got.*

Before, I'd lived in my girlfriend's flat, I hadn't needed any assets, not even things like a washing machine. We'd shared possessions, plates and everything. I thought my life was hers, forever. Now, I needed to rent a place. I knew I could afford it, so what was the problem?

The woman before me was frost dressed up. I knew about that, how people could change, but I still didn't like it, it made me nervous. I knew I'd never win her over.

'I have got savings,' I said stiffly. 'More than enough for the rent, as it happens.' I hated baring my soul like this.

'Well, that's good news,' she said, smiling. The smile went nowhere near her eyes. 'You can pay the rent for the house in advance. The whole six months.'

It was tall and rambling, in the centre of town, three storeys high, and I knew there must be something wrong, for a house this big to be offered this cheap. Well, not that cheap, but cheap enough for me to afford it. Even with all the rent in advance. I guessed it must be a wreck inside.

'How long has it been on the market?' I'd asked Gemma.

'I'm not quite sure,' said Gemma vaguely, twirling her hair around her fingers. 'About three months.'

'So why did the previous tenant leave?'

'I'm not quite sure,' she started to say, but stopped abruptly at the look on my face. 'She died, actually.'

'Ah,' I said.

'Not in the house,' said Gemma, quickly. 'She died in hospital, after a stroke. She was eighty-eight and deaf as a post, the poor old thing. She'd lived in the house all the time she was married.' She glanced ahead.

'The house is a bit neglected, sadly, and I know there isn't a washing machine, but at least that means you can choose your own.'

I laughed out loud, I couldn't help it. The woman was clearly a natural at this, she was already trained in estate agent speak. I thought she was very convincing, I guess I wanted to be convinced. The house had something, was in some ways perfect, tall and old and great for an office, as well as a home. I saw myself in my fantasy world, doing it up and making it smart, clients climbing the wide stone steps, pouring happily through the doors. Turning a shell into a home. And then I remembered.

There was no future. Not for the house, and not for me. Even now, I still forgot.

The sun went in and all of a sudden the day seemed cold and the house run down. Gemma and I were standing in the kitchen. I didn't like it. Gemma was right, it *was* basic.

'There *is* a fridge-freezer,' she said tersely, sensing my mood but still valiant, gesturing to an upright object, standing squat, in the middle of the room.

'What a strange place to put a fridge-freezer,' I said, indifferent.

'There's plenty of room in here,' said Gemma. 'I expect Mrs Parks thought to make it homely.'

Homely wasn't the word I'd have used. The kitchen was huge, with three old windows facing the back. They had very old glazing and strong iron bars. The glass was cracked and warped in the way that only old glass can be. Ignoring the dirt, I could barely see out. The floor was covered in cheap lino and the air of neglect was incredibly strong, I could almost smell it.

'Why don't we go upstairs,' I said.

2

Then – Miranda

The pub was busy, she hated it busy, she often longed for the quiet nights when nobody came. After Da had just died. But Da had run a successful pub, the people came back, the old regulars *and* the strangers, once they knew it was alright to come. Ma didn't mind, it kept her occupied, a pity hard work wasn't enough. If only her father hadn't died.

'You mustn't say that word, Miranda,' her mother would say. 'I don't like you saying that dreadful word.'

'But he is dead, Ma,' Miranda had said, 'and he's not coming back, now, or ever. He's dead, remember?'

She shuddered to think how cruel she'd been, but at the time she couldn't have cared, she'd wanted to make her mother cry, so they could find comfort, support in each other. Instead of being split by fear and dread, of poverty, loss and not having enough.

It made Miranda feel she'd died too. And that was the worst feeling of all.

Living in Curdizan Low was hard. There were so many pubs, most of them newer or smarter than theirs. Tom once said he'd counted them all, there were over two hundred in the whole city. Miranda snapped back.

'If you've the time to count all the pubs, you're far too idle, you should be in here, helping me out. Hurry up Tom and wash these glasses.' She hadn't seen Thomas again for days.

And now, tonight, he hadn't turned up, and her ma was in another of her moods, and had gone off somewhere, not for the first time. Miranda was on her own in the bar, and people were talking about the weather, so much warmer and wasn't that good? Miranda said nothing, these people were strangers, summer in the Low was as bad as the winter, worse sometimes. There weren't any floods or the freezing nights, or having to manage on poor coal, but the smells that came with summer were worse, the dung and the flies and the local abattoirs. She swatted an imaginary fly away. Then the woman with the coat came in.

She was young and thin and Miranda's height, and wearing a hat, which made her look respectable, almost, but no decent girl would visit a pub on a Saturday night, not on her own, and Miranda knew it. The first time she'd seen her, Miranda had thought she was someone official and had called for her mother to help her out. But it turned out the woman was nobody special, for all she was pretty, and now her mother had vanished again, just like the last time. Miranda glowered.

'I'll have a jug full, love, if you would,' the young woman said, adjusting her hat and her lovely hair, tucking the thick curls under the brim.

She doesn't deserve to have hair like that. She poured out the ale and slopped a little.

'Your mother not in the pub tonight?'

'What's it to you?' Miranda said. She didn't see why she had to be nice. They didn't need people like her in here.

'I'm only asking, love,' said the woman. 'I thought I saw her leave just now, as I walked in. Must have been somebody else I saw.' Miranda's eyes narrowed as she watched the intruder.

'I think she's gone out looking for Thomas.' Miranda wished she hadn't spoken, she shouldn't have told the cow anything, and both of them knew the words were a lie.

'I expect you're right, my love,' said the woman.

I'm not your love, Miranda thought, gritting her teeth and wiping the jug. *You're hardly only a few years older than me.* She didn't know why she hated Curtis – no, she did, it was what she implied, with her looks and her manner, and the things she suggested, hinted at even. *Go why don't you, and don't come back.*

The young woman left.

After she'd gone, Reg came up to the bar to see her. He was kind but dull and both of them knew he was sweet on her ma. He also worked part-time in the pub.

'You don't want to mix with types like her.'

'I wasn't,' said Miranda. 'I was serving her ale, like I always do.' A woman appeared, his sister Cath, she shooed Reg away and stood in his place, her eyes on Miranda.

'He's trying to tell you something, love.' Miranda waited.

'She's young, but a woman with men for friends. If you get my drift.'

Miranda nodded, she did get it. She'd known before they opened their mouths, before they started interfering. What she also got, but didn't say, was that Curtis had implied her mother was too.

3

Now – Aleph

I took to the house, in a strange sort of way, it was tall and thin and elegant somehow, with a road at the front, cobbled and quaint and steps leading up to the strong front door. The rooms were vast, with very high ceilings, and although the window panes were small, and barred at the back, light came in and showed up the dust and all the potential. There was plenty of room for an office upstairs.

The third and top floor I kept for myself, including a room with huge sash windows, which gave me a view looking onto the street. Maybe the street lights would stop me from sleeping. They didn't as it happened. I was often awake.

The street was in a good part of town, although Curdizan High had once been rough. Now it was fresh with refurbished streets and tarted up buildings, apart from mine. There were plenty of tourists wandering around. I lay in my bed that very first evening, looked at the sky through curtainless windows, and heard the shouts of drunken youths. I'd never lived in the centre before, was bemused by the noise, although not that troubled. The things that kept me awake were worse. I mourned the past, and along with the past, I mourned myself, my carefree self, who'd long since died.

I must have drifted off at some point, and was woken up by children's voices. I looked at my watch, it was half past two. *Christ!* I thought, *those kids should be in bed by now.*

I dragged myself up and peered outside, but all I could see were the street lights outside, no tourists, nothing, not even an urban fox or a dog. My house was on an old cobbled road called Old School Lane, a shortcut through from Narrowboat Lane, the main shopping street. Just past my house, at the other end, the Lane curved sharply round to the left and joined a street called Scriveners Road. The kids had obviously gone that way. I swore, loudly, thinking my chance for sleep had gone. I was right, it had.

Later that day, I went to the estate agent's to return the inventory, wondering if I might see Gemma. I walked through the door and as I did, my heart sank, for there at the desk was the woman I'd met the previous time. I read the badge attached to her shirt – Marianne Parks – it made me pause. 'The previous tenant was a Mrs Parks.' She knew what I meant.

'My mother,' she said. 'She died recently. And she was the *owner*. I'll take that.'

'There's not much on it,' I told Ms Parks, talking about the inventory. 'There was too much wrong to put it all down.' Realising then, how tactless that sounded. Marianne Parks didn't bother to reply.

'How are you finding the Old Schoolhouse?' she said, slowly, for once not looking me straight in the eye.

'Is that what it was?' I said, interested. A name like that could be good for business. The woman smiled.

'Thanks for the form, Mr Jones,' she said. 'We'll send you out a copy shortly.' She turned away, I was being dismissed. I headed for the door, thinking; I decided to pay a visit to the library. As yet no clients had found me in Curdizan.

'Have you heard them yet, Mr Jones?' she said. I stopped, short.

'What did you say?' I said sharply, turning around.

'Have you heard the children's voices in the night?'

'Yes,' I said. 'I heard them last night, about half past two. Parents these days are far too lax.'

'And were the children crying or laughing?'

'Neither,' I said. 'They were chattering loudly, in high pitched voices. I was half asleep when they woke me up. Tourists, I guess.'

Marianne Parks gave a slow, small smile, a smile that made me feel quite uneasy. But not as much as the words that followed.

'No, Mr Jones, they weren't tourists, or even the kids who live around here. The children you heard were the School Lane ghosts.'

4

Then – Thomas

I should have been helping Miranda in the pub, but instead I went up to Curdizan High, to look for Louise. The High's the part where the abbey is, as well as my school, although nothing about the place is high. I walked past the school and finally came to Pearson's Tenements, that's where she lives, but Louise wasn't there, surprise, surprise. I wasn't surprised, the place was a dump, but all the same, I had to look. The tenement building was tall and grim, tiny spaces joined by a stairway and open landings, the black of the open night in between. I thought they were more like rooms than landings, people's possessions scattered about, rooms on the outside. I thought of escape.

I once saw a woman jump from a landing, far too high from the ground to be safe, but almost worse, too low to be dead, and gone in a flash. They patched her up, as best as they could, and she even went back to her room for a bit, but she never walked the same after that and not long after, finally died. I didn't know it at the time, but her name was May, and she was also Louise's ma. I never did learn which room she came from.

It's a maze inside the tenement building, stair after stair to each new landing, the landings themselves being almost homes, with chairs or a table and a dog chained up and even the odd bit of carpet or rug. But the landings were cold, an outside cold and all exposed to kids like me.

I shivered, scared in the black of the stairway, I knew I ought to go back, and soon. Miranda would be wondering where I was. But I'd promised old Pike I'd find Louise.

'He's *Mister* Pike,' my ma would say, but she didn't know

Pike the way I knew him, he didn't deserve to be called *Mister*. He was cold, indifferent and sometimes cruel; he'd said if I didn't find Louise, he'd throw her out of the school for good, and she'd end up lost, like Miranda's ma. I didn't know what he meant by that, but I didn't much like the way he'd said it, and I liked Louise, she wasn't rough like most of the kids, and she lived in a flea pit, storeys high. If I had to live in Pearson's Tenements, in amongst all the privy smells, I'm sure I'd forget to go to school. School would be just a dream or something.

I reached a landing, the fourth or fifth, I didn't know which, so I tossed a huge stone over the edge, and counted until I heard it land. Although I'd looked, I hadn't found her. I'd even tried a few of the doors, but nobody seemed to know her name. A shadow slunk by and I held my breath, you're never alone in a place like this. I turned around, got ready to run, but a hand shot out and grabbed my collar, pulling me back, very sharply. Somebody's hand against my mouth. The somebody spoke.

'Tom, Thomas, you shouldn't be here, I haven't the time to look for you. I wouldn't have come, and won't the next time, it's only because your ma was worried.'

Ma, worried? That was a laugh. I snorted, loudly, and wriggled my collar out of her grasp. It was Miranda from the pub, looking wild as always, her eyes glowing bright in the light from the moon. She tossed her hair and I stared right back.

'How did you know I was here?' I said.

'I know you well enough by now. The sort of place you like to go. Each to their own, that's what I say.'

She looked around as we walked back down and hurried along the shabby street, all shadows and shade and stinking gutters. A rat rushed past and Miranda's nose twitched, as if to say, *You see what I mean?* I grinned in the dark, I liked rats and I liked Miranda, although not as much as I liked Louise.

'I presume you're coming back with me?' Miranda asked, as we stopped on the corner by Curdizan Church, the church that stood in the shade of the abbey. I nodded, sadly.

'Yes,' I said, torn between my longing for a pie at the end of my shift, and the word I'd given to find Louise. Shame on me, for the hot pie won. We hurried down Scriveners Road to the alley, through the alley to Convent Court and down to the streets called Curdizan Low.

'Don't be dragging your heels,' said Miranda. 'I'm supposed to be serving ale right now, and washing the glasses you didn't do.'

I smiled to myself as we hurried along. Collecting the glasses and washing them after was what I was paid for, and I liked my job at the Keepsake Arms. The money I earned from my job at the pub helped my ma, and it helped Miranda, her da was dead and Mrs Collenge was never around.

Miranda was good in the pub, I thought, cheerful and bright, but not too friendly, sharp enough to keep them drinking, spending their money, not talking to her. I wished again, like I'd wished before, that she was my sister and not just a girl who could boss me around. Neighbours and mates, that's what we were, even though she was all grown up. Miranda Collenge was eighteen.

5

Now – Aleph

Marianne Parks' words shocked me. *I've never believed in ghosts*, I thought, *so why start now?* Or at least, not the ones that weren't in my head. I cycled home in the fading light, forgetting my plan to go to the library, hardly aware of the world around me. Something had shifted inside my head. Starting again was proving to be what I'd guessed all along, another illusion. *You're never allowed to forget*, I thought.

I'd wanted to ask Ms Parks some more but she didn't seem eager to talk fully. The door had opened and someone walked in, another gullible tenant, probably, eager to part with some hard-earned cash. I left them alone.

I cycled away, vaguely troubled, and now with even more questions than answers. I rode with care down Narrowboat Lane, ducking my head when I came to the arch. I was almost home when a woman stepped out in front of the bike. I braked, sharply. The woman shrieked and her shopping and handbag fell to the ground.

Old School Lane was pedestrianised, which was just as well in the present circumstances. I dropped my bike and hurried towards her. The woman was struggling to pick up her parcels, margarine, bread and a bag of potatoes, all in one hand. Her other hand was glued to her ankle. *At least she's alive*, I thought, detached. My mind froze over.

'Are you alright?' I heard myself say.

'I think I've sprained my ankle,' she said.

When she finally removed her fingers, it was true the ankle seemed slightly puffy, a reddish colour, rather than pale. I picked up her handbag and gathered her food. 'My house is just here,' I told the stranger. 'Please come inside, I'll bandage that up.'

'Oh no, it's okay,' the woman replied, but her voice was faint and the no meant yes. I helped her make her way up the steps. Once inside, I steered her gently into the kitchen, and then to a chair, putting her shopping by her side.

'Would you like tea, or maybe some whisky?' I paused, waiting.

'Whisky, please,' she said smiling, her eyes darting all over the place. 'This is quite some kitchen, much bigger than mine. You've got so much space.'

'It's certainly different,' I said, dryly, passing her a mug with the whisky in it. 'I've just moved in so there aren't any glasses.' I sat down opposite the stranger and smiled.

'Aleph Jones? That's your name?' The woman was reading the estate agent's brochure; I'd put it there beside my tea.

'Yes, that's right. I know it's unusual, everybody says so.'

'A name to go with the house, I'd say. Quite unique.' She took a deep breath and looked behind her, stared at the hall. 'I'd love to have a look at the place; does that sound rude?'

A little bit forward, perhaps, I thought, but I wasn't offended, not in the least. Then she blushed.

'Not now, of course, not with the ankle. Climbing the stairs might be too much.'

'I'd offer to run you home,' I said. 'But I don't have a car.' I stopped abruptly. The woman smiled.

'I don't suppose you need one here, in the centre of town? Isn't this road pedestrianised?'

'Yes,' I said. 'But not round the corner in Scriveners Road. Would you like me to call a taxi?'

'When you're ready,' she said, lightly, and I realised then how lovely she was. Her hair was short and slightly spiky, her dark eyes chocolate, the Bournville kind. She was casually dressed, but quite impressive. I stood up abruptly.

'I'll do it now,' I said and vanished, and before very long the taxi was booked.

The rest of our time together passed quickly. She said she'd come into town to shop, I told her I'd meant to go to the library. I didn't say why.

The taxi turned up before I was ready and I noticed her looking around at the hall. I was suddenly seized by a crazy moment, the sort that defines one's life forever, and I asked this woman, who I'd only just met, to come back again and eat with me. 'Tomorrow?' I said.

'I can't tomorrow,' she said, softly. 'I'm going away for a few days' break. With Alice, my daughter.'

She watched my face as she said the word *daughter*, and it felt to me like some sort of test.

'Well how about a week tomorrow?'

We agreed on that and parted happily; she managed the steps to the street quite well. When I'd finally closed the door on my guest, my mind began to drift in reverse, recalling my chat with Marianne Parks.

'You asked if the children were laughing or crying, the School Lane ghosts. Why did you ask that?'

'It's just a rumour, Mr Jones.'

'Yes, Ms Parks, but what rumour?'

'They say it depends on who you are. The good hear laughter, the bad, crying, or even screaming. It's all rubbish, Mr Jones.' She sniffed loudly.

'My mother lived there most of her life, after she married, and she never heard the ghosts, not once.'

But wasn't your mother deaf? I thought.

Those were the thoughts that engaged my mind as I cycled back to the Old Schoolhouse, and caused me to fail to see Cressida Sewell. As time went on I recalled those words again and again, with good reason. I often heard the children at night, just around midnight and sometimes later. But from that day on, they were always sad.

6

Then – Thomas

Mister Pike was the same as always, bored and boring. I didn't know why he turned up at all, I thought it was kids who were meant to hate school. I did, often. But I also liked the porridge they gave us.

I shifted my bum on the hard wooden seat and played around with a couple of words. The work we did was far too easy, my ma had taught me to read already. I was proud of being able to read and write, most of the lads I knew couldn't count, let alone read. I wanted a better paid job than my da, he worked at the mill, when he was sober. A lot of the time he just didn't turn up.

The mill was everything in our street. We were right at the bottom on Haversham Road, our house backed onto the factory walls, you could the hear the generator's constant hum. Because our house backed onto the factory, it was dark at the back, there weren't any windows. There wasn't much light at the front either, the factory's silos towered above us and blocked off most of the sky and sun. Not far away was the factory chimney, belching out horrible smells all day. I hated our street.

I felt the sting as a huge piece of chalk bounced off my arm and onto the floor and under my chair. I seriously thought about throwing it back.

'Time to quit dreaming and starting working, Islip, unless you'd like to be out on your ear.' Pike was yelling as loud as ever but somehow it never made any difference.

'Plenty of lads would like to be you, sitting in the warm and dry all day. Lads who act a little bit grateful, not as if they can't be bothered.'

Warm? In here? He'd got to be joking. I glanced at my feet, which were bare as usual. Ma said I couldn't wear shoes in summer, or even in spring, the money for shoes just didn't exist. Despite all three of us having a job.

I felt a tiny twinge of guilt. Because I'd been late to the pub last night, I'd be docked some pay and Ma would be short, she was always short. My father drank it all away. She wouldn't be pleased that I'd turned up late and she'd no doubt give me some stick for that. But at least I had a ma to go home to, unlike Louise, whose mother was dead. I tried not to think of Louise anymore. Even more guilt.

It wasn't because Louise was missing, I'd done my best, I'd tried to find her, Louise was a mate, she loved to climb trees and beat me at conkers, and when it was hot we swam in the Blue. Our house and the factory were both by the river, which wasn't as good as you'd think it would be. Not when the days were really warm and the dung had been dumped by the corporation.

No, I felt guilty for something else. I hadn't gone looking for Louise at all, despite what I'd said to Miranda later. Looking for her was what I'd done after, after I'd given up looking for Alice. Alice was totally different to Louise; *she* was a girl, all flowers and hair, and pretty to boot. Strangely enough, that's why I liked her.

I was walking home from school one day, just pottering really, kicking at stones and picking up wood we'd use for the fire, and then in the distance, I saw Alice.

She was right by the gate that led to the church on Scriveners Road, Curdizan Church, and holding something in her hand. It was big and square and flashed in the light. She saw me looking, and put it away in her bag, quickly. *Posh*, I thought, and I couldn't resist walking closer. Her bag was blue and it looked so clean, as if it was new, and her blonde hair shone and wasn't tied back, *and* she wore shoes, all glossy and smart. None of the kids I knew wore shoes. *Slumming it,* I thought and scowled, jealous, and strangely angry, bitter and resentful. I wanted to live like them, I did, nobody wants to live in a dump. *Sorry Ma.*

I thought the girl would run away, she was far too smart, and I looked a scruff, with my shirt hanging out and my trousers baggy, and me being the third person to have them, but she didn't run away, she just stood there, staring, so I walked closer.

'I'm called Tom. Who are you?'

The girl didn't answer, just shook her head, so I tried again, a different tack.

'Do you live around here? That's my school, across the graveyard.' I pointed behind us. 'That's the door to the joinery workshop, some of the lads are training in woodwork.'

I thought she'd ask if I was one of the lads in training, but she still didn't speak, so I prattled on.

'There are also some lads who are going to be stonemasons, working on the church.'

I saw her glance across at the church and I laughed out loud and shook my head. 'Not *Curdizan Church,* the proper church, the abbey up there.' The abbey twinkled in the sun. She still didn't answer. I felt uneasy.

'Cat got your tongue?' I said impatient.

She shook her head, then pointed to herself and clamped her teeth shut. *Then* I got it.

'You're dumb,' I said. 'You can't speak.'

She hesitated slightly, then she nodded.

'Alright,' I said. 'I can write, can you?' She laughed at that and her blue eyes sparkled, as bright as the sky. *Of course she can write, you stupid prat. She's posh, and rich.*

'I don't have anything to write on,' I said. I felt helpless, useless somehow. Her smile widened.

But I do, she said, and although she hadn't opened her mouth, I could hear her voice as clear as a bell. It was light and fine and sounded like summer. And then she brought the thing from her bag.

7

Now – Aleph

I won't pretend I wasn't nervous, the day Cressida came for supper, that would have been a lie.

Things had been going well recently. Apart from Cressida, I had a new client, a Guinevere James, I was due to meet her early next week. It sounded straightforward, a business analysis, the kind of work I like to do. These days anyway.

I opened the oven door cautiously. My Indian meal was almost ready. All that was needed now was the guest. The doorbell rang.

Cressida stood at the top of the steps, holding mints and a bottle of wine. 'These are for you,' she said, smiling. I ushered her in.

The bells of the abbey rang out in the background.

'Thursday evening is bell ringing practice,' I said to Cressida. 'When I came to see the house, the bells were ringing, even though it was only morning. Gemma from Cloud House said it was a sign, so I thought, *right*, and took the house.'

Cressida smiled and we wandered into the vast kitchen.

'Something smells good,' she said sniffing.

'It's vegetable curry and rice,' I said. 'But I'll tell you now, I didn't make it. Top of the range from M&S or was that Waitrose? I can't quite remember.' Cressida laughed.

'I don't care, so long as it's good. Cooking's not your forté, then?'

I shook my head and she took the glass of wine I gave her.

'I see you've found your glasses, then.' Cressida smiled. 'What's it like living in a haunted house?'

'It's not the house, it's the street that's haunted. Or so I've been told. But how did you hear about the ghosts?'

'Everyone knows the old story, even the strangers and tourists do. But *I* was told they came from the house. This is the Old Schoolhouse?' Cressida queried.

'Yes,' I said, 'but as far as I know there aren't any ghosts. Not in here.' I must have sounded rather curt. Cressida put her hand on my arm.

'It's alright, I'll change the subject. It was just a way to break the ice.' I took a deep breath and smiled at her.

'I'm sorry,' I said. 'I'm feeling rather edgy tonight. Cooking always makes me nervous.'

'Even when you haven't cooked?'

I couldn't help laugh.

Later that evening, after the meal, we took our coffee into the lounge, which overlooked the front of the house. Like the kitchen, the lounge was huge.

'Such a beautiful room,' said Cressida softly. She looked around, clearly curious.

'In a terrible state.'

'Yes, right, I can see you need some new wallpaper, and maybe a carpet, but even so, you could do so much, if you had the time, and the inclination.'

But I do, I thought, and studied my guest. She was beautiful there, no doubt about it. I would almost say she belonged to the house.

But not with you, said the voice in my head. I couldn't allow myself to forget. The light that had shone, faded and died. But I still enjoyed the beauty of form.

Every movement she made was precise. The way she sipped her wine was an art.

An excellent choice, she said to me. Then she reached across and touched my cheek, light as a feather. I flinched, instinctively. She looked surprised and then amused.

'You had a speck of curry on your face, I had to remove it. I like order.'

Looking at the woman, I could well believe it. She was casually dressed, in trousers and shirt, but there was barely a thread or a hair out of place. Even the colour of her watch matched.

Now, you're being silly, I said to myself. *What kind of person makes everything match?*

Someone quite different from me, I thought. But, I still knew I wanted her there.

8

Now – Cressida

It hadn't been hard, Cressida thought, to persuade Aleph to let her stay over. The room she was in was bare but sufficient, it had a bed and a view of the courtyard, the former graveyard of Curdizan Church. And there, in the background, towered the abbey.

There used to be houses next to the church, Aleph had explained, late last night, as they'd both peered out of her bedroom window. He'd pointed to the left and Cressida had looked, but although she'd tried, she couldn't imagine the place in the past. There had been no moon and very little light, just the faint outline of Curdizan Church, now demolished, and the old church wall.

'Where did you say you'd recently moved to?' Aleph had changed the subject abruptly.

'Ebbenheart Green, about two miles out.'

'I've heard that's quite a good place to live. In the suburbs but almost rural, country lanes and quite a few trees.' He smiled, briefly. 'That'll be nice for your daughter, Alice.'

He'd taken well to her having a daughter, Cressida thought, he'd even asked some relevant questions, her age, her interests and then finally, the one that mattered, where had they'd lived before the move?

'Leverhulme,' she'd told him smiling, 'and I was very sorry to leave, but I needed somewhere a bit more central. And then, of course, I work in Curdizan. Convenience matters, being a single mum.'

'Sure,' said Aleph, looking thoughtful. Cressida smiled.

One day soon, she'd tell him the sort of woman she was and then his dreams would be all washed up. Not that he looked like a man with dreams, more like someone haunted by nightmares. *And* he'd been the perfect gent. She tucked into breakfast, suddenly hungry.

Breakfast, like supper, was served in the kitchen, and Cressida almost expected some staff, someone brought in from Downton Abbey like Mrs Patmore or little Daisy. Instead it was just herself and Aleph. Aleph leapt up when she walked in.

'I hope you slept well. Would you like some tea and toast?'

'I'd prefer some bacon and eggs, if you've got them.' Aleph's face fell and Cressida laughed. 'Don't worry, I'm only joking. Though I would like coffee, instead of tea, if there's some left?' As it happened there was.

They sat together, eating and drinking, as if they were friends.

'You're not having toast?' she said, amused, watching him polish off last night's curry.

'I don't eat toast,' said Aleph, shortly.

'What, never?' she asked, smiling, seeing the way his face turned grim.

'Never,' he said, 'I don't like it.'

And that's a lie, she thought, puzzled, looking at Aleph.

'I'm making a list of things you don't do. Drive, eat toast, is there anything else?' It was dangerous, this, but she didn't much care.

'It's a very short list,' he said, sombre, and where she thought he'd be curt or angry, he simply retreated into his shell. She studied the room.

'This kitchen needs a woman's touch. I wouldn't have placed that fridge-freezer there, right in the middle.'

'Neither would I,' Aleph agreed, finishing off the last samosa and washing the pastry down with tea. 'It's been in the middle since I moved in. I'll get around to shifting it sometime.'

She leant towards him, closer, intimate. 'I have to confess to something, Aleph. And not about the freezer's location. It's about my motive for coming here.'

Aleph blinked and looked surprised.

'You know when I stepped in front of your bike and hurt my ankle? I didn't really.'

'No?' said Aleph. He looked uncertain.

'I was thinking of coming to see you anyway. And blaming you for an injured ankle made it so much easier. Because I hoped you'd be kinder, more open.'

'Open to what?' His voice grew chilly.

'Late last night, we were talking about your counselling work, and you said you were particularly interested in speech and language. I'm sure you remember?' Aleph nodded and Cressida continued.

'Then you mentioned your *other* work, where you reverse recorded discussions, and from those reversals, pick up on things that people *don't* say. The hidden meanings behind their words. And how you use those to help people heal.'

'Yeah, I remember talking about that.' He wasn't giving her the slightest help.

'Well, I've got someone I'd like you to help. A child, actually.'

'I told you last night, I don't work with kids.' Aleph stalked off to the back of the room.

'Yes I know, you said, and I read it on your website, but that's why I told you that little white lie.' She hurried across the room towards him. 'I thought if I told you about myself, if you got to know me a little bit better, you might be prepared to make an exception, just this once.'

'No,' said Aleph, shaking his head. 'There are no exceptions, none, ever.'

Cressida begged, she didn't care, she knew she had to get a result.

'All I'm saying is think it over, please don't dismiss this straight away. I'm only asking because it's important. The girl who needs your help is my daughter.'

9

Then – Thomas

I felt I'd been in a dream for weeks. Miranda was acting rather strange, distant, distracted, and Ma was busy, something to do with her work in the laundry, or so she said. So, I thought, *Sod it, I won't go to school, not today, I'll have the day to myself for once. Mister Pike won't throw me out.* And then I remembered my mate, Louise. That's what he'd said he'd do to her, and now she'd vanished. I shook my head.

So what if he did throw me out? I wasn't alone like Louise had been, I'd find myself another job, to go with the one I already had, until I could get some proper work and earn decent pay, be a man. But until that happened, I'd do what I liked.

I sauntered jauntily down the street, aiming for the river and hoping to see some lads I knew, and maybe even cadge a smoke. *What Ma didn't see...* I thought, guiltily. But when I reached the end of the street I changed my mind when I noticed some of the curtains were closed. A sure fire sign that someone had died. I had to know who.

I hurried along Croston as fast as I could, turning right down Blackberry Close and went to see Ben, my undertaker friend. Ben was related to Reg and Cath who worked in the pub, and Tencell & Son was the family firm, but they thought they were too good for a firm that made coffins and buried the dead.

'More fool them,' Ben often told me. 'I make a good living, better than them.'

It was true that people were always dying, around here anyway. Curdizan Low was a grim place to live, although not as rough as Curdizan High where the tenements were and the drunks paraded the streets at night. Living the life Louise did was hard.

I pushed on the door of Ben's workroom, his house had once been a smart coach house, but now was almost derelict in parts, so he got the place for a snip, he said. It was mostly for work, the rooms upstairs were all rotten, although that didn't stop Ben sleeping there nights. The yard next door had a tap and a shed, the water for him and the shed for the horse. The horse was called Norah.

Ben used to call the shed a stable, just for a laugh, but I was surprised it was still standing. Inside the house, there were dozens of rooms, all of them dark, but none as grim as Ben's workshop, with its half-made coffins hanging on the walls. Ben looked up.

'I haven't the time to talk, Thomas, I'm far too busy. We've had one die, unexpected like.'

'That's why I'm here. I want to know who.'

'And what makes you think I'd tell you, lad?' He gave me one of his wicked grins.

'Getting your laundry done on the cheap, or maybe you'd rather look a scruff? Not that I'm sure I can tell the difference.' Ben swung his chisel round and I ducked. He laughed, loudly.

'I guess you won't leave me alone till I've said?'

'That would be right.' I hoisted myself up onto his bench and winked.

'It's Matt McCarthy of Terrace Hall Mews. He died last night, in his sleep, so I'm told. I've just been round to see the corpse. Flat on his back, like you'd expect.'

'Matt McCarthy?' I said, surprised. 'The bloke's not even sixty yet. He shouldn't be dead.'

What I really meant, was McCarthy was rich and nobody wealthy died around here. Not that there were many rich around here. Death was for the poor and hungry, not for the likes of Matt McCarthy.

'I can't believe he's gone,' I said. Matt McCarthy owned

several shoe shops, his wife was dead and he had no kids, so who would run the business now?

'He looked well gone the last time I saw him. But why don't you go and see for yourself?'

'I doubt they'd let me in for a look.' Just for a moment I thought he meant it.

'They might,' said Ben, looking thoughtful, 'if you pretended to be my apprentice. Tagged along, all good and quiet.'

'I'm far too young to be an apprentice.'

'You're far too young to be giving me cheek. Now are we going to his house or not?'

'Yes!' I said and made for the door. I wasn't going to miss a chance like this. I'd never seen anyone dead before, apart from that bloke they found in the river, and he barely looked like a man at all. Matt McCarthy was someone. We hurried along the road to the end.

The corpse was dressed in his shirt and shoes and even sported a loosened tie. His jacket was hanging over a chair, looking as if it needed a home. The man would have looked as smart as ever, except that he wasn't wearing his trousers. He looked almost vacant, not quite there, which of course he wasn't, although where he was, I wasn't quite sure.

'What did he die of?' I said to Ben. I knew most folk didn't die in their sleep, not without a proper cause.

'The demon drink,' said Ben, grinning. 'He drank too much, on too many nights and it did for his liver, and that was that. Remember that Tom, when you get older.' I frowned, silent. I didn't need telling to remember that.

I looked around the room we stood in. Terrace Hall Mews was a smart row of houses, not that far from Blackberry Close. The houses had railings and tiny front gardens, and bright brass rappers for knocking on doors. I'd never been in one of these before, but this one had been fitted out special. Ben bent down and whispered something in my ear. 'It even has an indoor bath.'

'No!' I said, and wondered if he was having me on. Most of us had to share a privy and an outside tap, all we had was the old tin bath, that hung in the yard and rattled in the wind. McCarthy's life had been so different, although not anymore, now he was dead. Death, it seemed, was the great leveller.

When we came out I glanced at the church which was next to Ben's place. A smaller version of Curdizan Church.

'At least he won't have to travel far,' I said, grinning and Ben laughed and punched my arm.

'And that, my lad, makes it easy for me.'

It was then I noticed Miranda's mother. She stood by the hedge that skirted the churchyard, slightly bent over, and wiping her face. She looked to me as if she'd been crying.

I turned away and ran after Ben, I didn't want him to see her there. I hadn't realised she'd known McCarthy, like my ma, she worked in the laundry, that's how I got the job in the pub. The pub didn't bring in that much money, so Miranda and her mother both had jobs. Which didn't explain her knowing the man.

All of a sudden I felt dizzy. I'd had no food since yesterday evening and that had been just a chunk of bread. But it wasn't just that which made me feel odd, I'd been feeling strange for the last few weeks, since the day I'd first seen Alice. I'd been hanging around after school, lately, telling myself I was looking for Louise. I hadn't seen her, or Alice either, but since that time, I'd felt kind of odd, as if I was living in a different world.

As if I wasn't quite here, anymore.

10

Now – Aleph

Cressida stood there pleading her case. I couldn't blame her.

I should have been angry, but she looked so stressed, as any mother would be, and as I waited, out it all came.

'She won't say a word, not a single word to me, ever. And she used to be such a talkative girl. I don't know what I'm supposed to do. It's driving me witless, day after day, always the same.' She paced the floor and back again.

'Perhaps she needs a speech therapist. Or an educational psychologist or a child psychiatrist. Some kind of expert who's right for Alice. She doesn't need me.'

'Do you think I haven't tried all those? I'm talking years not months, Aleph. Do you think I'd be here, asking you this, if I hadn't tried all the alternatives first? Can you imagine something so awful going on for so long?'

Yes, I can, actually.

'She's not like this with everyone else. She talks at school, to her friends, to the teachers, I've even heard her speaking in the classroom so a couple of times I rushed straight in, hoping to persuade her to talk to me too. And guess what happened? She just clammed up.'

'That must have been hard,' I said, softly.

'You should have seen the look she gave me. *I can't even trust you to leave me alone.* So that's the reason we've come to Curdizan. I thought a new start in a different town might help her improve, and then after that, I thought you might help, could help her start talking.'

'I don't know why you had that idea, I don't have skills in helping people speak. And as I've told you, I don't work with kids.'

'But you do have a special technique you use.' She waved a portable drive in my face. 'There's a sound file on here. Play it, please.'

I sighed heavily, and we went upstairs to find my laptop. I inserted the drive and found the file. Then I pressed play. Her daughter's voice filled the room.

'And the trees make sounds like light and dark, waving their way into autumn weeds, and casting off the spell of summer.' I stopped the file.

We stood silent, hearing the echoes of the words unsaid. I was wondering how I'd got to this place.

'She made that bit up herself,' said Cressida.

'The rhythm's lovely,' I said, smiling.

'She's always playing with words in class. Writing them down and reading them out, she's a natural, really. But what do I hear when she's out of school, when we're alone? Not one thing, not even a song. It breaks my heart.' Cressida paused. 'It's almost as if I'm being punished for something.'

'I'm sure that's not true,' I said mildly. Cressida shrugged.

'I need to find out what's the matter. That's the reason I've come to you. I know you do this special work, the work with recordings. Playing them back the wrong way...'

'In reverse.'

'Playing files backwards, and hearing the words that people don't say. If I can get her to talk to someone, then record it, I might find out what's going on. I'll have to get somebody else to do it, she won't talk to me, I know she won't.'

'But what if she won't discuss what's the matter?'

'I've no idea.' Cressida said, sadly. I felt my resistance fading fast.

'I'll give it a go,' I said, slowly, 'but I very much doubt a reversal will help. She'd have to give me something to go on. And, remember, Cressida, I've warned you already...'

'I know, I know. You don't work with kids.' She caught my gaze and smiled, grimly.

'Alice isn't just a kid,' she said.

11

Then – Thomas

I'd thought Alice was just like us, like me and Louise. Well, not like us, she was different, posh, but a kid all the same, who liked to laugh when things went right and ended up sad when things went wrong. But Alice was something else entirely.

She'd pulled the square thing out of her bag and I saw up close that it wasn't really square, but more rectangular. She pressed her thumb to the front, gently, the part she told me was called a screen, and the thing lit up with tiny pictures. On a blue background. She pressed again on one of the shapes and then there were letters, like on a typewriter. I knew about typewriters because Miranda said they had them at Chaucer's; she'd always wanted to work in their office. I told my ma, and she said the same, 'It's bound to be better than working in a laundry.'

My da, by the fire, had roared with laughter. 'You're not bright enough for that, Carol.'

Alice leant forward and touched the letters, one at a time, and words appeared in the space above them. 'Hi, I'm Alice.'

I was stunned, speechless, I couldn't think of a thing to say. I took a deep breath.

'Hello Alice, how are you doing?' She shook her head.

'Not like that, like this, stupid.' She grabbed my finger and at first I resisted, but she kept on tugging, and as I watched she guided my finger across the screen. I spelt out my name.

'Tom, to Alice.'

'Cool,' she replied.

'No,' I said, 'it's mild today.' Alice laughed, a genuine laugh, it was light and high and strong, from the heart. I realised then, that was what had been missing, she'd looked very sad. But she wasn't sad now.

'No, *cool* means, okay, good, I approve, not cool as in cold.'

'Fine. If you say so,' I said, thinking, *Really? How stupid*, but, of course, I was pleased she was talking to me. Sort of talking, anyway. She was writing again.

'Here, you take it, you have a go.' She passed me the thing and I stood there frozen, afraid I might drop it. 'Go on, try it, it's called a tablet.' Now, I *was* confused.

'A tablet is something you take when you're ill.'

'It's also a computer, a flat computer. This one's an iPad.'

'What's an iPad, or a computer?' I felt bewildered. Alice wasn't posh, she was out of my league. I realised I was still holding the tablet. I put my thumb to the top of the screen and dozens of pictures appeared before me, all in colour. That was crazy, totally amazing. They were faces, different people, and one of the people looked like Alice. With a small dark woman.

'Is that your ma?'

'Yes, that's my mum. Her name's Cressida.'

'You don't look anything like each other. Do you take after your father, then?'

'Yeah, a bit, but my father's dead.'

'Sorry,' I said. 'Mine is too.'

She smiled again, a bond had been forged. She leant across me and carried on typing.

'Can I take your picture?'

'Draw it, you mean?'

'No, *silly*. Take a photo, with my iPad.' She rattled the tablet.

'What, now?'

'Yeah, why not?'

I looked around. I couldn't see anyone else about. It was getting late, the kids had gone home and so should I, and the streets were getting much darker now. I wasn't talking about the light. When darkness fell in Curdizan High, the shady types came out of the shadows. I stared at Alice.

The iPad must be a camera, I thought. I'd never met anyone else with a camera. I'd heard about photos and someone I'd known had a portrait done, but that had been for a special occasion. I shrugged, curious.

She took the tablet out of my hand, and quickly held it in front of her face. I saw a flash.

'Not bad,' she typed. 'But wait a minute, where are you?' She pushed it across and pointed, carefully. I peered at the screen.

The view was there, just as I saw it, the gate, the back of my school by the churchyard, *and* in colour, that alone was enough to amaze me. But I was missing, not in the picture. I had been there, waiting and wondering what she would do, I'd seen the flash, and then I'd wanted to see the result, but I wasn't in it.

'No,' I said, 'that can't be right.' The picture first, there straight away, *and* in colour, and me not in it, it was all too much. I looked at Alice and backed away. This girl was different and I was afraid.

I turned around and ran like hell, down the road, past the churchyard and off to the right, through the alley, squeezing past some huddled bodies. I ran even faster down Convent Court, past the church hall, and I only slowed my pace at Croston. I kept on walking, heart beating fast until I reached Haversham Road and home. It really felt like home for once.

I knew I wouldn't have long in the house, I was due at the Keepsake Arms about now. I grabbed some broth and a hunk of bread and hurried outside to find the privy. Lucky for me it was empty for once. I sat on the seat, still shaking, craving some peace away from it all. I also felt guilty.

My da wasn't dead, like I'd said to Alice, he was probably down at The Tavern on Wenn Street, having a pint and holding forth. The drunken waste of space that he was.

'That's my lad,' he'd said to me once, when he'd heard about my job at the pub.

I'd said nothing, and neither had Ma, we'd both learnt to

keep our mouths shut when Da had been drinking. Da, when drunk, was a different bloke and Ma was the one who took the flack, mostly because I was young and could run. Lately, I'd bought a cricket bat, I'd had to bribe a lad for the thing, but I reckoned I needed it more than him.

I kept the bat by my bed each night, so the next time Da went to hit my ma, I'd be all fired up and ready to go, I'd give him a taste of his own medicine. Thinking about it made me sick, I didn't want to hit my da, not one bit, or anybody else, but sometimes you have to stand up for yourself. Or, if not for yourself, at least for your ma.

Then I remembered the girl, Alice. I hadn't been much of a man back then, running away because I was scared. Scared of the tablet and scared of her, scared of the look in those ice blue eyes.

I sighed heavily and left the privy, clutching the empty bowl and plate. I knew I'd have to go back and find her, not tonight, or even tomorrow, but sometime soon, before I forgot. I couldn't be weak, a cowardly type. I couldn't wait.

12

Now – Cressida

Cressida was sitting in Aleph's kitchen, feeling pleased and proud of herself. She'd won him round, he'd agreed to hear Alice, she felt like clapping or dancing around. Instead, she sat at the kitchen table, winding her way around the problems. Like getting Alice to talk to someone, about that day. Meeting Aleph wasn't just about Alice, but her daughter worried her more each day. She couldn't stand the silence much longer.

The post arrived with a hefty thump and she rose from her chair to go and look. The hall was one of the loveliest parts of the whole building, Edwardian tiles graced the floor and light flooded in through a stained glass panel. As well as a parcel, a couple of envelopes lay on the mat. One of the envelopes was edged in black. Cressida blinked.

She wandered back to the kitchen, slowly, clutching the post and poured more coffee. She also made some tea for Aleph. *Where had he got to?* Cressida waited.

'I've been thinking about some dates for Alice.' Cressida jumped. Aleph smiled.

'She can come next week, if that works for you. And then if you've got the recording ready...' He stopped, mid-flow.

Aleph scanned the post by his plate and picked the black-edged envelope up, slowly turning it round and round. 'It seems that leaving wasn't enough,' he muttered softly. Then he tossed it into the bin.

'Don't you want to read it first?' Cressida wished she hadn't spoken.

'It is *my* post.' said Aleph grimly.

'Yes, of course.'

He grabbed a seat and poured some tea, taking great gulps

and looking distracted. He looked across the table at Cressida. 'Why don't you tell me what happened that day? With Alice I mean. You never told me the full story. Why she suddenly stopped speaking to you.' Cressida sighed and nodded slowly.

'I'm not really sure, that's the trouble. Alice was meant to be going to her friend's. She had her phone and she knew where to go and I believe it's important to trust her. Then Annerley's mother gave me a call and told me Alice had never turned up. She should have been there and I was frantic.

'I rang all her friends, but everyone told me they hadn't seen her. So then I went out and wandered the streets, knocking on all the neighbours' doors, and speaking to all the people who knew her, but everyone said the same as her friends, they hadn't seen her. No-one knew anything. Then something happened, apart from Alice, and I had to stop looking, just for a while, but not before I'd enlisted help. I rang the police and they were worried, I knew they were, even though they wouldn't admit it.'

'But Alice came back later on?'

'Yes, that's right, in the late afternoon. She looked alright, all her clothes were creased, but nothing excessive, she said she'd been sitting in the park all day, and I believed her. The soles of her shoes were matted with grass.'

'Why didn't Alice go to Annerley's?'

'She said to me they'd fallen out, although Annerley denied it, insisted they hadn't. But that means nothing, kids will lie in a flash if it suits them. I think Alice was the one who was lying, I think she wanted some time on her own. She's very independent.'

'But to spend all day alone in the park?' Cressida shrugged.

'The following morning, I took her to the doctor's, just to be careful, but the doctor I spoke to said she seemed fine. A few days later the trouble started.'

'Was she still speaking when she came home?'

'Yes, that's why I believed it was nothing. But the very next day she acted withdrawn, and not long after, it was all downhill.'

'What about when she went back to school?' Cressida sighed.

'I didn't worry too much at first, I thought it would pass, like these things do. By the time I realised something was wrong, a week had gone by, and the staff couldn't remember anything, like how she'd been at the start of the week. And so the specialist visits began, but none of them made one jot of difference. The fact that she's normal at school doesn't help.' Aleph nodded.

'Alright Cressida, we'll give it a go. I'll meet Alice first, and after I've met her, I'll hear the recording of Alice talking, hopefully about the issue. But it could be a very short session indeed, when I meet her, if Alice won't talk.'

'She will,' said Cressida, 'although probably just about everyday things.'

'But if she won't talk to you, her mother, I very much doubt she'll talk to a stranger.'

'Yes,' said Cressida, 'that was a problem, until I twigged and bought her an iPad.'

13

Then – Miranda

Her mother's face was a wet weekend, all the time now. Miranda sighed. She normally craved her mother's attention, but somehow, lately, she just couldn't face it. Thanks to Tanya Curtis's comments. All her little insinuations.

Miranda knew she should have been happy. Today she hadn't been working at Chaucer's. Because they were always short of money, Miranda worked days at the sweet factory. Most of the girls who worked there loved it. Unlike her.

Miranda wanted a job in an office, Chaucer's preferably, and her ma was saving some cash for training, but she wasn't sure she wanted that money, now she thought she knew where it came from. She felt a sudden wave of shame.

She couldn't be sure her ma had been adding to her income that way, just because she went out nights. Why should *she* believe Tanya Curtis? Her mother worked all day in the laundry, along with Carol, Thomas's ma, and then at night, she was here to close up, throwing blokes out and cleaning the bar. Sometimes her ma worked the lunches, too, when Reg and Cath were off, or were sick. She deserved some time to herself in the evenings. She was probably sitting in somebody's house, having a chat, or taking a wander down by the Blue.

Even in very bad weather? thought Miranda. It didn't seem likely. So maybe the cow was right after all.

But now, tonight, her mother was here and making Miranda wonder again. She smiled at her ma. 'You look tired.'

'I am,' said Hannah. 'It gets to me sometimes, running a pub. More than the laundry, even though the work there's tougher. In this place, you're never off duty. You know how it is.' Miranda nodded. This was her chance.

'You know my job at the factory, Ma? Perhaps I'd be better off sticking with that? I can't see us finding money for training, anytime soon, just so I can work in an office. What do you think?'

Hannah sat down on a crate, weary. 'I don't want you to end up like me, stuck in a dead end job like the laundry. I've always said there'd be money for training, *and* I meant it. An office job is a good career. Better than spending days in a factory.'

And nights behind the bar, thought Miranda. She smiled at her ma.

'So can I go to the classes then?' Maybe Ma would be staying at home, to oversee Steve and Tom in the bar. Her heart fluttered, hope rising. But then she saw her mother's face.

'That's a little bit difficult now. Yes, you can go, but not at the moment. I've had some very sad news, you see.' Her face crumpled.

As sad as me being deprived of a future?

'The man who runs the shoe shops is dead. Matt McCarthy, the one who lives in Terrace Hall Mews.'

'That old bloke?'

'He's only a little bit older than me. Was, I mean.'

'Ma, the man was nearly sixty.'

'Fifty-four, that's quite a bit younger. Carol and I did all his washing, we knew him quite well, like a friend, almost.' She blew her nose and turned away. 'That's why I often went out nights, he liked his clothes back straight away, he hated them being in the laundry too long. Bit of a snob, was Matt, really. We used to do his lads' uniforms, for both of the shops. He liked to see them all dressed up, reckoned the look was part of the sale.' She smiled weakly, a wave of tenderness crossing her face. Miranda's heart sank.

So, not as bad as the tart had implied, only the one, but one was enough, around these parts. The fact that the bloke was a toff didn't help.

And Ma having a pub to run. Her reputation was everything. Miranda studied her mother afresh.

'So now he's dead, will we be worse off?'

Her mother flinched and lifted her chin. It suited her more than tears and mopes.

'You'll get to go to the classes, Miranda, you see if you don't. I'll just have to find another way, apart from the washing. Matt used to give us tips now and then.'

Sure he did, Miranda thought. 'Don't worry, Ma, the classes can wait. But you ought to ban that tart from the pub.'

'Which tart's that?' said Hannah, distracted, and not really paying attention to her daughter. Miranda followed her mother's eyes, she was gazing across at the mantelpiece, no, more at the shelf above the mantel. She gasped with surprise. The boot that sat on the shelf was gone.

Putting a shoe in a newly built pub was meant to ward off evil spirits. Her ma had said she'd discovered the boot when the men were fixing the pipes, out back. She'd put the boot on display in the parlour and said it would bring them luck and more. It hadn't been long after Da had died. They'd needed that luck, they really had.

And now the boot had disappeared.

Miranda felt a wave of despair. She wasn't normally superstitious, but a thought had wandered into her head, and she didn't much like it. She remembered thinking when she first saw it, that although it was old, the boot wasn't *that* old, it couldn't have been as old as the pub. But maybe the boot hadn't come from the pub.

Perhaps it had come from McCarthy's shop.

14

Now – Aleph

I could see the black-edged envelope bothered her, her eyes had followed it right to the bin, and if Cressida could have taken it out, opened it and read it, I'm sure she'd have done so. She didn't know I'd take it out later. I liked this woman, I really did, I wanted to make things right for her, and also for her daughter, and I knew she needed an explanation. It didn't have to be the truth.

'That envelope came from my ex-girlfriend, Gerry.'

'It's none of my business,' said Cressida, quickly, but looking more than slightly intrigued.

'I know,' I said. 'I want to tell you, really I do.' *Lies, all of it.* I took a deep breath.

'Gerry, my ex, she won't forgive me for certain mistakes. So every year, since we broke up, she sends me a card.' I paused, waiting.

'Weird,' said Cressida. She gave it some thought. 'But how do you know the cards are from her if you haven't even opened the envelopes?'

'This is the fourth, the first one I opened. And what was inside wasn't that pleasant, it was awful actually, so now I don't bother. As you can see, they're quite distinctive.'

'How strange,' said Cressida, knocking back her coffee and getting to her feet. I wondered if I'd scared her off.

'So can I bring Alice to see you next week?'

'Of course,' I said. 'And thanks for coming for the meal last night. I'm glad we had the chance to talk, even if it wasn't an accident.' I grinned, suddenly.

'Yes,' said Cressida and returned my smile. But I saw the smile didn't reach her eyes.

After she'd left I stood in the hall and looked at my hands, they were almost steady. *Perhaps I'm getting better*, I thought. I doubted it somehow.

I wandered back towards the kitchen and stopped at the door and looked inside. There wasn't much I could do with the units, or the tired old lino covering the floor. The fridge-freezer which sat in the middle was a different matter, I could push it back up against the wall, which was probably where it had been in the first place. The gap by the door was made for the thing. I'd do it now.

The job proved harder than I thought, the freezer was huge and solid as a rock, so when I'd finally got it in place and plugged it back in, I thought I'd done the worst of the work. I'd forgotten about the clearing up. Decades of dirt would take some shifting. I paused, puzzled.

Where the freezer had been was clean. Yes, there was dust, the odd bit of food, and also what looked like a smear of grease, but weeks or maybe a month of dirt, not years or decades. Someone had moved the freezer recently.

Why would a person do that? I wondered. I stared down at an enormous trap door. *A cellar!* I thought. I'd never asked Gemma about a cellar. It was obvious, really, in a house this age.

The trapdoor was old with a big steel hoop, and looked substantial, but I believed I was up to the job. I wondered if I should go down now. Cellars don't generally frighten me and the thought of the possible treasures appealed. I grabbed a torch and was ready to go.

The trapdoor proved a piece of cake, the wood was old and partially rotten. I made my way down the rickety stairs, looking around the walls for a light switch. Unfortunately, there wasn't one. The cellar was dark and fusty-smelling.

Reaching the bottom, I paused briefly, shining the torch for illumination. Right at the back were several windows, but they were no help, they were covered in grime. I wandered around the empty space, scanning the room to see what was there. Two of the walls had wooden shelving, the sort that could have been used for wine. Sadly, I couldn't see any wine. This cellar was proving a real disappointment

A jar was sitting on one of the shelves, full to the brim with a dark brown liquid. Whatever it was, it wasn't urgent. I wasn't going to open it now. *Maybe tomorrow*, I thought, vaguely.

My tour of the cellar was almost complete. I saw some planks of wood in the corner, and next to the planks, a smallish door. I guessed the door would lead to a cupboard but I couldn't be bothered to open it now. On the way out, I saw something on top of a shelf, I couldn't see what without a ladder. I stretched my hand out to reach the shelf and my fingers touched something smooth and cool. I gritted my teeth and grabbed the object, shining the light of the torch on the shelf.

The torch showed up the damp of the walls and the dark red flaking paint of the wood. But what intrigued me most of all was the thing I was holding in my hand.

A dark brown boot.

15

Now – Aleph

Most of the work I did was typical, failed relationships, self-esteem issues. I was a counsellor after all. But after my life had gone downhill, I needed a change, I needed to branch into something new. While keeping the bread and butter going. That's where analysing speech came in. I even thought it might help *me* heal.

I'd made some recordings about what happened and played them backwards, in reverse, listening hard for words or phrases. Trying to find those thoughts unexpressed, when played forwards. Nothing came up. Terence Lyle, the man who was my professional supervisor, acted surprised, but I still believed the approach would work, for some clients. Like Guinevere James.

Guinevere James ran an internet business, she was doing quite well and some of her clients wanted to invest. She thought the investment could help her expand, but wanted to be sure they were on the level. What if they'd planned a take over, once their feet were under the table?

'That's why I've come to you, Aleph.' I nodded, sagely.

'You did warn them, before the meeting, that you were planning to record the discussion? And what was going to happen afterwards?'

Guinevere nodded, and gave me a list of names and signatures, giving permission for the file to be analysed. I smiled, reassured. It was crucial this was all above board.

I'd talked about this aspect with Lyle. 'No-one would give their permission,' I'd said, 'if they had a corrupt agenda. For therapy, yes, because no-one would know what the file would reveal. But business is different. They wouldn't want people to know what's there.'

'Assuming they think the process works.'

'But isn't that rather unethical? Because we know it works, even if they don't.' Lyle just laughed.

'You're too naive for this kind of work. We've already told them what might happen. If they don't believe it, that's their decision. Or maybe they think it's worth the risk. It all depends how much is at stake. If they refused to cooperate, Ms James might walk away from the deal.'

I wasn't completely happy with that, and years ago, I might not have done it. But I wasn't the man I was back then. I enjoyed doing the business recordings, they were simpler than the therapeutic ones, and far less stressful. And mostly they said the same, both ways.

My client and I were sitting in the office, I'd managed to get a desk and some chairs. Guinevere James looked calm and at ease, I'd already made her several teas, her eyes were sharp, alert and interested. She wasn't my idea of a businesswoman, with her bird's nest hair and colourful clothes but I liked her manner, which was brisk and practical. She was very different from Cressida Sewell. I smiled, warmly.

'The way it works, as I've said, is this. People discuss whatever's the issue, say what they think and that's recorded. Then it's played back by me, in reverse. Most of what I hear then is gibberish, but every so often a phrase appears, and I listen carefully to hear what's said. Sometimes it's just the same both ways, not the words themselves, but the feelings behind the words being said. If so, that's good, it means the client means what they're saying. Sometimes however, it's not like that.'

Guinevere James nodded, silent. I knew she was looking for some sort of insight. Did she hope they'd be on the level, or was she looking for some kind of dirt? People often said they were ready for the truth, but when it came down to it, they usually weren't. I glanced at Guinevere.

'Forwards and backwards can be consistent, but sometimes

reversals are very different – a contradiction of what was said forwards. The subconscious speaking and telling the truth. Or, at least, that's the theory behind the work.' I paused for a moment. 'And there's more.

'Reversed recordings can give extra insight, add more information to what was said earlier, when the file was played forwards.' It all helped me see the picture. 'I think it's time we made a start.'

I'd already played the file, both ways, so I knew what was on it, and what to expect. What I didn't know then was how she'd react. She watched me choose Reverse on the program, then click Play to start the sound file. A few seconds later I paused the file. 'There,' I told her. 'There's your first one.'

My client looked startled. 'I didn't hear it.'

'I'll play it again,' I said, and did, this time slowed to 80%. 'It takes a while,' I told her, gently, 'to get your ear in, when you're first starting. Try it now.' This time she heard it.

'*It should be good for us,*' he said. The words were garbled, sounded distorted, but nevertheless a definite statement. At first, a file that's played in reverse sounds just like noise. But after a while, with the appropriate training and endless practice, you learn to pick up the phrases easily. Guinevere nodded, looking triumphant.

'I definitely heard it.' We sat and listened to more of the same.

'*We need something different,*' a man's voice told us. 'You certainly do,' said Guinevere, smiling.

'*A good way to go, yes?*' said a voice. A different voice from the one we'd just heard. My client was proud and glowing, exultant. I guess she didn't want dirt after all. Then came something she wouldn't like.

The words were curt, staccato, almost. '*Not good news; when it hits,*' he said. She looked startled.

'Did he say what I think he did?'

'I'm afraid so, yes.' I played the phrase for her one more time. My client looked grim, angry, almost.

'What does that mean, do you think?' she said. But I knew she'd understood the point. What they were saying wasn't what they really felt.

'You can't let your feelings count,' said a voice. Then, *'Do what you have to,'* followed by silence. My client jumped up.

'Is the rest of the recording all the same? How much further is there to go?'

'Most of it, yes, and twenty minutes.'

'I think I've heard enough for the moment.' She stood there glaring, staring at me. I didn't move.

'Look Mrs James, you're clearly upset. I really don't think it's a good time to leave. Please sit down and we'll talk it through.'

'I haven't the time to talk it through. I heard what he said, that's enough for me. And you've just said it's all like this. I don't want to hear it, not right now. Are you going to give me a transcript?'

'Of course,' I said, 'I've got it right here. It also discusses the metaphors. I think I explained to you what they were.'

'Sod the metaphors,' Mrs James said. She snatched the transcript out of my hand. Then she sighed, and sat back down.

'I'm sorry,' she said, looking embarrassed. 'I realise it isn't your fault, Mr Jones. I guess I didn't believe it would work.'

'You and most of my other clients.' I smiled, sympathetic.

A short while later, I watched her pick up the transcript carefully, tuck it into her oversized bag.

'You know you're not alone, Mrs James. Few people think it works at first. It seems quite bizarre the first time it happens.'

'It came as a shock,' my client said, 'and not just hearing the things they said.' She took some money out of her purse. 'Is it alright if I pay you now? I've got the cash.'

I nodded, understanding, I'd seen it before. She'd wanted those guys to be on the level and now they weren't, she felt betrayed, *and* embarrassed. So many people felt the same.

Life's a bitch, I thought grimly, and shook her hand as we said goodbye. We stood on the doorstep, taking in air.

'Isn't this place the haunted house?'

Not again, I thought, frowning. 'Not the house, it's the street that's haunted. Or so I've been told.'

'The School Lane ghosts,' said Mrs James, nodding. 'But isn't it true they lived in this house? And maybe even died in here?'

'I wouldn't know,' I said coldly. 'Nobody's said so.'

'Well,' said Guinevere, turning her back. 'Perhaps I'm wrong.' I couldn't let her leave it like that.

'How did you hear about the ghosts?'

'Marianne Parks at Cloud House told me.'

I cursed the woman in my head. 'Marianne Parks tells everybody,' I said bitterly.

'Well,' said my client, smiling, briefly. 'She is my cousin.'

16

Then – Thomas

I passed my school and Louise's tenements, and walked under the archway to Narrowboat Lane; it was anything but. The street was wide and packed with shops. I could follow it all the way to the market, and late on a Saturday, that's what I did. I'd often go there and rummage around the stalls for scraps, vegetables mostly. My ma would add the best to our meal and sometimes Wilks, a mate from school, would pass me a bone, which would make great broth. Today, however, my plans were different.

'You'll never find that boot in a shop,' I'd told Miranda, certainly not in McCarthy's shop. There's only the one and it's far too old.' Miranda looked angry and tired as well.

'Yes, thank you Thomas, that's probably true, but I'd still like you to look, alright? It's a dark brown boot with buttons on and a good deal smaller than the ones I wear.' She lifted her skirt to show her shoes.

'I never knew you had such big feet. And I have seen the boot before, remember?'

Miranda laughed, but not with pleasure. 'I'll have less of your cheek, if you don't mind, Thomas,' she said, sharply, clipping the side of my head as she did so. I winced with surprise but said nothing. Miranda looked sad and very troubled. Later that day, I went looking for the boot.

I assumed someone had stolen the thing, but just for a lark – even the poor need more than one boot. I'd forgotten to check which foot it was for but that was too bad, I couldn't go back and ask Miranda. I knew I wouldn't find the boot, but maybe trying would make her feel better. I didn't believe it.

Having the boot was meant to be lucky and losing it now

could only mean trouble, but I remembered Miranda once saying, 'We all make our own luck, Tom, and don't you forget it.' I never had, though I doubted the same was true for Miranda.

I peered in Matt McCarthy's window. It was gone half past five and the shop was empty, apart from the stock and maybe my mate. The left hand window was stacked with shoes, and some of the shoes on display were boots, but none of the boots I saw looked right.

Round our way, buying new shoes was rarely an option. My ma always had our shoes repaired, when we wore them, which wasn't that often. Repairs were cheaper and well worth doing. But even I had a 'new' pair sometimes, passed on to me by somebody else; if I was lucky the 'new' shoes fitted.

I pushed on the door and wandered inside as the bell tinkled, sauntering up to the glass counter, grinning.

'Evening Percy,' I said, nodding. 'I'm looking for a boot.'

'Are you sure you don't mean a needle in a haystack?' Percy Thomas had been at my school, but as he was older, he'd left last year. I remembered Percy on account of his name, Thomas I mean, and because he allowed me to boss him around. More fool him.

I described the boot to my old school mate and he pulled down a few to show me the styles. 'How about these, or these or these?' Ten pairs later we were bored to tears and I hadn't seen anything like the boot. I glanced up again, at the shelf of repairs.

'Let me see that one there, on the right.'

Percy reached up and passed down a boot. 'That's not one of ours, you won't get a new pair. It's in for repair, the style's out of date.'

'I don't need a new pair, I just need this. Whose boot is it?'

'Now, you know I can't tell you that, Tom, lad.'

'Not even for a brand new packet of fags?'

His eyes lit up and he checked the tag attached to the heel. 'You really mean it, about the fags?'

'True as I'm standing here in this shop.'

My old school mate lived at home with his ma, and she took every penny he earned and more. He was far too soft, or soft in the head to hold some back for life's small pleasures. I reached across and grabbed the boot. 'Thanks, old mate, you won't regret it. I promise to come back soon with the fags.'

'Tom, wait, where you going?'

I didn't bother answering Percy. He might have been soft but the lad was huge, the only advantage I had was speed. I left the shop and hurried along the road to the archway.

Once I realised I wasn't being followed, I slowed right down to a walking pace, thinking how pleased Miranda would be. I couldn't believe I'd actually found it. Then I remembered to check the tag. Now I'd know who'd taken the thing.

I stopped abruptly and read it again. The name hadn't changed, it was still the same.

Well, I thought, and carried on walking. *That is a surprise.*

17

Now – Cressida

Alice was late home from school, *again*. Cressida tried to control herself, not to get angry and scream at Alice, but past experience made it hard. When Alice was late, how did she know Alice was late, rather than missing? It was hard not to worry, especially now they lived somewhere new, with Alice going to a brand new school. Especially after that terrible day.

She'd never gone missing in Leverhulme. Except that once.

When Alice was late, the time before last, Cressida checked where she was with the school.

'She left with the others, I saw her go.' Cressida frowned. That was the day she was three hours late.

'You'd better not make a habit of this.' Cressida heard herself almost screeching, she hated the way she lost control. She'd promise herself not to do it again and then she would, the very next time.

'I only went for a walk around town,' Alice informed her, using her iPad, looking bored, as if she was the adult. 'Can I do my homework now?' Cressida sighed.

'That's why I gave you the smartphone, Alice. So you can text me where you are. So I don't worry.'

'I've told you before, Mum, there's no need to worry. I'm not a baby.'

'So act like an adult and use the phone. I'd rather not have to collect you from school.'

Alice frowned and gave her that look, the one that said, *You damn well won't.* Cressida sighed. Kids today had so much attitude, Alice especially.

'So what time will you be home tomorrow?'

'I've no idea, it depends on the others. I'll send you a text, as soon as I know. But I will be home before it gets dark.' As if she was making a big concession.

'See that you are, and remember the text.' Cressida left her alone with that, but she knew she had to keep tabs on the girl.

Cressida watched her daughter leave, she saw her stop and talk to her friends. The sight of that hurt a hell of a lot. *Why can't she talk to me?* she thought. The girls crossed the road together as one, arms all linked as they ambled down the hill to the town, leaving the school gates far behind. Alice was laughing and using her phone. Cressida checked; if Alice was texting, it wasn't to her.

The girls were happy, laughing and talking and jostling each other. Cressida followed, slightly behind, just about keeping her rage in check. How could Alice talk to her friends *and* to her teachers and not to her? Maybe Alice *was* putting it on?

No, she thought, *that can't be true, no-one could keep the pretence up that long.* She'd asked Alice dozens of times, if she'd upset her, but each time she asked, Alice said no. Yet something must have caused the reaction. Cressida knew that day was the key. That terrible Sunday Alice had vanished.

She followed them all around for a while, tedious stuff, shopping mostly, looking at clothes and fancy bags. A couple of times she was nearly spotted. The girls then sauntered across to the market, gathered together, then broke apart, each one going in a different direction. Cressida watched Alice waving goodbye. Her friends had gone and she was alone. It was just after six.

Alice wandered through the market, Cressida doing her best to follow. Most of the stalls were closing up and the light of the day was fading fast. Stallholders loaded their cars with goods while Cressida walked between crates and stock. Alice turned off onto Convent Court, near the church hall which was barely used, and made her way towards the abbey. Where was she going? Cressida wondered. Then Alice wandered into an alley. Cressida panicked and hurried after her. She didn't like Alice being alone in there.

She followed her daughter through the passage, ending up on Scriveners Road. The light had almost gone by now. She watched as Alice rounded the bend and suddenly realised where they were. *This is the street where Aleph lives.* Cressida was still getting to know Curdizan.

She watched as Alice passed Aleph's house, and headed for the archway to Narrowboat Lane. She didn't like Alice going this way. For all the area's modernisation, the path to the archway was badly lit, a former haunt of prostitutes. *Who was it told me that?* she thought.

Alice paused and Cressida stopped, stepping back quickly into the shadows, Alice was typing on the iPad, laughing and holding the tablet up high. As if she was trying to take a photo. *Why here, of all places?* Alice turned the tablet around, as if she was showing the screen to someone. Cressida gasped and hurried forward. Alice was obviously not alone.

Cressida rushed towards her, shouting, 'Alice, it's me.' Whoever was with her could be trouble, and Cressida couldn't take that chance.

'Mum,' typed Alice, 'What a surprise! I'd like you to meet my friend, Tom.'

Cressida looked up Narrowboat Lane, but all she could see in the fading light were a couple of women strolling away. She couldn't see any men or boys.

'He's always running away,' typed Alice. 'I don't think he likes me taking his photo. Not that it ever comes out when I try.'

'Here, let me see.' Cressida grabbed the iPad quickly, wanting to check that Tom was a boy and not a man, and a threat to her daughter, but there weren't even any boys in the picture. She saw the street with its trees in bud and a couple of women in rather quaint costumes, and a lot of closed shops but that was all. Cressida sighed.

Alice believed she'd been talking to someone, that was

evident. A boy who didn't seem to exist, on the screen or in the street. Could this be a part of the problem?

18

Then – Thomas

I hadn't expected to see Alice, not by the archway that led to the school. I don't know why not, it wasn't that far from where we first met. I guess I was thinking about the boot, and feeling rather proud of myself. But when I saw Alice, it all came back, how I'd run off the last time I'd seen her, and then I didn't feel quite so proud. Alice smiled and her face lit up.

'Hello Tom,' she typed on the tablet. 'Great to see you. How are you?'

'Fine,' I said. 'But I can't stop now, I've got to get home, My ma's expecting me straight away.' I watched her face fall, and then I felt guilty *and* regretful, it wasn't as if I didn't like her. So I thought about how to make amends.

'Why don't you try for another photo?' I nodded at the tablet.

'Sure,' she typed, and held the thing up for me to smile at. Then she showed me the photo she'd taken. 'What do you think?' My heart sank.

'You've got a definite knack for that,' I said frankly, admiring the view and the blossoming trees. She'd even managed to capture the light. Alice said nothing, she'd already seen what I had noticed, I wasn't in it. Yet again.

I told myself I didn't care, I didn't know how the damn thing worked, how the picture came out, straight away *and* in colour. I'd never seen colour in a photo before. But it made me proud that Alice could do that. Then I had a thought.

'Will you take my friend's photo? Another friend,' I added quickly, grinning and thinking, of course, of Louise.

'Sure,' said Alice and as she answered I saw this woman running towards us. She was almost invisible, almost not

69

there, but I guess that could have been the failing light. And she was wearing the oddest clothes. I could see at once, she wasn't happy. *Right, Thomas, lad, it's time to move on.*

'Sorry Alice, I've got to run. I'll see you around, hopefully soon.' I doubled back and made my way down Narrowboat Lane, I knew these streets like the back of my hand. The woman would never catch me up.

Going the long way took a lot more time, it meant I was late to the pub again. I skipped going home and rushed through the door of the Keepsake Arms, gasping for breath. I needn't have bothered, the place was empty. I noticed Miranda looked amused.

'Where have you been until now, Thomas? You're starting to make a habit of this.'

'You wouldn't believe me if I said.'

'Why don't you try me? I'm bored as anything, stuck in here. The least you can do is keep me amused.'

'I think I've seen a ghost,' I said.

Miranda was thrilled about the boot. 'You're definitely sure this is the one?'

'Of course I'm sure, I've read the tag. Guess who left it to be repaired?' I felt a tiny twinge of fear.

'My mother,' she said and looked so sad. 'That boot had been on the shelf for years. I can't imagine why she did it.'

'Well, at least you know they've done a good job.' Miranda ignored me.

'You're sure it was McCarthy's shop? Not David Rennin's across the road?'

'Of course I'm sure, a mate of mine, works there. We had a good chat.' I paused, thinking.

I knew I was only a lad to her, but I'd had to grow up fast in the Low. I saw by her face that something was wrong, more than just a boot going missing or some ridiculous superstition. She looked troubled.

'You're far too young for this Thomas, but there's no-one

else I can tell but you. Apart from your ma and I'm not that sure she isn't involved.'

'You'll have to tell me now,' I said. 'Involved in what?' Miranda nodded and scanned the room. The bar was still empty apart from a man, and Reg and Cath, over in the corner and supping ale. Steve was out back, stacking crates.

'Come with me then, Thomas, and hurry.' I followed Miranda up the stairs.

She didn't stop when we reached the first floor. Two floors up, we went through a door and up more stairs to the pub attic, a narrow, cramped space which was cluttered with stuff. Miranda went in and I followed.

I watched her move some chairs and a table, stopping at something I couldn't see, half hidden behind a huge sideboard. I followed quickly and found Miranda staring at a trunk. As I watched she levered it open, clearly something she'd done before. I peered in.

The trunk was filled to the brim with shoes. Unlike the boot, they were all brand new.

19

Now – Aleph

Guinevere James had got to me. Not the recording, that was expected, but what she'd said after, about the ghosts, that they'd lived in this house. And if Parks was her cousin, she would know. Presumably. I swore, loudly.

Forget the ghosts, I told myself. *They don't matter.* But all the same, the house felt cold. I stood in the hall, silent, thinking.

Nobody died in here, I thought. *That's what Gemma Pearce said. Even the previous owner didn't.* But, realistically, was that likely? The house dated back to the 1850s, somebody would have died in here. The question was, who?

And was it important?

A loud crash shattered my thoughts. I hurried down the hall to the kitchen, my heart pounding and nearly tripping over the boot, which was lying in the middle of the kitchen floor. The trap door leading to the cellar was open. How had that happened?

I hadn't left the windows open, and even if I had, the draught must have come from down there, not here. I took a torch and went to look, with more than a little trepidation. I didn't think it could be a burglar. I was right, it wasn't. And the windows down there were barred and closed.

I looked around the cellar carefully, striding across to the cupboard door, the one I'd not opened the previous time. Maybe it led to some kind of vent. I tugged, firmly and the door flew open, nearly sending me flying backwards. I shone my torch inside the space.

There were three narrow shelves inside the cupboard, all of them bare, but heavy with dust. I groped around underneath the shelves and at the bottom I felt a draught. Nothing of any consequence. I sighed, defeated and got to my feet.

I don't believe in ghosts, I thought. I kicked the cupboard door to close it, and hurried back up to the light of the kitchen, scanning the cellar with the torch as I left. There was nothing to see, wherever I looked. But the air was thick with cold and fear.

I could hear the sound of my phone ringing, where I'd left it, on the table. I nudged the trapdoor shut with my foot.

'Just ringing to check that everything's fine,' Cressida told me, sounding disturbed.

But is it? I thought, grabbing a chair and staring at the trapdoor. 'Is anything wrong?'

'Alice has got an imaginary friend.'

I laughed out loud, relieved at such a trivial tale.

'It's not funny,' said Cressida, angry. 'She's far too old for that sort of thing.'

'So how do you know this friend's made up?'

'She says he's called Tom and he doesn't wear shoes and always looks shabby. Have you come across any boys like that? Then she complains he never shows up in the photos she takes. And it's true he doesn't, I saw one myself.'

'Perhaps she's just a bad photographer.'

'Oh, come on, Aleph, kids these days are used to such things. They all know how to take a photo, it's simply a matter of point and click. The street was there, there were even some trees, but I didn't see Tom. By the time I'd caught her up and checked, Tom had vanished into the night. Supposedly. That's why I think she made him up. That and his clothes.' Cressida paused.

'What am I going to do about Alice? She really believes the boy was there.'

'Couldn't he be a boy from school?'

'I know there isn't a Tom in her class, but that doesn't mean he's not in her year. But it doesn't seem like he's real to me, if he was real, he'd have been in the photo. All I saw was Narrowboat Lane.'

'Why don't we talk about Tom tomorrow, when Alice comes round in the afternoon? You won't forget to bring the recording?'

'I didn't have time to fix up the chat with Alison Clipper. She's one of the mums that Alice knows. I thought tomorrow, you could just meet Alice and then, next week, I'll bring the recording. And before you ask, it's all above board, I've spoken to Alice about what's happening.'

'Good,' I said. 'It's important she knows.' I leant down and picked up the boot. My mind was still on the trapdoor incident.

'And that's not all,' Cressida was saying. 'I asked Alice what Tom was wearing and she reported, "The same as the last time." Which was one more reason she thought he was poor. So I said, "Maybe it's his school uniform," and Alice shook her head and smiled.'

'"Not like any I've ever seen." And then she said he was holding a boot.'

'What?' I said. It was all I could do not to drop the phone.

'That's what she said. It was small and brown and rather old fashioned. You know the sort, that's done up with buttons.'

'I certainly do,' I told her, grimly. 'It sounds just like the one in my hand.'

20

Then – Miranda

Miranda watched Tom stare at the trunk. 'I only managed to open it this morning.'

'They look like the ones in McCarthy's shop.'

'That's because they're McCarthy's stock. But these never found their way to the shop. I don't know what I'm going to do.'

'Why don't I ask my ma about them? She and your mother did his laundry. Maybe he asked her to store them here.'

'That doesn't sound very likely to me. No, I'll talk to my ma first. They are in her pub, after all.'

'Sure,' said Tom, sounding worried. Both of them knew the shops had stockrooms, there wasn't any reason to store them up here. Miranda knew it all smelt bad.

'Miranda?' called Cath. 'You're needed down here.'

Miranda slammed the trunk lid shut. 'Coming,' she said, and glanced at Tom who averted his eyes. For once the lad had nothing to say. Together they trooped back down the stairs.

The following day she spoke to her ma.

'The boot that went missing off the shelf? You removed it.'

'Yes, that's right. I wanted to get it smartened up. The boot is meant to be for luck and I thought ours was on the way out. Business has been a bit slow, lately. So I took it along to McCarthy's shop and gave it to Percy who said he'd repair it.' A shadow suddenly crossed her face. 'They're still wearing black in the shop, you know.' Miranda ignored her.

'You've wasted money repairing a boot we can't even

wear? You said to me the takings were down, and yet you think we've got money to burn.'

'It didn't cost us a penny, Miranda. Percy said he'd do it for nothing, in Matt's memory.'

'So it's Matt, now is it?' Miranda said, folding her arms and staring at her mother. 'All very cosy, I must say.'

'I worked for that man for years, Miranda. I think I'm entitled to call him Matt. And as for the boot, for me it's a keepsake. From years ago, when I first knew Matt. And as you know, we're the Keepsake Arms.' She smiled feebly.

'Now hang on Ma,' said Miranda, confused. 'I thought the boot was found in the pub. By one of the blokes who fixed that pipe.'

'That's not quite true,' said her mother, colouring. 'I was given the boot by Matt McCarthy. I liked the story of a lucky shoe.'

'You were given it when?' said Miranda, coldly. She could feel the heat of her anger growing, the thought of what her da might have felt.

'A few years back, when your da was in trouble. Matt was a brick, helping us out, just like he did when your father died. I couldn't have managed without his help.'

I'll bet you couldn't, Miranda thought. *To think that tart had been right all along.* 'So all this started before Da died?'

'All what started?' Her mother's face paled. 'Oh, no, Miranda, you've got it all wrong. That's not how it was, I was gutted, lost, when your da passed away. I liked Matt, of course I did, he was good to me, kind, but not in that way. Your da was the only one for me.'

Sure, thought Miranda who wasn't convinced by what she'd heard 'So tell me ma, while we're talking about it, did Matt give you the shoes in the trunk, or did you take them all by yourself?'

And hated herself for feeling triumphant when her mother gasped and fell to the floor.

21

Now – Aleph

I know it was stupid, unrealistic, but when I left, I hoped they'd stop. I thought that maybe once I moved, to a different town and started again, they wouldn't find out, or if they did, they'd let it be done, and then, at last, I'd be free to start over. Or at least as free as my mind would allow. But they didn't stop.

The envelope sat on the mantelpiece.

When Cressida left the other week, I'd rescued the envelope from the bin, and put it up there as a kind of penance. I knew it would have to go in the box, along with the others, but for now I let it sit on the shelf, reminding me of what I'd done, and how I'd never forgive myself. And neither would they. I sighed heavily. The doorbell rang.

I whipped the envelope off the mantelpiece and stuffed it behind a cushion quickly. I couldn't have Cressida seeing it again. Or even Alice.

Alice was not what I thought she'd be. She was tall and blonde with ice blue eyes and not one bit like her mother to look at. She seemed cool, detached and in control, as if she was making some sort of judgement. She probably was. I tried to smile but it came out wrong and the girl looked away and stared at the floor. Her clothes were pretty, a very pale pink, with flowers and frills, but the clothes didn't fit the girl I saw.

'Hello, Alice, it's good to meet you.' She ignored my hand and didn't even type me a message on her iPad. I wondered why I'd agreed to this.

I led my guests towards the kitchen. After yesterday's trapdoor incident, I had my doubts about using the kitchen, but my office was small and the kitchen had mugs, a kettle some biscuits. At least I'd remembered to hide the boot.

Crazy, I'd thought, *the boot means nothing*, but all the same, I'd still hidden it. I didn't want Alice freaking out. My whole perspective on life had changed in the last few years. The world didn't seem that safe anymore, or even meaningful. All those things that everyone did, going to work, meeting friends at the weekend, gossip and chatter, all seemed fake. I knew that mostly those things were important, kept people connected, but nobody said what they really thought. Suddenly, I felt warmer towards Alice. Maybe, as someone who didn't speak, she felt the same, felt excluded. I turned around and saw her standing, staring at me. But it wasn't me she was staring at, her eyes were glued to a place behind me. Where the trapdoor was.

Quick as a flash, her iPad came out. Cressida and I rushed to her side.

'I'm not going in the kitchen, Mother.'

'What?' said Cressida, disbelieving.

'Can't you hear them crying, Mum? They're driving me mad.'

'Don't be silly, Alice, please. There's nobody crying.'

'The children,' I said to Cressida, quickly. 'I think Alice can hear the children.'

Alice ignored me and went on typing. 'It's terrible, Mother, sad *and* tragic. I'm not staying.'

'What children? There aren't any children.' Cressida, puzzled, was looking around.

'Enough,' I said, and ushered them out, suggesting to Cressida they go upstairs. Alice and I had a little tussle; she clearly wanted to leave the house.

'Upstairs, now!' Cressida said and Alice gave in, gritting her teeth and scowling at me. But she made us go first.

When we finally reached my office, I reminded Cressida of the old story. 'Old School Lane is supposed to be haunted, you were the one who mentioned the ghosts when you came round. Don't you remember? People have heard children laughing *and* crying.' I looked at Alice.

'One was distraught,' she typed on the screen. 'I couldn't bear it, hearing him cry. It went on and on, it was terrible, dreadful.'

Cressida dragged me onto the landing. 'Do you believe it?' she said, sharply.

'I don't believe in ghosts,' I said. 'Mostly it's just imagination, or maybe a trauma, disturbing the mind. But, I have to say, I've heard these children, usually crying, and just this week, a client hinted at children's deaths. In this house.'

'And knowing that, you let Alice come here?'

'I don't believe it, it's only a story.'

'But I'm the one who makes those decisions, the ones about Alice. Especially with Alice being so fragile. Didn't you even think to mention it?'

'I'm not fragile, Mother, please.' Alice had followed us onto the landing, was typing rapidly as we watched. 'I just don't feel like talking right now.'

'Right now, being the last four years?'

'I go to school, I do my assignments.'

'And you don't mind talking when you're at school. It's only at home you don't want to speak, only to me. Maybe it's won't, not can't, Alice. Maybe you're just being stubborn and spoilt. Perhaps if I took that thing away, then you'd start talking.' Alice gripped the iPad tighter.

'Cressida, don't...'

'Stay out of it, please, she's not your child.' Alice sighed and typed rapidly.

'It's always all about you, isn't it? It's not that I'm not speaking that matters, but only that I'm not talking to you. You can't bear thinking you're not in control. That's what you care about, really, Mother, not about me.'

'How dare you say such terrible things, and in front of a stranger? When I think what I've done for you, the worry I've had.' She made a dive for her daughter's hand but Alice was fast, too fast for us both and tucking her iPad under her arm, she hurried downstairs and out of the door. Cressida followed as fast as she could. 'I'll be in touch,' she hissed as she went, giving me a cursory wave.

By the time I'd made my way down the steps and onto the street, Alice had gone and Cressida was running around the corner, rapidly vanishing out of sight. *Christ, what a mess!*

I walked back up the steps, to the door, when a sound below made me turn around. Alice emerged from the lengthening shadows. I peered down at her over the railing. 'Alice,' I said. Her eyes met mine.

'There's something you need to know, Aleph.' My heart was thudding, thumping like mad.

'I was there, the day that it happened. Just in case you don't remember.' And before I could answer she'd turned away and hurried off in pursuit of her mother.

I turned around and went inside, feeling light headed, the palms of my hands were visibly sweating. I leant against the door, thinking. I wondered if what she'd said was the truth, and if it was, what it might mean? I didn't know the answer to that.

But I had noticed something else about our unexpected, little exchange. Alice hadn't used her iPad once.

22

Then – Thomas

I was on a mission, and it felt important. Miranda had something that needed doing. And I was the one to do that something. Or at least get it started, like when I'd been to see Percy Thomas.

Ben was having a cup of tea.

'Hi there, Tom, how are doing?'

'Fine,' I said and grinned at my friend. 'Is there any tea for a mate?'

Ben laughed and poured me a mug. 'It's pretty well stewed, don't let it go cold.'

I took the drink and peered outside at the church next door. There were too many graves. It wasn't as smart as Curdizan Church.

'Is it true what they say, that it's all full up?'

'It certainly is,' said Ben, nodding, he'd finished his tea and was hammering nails into a coffin. Undertakers are always busy. Or, at least, around here. The Low wasn't the healthiest of areas.

'But Matt McCarthy's got a spot.'

Ben paused for a minute and looked at me. 'I never thought you were stupid, Tom. Despite what I've heard.'

'What do you mean?' I said, sharply and then I grinned. 'You mean because the guy was rich he's able to have a place in the graveyard?'

'The penny's dropped at last,' said Ben.

'So where are they going to bury the rest?'

'Curdizan Church, the one by the abbey. And the rest in the field across the Blue.'

'Now, that is a joke,' I said, laughing. 'You're having me

on.' Ben nodded.

'Yes, but not about Curdizan Church.'

'That's quite a way to take a body.'

'So, why should I care?' said Ben, grinning. 'The further they go the more it costs, although being so poor, they rarely pay, so maybe I should care after all. What do you think?' He paused, considering. 'Why are you here?'

This was where things might get tricky. 'I gather you've got some storage space.'

'And what if I have, what's that to you?'

'I wondered if you'd store something for us.'

'Depends,' said Ben, 'on what it might be.' He put down his hammer. 'Come on, I'm waiting.'

'It's only a trunk.'

'A trunk,' said Ben. 'So what's inside it?'

'The owner would rather I didn't say. But nothing you need worry about.'

'So the owner's really the owner, then, is she?' I stared at Ben, incredulous.

'How did you know the owner's a she?'

'Got you!' said Ben and I cursed him then, swearing out loud. 'I suppose the owner's Miranda Collenge?'

'Yes,' I said, 'that's right, she is.' *Sort of,* I thought.

'Well, lucky for you, I like Miranda. More than most girls I know, as it happens.'

'Miranda's too good for you,' I said.

'And far too old for you, Tom. Happen you think she'll wait for you? It'll be a long wait, that's what I say.' Ben grinned.

'She's just a mate, like an older sister,' I said, embarrassed.

'More like a parent from where I'm looking.' I scowled again, knowing I was beaten.

'I'll store her stuff on one condition, you let me look inside the trunk first. I can't be handling stolen goods.'

'They're not stolen,' I said, sharply, thinking the shoes were more like a gift. A gift received in advance of permission. I crossed my fingers.

'I'm waiting,' said Ben.

'I can't,' I said. 'I've given my word and I won't break it. That's the deal. You'd have to promise not to look.'

'No way,' said Ben, shaking his head. 'It's my building, and my reputation.'

'Well, sod you then,' I yelled, leaving. 'I guess we're not the mates I thought.'

I wandered, woebegone, down the street, passing the church with its spindly hedge. I peered between it into the graveyard, grave upon grave, with no space to speak of. Even when they were dead and gone, the poor very often had nowhere to go. And what about the trunk of shoes? What on earth would we do with them now?

'What did she say?' I asked Miranda later that day. I knew she'd meant to talk to her mother.

'What do you think she said?' said Miranda. 'She thought the trunk would stay a secret, hers and your mother's, hidden in the attic. She never expected me to discover them. God knows what they think they were doing.'

I hung my head, unable to speak. It was hard to know about Mrs Collenge but knowing my ma was involved was worse.

'My da is useless at bringing home cash. He might have a job, but he spends it all on booze and fags.'

'You don't have to make excuses to me. I know how it is, Tom, really.' Miranda was sharp and I couldn't blame her. We were the ones who were stuck with the problem, getting rid of the stolen shoes, while those responsible left it to us. I didn't feel such a clever lad now.

'You know what made me really angry?'

'What?' I said, not wanting to know.

'My mother said we could simply sell them, just as they'd planned to do all along.' And then she said, "Matt wouldn't mind, he was such a dear. I wish you'd known him better,

Miranda." She actually said he was "*such a dear*". My father's only been dead four years.'

'That's quite a long time,' I said mildly.

'It is for you,' Miranda retorted. 'Seeing as how that's about your age.'

'So you did explain why we couldn't sell them? How if we did, it would look like theft, now that he's dead and someone would notice.'

'Of course I did, you stupid boy. But then she said, "Just leave them in the trunk."'

'For Reg and Cath and the others to find!'

'Exactly,' said Miranda, 'a stupid idea.' She paused, looked worried. 'Although, knowing Reg, he's already found them and sold more than a few on to his mates.'

'So what are we going to do now?'

'We'll have to think of another alternative, now Ben Tencell's said he won't help.' She scowled briefly, probably at Ben, but maybe at me. 'We need a secure hiding place, until I can talk to Percy Thomas. Persuade him to take them into the shop.'

'Let's tell him now,' I said eagerly. Percy wasn't such a bad old stick.

'Not on your life,' Miranda threatened. 'Because if you do, you'll be in that trunk, instead of the shoes, and you won't be coming out very soon.'

23

Now – Aleph

I try not to think of the little boy's name, knowing his name made it so much harder, made him more of a real person, even though he was real enough. I knew I'd never be able to forget. Most would say that's how it should be. I'd been driving along the Leverhulme Road, on a sunny Sunday morning in spring. I wasn't that fond of spring anymore.

I must have been going about the speed limit, around thirty or maybe less, but definitely not more, I'm sure about that. I'd just set off from my girlfriend's flat, I was still eating toast as we'd just finished breakfast. We'd also had another row.

Gerry was blonde, she liked good clothes, and her car was new, it went with her look, which was clean and glossy and well-presented. I thought I was part of that image too, but after the accident, all that changed, I was tarnished, damaged and definitely over. I didn't fit the look or her life.

'I think it's time we had a baby,' she'd said that morning, not for the first time, but much more decisive than when we'd last talked. I couldn't help thinking she made it sound like a supermarket purchase, something you went and picked off the shelf.

'Soon,' I said, not really focused or paying attention. *Sometime next year, or the year after that.*

'It's always soon or sometime with you.'

'You've never seemed overly bothered before. I thought it was something we'd planned for the future.'

'Of course I'm bothered, why wouldn't I be bothered? I've just been subtle, not pressuring you. A nice little girl, with silky blonde hair, of course I'd like one, why ever not?'

'A blonde little girl all pretty in pink? You just want a carbon copy of yourself.'

'What is it with you? You know I hate pink. You make it sound like a crime to care. You've never minded my blonde hair before. Or anything else about me, either.'

'I don't,' I said. 'You know I like the way you look. I like your hair and I like kids too. Just not at the moment, that's all I'm saying. Damn it, Gerry, we're only young.'

'We're not that young,' she said, slowly. She was right about that. And I guess for a girl, the clock always ticks.

'I didn't say no. I said, just not now.'

'And that's what you said the last time I raised it, will probably the next time, and the time after that. And ad infinitum.'

'That's really not fair,' I said, sharply 'you haven't mentioned it all that often.' But she had of course. I just hadn't wanted to hear the words. I picked up the car keys and grabbed some toast. 'I think I'd remember about the blonde hair,' I said sharply.

'Piss off,' said Gerry, so I did just that. And wished I hadn't, ever since.

I thought I'd go to the office for a bit. Those were the days when I worked in a team, felt I belonged, was part of a group. I enjoyed my job, was liked and respected, admired sometimes, when I worked with a client who was more than challenged and managed to help him turn things around. I was proud of my skills, arrogant almost. Now all that was gone.

Because it was Sunday the roads were quiet. I knew the route I was taking well, I'd lived there several years before, before I'd moved into Gerry's place. There weren't any corners or tricky little side streets. There were lots of parked cars which narrowed the road, so I drove carefully, leaving room for other drivers. I hadn't been drinking, I hadn't been doing anything wrong. Except thinking about my future.

I was driving along with the window open, the sun in the sky, thinking about Gerry and about having a kid, and wondering whether the kid was the problem, or whether it was Gerry. That brought me up short. I grabbed my toast from the passenger seat and chewed on it slowly, thinking, deciding. My car rolled forwards a few more feet, and then I saw a flash to the left, it was barely more than a sliver of colour, and then I felt the thud of the impact and knew that something terrible had happened. Something far too bad to undo. I slammed on the brakes. It was far too late.

I don't remember a lot after that. The police informed me I left the car, went round to the child, a boy, who was dead. He was only young, he hadn't a hope. The witness, an elderly man, I was told, had seen it all, been powerless to help. I'd driven past him a few yards back. He rang for the ambulance, then the police.

'The boy ran out from behind a car, suddenly, abruptly. The driver couldn't have done anything about it.' The boy I'd hit was only small.

The man also said I was driving carefully, looking alert, with my hands on the wheel. I thought of him then as my guardian angel, and thanked him again and again in my head. Now, I wish I'd gone to prison. It wasn't my fault, they all said that, but I didn't get that – when it had happened, I'd been thinking about my row with Gerry, not little boys dashing into the road. I'd picked up the toast, I remembered that, so what if my hand wasn't on the wheel? The man was old, perhaps his eyesight wasn't that good? And as for me, I couldn't remember.

Everyone said I'd had no chance, the boy was young and had just dashed out. But what makes a kid so young do that, and what were his mother and father doing? Shouldn't he have been at home with them?

Because of the witness and the evidence, I didn't get charged or taken to court. In theory my life should have stayed the same, the same old job and the same old life. But that was never an option for me. The child, whose name I'll never forget, whose parents refused to talk to me, who never answered my letter, is always there in the back of my mind, wherever I go and whatever I do. I never stop thinking about the child, and the life I ended.

My own life ended too, on that day. My job fell apart, I no longer coped very well with the clients, when my position seemed much worse than theirs. I hated my friends for wanting me to 'move on with my life', and for being so glad I was found 'innocent'. When Gerry finally chucked me out, I was almost relieved. I was no longer suitable father material. I think it took her three weeks to decide. I knew I'd have to start over again.

At first, I stayed in Leverhulme, getting a flat in a different suburb, but that was just too close to home. So then I moved to London for a while, thought about Spain or even Australia, but none of the options seemed to work. In the end, I came back to the region and moved to Curdizan, which is near Leverhulme, but not too near, living in the shadow of churches and ghosts.

I don't believe in ghosts, I thought. Except the ghost of the child I killed, a lost little boy who never went home.

I stared at the black-edged envelope. The cards didn't come from my ex, Gerry. They arrived each year on the anniversary of the day it happened, the day I killed that little boy. I'd only ever opened the first one and that was enough. I knew I should have thrown them away, kept throwing them away as each one arrived, or told the police, or told someone, but instead, I put them all in a box, a box with a lid, an old shoe box.

And never, ever, ate toast again.

24

Now – Cressida

Martha had been her friend for ages, for at least five years, and had stuck by her when things had got tough. Being on your own with a kid wasn't easy, even a kid as bright as Alice. Especially a kid as bright as Alice. Cressida sighed.

'Coffee and scones?' Martha asked her.

Cressida watched her friend lay the table, put out jam and mugs of coffee, extra strong, especially for Cressida. Martha's kitchen was nothing like Aleph's. The small pine table, the bright blue curtains dotted with gold, the window that looked on a perfect garden. Paradise in England, Cressida thought, although one that was earned and achieved with effort.

'Len's at the yard,' Martha informed her, pulling her chair right up to the table. She hoovered up some crumbs from the cloth and dusted them carefully onto her plate. 'He can't keep away, now the weather's improved.'

Len was Martha's loyal husband. The man had a small and ancient boat. He was gradually making it more than viable. *Better that Len is out,* thought Cressida.

'I'm taking the sound file to Aleph soon, the one of Alice talking to Alison. I've no idea what's going to happen.' She sipped her coffee. *God, that was good.*

'So it's Aleph, now?' said Martha mildly, the soft enquiry not hiding her thoughts. 'Are you sure you're not being taken in? We know that man can spin a tale.'

'It's not like that, you know it's not.' She rested her hand on Martha's, briefly. Martha quickly snatched it away. Cressida paused.

'I think you ought to face the truth. I don't want a man in my life anymore, or even a woman, not at the moment.'

'It isn't healthy to be alone,' Martha told her. 'Having Len has been marvellous for me.' She passed more scones and Cressida took one.

'I'm not alone,' Cressida told her. 'I've got my daughter, Alice, remember?' Her friend didn't answer. Cressida went on.

'I was there when the post arrived, including your envelope, the black-edged one.' She stared at the fine lace tablecloth.

'And how did he take it?' Martha asked her.

'Not that well, as you can imagine. He told me his former partner sent them.'

'Shades of a guilty conscience, I'd say. He doesn't know you knew he was lying. Unless he thinks she really did.'

'He might,' said Cressida. 'She did dump him.'

'Hardly surprising. Gerry's the sort who likes things shiny. Trouble and Gerry don't mix very well.'

'Aleph doesn't mix with anyone now. Or, so I gather.'

'I bet he's got his eye on you.'

'Maybe,' said Cressida, 'he's certainly friendly. Wasn't that what you wanted to happen?'

'So long as he doesn't pull you in. Can you be sure he won't, Cressida?' She rose from the table and stacked the dishes, then walked to the sink and began washing them.

Cressida studied her friend's profile. She was struck by how her pregnancy was showing. Martha turned round and saw Cressida staring.

'What are you thinking, looking like that?'

'I'm thinking it's time you stopped all this, now that you're pregnant.'

Martha frowned and wiped her hands. 'You mean, you think it's time I moved on?'

'That's right, I do, now you've got a new baby coming. It's the perfect time to start again.'

'I can't just paper over the cracks, pretend the man didn't do what he did. Replace what I lost with something else.'

'I wasn't saying that,' said Cressida, slowly.

'Oh yes, you were, that's what everybody says, even my husband says it sometimes. You'd rather I just moved on and was happy.'

'And is that such a terrible thing?' Martha paused.

'No, not in itself. But I'm just not ready to let go yet. The cards are done, they've run their course, and from what you've said, they didn't work. But as for the rest, we'll stop when I'm ready. Tell me you won't give up on me now?'

'No,' said Cressida, rather reluctantly, thinking she didn't have much choice. *I'm doing it for Alice*, she said to herself.

Martha leant forward and stared at her friend with a fixed expression. 'I agree, Cressida, it's time to move on. But not before we've told him the truth.'

25

Then – Thomas

I was still bothered about the shoes. Especially now I knew Ma was involved. But I knew much better than to mention them, to her or my da. Miranda and I had to deal with it, and we still needed a place to hide them. Miranda's idea was once we'd hidden them somewhere else, away from the pub, we, or I, could take them back to McCarthy's shop, a few at a time.

Had it been me, I'd have thought of a story to tell Percy, and shifted the whole damn lot at once. But Miranda refused to go that way.

'If someone finds out, and it only takes one, my mother's position in our pub will be ruined. They might not even say much to her face, but the talk would be rife, then trade would suffer and where would we be?' She looked at me keenly. What could I say?

'You'd be out of a job,' she said, curtly. Which also started me thinking a bit.

The next morning, I didn't go to school until later. Which meant missing breakfast, a great sacrifice. I went to the market, my ma shops there, and I knew a bloke who wanted a lad to help with deliveries. I could work Saturdays and maybe some very early mornings, and still do the glasses in the pub each night. But I knew if Mason gave me the job, it'd lead to more work, and more after that, and before very long, I'd be working for him, and not with Miranda at the Keepsake Arms. I felt guilty.

But, I couldn't be sure my job there was safe, and I needed to work, my da was such an awful provider, a waste of space who drank too much. I opened the door of our classroom warily. Pike looked up.

'Where do you think you've been, Islip?'

'To see about a job,' I said, brightly, looking at Pike and hoping he'd give me a break for once. The other kids stopped what they were doing and watched me keenly. They liked it when Pike picked on me, it meant they were off the hook for a while.

'And how did you do?' said Pike, sneering.

'I got the job,' I said grinning, in spite of myself.

'You got the job!' He turned to the rest of the class and laughed. '*He* got the job. It can't have been much of a job, boys can it?'

'No, Mr Pike,' they all chorused. I felt myself go red with anger.

'In fact, *Mr* Pike, it's a very good job, and I'm proud I got it, pleased as punch. The man who's going to be my boss, he says he thinks I'll be great at the work.' *Bad mistake.* I knew it the moment I'd opened my mouth.

'Oh, he does, now does he? Well I guess he'll be a fool tomorrow, or whenever he takes you into his stable. So what are you doing here now, Islip, if you'd rather be somewhere else?'

'But I like being here, Mr Pike, honest, the job is just a little extra.' It wasn't true, I hated school and I liked Pike less, but I did like the food and I liked learning. I wanted to learn as much as I could, so I could get on, when I was a man. Which made me think of Alice and her iPad. I took the chance.

'Have you ever seen an iPad?' I said to Pike, as I walked to my bench. 'It's a big square thing for writing on. With all the alphabet on as well.' He looked incredulous.

'It's, "seen an iPad, *sir*?"', he snapped at me, 'and no I haven't, and I don't particularly want to, either. What I do want, Islip, is someone who turns up on time for lessons and doesn't start giving me cheek each time.'

'I'm not,' I told him, feeling indignant, but Pike raised his hand to silence my words.

'That's enough!' he said. 'You can go downstairs to the joinery workshop and stand outside for the rest of the morning. That'll teach you to turn up late for your lessons. I'll let you have dinner, *if* you're lucky. Go on, Islip, get out of my sight.'

I scowled as I left and made a gesture and Pike saw it. I knew I wouldn't get dinner today. My pleasure in my job was fading fast, I was already hungry and going on starving.

The school was based at the top of the house. I trundled down to the joinery workshop which was on the ground floor and had a back door which led out to the churchyard. I peered carefully into the room. Pike might be grumpy and sometimes callous but the man who ran the workshop was worse. According to Jake, who was one of my mates, you never crossed Wetherby Eisen twice. Or if you did, you vanished for good.

'You're pulling my leg, Jake,' I'd said and Jake had grinned, as if to say, 'Sure,' but I still suspected he'd told the truth.

When I looked in that particular day, Jake was standing by the sink, which was next to the door that led out to the churchyard, where Pike had told me to stand, looking stupid. Everyone hated being told to do that, the girls because they were scared of the graves, the lads, because they were scared of Eisen. Jake looked up and saw me approaching. He frowned and gestured over at Eisen, who I could see was talking to someone. *Another poor sod who's got into trouble*, I thought grimly. But no, when I looked, I saw it was Ben. I started walking towards them, unthinking.

'Tom, come back!' Jake hissed and I stopped, and made my way back towards him, reluctant.

'You're a fool if you think you can go over there. Eisen's in a foul mood, today.'

'But that's Ben Tencell, he's a mate,' I told him. 'I don't want him thinking I'm rude,' I said.

'And will he be here tomorrow?' said Jake. 'When Eisen decides to lock you in the basement?'

I shivered suddenly, and said nothing, understanding the point at last. Eisen liked to torment his pupils, even more than *Mister Pike*, and any slip of an excuse would do. I didn't need that sort of trouble. I turned away and went outside.

The graves mocked me, with their flat, stupid faces, asking me what I was doing in the churchyard and telling me I was as useless as them. I wondered whether I should wait for dinner. If I just scarpered until tomorrow, what would it matter? The smell of the slaughterhouse drifted over.

Minutes later, Ben strolled past, walking slowly down Scriveners Road. He stopped when he saw me, frowned then grinned. 'What are you doing out here, Thomas?'

'It's a long story, you don't want to know. What were *you* doing, talking to Eisen?'

'It's *Mr* Eisen, to you, remember.' Ben grinned again, and I grinned back, glad to be here and talking to a mate. 'We were talking supplies, not that it's any of *your* business. He knows of a place I can get more wood.'

'Right,' I said. 'Pike told me off for getting a job, or asking questions, or giving him cheek, any of these, or just for existing. Who knows with Pike?'

'I thought you had a job in the pub?'

'Now I've got two, we need the cash. I don't like Pike, he's a miserable sod and always looking to get one over.'

'Well, take it from me, I saw you before in the joinery workshop and Wetherby Eisen's harder than Pike. You stay away from Wetherby, Tom. He's a mate of mine, I know what I'm saying.'

'But it's fine for you to be mates with him?'

'It's business, Tom and business is different, besides, I'm a man and you're just a lad. Blokes like Eisen eat lads for breakfast. I mean it, Thomas. Stay away from the man.'

26

Then – Miranda

When Miranda got back to the pub after work, it was well after seven and she was shattered. There had been a demand for rock at the factory, which had meant more work, and Miranda had jumped at the extra hours, but her ma would be worried, or should have been worried, assuming she'd troubled herself to care. Miranda sighed.

Her ma hadn't been the same for ages, not since Matt McCarthy had died and then even worse since the shoes had been found. He ma was slowly falling apart and on top of all that the takings were down. What had happened to the mother she'd known?

As she drew closer to Dogleg Lane and the Keepsake Arms, she could hear a noise, the sound of music and ribald laughter, and Miranda's heart sank as she guessed where it came from. She paused, then pressed on. As she walked in she was pushed aside by a couple of strangers, apparently eager to reach the bar. The woman stopped and reeled a little, already tipsy.

'We're looking for the singing room,' she said to Miranda.

'What did you say?' Miranda replied.

'The room where the dancing and singing is, love.' The man spoke this time, he at least seemed more or less sober, until he gave a very loud belch.

Miranda pushed past them into the bar, where Reg was supping a pint of ale.

'What's going on?' she shouted, furious. The racket in here was even worse.

'It's nothing, Miranda,' Reg said, grinning, 'your ma's just trying to make a few shillings. It would help her though, if you came home sooner.'

'I haven't that long since left the factory, so don't you start giving me a hard time. What do you mean, make a few shillings? What's she done now?' Half of her didn't want to know the answer.

'It's only a bit of singing and fun. Your ma's moved the parlour upstairs for the night, so the room can be used for music and dancing, just for this evening. It's a music night, for special guests only.'

'Special guests only! You can hear that racket up by Pasenheuse. *And* you need a licence for music, I thought you knew that.'

'Your mother's the one who's in charge, not me. I don't know nothing about any licence, you'd have to ask your ma about that. But the singer's only a waitress really, she's helping your mother to serve the ale, and only singing to keep people happy.' He winked at Miranda who swore loudly; *she* was the only sane one amongst them. She went to the parlour; was back in a flash.

'There's a woman's dancing on the table in there and it's not even Saturday! I can't believe my mother did this. Where the hell is she?'

'Don't ask me,' said Reg, grinning, 'but I'd try outside if I were you. The noise through there probably drove her out.'

'And whose fault's that?' Miranda snapped back, dashing outside and heading down the passage to the yard at the end. Her ma was sitting on the back doorstep, holding a fag. Miranda was stunned.

'Since when did you take up smoking, Ma? And there's a woman dancing in there!'

Her ma glanced up and smiled at Miranda. 'Smoking is legal, the last time I heard, and dancing is too, as far as I know. You let that woman have her fun, it'll soon be morning, and she'll be working as hard as ever.'

Miranda walked a bit closer to her mother. 'I'm not that sure I know you lately. We used to run a respectable house, and now there's someone dancing on the table and a racket fit to disturb the dead. I could hear the music streets away.'

'So what if you can? The people in there are enjoying themselves.'

'This isn't the sort of pub we run. I don't know why you've decided to do this.'

'For the money, Miranda, why else would I do it? Didn't you hear what I said the last time? The takings are down, there are too many pubs in this part of town, it's hard to get business.'

'You could have fooled me, it's heaving in there!'

'Then you should be pleased, we'll make more money, unless you want us to lose our home. You know Tom's father, Scotty, came in? He loves the singing nights, he said, he's going to bring all his friends the next time.'

'That's what we need,' Miranda sneered. 'More of life's dross like Scotty Islip.'

Hannah Collenge stared at her daughter. It made Miranda feel uncomfortable. Her mother frowned.

'I never took you for a snob, Miranda. You used to be a good-natured girl, warm and friendly and not one to judge. But now you've turned all prim and proper, and all because of a bit of dancing. It must be the factory that's made you like that, because I certainly haven't.'

Oh yes, you have, Miranda thought. *It all began when your standards slipped and you gave yourself to Matt McCarthy. And then you went and took those shoes.*

She grabbed her ma's shawl which lay on the step in a crumpled heap. The shawl was good, from her father's day, and made with wool, it was thick and warm.

'You can think and say whatever you like. But first thing Monday, I'll be going to the pawnshop and taking this shawl and a few things more. It might be grim, but at least it's honest, and it's what folk do, in our position. Instead of running a bawdy house.'

As she climbed the steps to her room, she thought about

what her mother had said. She wasn't stuck up or looked down on others, she only wanted to keep things right. But as she opened her bedroom door, trying to ignore the noise from the parlour, she couldn't help hearing the voice in her head, which wondered if her mother was right.

27

Then – Thomas

Wherever I was, I always seemed to be late for something. I was late leaving school because Pike insisted I finish my work, as I had, he told me, "wasted my time, talking to mates while standing in the churchyard". 'Forgetting', of course, that he was the one who'd sent me down there. So, now the night was drawing in, and I knew Da would be home for his tea, so I thought I'd go up to the tenements again and look for Louise. And if I saw Alice while I was looking, well that was a bonus.

Pearson's Tenements were bleak, as always. They seemed to cast a terrible shadow, dark and forbidding, looming over the street below them. Not that the people passing by noticed. Most of those wandering down the street were drunk. I noticed a woman round by the back. She was filling a pail from a tap by the privies.

'Have you seen Louise?' I asked her. 'She's a friend of mine and May's daughter. She hasn't been seen at school for ages.'

'Not for weeks,' said the woman, offhand, ignoring my smile and watching the bucket as if it would vanish. Now I *was* worried.

'Do you happen to know which floor she lives on? Then I could go and ask the neighbours.' *Someone must know where Louise had gone.* The woman turned round and gave me a glare.

'No, I don't, but even if I did I wouldn't tell you. I don't know you from Adam, do I?'

'I'm a friend, from school, we're mates, honest. I'm only trying to find Louise.'

'If you were her friend, you'd know where she lived.'

'She didn't want to tell me,' I said. 'Because...' I stopped, I couldn't say it. Because she was ashamed of her home, I meant, ashamed of living in Pearson's Tenements.

'I really am her friend,' I said. 'Someone from school asked me to find her. One of the teachers, a Mr Pike.'

The woman gave a snort of laughter. 'So that's why you're asking, because you've been told to. Well, you listen sonny, the kids round here don't go to school, they've something better to do than school and that's get a job. I don't suppose you've heard of that?'

'Of course,' I said, 'I've got a job, in fact I've got two.' Well, I would have soon.

'And yet you've time to gossip with me. They must be easy jobs, I reckon. Haven't you got a home to go to?'

'I'm trying to find my mate, Louise. I've already said.'

'And I've just said she isn't here. And as I'm on the same floor as her, I reckon I'd know.'

'So you do know where Louise lives, then?'

The woman laughed. 'You've caught me out. I'll tell you something, for nothing lad, seeing as I reckon you're telling the truth. Your mate Louise is gone for good, she won't be back, some people moved into her room, recently. Irish they were. I suppose you know what happened to her ma?'

'I do,' I said, and I saw by her face she was disappointed, I'd done her out of a gory tale. 'But what about Louise's things, what happened to them?'

'I expect the Irish have got them, my lad, unless she took them with her, of course. But no more questions, I've got to get going. It's a long way up from where I'm standing.'

'I could help,' I said quickly, and I saw by her look that she'd guessed my intent, to follow her up and find out which of the rooms was Louise's.

'Not on your life,' she said, sharply, so I moved to one side as she passed with her pail, keeping well back from the sloshing water and finally hiding in the shadows, to watch her climb the many stairs. It took a long time, and because it was dark, I almost lost her more than once.

Three floors up, I started to follow her, acting with stealth to keep out of the way. When she finally reached the top, I hid out of sight and watched her stagger along the passage, then push on a door on the left hand side. I emerged slowly. I could see that there were several doors, hers was the second on the left hand side. Which meant Louise's was one of the others. I went back down.

When I stepped out onto the street again, Alice was there.

'What are you doing round here?' I said.

'I've just been in there,' she typed rapidly, nodding at my school which was some yards behind us.

'Oh no you haven't,' I said, grinning. 'I'd know if you had, that's my school, not yours.'

Her eyes narrowed, as if she was thinking. 'It's a house, not a school, although maybe it's both.' She looked at me closely as she was typing. 'Are you the sort who tells lies, Thomas? I wouldn't have said so, if I'd been asked.'

'Not very often, only when I need to. What about you?'

'Of course,' she typed. 'It's necessary, sometimes, especially right now.' She grinned at me, as if she knew a secret. 'Where do you live?'

'Down in the Low, on Haversham Road. Right by the flour mill, you must know that.'

'Of course I know it. That's ages away.'

'Not if you go the way I get there, round the corner, and past the church, then through the passage and down the road. It doesn't take long.'

Alice nodded. 'I know the passage, I've just been through it. But there isn't a church there, not anymore, not where I live.' She paused and smiled and her blue eyes glinted. 'Like the school, it's long since vanished, changed completely.'

'Of course there is, you must be blind! Here let me show you, it's just round the bend. Then you could come to see my house.' Alice considered and shook her head.

'I've got to get home.'

'So where's your home if it's not around here?'

'Ebbenheart Green, it's a fair old walk.'

'That's really nice, all fields and trees. We picnicked there with the church group once. Not that I go to church often,' I added hastily.

'There aren't any fields in Ebbenheart Green.'

'What?' I said and stared at Alice. Was the girl blind, or stubborn or stupid? It didn't matter which, I still liked her. I took a deep breath and stood a mite taller.

'Are you coming round to my house, or not?'

28

Now – Cressida

She knew she wasn't handling things right and talking to Martha had only confirmed it. Martha was set on her own agenda, and she had been happy to do what she asked. But now, Cressida was thinking about Alice, especially after the other night. The row, then Alice running away – from children's voices? No, from her mother. Cressida had to admit the truth. Then what happened after she ran. *It was all very odd.*

Cressida had wandered into the courtyard, once the churchyard of Curdizan Church. The council had made it all quite attractive with paving and trees and some new wooden seats in dead people's names. It was easy to see where the gravestones had been, some of the slabs were still in the ground along with the path which had led to the church.

Cressida paused. At first, she hadn't seen Alice anywhere, had despaired of ever finding her here, but then when she walked back up to the road, she noticed Alice right up ahead. But Alice wasn't alone anymore. Cressida stopped.

Where were Alice and the boy going? This wasn't the way to Ebbenheart Green.

She followed them further along the street, keeping well back, and watched as Alice crossed over the road. The boy was leading her down a passage. Could this be the boy called Thomas?

She hadn't been down the passage before, but she didn't have time to study her surroundings because before she knew it she was out the other side and doing her best to keep up with the kids. On the left of the street was an old church hall, clearly disused, and then she'd left the part of the city she knew quite well and had wandered into a different landscape.

A derelict one.

Cressida wanted to stop and look, but she couldn't stop now, because Alice and Tom, if Tom he was, were still walking, and quickly at that. Alice was typing as she walked, clutching her iPad close to her chest. This place was just a pile of rubble. Apart from a church, ahead on the left.

'That's Blackberry Close,' said a voice from the right, and she looked down sharply at a tired old man who was sitting on the pavement, sucking on a pipe which had clearly gone out. He grinned at Cressida, a toothy smile, and somewhat eerie, his white teeth glowing in the almost-dark.

'I can't stop, sorry,' Cressida told him. 'I'm following them.' She gestured ahead to the vanishing kids.

'Following who?' said the old man, mildly, dropping his pipe on the ground with a clunk. Cressida sighed.

Drunk, I guess, she said to herself. She didn't have time to spare for pity.

The site had obviously once been bulldozed. There were broken-up walls and mounds of rubble that no-one had bothered to take away. There were even a couple of buildings still standing, apart from the church and whatever was beyond it. On the right was a pub, it looked more like a house, but a sign still swung from above the door. The Keepsake Arms, the sign informed her. Cressida stopped. She'd lost Alice in the fading daylight and even the man on the pavement had vanished. It was almost dark and rather creepy. Cressida sent a text to her daughter.

'Alice where are you? I'm walking back towards the church, but I can't see a thing in this wretched light.'

'Sorry Mum, I met up with Tom. I'll be at the abbey in about ten minutes.'

Not that church, Alice, thought Cressida, sighing and looking around. It wasn't that hard to imagine the past, how the place might have looked a long time ago. Row upon row of narrowing streets, cobblestones and small-paned windows, kids on the pavement and men at the pub. She glanced across at The Keepsake Arms. It looked a homely sort of place, probably shabby, but bigger than most. It can't have been easy, living back then.

Cressida wandered towards the church. Blackberry Close was nothing to speak of, broken down pavements and then came the church, a solid old thing. The building next door was still standing, a yard to the right, the house to the left. The house had the look of an old coach house, peeling black paint and a huge old door. The cellar windows had bars behind them, upstairs all the curtains were closed. Cressida shivered.

There was something creepy about the house, which was odd, she thought, because Aleph's house was meant to be haunted, and yet she'd felt nothing, nothing at all. In contrast, this house had an unpleasant feel.

Cressida sighed, thinking of Aleph and mentally dragging herself from the past. The next few weeks would be more than difficult and she would have to deal with that. Hearing what Alice might reveal.

29

Now – Aleph

Cressida looked as lovely as ever. She wandered into the sunlit hall and passed me the sound file, smiling grimly.

'I hope this works, I'm at my wits end.' I didn't answer. What could I say? You never could tell with this kind of work. Something would happen, but who knew what?

'There's coffee,' I said, 'in the office upstairs. Let's go up.' She did as I said.

My guest sat down in the nearest chair. 'This is quite a desk you've got in here. I thought that the last time. Where did you get it?'

'The charity shop on Narrowboat Lane.'

'Really?' she said. 'I'd never have guessed. But then, there are so many to choose from. Charity shops, I mean, not desks.' She laughed, feebly. Cressida was nervous and I was too. God knows what we'd find today. I didn't like doing the reading blind. Usually, I heard them in advance. And that wasn't all.

I hadn't had a peaceful night. I'd been up and down, pacing the room, hearing the sound of children crying. I'd hear them cry, look out of the window, see nothing, then go back to bed, waking up to hear them crying. This went on until almost five, then about six, the bin men turned up. I wasn't exactly on top form.

'How do you want to play this thing?' I said to Cressida. 'No pun intended.'

'Why don't you listen and do what you do, and then perhaps we can talk, later?' Cressida was edgy, she'd already heard the file the right way, just not in reverse. I smiled calmly.

'Don't expect too much this time. This is just an initial recording.' Cressida nodded.

I started us off by clicking Play. The first voice I heard was Alison Clipper's, one of the mothers, who'd sat with Alice and made the recording. The school hadn't wanted to get involved. That's why Cressida had asked a parent.

'You know why we're having this chat today?' Alison Clipper was talking to Alice.

'Because I won't talk to my mum, said Alice. She thinks she's upset me.'

'Is that true?'

'No,' said Alice. 'Of course she hasn't.'

'So why won't you talk to your mother, Alice? It's quite a long time not to talk to someone. You know that day, when you ran away, that Sunday in summer, did something happen to make you scared or to make you angry, and stop you talking. If that's what happened it's okay to say.' Alice didn't answer. Mrs Clipper sighed.

'We're all trying to help you Alice.'

'I hate talking about this stuff. Everyone always says the same thing. I told my mother I'd talk to you, but only if it was the way I wanted.' Her voice was tight, controlled, like an adult's.

'We only want to do what's best.' But Mrs Clipper's voice belied her words.

'I'd like to talk about Tom,' said Alice.

I started, surprised and glanced across for Cressida's reaction, but she shook her head and whispered, '*Listen.*' The file rolled on, I *was* listening.

'I've only known him a couple of weeks. He's about my age and lives in the Low.'

'How did you meet him?' Alison asked. She seemed relieved that Alice was talking.

'I was standing right by Curdizan courtyard, where the church used to be, in Curdizan High, when Tom turned up so I showed him my iPad. Then I took his photo.'

'And, did he like it?'

'That bit was weird, Tom wasn't in it, even though I knew I'd included him in it. And, no he didn't like it, not when he saw he wasn't in the picture, it made him take off. Then, when I tried on a different day, the same thing happened. Tom wasn't happy.'

'So, has your mother met this Tom?'

'No, not yet, I've barely got to know him myself. I wasn't expecting to see him the last time, but then he turned up and wanted to show me the place where he lives. It's down in the Low, on Haversham Road. That's by the mill, where the Blue runs past. It wasn't very nice. The houses are small and ugly and cramped, that's how the mill owner makes his money. He crams people in and gets money from rents *and* cheap labour.'

Mrs Clipper coughed, I wondered if that was because she was speechless. 'He's quite a sharp lad, your Tom, isn't he?' She paused briefly. 'I was told that there weren't any houses in the Low, or at least not now. That it's all derelict. Isn't that true?'

'Not where Tom and I were, no. There were loads of houses, a church and a pub and of course the factory. It's a whole different world, Mrs Clipper, believe me.'

'It certainly is,' said Cressida grimly, reaching across to pause the recording. 'Have you been to the Low lately?'

'I've never been to the Low,' I said. 'I haven't lived here long, as you know.'

'Well, take it from me, it's a building site. I followed Alice and Tom that night and she's right, there's a church and a pub and the factory, what's left of it anyway. But there aren't any houses on Haversham Road.'

'She's obviously making it up,' I said. 'But what about Thomas? You said he was an imaginary friend?'

'That's what I thought, but that was before I followed them there.'

'You actually saw him there with Alice?'

'I did, yes, although only at a distance. It was definitely a boy, although it could have been anyone.'

'And yet he wasn't in the photo she took?'

'No,' said Cressida, 'I checked and he wasn't. Don't you think that's rather strange?'

30

Then – Thomas

Seeing Jake had got me thinking. All of the lads were scared of Eisen. He often threatened to lock them up, put them in the basement, if they were bad. The basement of the school was really a cellar. *A cellar,* I thought. A perfect place to hide the boots.

There was probably hardly anything in it but if I was lucky, there could be a cupboard. And the school wasn't far from Narrowboat Lane, where Matt McCarthy's shoe shop was. *Perfect,* I thought. Assuming the shoes weren't found by Eisen.

That day at school, I thought about being a bit of a nuisance, so Pike would send me down to the churchyard, so I could check out the basement idea. But in the end I scrapped that plan, I needed to keep a lower profile, I didn't want to lose my place at school. Apart from the lessons, I got free food and was out of the rain; I'd have to find a different way.

I waited until the school day was over and slipped downstairs to the joinery workshop. The door to the churchyard was firmly shut, but Jake was still there, sweeping up nails.

'You can't keep away from this place, can you?' Jake looked amused.

'I want to know what's in the basement.'

'You, most likely, if Eisen comes in and finds you here. You know you're not meant to be down here. Not without Pike's express permission.'

'Then tell me, quickly. What's in the basement?'

'Little and nothing, as far as I know. A disused kitchen, that's used on occasion. Planks and nails, a few rotting bodies, how should I know? I've no idea, I rarely go down there. I'm a good lad, the best I'm told. Why do you ask?'

'Never you mind. What about Eisen? Does he go down there?'

'Not that I know of. Sometimes he sends the younger lads down, to fetch up some wood or some nails from the cupboard. But most of the wood is kept out there, along with the tools.' He gestured outside to an old stone shed that sat in the churchyard. I grinned at Jake.

'Great, I owe you. But don't tell anyone I was asking questions.'

'Don't tell anyone what? said Jake. We grinned at each other. But I'll be claiming the favour back.'

I nodded, agreeing, Jake was a mate, and your mates were precious, you didn't get many, not around here. I sighed, thinking. Now, I'd thought of another problem. How to get all those shoes up here, and into the basement, without being seen.

As it happened, Ben had the answer.

'Found a place to store your trunk?' Ben asked me, when I went to visit him at his workshop, later that day. 'Or should I say, Miranda's trunk?'

'It's Hannah's actually, Miranda's ma. And maybe I have, but there's still a problem. And as you don't want to help us out, you won't be asking me what that is.'

'I didn't say I wouldn't help you. I just said I wanted to know what was in it.'

'I can't tell you that, that's private information, between me and Miranda.'

'Right,' said Ben, looking amused. 'If you say so. So, then, what's the problem?'

'Getting the trunk from here to there.' There's such a thing as too much pride. Ben looked smug.

'You want me to give you a lift on the cart. Well, as you're a mate, I can do that for you. For a fee of course.'

'A fee?' I said, my heart sinking. 'How much would you be

wanting then?' I was totting my wages up in my head, including the ones from the job I'd just got. The one I hadn't even started yet.

'A quick look at what's inside the trunk. It won't even cost you a packet of fags.' He grinned, broadly and I wished I had a shoe in my hand, so I could throw the thing at his head. And hit him, hard.

But, of course, I wasn't wearing shoes.

I saw Miranda later that day, in the pub's parlour. She was on her knees, scrubbing the carpet for all it was worth. She didn't look happy.

'I thought you had a woman did that?'

'The cleaning, yes, that's Mrs Hemhirst. But she said she doesn't do cleaning carpets, not the sort that are stained with sick.'

'I thought the drunks all stayed in the bar.' Miranda looked up.

'That's right, Thomas, and so did I. Until my mother flipped her lid and decided to run a music hall. Now, we have singing and dancing in here.'

'Really?' I said, starting to smile. 'Don't you need a licence for that?'

Miranda sat back and glared at me. 'Was there something special you wanted, or have you just come here to cause me hassle? Because if it's the last, then shove off now, I'm far too busy. No, forget I said that, you clean the carpet, I'm fed up with being the pub skivvy.'

I caught the rag she threw me, and more, a whiff of something, it didn't smell good. 'I came to give you the good news.'

'I've found a place to store the shoes. Until we can take them back to the shop. And Ben's offered to help us move them, on his cart. I reckon we can take them as soon as you want.' I smiled, proudly.

Miranda got to her feet, looking weary. 'I think you'd

better come with me.'

'Why, where are we going?' I asked her. She didn't answer.

I followed Miranda up the stairs, each flight taking a little bit longer. Several years later we reached the attic, ducking our heads as we crept through the door. The glow from her lamp lit the room, barely.

'See that trunk with the shoes over there?' I nodded slowly.

'Well, go beyond it, past the old suite. Right behind it, you'll see what I mean.'

I did as she said, it took me a while, the shadows were worse, away from her lamp. I stubbed my toe as well, for my pains. Two more trunks were lurking in the corner. She made way her forward, to stand beside me, pulling at the lids to reveal their contents. I couldn't help it, I gasped with surprise.

Dozens more shoes nestled within.

31

Now – Aleph

The lack of sleep was getting to me, it had only got worse as the day wore on. But now it was time to reverse the sound file. I smiled at Cressida.

'This is when we hear what she thinks. *Really* thinks, as opposed to what she tells you she thinks. Assuming that you believe it works. Not everyone believes it does.' Cressida nodded.

'I'm willing to give it a go,' she said.

'We might hear the same backwards as forwards, or we might hear something we didn't know before, or we might hear something totally different , a contradiction of what was said forwards. If the two versions contradict, the reversal is much more likely to be true. Do you understand?'

'Yes,' said Cressida, 'although I'm still not convinced that doing this will help.'

'Well, let's just hear what Alice has to say. It'll give us an insight into her mind.'

'She's just being stubborn, or maybe she's ill. I can't see how this process will help.'

'You said you'd give it a go,' I said. 'It's vital you don't prejudge what happens.'

'I know,' said Cressida, looking doubtful. 'It's just, I'm rather sceptical.'

'Fine,' I said and clicked on Play. Time to hear things from Alice's perspective.

When Alison Clipper asked about Tom.

He's a friend, said Alice.

'So that bit's true.' I gave her a look.

Tom didn't know what an iPad was.

119

'Maybe his family can't afford one. I hadn't used one before I bought hers.'

'Right,' I said, through gritted teeth. I wished she'd shut up.

That's because Tom is dead.

'What?' said Cressida. 'Stop that, now.' I pressed Pause.

'Did she say what I thought she did?'

'Yes,' I said. 'It probably means they've fallen out. He's dead to her.'

'No,' said Cressida, 'that's not right. Alice and Tom are still good friends, she mentioned him only yesterday evening.'

'Reversed words tell the truth,' I said. 'It might be veiled but it is the truth.'

'So what does that mean?'

'I don't know. Let's listen to the rest.'

Streets of houses, row upon row. A horse in the yard. Next to the old-fashioned coaching inn. With its black and newly-painted door.

A woman outside the Keepsake Arms. I think the woman's called Miranda.

This is Tom's world but... Tom is dead.

His world's dead. I can't tell Alison Clipper that.

'She certainly can't,' said Cressida softly. She reached across and paused the recording.

'You're the professional, you explain.' She glared at me.

'I can't,' I said. 'I only know what I've already told you, the words that are said in reverse aren't lies. Except, there's one thing.' I paused, thinking.

'You said the Low was mostly rubble. Only one pub and no houses at all on Haversham Road?'

'Yes,' said Cressida.

'That's not the way Alice saw it. From her perspective, the Low still exists. The houses, the people, there's even a horse, and a woman called Miranda. When you went there did you see Miranda?'

'I only saw Alice and a drunk on the pavement and plenty of rubble. And of course there was Tom.' Her voice trailed off.

'But she saw a place which was vibrant with life. Bustling, breathing, even the paint on that door was fresh.'

'The coaching inn door.' Cressida said. 'That building was there.'

'And was the black paint on the door fresh?'

'No, of course it wasn't. It was faded and peeling and barely black, most of the door was just tired old wood. The paint had long gone.'

'That proves it, then, Alice didn't see the place you saw, she saw the Low as it used to be, a long time ago. She saw the past, with Tom in it. And if she saw the past and Tom in it, then in the present, Tom would be...'

'Dead,' said Cressida, and our eyes locked.

32

Then – Thomas

Pearson's Tenements were worse by daylight. The light only made the building look derelict, dirty and shabby, and worn at the edges. I didn't want to go there, not anymore. But I had to try to find Louise. This time next week, I'd be doing two jobs, working for Mason as well as the pub, with the school in between, it had to be now.

I made my way to the fifth floor, slowly, trudging, not walking, looking around for rats and dogs. I saw two dogs, tied to some railings, but not any rats, the daylight was probably keeping them away. I sighed heavily.

When I finally reached the top, I couldn't see much, just a long string of washing, blocking my view. I pushed my way through it and began trying doors on the left hand side, as quick as I could. The first one I tried opened easily.

It was damp and dark, with very little light, apart from the light from a tiny window. It made our house seem like a palace. We had *four* whole rooms, if you count the scullery, which Da always did, he said he paid for it, same as the rest.

Under the window a man was snoring, asleep on a mattress, he barely stirred as I wandered around. I couldn't see anything girly at all, no shoes or clothes or the kind of touches my ma likes to make, fancy chair backs and loads of ornaments. No, there was nothing. I went back outside.

The next door along belonged to the woman I'd met before. I gave it a miss, at least for the moment. Then a lad emerged from a doorway opposite. He glared at me.

'What're you doing up here?' he said.

I studied the boy. He was shorter than me and far more scruffy, with wild brown hair.

'I'm looking for a mate, she's called Louise. I'm trying to find which room she lives in. Any idea?'

'There's no Louise here,' he said abruptly, and tried to get past me, but something about his manner felt wrong.

'So let's have a look, to prove you're right.' I hurried towards the door he'd come out of and gave it a shove.

'What do you think you're doing, mate? You can't go in there.' The boy turned around and grabbed my arm. 'I'll set my da on you, laddie, and then you'll regret you came up here.' From the sound of his voice, I reckoned he was Irish and the ones around here were known for their tempers. I knew I'd have to be quick at the job. I scanned the room as fast as I could, it was more or less empty, with the same poor lighting as the one I'd just been in, and the same dank smell and a mattress in the corner. Along with a pile of women's things. I made straight for them.

'Hey, now, you, come away from those things, they're my ma's, right enough.' The lad was now giving vent to his anger, kicking at my ankles but I didn't much care. I held up a cardy, Louise's cardy.

'Sure they are,' I said to the lad. I recognised the thing, it was old and tatty, she'd worn it for school and I'd teased her about it, every day. Said it was made of holes not wool. It made me feel choked.

I bundled the cardigan under my arm, along with a dress I thought was hers too. Then I turned on the lad and grabbed his throat. 'Why don't you tell me where you got these?'

He made some sort of animal noise, so I eased off the pressure and asked him again.

'They were here when we got here, honest they were. We've haven't been here for more than a month, we were lucky to get it, that's what we thought.'

'I'm looking for the girl who wore these clothes. I want to know what you've done with the rest.'

'I haven't done nothing, and neither's my da. A man came around and took some away, such as there was, apart from what's there. I reckon he thought those things wouldn't sell.'

'And who was the man?' I said to the lad.

'The rag and bone man, perhaps, I don't know. He said she wouldn't be needing the things. Da didn't argue, I think he was pissed and not quite with it. My da said later, it was a pity they'd gone, my ma had wanted to keep the best stuff. She said she'd turn them into some shirts.'

'I ought to string you up,' I said. 'That's theft, that is, and she's my mate.'

'We're not the ones who stole the things, the stuff was here when we arrived, and see, it's still here, apart from the things the rag and bone took. He didn't even pay us hardly anything. Here, they're yours.'

He shoved the last of her stuff towards me, a thick, scruffy scarf, also full of holes and I stumbled backwards, releasing my hold. I gripped the things tighter.

'That's all there is, you're sure of that?'

'As sure as I'm talking to you right now.' The lad was rubbing his neck and coughing. 'But my da's due back so you'd better leave now.' I took the hint and left then and there, running downstairs at a flying pace. I passed a man on the stairs, coming up, I'd swear he had an Irish face. I knew I had to get out of there fast.

Once I was safely back on School Lane, I took a deep breath and sighed with relief, but the pleasure at being outside didn't last. I might have found a few of her things, but I still hadn't found Louise herself. And if what the lad had told me was true, she wouldn't be needing her clothes anymore, according to the man who took the best. It gave me a cold feeling inside.

I didn't like to think what that might mean.

33

Now – Aleph

Cressida and I were standing on the street, on Scriveners Road, where the church used to be. It was empty of people and almost of pigeons. I turned to Cressida. 'What do you think we ought to do?'

'I'm just remembering something else. Alice said Tom lived ages away, but he said no, it's just "past the church, then through the passage and down the road." He meant this church, here.'

'But there isn't any church here, not anymore.'

'Quite,' said Cressida.

We wandered aimlessly down the road. Or so I thought. Cressida spoke.

'They crossed the road about here, I think, and they, we, went down this passage.'

We stared at the alley, it was grim and unwelcoming. 'I'd never been down this alley before. I don't believe I knew it existed.'

'You and half of Curdizan probably. The more fortunate half.'

'Maybe so, but Tom knew it, he used it regularly. That's the impression I got from Alice. It comes out by an old church hall.'

Cressida hurried along the passage, and I followed, catching her up on Convent Court, by the old church hall, the one she'd just mentioned. It was virtually derelict.

'Going through the passage is a much quicker way to get down here. And if we turn right down Pasenheuse Road, we can get to the Low and Tom's old home.'

'Let's do it,' I said, and we set off walking.

Soon we arrived in the old part of town which was not much more than a building site. I stared at the remnants of yesterday's streets and felt very sad, the place was a dump, but once it been a home to hundreds. A whole community, living and breathing and dying down here. Facing hard things we knew nothing about, I could smell it in the air, the scent of the river and the stench of dung, the dust from the factory, shadows in the sky and the drains overflowing. Blood in the gutters on abattoir days. How did I know this? I hadn't a clue.

I suddenly thought we ought to go. So I turned to Cressida who was right by my side, silent and watchful and staring at a building that could have been a pub.

'It's the Keepsake Arms,' said Cressida slowly.

'Do you think you really saw Thomas?' I said, considering.

'I did,' said Cressida. 'He looked as real as you do now.'

'So if you saw Tom, and Tom is dead, then you and Alice must have seen a ghost.'

'Right,' said Cressida, paling slightly.

'But there's something else,' I told her, thinking. 'Alice saw even more than you. You saw a ghost but she saw a ghost town, a bustling place that once existed. How did that happen?'

Cressida didn't even try to answer.

34

Then – Miranda

Miranda sighed as she carried the pot. *My mother thinks she's the local saint. The laundry, McCarthy, dancing on the tables and now she's making soup for the poor. And I thought we were the ones who were poor!*

She paused briefly on Convent Court, taking a rest outside the church hall. A pity that wasn't where she was going. The pot was heavy, full of soup and she carried two loaves under one arm.

'Others give money but we can't afford it. That doesn't mean we can't do our bit.'

'We've done our bit for the church already. The church down here on Blackberry Lane.'

'But they still need help at Curdizan Church. The vicar's wife's ill and there's plenty more soup. And Mary-Ann Parks could do with a hand. I thought she was your friend, Miranda. I don't know why you're making a fuss.'

'Perhaps because I work at Chaucer's *and* at our pub. And now you want me to work on a Sunday.'

'A few extra hours, Miranda, that's all. It's not a big deal.'

No, it's not, Miranda thought, *not in itself. But added to the jobs, and all the small chores and managing people when Ma was off out, it was more than enough, especially today, at the end of the week.* Miranda's feet ached.

She wiped the rain away from her face, it was pouring down, and she staggered carefully into the passage. At least the alley would be quiet today, with less of the usual passing trade. She squeezed her way onto Scriveners Road, being careful not to drop the bread, and as she did, she noticed a couple of people in the distance. The man was tall with his hair tied back and his shirt was white, which was rare in these parts. *They'll be up to no good.*

The people who lived around here could be trouble. But the man looked rather well dressed, all the same, and the bloke who was with him was clearly not skint. He was obviously younger, maybe a boy. Miranda blinked, she couldn't believe it. The younger bloke was a woman in trousers! She needed to get away from this place. But first she must do what her mother had asked. Where was the church? She couldn't see it, damn all this rain! She blinked and sighed and looked again. There it was! She'd better make haste, before she went mad.

The soup kitchen was held in the schoolhouse, down in the basement, which was hardly ever used but at least there was a sink and a tap that worked, and the lads had brought tables down from the workshop. Miranda looked round, the place was crowded, she'd never seen such a crush as this. She squeezed herself past the burgeoning queue.

'I'm glad you've arrived,' said Margie Mace, who worked part-time in the laundry with Carol, Thomas's ma. 'We've got some more pots but at such short notice, we didn't have time to get a vat going. I'm not sure we're going to have enough.'

'Well, this should help,' Miranda said. 'It's vegetable broth and stuffed with veg and I've brought some bread, just a couple of loaves.' She lifted the big pot onto the table.

'That's just what we need,' said Margie, smiling, prodding the loaves, then tearing them up into generous portions. The vicar's daughter served up the soup.

'Isn't this thick? That must be all the good that's in it.' She smiled at Miranda.

Miranda smiled back, Mary-Ann Parks was a friend of hers, despite the woman being several years older. She felt much better, now she was here and out of the rain.

'Aren't you a pet, bringing all this soup, and your mother is too for making it all. I can't believe you carried it here.'

Neither can I, Miranda thought. 'It might need a little reheating,' she said.

Mary-Ann nodded and tried a spoonful. 'No, it's just right. Some of the people who come here are old, we try not to make the food too hot. You'll stay for a while, and have some too?'

'I can't, I'm afraid, I've got to get back.' She stared at the people filling the room. A girl squeezed past, and manoeuvred her way to their side of the table.

'Miranda, I don't think you've met my sister? This is Clara, the baby of the family.'

Miranda smiled and held out her hand but Clara ignored it and scowled at her sister.

'She looks more like you than me,' she said. Mary-Ann laughed and nodded at Miranda.

'Perhaps,' she said. 'It's the hair and the height. Don't you think that's it, Miranda?'

'Perhaps,' said Miranda, who hated the thought of being just like another. Though Mary-Ann Parks was pretty enough. Clara scowled and walked away, clearly resenting Miranda's presence.

Miranda grinned and looked at her friend, noticed the necklace around her neck. A simple string of turquoise beads. 'That's rather pretty,' she said, pointing.

'Oh, it's just a token I got from someone.' Mary-Ann blushed and seemed embarrassed.

An admirer, I'll bet, Miranda decided, meaning to ask her mother later. Her ma was always good for the gossip, being so thick with Carol Islip.

'It's time I was off,' she said to her friend, seeing the queue was growing apace. 'I'll be back next week to collect the pot.'

'We're all very grateful, love,' said Margie, handing a portion of broth to a man. He spilt it all, with his unsteady hands, then spilt some more when he burped loudly. Miranda sighed and turned away. *Thank God my mother can't see the waste.*

When she emerged at the top of the stairs, it was still

raining, and almost like evening; despite it being day, the rain had blocked the light from the sky. Even the abbey seemed overshadowed. *And to think I thought the Low was bad,* Miranda considered, hurrying down the dank alley as fast as she could. She couldn't wait to get back to the pub.

As she left, she recalled the people she'd seen coming up with their strange, fancy clothes and their alien looks. She looked around, but of course they had gone. *They must have been a mirage,* she thought. *Time to go home and have some soup.*

35

Then – Miranda

Miranda was working alone in the parlour. A woman came in, in a deep blue coat and Miranda's heart sank, for she knew the coat and the woman inside it, it was Curtis, the tart. Miranda had just finished settling one fight, between two older women who ought to know better. And then there were the men who'd blocked the door to the pub.

'We're only singing gospel, love.'

'And we're not a church, we're a public house. Come back when you're done, for a pint, why don't you? *Then* you'll be welcome.' One of them laughed but the others looked blank. The older man scowled.

And I'm trying a make a living!

So the last thing she needed, now things had calmed down, was Tanya Curtis turning up, no doubt to make trouble, if she could. Miranda swallowed and took a deep breath.

'What can I get you?'

'Ale, please love, like I always have.' She ignored Miranda who reached for her jug, and put the container down on the counter. 'I've come for a little chat, Miranda. About your mother.'

'I'll get her now,' Miranda said, turning her back on the woman at once. Though she doubted her ma was in the pub.

'I don't need to see her. It's you I want to talk to, love.'

Miranda stopped and turned around. 'Well, make it quick, I've a pub to run.'

'You could have fooled me.' said the woman, laughing. She glanced around the empty room. The fight and the singers had put people off.

'Say what you've come to say to me then, then leave us

alone.' Miranda's voice was tinged with steel.

'You'll have heard, no doubt, about Matt McCarthy. How he dropped down dead and was buried last week.'

'Of course I've heard.' This didn't look good.

'So you'll also know your ma knew him, although *how* she knew him, I wouldn't like to say.'

'And how is this your business, exactly? I think you'd better be leaving now. I don't want to have to throw you out.'

Curtis laughed and shook her head. 'I doubt you could, I'll leave this place when ready, sweetheart, and that's not yet. I know you'll want to hear this.'

'I very much doubt it,' Miranda muttered, under her breath.

'Before your ma turned up at Matt McCarthy's, doing his washing, and more probably, *I* was his friend, and a very good friend, for a very long time. And he said, to me, that when he died, he'd see I was right, and leave me something, so I wouldn't want for food or coal. But Matt McCarthy broke his word, he didn't leave me a single penny, I reckon, because he was sweet on your ma.'

Miranda felt hot but she brushed it away and stared at Curtis. 'If that's your cue to ask for money, you're wasting your time. He didn't leave us a penny either, and as far as I know, there wasn't a will. It's none of your business, as it happens, but I'm sure you can see we're not well off.' She waved her hand around the room, at the threadbare chairs and the worn carpet, even the net at the window had holes.

'He might not have left you money as such, but you and I know your ma got a legacy. And we also know she took possession, of that *gift* before the man died. Which means it wasn't rightly received, seeing as she took it without permission. Or, should I say, took *them*, not it. You know what I mean.'

'Oh no I don't,' Miranda lied. She'd followed the woman's eyes to the fireplace, had seen them rest on the empty shelf. She meant the shoes, she knew she did. But how did she know? Miranda was scared.

'I think you do, and I do hear what you say about poverty.' Casting her eyes around the room.

'I never mentioned the word *poverty*,' Miranda bit back.

'You didn't need to mention it sweetheart, I can see it. But there's poor and poor, if you get my drift, and you and your ma have a thriving business. When your ma's willing to put in the effort.'

'How dare you say my ma is lazy,' Miranda said hotly, making her way around the counter.

'I never said that, you were the one who mentioned the word. All I said was your business had prospects. And you're not the kind who puts a *foot* wrong. So I'll be back in about a week, by which time you'll have thought it through and found a solution, so we can come to a little arrangement.'

'Oh no we won't,' Miranda muttered, but the words were soft and barely heard. She watched as Curtis strolled to the door, staggering slightly, a lopsided smile on her lovely young face. Right by the door she turned around. 'If I was you, I wouldn't trouble your ma with this. I think she's got enough on her plate.'

As she closed the door with a mighty clang, Miranda collapsed. *It never rains but it pours,* she thought.

What on earth was she going to do now?

36

Now – Aleph

I was still thinking about the ghost town, otherwise known as Curdizan Low. I wondered vaguely if Cressida and Alice were having me on. Perhaps this Tom was a make-believe boy, and Cressida and Alice were in on the joke. I didn't believe it.

I hadn't seen Tom but I had heard crying, and I had been at home when the trapdoor flew open, and all by itself. It hadn't happened only the once.

The third time it happened I moved the fridge-freezer back to the middle, over the spot, to make it stay closed. Maybe that's why it had been where it was. I felt lousy.

This was my third bad night in a row, and the crying and screaming went on and on. I had a distinctly uneasy feeling. I stared at the boot which was sitting on the shelf, looking benign. What do you know? I said, angry. The boot said nothing. But the voice in my head was telling me to leave. If only I could.

That wretched woman, Marianne Parks, had forced me to pay all the rent up front. A whole six months and no way out unless I wanted to lose the money. It was too damn long, but I knew I'd have to stick it out. And find a couple of well-paying clients. Then the doorbell rang.

I wasn't expecting a client now but Guinevere James was standing there. I smiled warmly. 'Hello, Mrs James, I'm glad you've come back. Did you want to discuss the recording?'

She didn't respond to my question right then but followed me in, divesting herself of her coat as she went. She was also wearing a tartan scarf. The scarf stayed on as Guinevere James sat down at my table, and watched intently as I made some tea. Most of my guests so far had drunk coffee. Guinevere

James was obviously different. 'Thanks Mr Jones, that's just how I like it.' She paused, waiting. 'I have to admit, I'm rather nervous.'

'There's really no need,' I said, smiling. Clients, I found, often had insights, that came along later. An insight might throw up something important, something they needed to discuss with me. I sat there, waiting, patient and focused.

'I came to see you under false pretences.'

'Right,' I said, and waited some more. *Whatever now?* I said to myself.

'There is no internet business,' she said. 'Or any investors who might want to own it.' She looked me in the eye and swallowed. 'I made it all up.'

'You what?' I said. I took a deep breath. 'And all the people on the recording?'

'They're colleagues at work.'

'And this work is as a...?'

'Journalist.'

Damn, I thought. *I should have known it, given my history.*

'So this is about my private life?'

'Your private life? I don't know anything about your life, outside of your work, and not a great deal more about that.'

Oh shit, I thought, and cursed myself. If that was the truth and she really knew nothing about my past, I knew she soon would, being a journalist, now that I'd gone and flagged it up. I swore, silently.

Guinevere James was still talking.

'I came to you to test out a theory, to see what would happen if I put it into practice. And I have to admit, I was surprised.'

I nodded, understanding. 'You thought reversals didn't work,' I said, 'and then when yours did, it shocked you to hell.' I remembered the things her colleagues had said, played backwards.

Not good news; when it hits, he'd said. It certainly wasn't, my client was a fraud, not the person she'd pretended to be.

Then there was something about not letting feelings get in the way. Then, finally, came the clincher.

Do what you have to.

I looked at James. 'These people of yours, they were talking about me and not about you. I thought these men were your business partners, talking about their underhand schemes to steal your business. But in fact they were your journalist colleagues, talking about me and about what you were doing. That's right, isn't it?' Guinevere nodded. She had the grace to look embarrassed.

'When I heard them say those words, I was shocked to the core, I felt as if we'd revealed ourselves. I didn't dare hear any more that day. I hoped you wouldn't have guessed what we'd done, but I had to get out, and pretty damn quick.'

'You needn't have worried,' I said, curtly. 'I believed what you said, I took it on trust. I assumed the words were about your company.'

'I know that now,' said Guinevere James. 'I'm so sorry. I feel terrible.'

'So why come back?' I said, coldly. 'I'm sure it's not to apologise to me. I presume your paper's printed the story?'

'We scrapped the story, Mr Jones. I'm here because I need your help.'

'You said that the last time,' I told her, sourly. I wasn't going to give this woman any help.

'But this time it's completely different.' Guinevere James unravelled her scarf and hooked it round the back of the chair. 'I want you to help me solve a murder.'

37

Then – Thomas

I'd washed the glasses, cleared the tables, swept out the yard and still she looked grim. What was the matter with Miranda tonight?

Once the punters had left the pub, she dragged me aside and into the parlour. 'Thank God there's no singing or dancing tonight.'

'Well, I see your ma's out, so why would there be? I gather she's gone across to the church, the one near Ben on Blackberry Close.'

'I expect it's about the soup kitchen, it's her latest project.' Miranda scowled. 'It's not as if she's not needed here.'

'She probably feels guilty,' I said mildly. 'Other folk not having quite as much.'

'And so she should,' Miranda said, walking around the room in circles. 'Guilty as hell for what she's done.'

'Shh,' I told her, feeling anxious. 'Cath is still in the back kitchen.'

'You've no idea what she's done, Thomas. No, let me rephrase that, what she and Carol, your mother have done.' My stomach began to feel mighty strange.

'It's about the shoes?'

'Damn right it is. You know you saw there were two more trunks?'

'There aren't any more?' I said, incredulous.

'No,' said Miranda, 'but I almost wish that was all it was. It's much worse than that. The tart knows.'

'You mean Tanya,' I said, mildly. 'The woman with the coat and the curly brown hair. That's always escaping from under her hat.'

'Since when did you start noticing Curtis?'

'My ma was the one who pointed her out. She said she sometimes comes into the laundry, brings in the washing, but Ma said she's really stealing stuff, picking up things other people have dropped.'

'That wouldn't surprise me,' Miranda said, sourly. 'But no, it's worse, she knows about the shoes.'

'But how?' I said. 'I can't believe she's been in the attic.'

'I doubt it,' said Miranda. 'My guess is that Reg or Cath must have told her.'

'Bastards,' I said.

'Right,' said Miranda, 'that's exactly how I felt.' Any other time she'd have given me a clip for swearing at my age, but not this evening.

'And if I can prove it,' Miranda went on, 'whoever it was, they'll get the sack, and on the spot, although we'd never find a replacement. But the thing is, Tom, those shoes have to go, as long as we've got them here we're at risk. She said she's coming back in a week, and wanting money to keep her mouth shut. I don't want to pay her and we don't have the money to pay her anyway, and without the shoes, she can't prove a thing.'

'What does your mother think we should do?'

'I haven't told her, and I'm not going to, she's barely with it, these days as it is. Moping around over Matt McCarthy.' Miranda gave another scowl. I thought, fast.

'I told you before, we can use Ben's cart and take them to Percy, Percy won't talk. He loves secrets, his life is so boring, he's desperate for secrets and thrills and intrigue. You've nothing to fear from Percy or Ben.' But Miranda was shaking her head firmly.

'I'm not going to use that cart,' she told me. 'There are three trunks now, and even if we managed to get them in there, someone would notice us driving them away, or getting them out at the other end. Narrowboat Lane is a very busy street. That cow is always lurking around. I wouldn't want to risk it, Tom.'

'We could do it at night,' I said, hopefully.

'And what sort of noise do you think that would make, cobbles and hooves? Even at night, someone would hear us. I don't want to get Ben Tencell involved.'

'I thought you liked him,' I said, grinning.

'I do,' she said, 'as a mate,' she added and her face coloured up, which made me smile. 'But I still don't want his help with this.'

'We have to ask Ben,' I said firmly, 'you know we can't move those trunks on our own. Please let me ask him, for advice at least. He'll want to help, I know he will.'

'But will he keep it to himself?' she said. 'It's not just my ma, there's yours as well.'

As if needed telling, I thought. I looked Miranda straight in the eye. This was the way to do things properly. 'He will as it's you,' I said, insistent. 'I know he won't tell a single soul.'

38

Now – Aleph

Killing the boy was a dreadful thing, and not being able to recall what happened, made it worse. The old man had been my faithful witness, he'd said I was innocent, driving correctly, not going fast, and I knew I wasn't drunk or drugged. But something, shock or fear or guilt, had blanked my mind and I couldn't remember what I'd been doing. Which made it much worse.

The child had been killed and I was alive, and yet I was dead, although I still breathed. Because of the death of an innocent child, because I felt guilty. And also because I couldn't remember: not knowing how made me wonder. What if the man had been wrong all the time?

The witness had said that the boy had ran out, but how could I be sure that was true? When people aged their sight deteriorated, his vision might not have been all that it could be.

And I believed the toast I'd been eating had been on the seat. Or if it hadn't, maybe I'd eaten it seconds before. But what if I'd taken my hand off the wheel to chew on the toast at the crucial time? No-one had found any toast in the car, or if they had, they hadn't told me. But I couldn't be sure exactly what happened.

All that I knew was that I'd stormed off after rowing with Gerry and that thoughts of the row had been playing on my mind. How both of our lives had revolved around her and how much I hated the way things were. How we moved when she wanted, had sex when she wanted and now we were going to have a baby to please her. *I* had wanted an equal partnership but ended up with a tragedy that destroyed two lives. And no little girl with long blonde hair.

'I don't think I'm the man for the job,' I said to Guinevere, several days later. 'You don't know very much about me.'

'I know *all* about you, now, Mr Jones, and believe me, you're the man for the job.'

'So you *did* know about my private life.' She coloured up then, but kept my gaze.

'I checked you out, but I hadn't before. I chose you because of your skills with recordings. Reverse recordings.' She smiled lightly.

'So what exactly do you want doing now?' I sighed bleakly, this woman was a journalist, ergo, trouble. I didn't want to read about my life in the paper, my life was hard enough as it was, without the addition of fresh publicity. This felt like blackmail and I said so. Guinevere James looked genuinely startled.

'Oh no, Mr Jones, you've got it all wrong. I won't be sharing your story with anyone. But I like to know who I'm working with. It gives me some sort of reassurance.'

She smiled, suddenly, and I thought at once, *she's a person I can trust. Like hell you can*, said my other voice. I couldn't trust anyone, not anymore.

'I'll listen,' I said. 'That's all I can promise.' She nodded, content.

'You remember when I last came to see you? I asked you about the School Lane ghosts?'

'I do,' I told her, suddenly wary.

'I mentioned my cousin, Marianne Parks.'

'I've met Ms Parks.' *And I wish I hadn't.*

'Marianne Parks has a personal history with this house. Her mother lived here so she'd like to find out a bit more about it. I believe you've heard these children's voices.'

'I've heard something,' I told her, tersely. *How the hell did she know that?*

'And, as I understand it, this work you do, the reversing of sound files, can work on crying, as well as on voices.'

I nodded, warily. 'That's only what the research informs me, I've never done any crying reversals. To be honest, Mrs James, I'm highly sceptical.'

'Ms,' she said, and I raised my eyes.

'Ms, Mrs, the point is, Guinevere, I can't guarantee I'll find anything of use.' I already knew where this was leading and I didn't like it, not one little bit.

'Then think of it as humouring me. You'll be very well paid for your time – Aleph.' She grinned, shamelessly but I couldn't smile back. I waited her out.

'If I was to give you a sound recording of a child crying, do you think you could check it for – reversals?'

'I could,' I said, 'that wouldn't be hard. But I think you're pulling a fast one, Guinevere. I presume these are meant to be ghosts crying?'

The journalist smiled and got to her feet. 'Please call me Ginny. I'll get the file to you very shortly. And thanks for your time.'

'But, wait a minute, we haven't finished.' I was chasing her down the hall as I spoke. 'You told me you had a murder to solve. What about that?'

Guinevere smiled as she opened the door. 'All in good time, Mr Jones,' she said. 'All in good time.'

39

Then – Thomas

'She won't let us use the cart,' I said. Ben looked up.

'Won't let *us* use the cart, you say? Since when did I invite you along?'

'When you decided to help Miranda. Now we're a gang, a gang of three.' He looked thoughtful.

'So why can't we use the cart?' he said.

'She reckons it's far too noisy at night. And during the day there are too many people. Like Tanya Curtis, Miranda says.'

'And Miranda knows best?' Ben was amused.

'They are her things,' I told him hotly.

'Or rather, they're not, that's why there's a problem. Even if I don't know what *they* are. But you want me to find a solution?'

'If you can,' I said sharply, not that sure that I wanted his help. Ben and Miranda could both be a pain, they were very well suited. I scowled, sourly.

'Cheer up, Tom, I know what to do. It won't be easy, but you like a challenge, or so you keep saying. Close the door, I've something to show you.'

I did as he said and pushed the door to. All of a sudden the room went dark. I understood why he kept the door open. Saved on the light.

'Now fetch that lamp from the shelf over there.' I brought him the lamp, my eyes were becoming used to the dark, and Ben lit it quickly, and opened a door. I followed him into a tiny room. I'd never been in this room before. There was barely enough space to turn around. He moved a heavy old desk aside, and there, beneath it, was an old wooden trap door. He lifted the lid and beckoned me over. 'Follow me

149

down, and watch your step.' I shook my head.

'Not on your life,' I said firmly. 'That's a cellar.'

'Give the lad a prize,' said Ben, laughing. 'That's why they send you to school, I guess. He grinned at me. I thought you wanted to help Miranda? Or do I to have to do this alone?'

I shook my head and gritted my teeth and followed Ben warily down the ladder. It was dark in the cellar but dry, more or less, which made me feel better, until he vanished into the black.

'Ben! Don't leave me.' I sounded terrified, damn it, I was.

'Are you a man or a mouse?' said Ben, reappearing with the lamp. I watched as he moved a pile of bricks along with some planks. Behind the wood was what looked like a tunnel.

'Mind you keep up,' said Ben, sharply and I didn't argue, there was no way I was going to be left behind. Six foot in, he stopped abruptly and I nearly collided with his back. He swung his lamp around the space. The floor was made of uneven stone and the ceiling to the tunnel was low. The walls were damp with condensation. I shivered suddenly.

'This tunnel goes under the churchyard, next door. And from that church to Curdizan Church and then to the abbey, or so I've been told. It was used to get treasure away from the place, when the churches were sacked, or so I believe.' I must have looked blank.

'A little before your time,' said Ben. He grinned at me.

'We won't be going as far as the abbey, we'll be stopping just before Curdizan Church.' He looked around the space carefully. 'My guess is that these are just sewage tunnels, for mopping up rain and other delightfuls. But, of course, we'll probably never know.'

'I'm freezing, Ben,' I said, pleading. 'Could we have the lesson another time?'

'Guess what's next to Curdizan Church?'

'I've no idea,' I said, sighing, gritting my teeth to stop them chattering, 'unless you mean my school, of course.'

'I do,' said Ben. 'There's a route from the tunnel straight to the school, and that's how we're going to move the trunks, along the tunnel and up to your place. You wanted them near the school, you said. What do you think?'

'That's great!' I said, suddenly exultant and not understanding how much was involved. 'But how do you know it goes to my school?'

'Because I've used it before,' said Ben.

40

Then – Thomas

I always seemed to be late for school, just like today. 'Bunk up,' I said, 'you're in my seat,' to the lad who'd nicked my place in the row.

Ned gave me a scowl but he moved along and let me squeeze in. 'Carson's gone missing,' he told me, softly. 'I reckon that's three, and that's just the ones I've been told about.'

'Three?' I said. I only knew about Alec Mimson.

'And your Louise,' said Ned, slyly.

'She's not my Louise,' I told him, sharply. 'But I did find her things, well some of them, anyway.' I suddenly felt glum.

'Like what?' said Ned, perking up at the gossip.

'A dress and a cardigan, in her room. The lad who was there said a bloke took the rest, but I don't know who or why he took them. It could have been the rag and bone man. I'm afraid she's gone for good.'

'Along with Mimson and Carson, then. All of them vanished, just like the wind. Don't you think it's odd, Tom?'

'Yes,' I said, 'and 'I won't stop looking, but I don't know where I'm supposed to look. And Louise always said, oh, it doesn't matter.'

'Go on then, tell me. What did she say?'

'She said she might have to up sticks and go, if the money ran out and she couldn't get more. But she said if she did, she'd leave me something, some sort of keepsake.'

Ned smirked and I wished I hadn't opened my mouth.

'You're sure it's not a cardy?' he said.

After school finished, I made my way round to the pub,

quickly, eager to be on time for once. Miranda looked up as I walked in. 'You're very early, what's the matter?' Then she gave me a stick of rock.

'What's this rock for, bribery? Want me to scrub the floor, or something?'

'Spoils from work, it's crushed at the end so we can't sell it. I expect it'll taste just the same, Thomas. Can't stand rock myself, anymore. Seen too much of it, every day.' She shuddered and sighed and turned away.

'I've got some news on the shoes,' I said.

'Shh!' Miranda said, looking around. 'The way you're talking anyone could hear.'

'There's no-one in here but us,' I said. 'Ben's said he'll help move the trunks.'

'And how, exactly?' Miranda asked. 'I've already said we can't use the cart.'

'We're going to use a tunnel to move them. It goes from his place to Curdizan Church. You know the church, it's next to my school.'

'Of course,' she said. 'I was up there, recently, serving soup to the needy poor. The vicar's daughter's a friend of mine.'

'Is she?' I said, grinning at Miranda. 'Friends with connections, aren't you the one?' Miranda scowled and went on talking.

'Ben says the tunnel runs right to the school. We can hide the shoes in there. As you know, it's not far from the shop.'

'So where are we going to hide them exactly? Once they're finally in the school?'

'We can store them in the old kitchen, the one underneath the joinery workshop. There are loads of empty cupboards in there.'

'Oh no, we can't,' Miranda told me. 'That's where the soup's handed out on Sundays.'

'Hell,' I said, 'I didn't know that. Well, maybe we can store them in the tunnel. They're only shoes and not very heavy. It's not going to be for long, anyway.'

'No,' said Miranda, 'damn right it isn't.' She stood there frowning, she always seemed to be grumpy lately. I couldn't see why she was so bad-tempered, I didn't think Tanya Curtis was a threat. So I told Miranda about Louise. *Then you'll know who's badly off.*

'And now he says a few kids have vanished, don't you think that's odd, Miranda?'

'But who says, Thomas? From what I hear, it's only your mate, and as far as you know he could be wrong.'

'Ned's never wrong,' I said stoutly. 'He keeps his ear to the ground, does Ned. And Louise did say she'd leave me something, if she went away.'

'Like what exactly?' Miranda sounded sceptical.

'Her necklace,' I said, feeling embarrassed. 'And yes, I know, it doesn't sound likely.'

'It doesn't sound likely at all, Thomas. But as you've mentioned it, go on, tell me.'

'She used to wear it for school some days, it's a long, thin string of bright blue beads. The girls weren't meant to wear jewellery at school, so she used to wear it under her blouse, so Pike wouldn't see.' I stopped prattling. 'What's the matter?'

'Bright blue beads on a string you said?'

'Yes, why, have you seen it?' My heart started thumping.

'Yes,' said Miranda, 'I saw it on Sunday. Hanging round somebody else's neck.'

41

Now – Aleph

The following day Ginny came back, bringing the sound file. While she was there, I listened to it quickly, playing it forwards, the normal way. All I could hear was a child crying. It was very depressing.

'I'm very grateful, Aleph,' said Ginny, 'and so is my cousin, Marianne Parks.' I couldn't help disbelieving that statement.

'You're not going to go to print with this?' I could see the headline right away.

Deluded child killer talks to the dead.

'No, I've told you, this is nothing to do with the paper at all. My cousin, Marianne has always been troubled by her family history. And that of the house, your house, I mean.' She paused, waiting.

'Alright,' I said. 'I'll have your results by tomorrow, Ginny. But there won't be any transcript with this and nothing I say will be recorded, by you, that is. Do I make myself clear?'

'You do,' said Guinevere, getting to her feet. She smiled at me as she walked down the steps. Why did I have this ominous feeling?

I did the work in the early evening and It wasn't pleasant work hearing the sound of a child crying. Over and over and over again. Of course, I'd heard such crying before. But somehow the recording made it real.

Difficult themes would often come up as a part of my work, but I had the chance to assist the client, help them through, or sometimes, anyway. Lately, though, I'd been feeling drained. *Since the accident,* that's what I meant.

Lyle, my supervisor, would probably have said I was giving

too much, not keeping to the boundaries as I was meant to, and I knew the man was probably right. I also knew that now, *afterwards*, I probably wasn't cut out for this work anymore. But I still had to eat.

I played the first half of the sound file first. It was mostly blank, with a few low sobs and not a lot else, sad and grieving, rather than desperate. It didn't sound much like a ghost to me. But neither did the sounds in the street at night, I'd thought they were tourists. Then I tried that section in reverse.

I want to see you. It's been so long.
I wanted to say hello again.
But now you're gone. I'm gone too, silent and lost.
Part of me has gone forever. But what can I do?

The simple words moved me so much, I really felt the pain of the child. *But could it really be a ghost? It didn't seem likely.* Perhaps I ought to record one myself, rather than trusting Guinevere James. I played the rest of the file to the end. This was much more difficult to hear.

It was all his fault. He took you away.
Then I was scared. Now I'm lost too.
I want you back. And I want me back. And I want...
This awful time to be over.
But it can't be over. And I can't go back.
Because you're dead.

The recording came to an end with a whine. I clicked to press pause.

So who exactly was dead? I thought.

42

Then – Miranda

She asked her ma about Mary-Ann, if Mary-Ann Parks might have an admirer.

'She's going to marry Wetherby Eisen.'

'The man who runs the joinery workshop at Thomas's school? You got to be joking.'

'I'm not,' her mother said, and smiled.

'But, she's the vicar's daughter,' said Miranda. 'It wouldn't be right, her marrying him.' Her mother laughed.

'What do you know about right and wrong? The vicar and Eisen are thick as thieves. He helped the man get a start with his workshop. And haven't you got any eyes in your head? He's not bad looking, is Wetherby Eisen, for all he's not the landed gentry.'

'His hair's almost black, you call that good looking? I prefer my lads with fairer hair and a little more charm.'

'Like Benjamin Tencell, I suppose.'

'Oh, give it a rest, Mother, please. I suppose you've been talking to Thomas again? Never mind Ben, what about Eisen? Has he been going with Mary-Ann long? She's never said.'

'About three months, or so Carol told me.'

'She wouldn't be in the family way?'

'And how would I know if she was, Miranda?'

'I'm sure you know all there is to know, Ma. Seeing as how you're thick with Carol.' *Except about our plans for the shoes.* She frowned, considering what she should do.

There'll be time enough to tell her later. When they've finally left the building.

I can't see us getting away with this,' Miranda insisted,

opening the door to her partners in crime. Tom charged in, followed by Ben.

'Keep your voice down,' Ben retorted. 'Your mother's in bed and asleep, I presume?'

'She should be yes, on the brandy I gave her. She didn't even notice me do it. She'll have a bad head when she wakes in the morning.' She frowned, guilty.

'I gave her an extra tipple in her cocoa.'

'So they've all gone home, apart from your ma, and you've dragged all the trunks to the door of the attic? Ready for us to bring downstairs?'

'I'm still not sure we should be doing this.'

'But you don't have a better idea, do you? Ow, that hurt.' Tom rubbed his ear.

'It'll hurt even more if you don't shut up.' They had finally reached the top of the stairs.

The journey downstairs from the attic was a nightmare. Taking three trunks meant three separate journeys, with Ben always taking the worst of the weight. Miranda gripped the other handle, while Tom stood back and acted as lookout. *We'd have been better off leaving him at home*, thought Miranda, but she knew how much he wanted to help.

And he would have helped, Miranda knew, if they managed to get the trunks to the tunnel, and then to the school, or anywhere suitable far from the pub. They went outside and across the road and staggered down to Blackberry Close leaving the other trunks right by the door. *If anyone goes to the pub's back door, then the whole game's up*, Miranda thought.

But the night was dark and there wasn't a moon, and at the beginning things went fairly smoothly. Until Ben tripped and a lid flew open. Shoes spilled out all over the road.

'Ah,' said Ben and grinned at the others. 'So that's what's inside the trunks, I see. I wondered, because Tom had said they'd be light.'

'I thought I told you to fasten them down.' Miranda hissed

160

and glared at Thomas.

'I did,' said Tom, 'I swear on my life. It must be the ghost who came and undid it.'

Miranda sighed as Tom laughed and watched as he scrabbled around for the shoes, stuffing them back in the trunk, quickly. Then they moved on. Forty minutes later, including a tricky descent to the tunnel, that part was done.

'Isn't it time for a little rest?' Tom whinged.

'No, it isn't,' Ben insisted. 'We have to move on as fast as we can. We can't leave the shoes in the tunnel overnight.'

'So where are they going ?' Miranda enquired. She recalled her previous chat with Tom.

'I thought there were going in the school basement?'

'As I told Thomas, it's used on Sundays for the soup kitchen and anyone could find them if we left them there. Tom said we could leave them in the tunnel. Didn't you Tom?'

'Leave me out of it,' Tom insisted, glaring at Ben and then at Miranda.

'Why don't we worry about that later?' Ben said tersely, grabbing the handle of the nearest trunk and gesturing to Miranda to take the other. 'We're still a long way from our destination. The night's getting on.'

'Isn't it just?' Miranda said, sourly.

Moving the trunks along the passage was far from easy. Curdizan Low to Curdizan Church was quite a good walk and slightly uphill, without the strain of carrying trunks. The tunnel was as black as pitch. Tom walked ahead with the lamp to guide them. *So we did need him, after all.* Miranda smiled.

'I'd have preferred to have stored them in your workshop,' Miranda told Ben as they staggered along.

'But you weren't prepared to say what was in them. I needed to know, if I was storing them.'

'I don't see why. What did you think I was keeping inside them, buried treasure? I think you ought to have trusted me more.' She sighed, loudly. The question now was, could she trust *him*? Then something soft brushed past her leg. Miranda shrieked.

'You never said there were rats down here! Are we nearly at the church?'

'I reckon we're probably near the church hall. It won't be long now.'

'And about time too.' They paused briefly. They were walking each trunk a few hundred yards, then going back for the second and the third. It was really hard work and slow at that but at least they could see they were making progress.

'We should have brought a sled,' said Tom. 'Or even dragged the trunks on some planks.'

'I thought of that,' said Ben, mildly. 'But the floor's uneven, and we'd have to have sorted the planks out first, or found a sled. You said the trunks weren't very heavy, so I didn't think they'd be too hard to carry.'

'Not for a bloke,' said Miranda, grimly.

'Here we are,' said Ben, suddenly, and Tom gave a cheer and did a little dance. Miranda paused and looked around. Right up ahead were the steps to the crypt of Curdizan Church. But before the steps, to the left, was a door.

Miranda watched as Ben walked over and tugged on the door, it opened easily. 'Done it before,' he said grinning.

'You haven't yet said how you knew about this place.' Ben didn't answer; just walked through the door and into the passage. Miranda sighed.

She followed him carefully through the gap. 'Thomas, come here and bring the lamp!'

Tom passed it over and Miranda shivered as she noticed how much the walls had closed in. This passage would lead to the school basement. *I hope it's not far,* she said to herself.

'I'll go and open the door at the end.' Ben disappeared and Miranda could hear his footsteps receding.

'I never wanted to store them in the basement,' Miranda insisted as she and Tom waited, and waited, and waited. Nothing, just silence, not even a rat. And then she heard the sound of swearing.

'Ben?' she called out. 'We can hear you up there and we're fed up with waiting for something to happen. Aren't you coming back?'

Her words echoed in the lonely tunnel but no-one replied, not even a ghost. Ben had taken the lamp with him so there wasn't a lot to see either.

'I hope he's not going to be long,' said Thomas.

'You and me both,' Miranda agreed. Then Ben reappeared, not looking happy.

'Now what's the matter?' Miranda asked him. She barely dared ask.

'The door to the basement won't open,' he said. 'Unfortunately, I think it's still locked.'

43

Now – Aleph

The next day I saw Ginny again. By then I'd had a change of heart.

'I've made a transcript,' I told her curtly. 'Without any names, to say where it's from. I don't want any trouble from this. You do understand?' Guinevere nodded. She skimmed the transcript, reading the words.

'Marianne will be thrilled with this.'

'Thrilled, how?'

'She's known that something was wrong for years. She's wanted to find out the truth for ages. Now, at last, she's got something to go on.'

'When I saw Marianne Parks at the office, she told me all the rumours were rubbish. She said there weren't any ghost children.'

'Of course she did, she was testing the water. She didn't want to look a fool, did she? Especially not in front of a stranger.'

I wasn't amused and I told her so. Ginny shook her head.

'Nobody's made you look like a fool. I'm paying for your services, this is business. Though, had I been you, I'd have wanted to hear the full story.'

'What story?' I said on cue, wishing as I'd said it, I'd kept my mouth shut. I realised I was taking the bait. I *didn't* want to hear her wretched story, unless, of course, it affected the house. But I did want the crying to stop. I needed the sleep, *and* the work, so I could find somewhere different to live. I folded my arms.

'Alright, Ms James, you win, this time. Tell me the story, you've got my attention.' Guinevere grinned.

'A woman was murdered a long time ago, but no-one was ever charged, or found guilty. Her family assumed she'd run off with a lover, her body was never recovered at the time. Then years later, a body turned up, but her parents were dead by the time that happened. And years had passed, if you see what I mean.' I nodded, understanding.

'The corpse would have decomposed by then. That must have been hard,' I said, softly.

'It was for Marianne Parks,' said Ginny. 'She was the one who found the body.'

'Right,' I said. Well, that was a facer. *No wonder the woman was obsessed with ghosts.*

'And not just that,' said Ginny, carefully, with what I saw was a touch of relish. 'She found the body in your cellar.'

44

Then – Thomas

'You *are* joking,' Miranda said.

'I'm not,' said Ben, 'I've tried the door twice. It's definitely locked. But *you* try it. And as for you,' he glared at me, 'you said you'd ask someone to unlock it.'

'I did,' I said, 'I asked Jake. He swore he'd do it before he left.'

'You've involved someone else, without my permission?' Miranda looked furious. Ben shook his head.

'No he hasn't, he was asked to leave the door open for me.'

'And that proves what?'

'I've my own reasons for using the tunnel.'

'And very obviously, secret reasons,' Miranda retorted. She didn't bother to ask what they were. They both looked unhappy and I was fed up. When I next saw Jake, there'd be trouble for sure. Miranda spoke up.

'So what are we going to do with the shoes? We can't take them all the way back to the pub. I think we should leave them right here in the passage? Just for a while.'

'I've told you before that's just not possible,' Ben said quickly. 'This is what we're going to do.' He looked at me and grinned broadly. 'This is your chance to do your bit.'

Climbing the steps to the crypt was easy. The door wasn't locked, which Ben seemed to know.

'Go up to the church and into the churchyard, then double back towards the school, crossing the graveyard.' I did what he said, it was all straightforward, more or less. But when I finally reached the school and tried the door to the joinery workshop, it was, of course, locked.

'There's another door by the big stone shed that leads to the basement,' Miranda had told me, but that was locked too, as we'd imagined. I knew I'd have to take the third route. My heart sank at the thought.

'There's a window at the side which doesn't close properly. Squeeze your fingers through the gap and adjust the catch. You might need a strong stick for that, you'll find one close by. And no, don't ask, just do what I say. Then pull the sill down and haul yourself over. It's easy as pie.' Or so said Ben.

I did what he said. It wasn't easy.

First , I needed some crates to stand on, I wasn't that tall. Then, when I'd finally pulled the sash down, heaving myself through the window was hell. I tumbled in and landed on a workbench, which hurt, a lot.

'Rats, bats and curses,' I said.

'What if someone sees me climb in?' I'd asked Ben, earlier.

'They won't,' he insisted, 'or we'll be in trouble. This is your chance to prove yourself. We're relying on you, Thomas, remember? Aren't we, Miranda?'

'Yes,' said Miranda, but she didn't seem sure. I was dreading it all, I knew I couldn't fail.

Even when I was outside the window, complete with the crates, and the stick for the catch, I'd had to hang around, there were drunks going past, and then a group of women, staggering together, waiting for them to go past took ages. And meanwhile, it was getting lighter. Then I was in.

Next, I had to get down to the basement. 'That bit's easy,' Ben had told me. 'Just lift the trapdoor and go down the steps, that'll be a breeze.'

Easy wasn't the way I'd describe it. The trapdoor was heavy and difficult to lift. I had to use some wood as a lever.

'You should be doing this job, not me,' I'd said to Ben earlier. He shook his head.

'If I was seen, I'd end up in jail. I can't take the risk.'

And I can? 'Can't we both go?' I'd said to him then. 'You

could just act as a lookout or something.'

'And leave Miranda alone in the tunnel?'

'I don't mind,' Miranda said quickly, but I knew that wasn't true, she was scared of the rats, and Ben was a gent, he wouldn't have left her alone in the dark. Miranda refused to leave the shoes. *Anyone would think her ma's name was on them.*

Or my ma's name, I thought, bitterly.

And then I was there, alone in the basement, at the bottom of the steps. I couldn't see a thing, but I could hear Ben's voice, inside my head, telling me what to do, as usual.

'Use the steps to get your bearings, then walk towards the door to the tunnel.' I started walking, slowly, steadily, stumbling twice over pots and pans and then, at last, I found the door.

'What will I do if the key's not in it?' I'd said to Ben earlier.

'It will be, I'm sure, they've obviously locked it. They've probably left the key in the lock.' I hoped to God he was right about that.

I hadn't a clue where the key was kept, I'd barely known the door existed, until Ben had told me to talk to Jake. I pressed my hands around the frame, using touch to find the keyhole. I finally found it, but there wasn't any key. I couldn't believe it. I could have cried.

I scrabbled around on the floor for the key, just in case it had fallen out. Of course, it hadn't. Not for the first time, I longed for a lamp, at least with a lamp I could look in the drawers and find the key.

'You can't take the lamp,' Ben had insisted.

'If I wasn't in the dark I'd be so much quicker.'

'And how would you get the lamp through the window? It's far too dangerous, and somebody passing might see the light.'

I didn't answer.

It was black as pitch as I walked round the basement, my eyes were adjusting, but only gradually. A small scrap of light came down from the workshop, but not very much and a little bit more seeped in through the windows, but they were so smeared with dirt they were grey. From what I could tell, daybreak was coming and that was bad news for our small gang of three. The joinery classes would soon be beginning and Wetherby Eisen would see the raised trapdoor. Then he'd see me and I would be toast. There'd be no more school, and no more porridge and no more chances of finding Louise. And then I'd never see Alice again. I needed that key, but where the hell was it? And then I heard an enormous crash, as something heavy fell over upstairs.

45

Now – Aleph

'In the cellar?' I said, feeling faint. Almost as if she'd knocked me over.

'So I believe,' said Guinevere James. 'Is there any more tea in the pot for me?'

There wasn't so I made more, just to please her. As a diversion, it wasn't working. To think I'd actually been in the cellar. I turned to Ginny.

'Where exactly was the body?' My guest shrugged casually.

'I'm not quite sure. I have to be careful when I mention it, it's a sensitive issue.'

'And to think she dared to rent me the place.'

'I don't think the woman was *murdered* in your cellar. I only said that's where she was found.'

'But, still, her body had been in the cellar, rotting away. I should have been told, I really should.'

'And would you have taken the house, if you'd known?'

'No, of course I wouldn't.'

'I rest my case. My cousin is all alone in the world, apart from me and she's not the easiest of people to get on with. This house and the story of the murdered woman have been a worry to her all her life. I think she's starting to run out of answers. Which is where you come in.'

'She could have tried booking a course of therapy, like a normal person, instead of all this business with ghosts. And answer me this.' I paused briefly.

'When I told Ms Parks I wanted the house she made me pay six months' rent in advance. If she was so desperate to move it on, then why not rent it to me more cheaply, or let me pay on a monthly basis? Surely that would have made more sense?'

'I'll tell you why not. She wanted to be sure you'd stay for a while. She didn't want someone who'd hear the rumours and leave straight away. She thought if the tenant stayed there for a while, then when they moved on, the fact that they'd stayed would help with the sale. Or to get more tenants.'

'I'm afraid there's a problem with that,' I said. 'I didn't just "hear the rumours", as you put it. I heard the ghosts, the children crying, and I know a woman who thinks she's seen one. I've no idea what's going on, but you said a *woman* was murdered in here. But this is the audio file of a child. I don't see how that fits with the woman.'

Ginny looked pensive. 'There's more to all this than I've told you so far, and all of it happened around the same time. When this was a school, some children went missing, or so rumour has it, and nobody knows what happened to them. There were lots of suggestions, but none of them were proved as there weren't any bodies.'

'But are you sure?' I said, sourly.

'As much as I can be. But when the woman's body was found, decades later, a lot of people thought whoever had killed the woman, had killed the children too, but why, we don't know, for any of it. According to the legend, the children are crying because they're scared and afraid they'll be killed, or if they are ghosts, maybe *have* been killed. Murdered in their beds, or perhaps somewhere else, just like it said on your audio file.'

'Now, wait a minute,' I said hotly. 'The audio file did not say that. The child we can hear says they're missing someone and wanting to see them and the person isn't there.'

'Because they're dead.'

'Well, yes, that's true. But death can come in a lot of ways, not just murder.'

'But in your transcript, the child blames someone for their friend being missing and the first child is scared. Like the children of the past were scared of the man.'

'And which man's that?' I said, exasperated.

'Wetherby Eisen. There wasn't any proof he killed the woman, but everybody thought so, or at least they did once her body had been found. He could have been involved in the children's deaths too.'

'Assuming any children died at all.'

'But if they didn't, how come they never turned up alive?'

'But no-one found any bodies either. You said that.' Guinevere sighed.

'We could go on arguing about this all day. The point is, Aleph, most people think he killed the woman, the woman whose body turned up in your cellar.'

Thanks for reminding me.

'As for the kids, there's a very strong link. The missing children went to the school which was in this house, and Eisen ran the joinery workshop. And the joinery workshop was —'

'In this kitchen,' I finished for her. A lucky guess but it seemed obvious. 'With the cellar below it.'

'Exactly,' she said. And smiled broadly.

46

Then – Thomas

There was little point in trying to hide. Someone was up there and I was down here, and of course, I'd left the trapdoor open, I'd needed the light. I had to act fast. I squeezed myself under a workbench quickly, crushed between the wall and the sink, and tried not to breathe, or at least, not much. I could hear his footsteps moving around. And then I heard him descend the stairs. I noticed the man was very light-footed.

I heard him open a drawer nearby and make his way to the door to the tunnel. The man was only a few feet way. Assuming it was a man, of course. The footsteps stopped.

'Tom? Is that you?'

'Jake!' I shouted, very relieved, dragging myself from under the bench and standing up front of my mate. 'Thank God it's just you! I was scared half to death, wondering if it was Eisen or Pike.'

'Well, it's not, it's me,' said Jake, grinning. 'I take it the open window was you?' His flickering lamp showed up the shadows and his smug little face.

'Yes,' I said, 'but if you had left the door unlocked, it wouldn't have happened.'

'Yes, sorry, I forgot, but there's no harm done, and here I am, along with the key.' He brandished it proudly.

'There's no harm done? We've waited for ages to get in here, and I've been struggling alone in the dark. There are people back there who are waiting and wondering where I am.'

'Yeah, right,' said Jake, he didn't seem bothered. 'I couldn't come back the moment I remembered, I had to avoid all the drunks and lovers. So I said to myself I'd get up early, but when I got up my aunt was awake, so I had to wait till she'd gone back to bed. It took forever.'

'Don't you live with your ma and da?'

'No,' said Jake, 'my da ended up in the loony bin and my ma's well dead so I live with my aunt, she's Tanya Curtis.'

'Curtis?' I said, and I suddenly went cold.

'Yeah, don't worry, she didn't hear a thing. She'll not learn about your adventures from me.'

'She'd better not,' I told him, grimly, thinking I'd have to keep my mouth shut. Miranda would have a fit if she knew. 'Have you got that key to the door then, Jake? I have to get on.'

'Here,' said Jake, and chucked it across. 'I don't suppose I can wait and watch.'

'You damn well can't, as you've let me down, and not just me, my mates as well. But don't worry, I'm still grateful.' Jake grinned, broadly.

'I reckon that's two favours you owe me.'

I threw him an almost-full packet of fags and his eyes lit up. 'You can have these for starters, so long as you promise to keep your mouth shut.'

'I've said I will, you can trust me mate.'

I raised my eyebrows, showing my doubt and Jake scarpered, as quick as a flash. I watched him scamper up the stairs and heard him easing the trapdoor down. He might be small, but Jake was wiry and stronger than me, tougher as well. I heard him slip the bolt into place.

Then I had a moment of panic. If the key didn't work I was trapped in here.

I'd barely turned the key in the lock and leapt out of the way, when the door burst open and Ben charged in. 'Where the hell have you been?' he said.

'In here,' I said, 'and for far too long. It's hard to find a key in the dark when you can't see enough to look in the drawers.' I didn't feel in the mood for a grilling.

'But the key's in the lock,' Miranda insisted, squeezing past Ben and into the room. She swung the lamp around the basement.

'Jake forgot it. He's only just brought it, minutes ago. I thought I'd be stuck until Eisen turned up.'

'Just as well you weren't,' said Ben, looking grim. 'Well, now that we're here, we need to decide where to hide the shoes?'

'I've already said we can't hide them in here,' Miranda insisted. 'Someone would open the cupboard and find them. It might look all abandoned to you, but every Sunday this place is a kitchen for feeding the poor. I think we'll have to store them in the crypt.'

'Oh no we won't,' said Ben, abruptly and I wondered why not but I kept my mouth shut. Then I remembered the crates I'd seen, stacked in a corner, as I rushed on through, on my way to the churchyard. *Odd*, I'd thought, *I wonder what's being stored in them?* But I hadn't been able to investigate then, I had much more pressing matters to deal with. Like keeping Miranda and Ben happy. It wasn't working. Miranda was looking as red as her dress. Red with rage.

'That's a nice frock you're wearing,' I said, seeing the fabric shimmer in the light. I was trying and failing to calm her down. It only seemed to incense her further.

'It was until I ripped it earlier. I must have caught the hem on my shoe.'

'You shouldn't have worn it this evening, then. Wearing a posh frock on a trip like this, that was just stupid.' Ben sounded grumpy.

'It's not a posh frock, it's only the thing I wear at the pub.'

'It looks like it's satin and that's posh to me. And now you've gone and torn it, quite badly. I doubt it'll ever be the same.'

Miranda bit her lip and said nothing, and I recalled how earlier this evening, yesterday now, when Miranda had been on her shift at the bar, she hadn't been wearing the dress at all.

She'd worn the dress tonight for him. To walk in a dark, filthy, tunnel. Aren't girls stupid?

'What shall we do about the shoes?' Ben was rapidly losing patience. And I knew time was running out. We had to be quick. Miranda spoke up.

'Why don't we move them to the shed outside? There's only some wood and the tools in there. That's right, isn't it, Thomas?'

I grinned at Miranda, nodding agreement. She was acting as if Ben didn't exist.

'That'll be alright,' Ben added his comments, 'if they stay in the trunks and we move them soon. I very much doubt if Wetherby would notice.'

And then, finally, things went smoothly. We unbolted the door that led to outside, climbed the steps and stood in the churchyard. Moved the trunks across to the shed, one at a time, all of us feeling exceedingly weary. Ben then moved a few planks across them, leaving some space for me to get through.

'So you can take the shoes to Percy,' Miranda confirmed.

'As soon as you can,' Ben interjected. Miranda said nothing but pursed her lips.

After our delayed but successful venture, Ben then said, as he brushed himself down, 'I think this calls for a celebration. How about a kiss for luck?' He looked at Miranda, waiting and hopeful.

'Perhaps when's Tom's got rid of the shoes.' Miranda said and looked at me. She smiled briefly and I grinned back. Both of us knew it could take a while.

47

Now – Aleph

As soon as Guinevere James had gone, I grabbed a jacket and cycled to the library. I was hoping to shed some light on the story, hoping to find that Ginny had lied. My first attempts seemed doomed to failure.

'The body was found mid-twentieth century, and she was murdered? We've several books on local murders.'

I skimmed them all, there was no mention of my house at all, or even the street. So, what to do next? I found the assistant.

'Her body was found in the Old Schoolhouse.' I was rather reluctant to give this away, knowing they'd probably make the connection and realise I lived there. Curdizan wasn't the largest of towns.

The archives assistant paused and smiled. 'You should have told me that straight away. The local paper had loads on the murder. I'll get the editions now, if you want.'

'Editions?' I said, my heart sinking. 'Aren't the papers on microfilm?'

'No, not this one. But lucky for you it's weekly, not daily.'

I saw what he meant when he brought up the papers, dozens of copies, bound up in a volume the size of a house. They came on a trolley.

'There's a year in there,' I said dismayed, looking at the book and staring in horror at the tiny print and narrow columns. Just reading a page could take an hour. 'I don't suppose there's an index?' I said.

'You've got to be joking. But a student was studying the murder recently. I can tell you where the articles are.'

It was strange reading about my house in an earlier time,

before I was born. There was even a photo and a copy of a drawing from around the turn of the twentieth century. The house looked much the same as now, but the street looked different, the road was cobbled, and some of the nearby houses looked grim. Tenements, mostly, and round the back, Curdizan Church, and right behind that, Curdizan Abbey. I felt rather sad.

So much had since changed, no church, no graveyard and only a rather twee courtyard instead. Since the awful accident happened, I'd thought a lot about time and change, how time moves on, and can't be rewound, however much we would like to rewind it. My house might have looked the same then as now, but then it had been a school for the poor, and surrounded by those who lived in the dark. I knew the area used to be rough. I thought briefly of the churches behind it, the beautiful abbey with its gothic spires and Curdizan Church, so solid and strong, yet overshadowed. I wondered what the vicar had been like. He would have a difficult job, the place had been rife with prostitution, and brawls that continued into the night. A place where the children wore no shoes.

And bread wasn't just a part of a meal, or so I'd been told.

Time had moved on and so had the street, but was it a good place to live, even now? I had my doubts. I settled down to the in-depth reading.

The writer relished sharing the details, including where the body was found. Behind a cupboard in the cellar, he told us, I knew where he meant, there was only the one. All I'd found were a number of shelves and a feeble draught. I obviously hadn't looked hard enough.

Marianne Parks *had* found the body. She'd only been five, it must have been a shock, a life changing moment, assuming she remembered what happened that day. According to the paper, the body was wedged in some kind of passage, behind some wood which had blocked off the entrance so no-one had known the passage was there.

A child couldn't move that wood, I thought. But then I learned the family were having the bathroom improved, and a builder went downstairs to check on the plumbing.

I bet he opened that cupboard, I thought. Maybe he'd found some pipes or something that needed some work and had used his drill or some sort of tool. Presumably taking out the shelving first. And, in so doing, disturbing the wood that had been there for years. But not enough to spot the body.

Then a few days later a girl of five went down to the cellar with her mother and father, who were checking for damp and maybe checking the plumber's work, and she, curious, opened the smaller door to the cupboard. And nearly died when a large plank of wood, which was stacked by the wall, and very badly balanced, toppled from its place and landed beside her. *The builder should have put the shelving back.*

'It only just missed me, Daddy,' she said. And because she missed the flying wood, and was only young, she hurried behind it, into the passage, to see what was there. And found the woman's body on the ground. Her parents were stunned.

The victim had worn a cheap necklace, a long thin string of blue coloured beads. The beads had been crucial to the investigation, along with what little had remained of her clothes. The victim was believed to be the vicar's daughter, and people remembered her going missing. They also remembered her wearing the necklace, not that long before she vanished. Finding witnesses hadn't been easy, the girl had vanished decades before. Her father, the former vicar of the church, was long since dead and so was her mother as well as most of the people who'd known her. Those who were left were hard to track down. Her sister Clara had been alive, but had lived abroad for a number of years and didn't come back for Mary-Ann's funeral.

The woman had vanished decades before, along with her lover, Wetherby Eisen. Eisen was believed to be her killer but no-one had managed to track him down. They probably hadn't tried that hard, even though they'd believed he was guilty. The girl was dead, her parents were dead, and a long time had passed, so nobody cared. There were presumably, more urgent cases.

After she'd vanished, her father, the vicar, had retired from the parish, under a cloud. It was thought she'd eloped, which at that time in history was something of a scandal, especially given her father's job. When, decades later, her body turned up, it appeared she hadn't eloped after all, the woman had been murdered, presumably not that far from her home, with her parents at the vicarage. I paused, thinking.

If Wetherby Eisen *had* killed her, she probably *was* murdered in my cellar. Or at least, in the passage behind the cupboard. Eisen's workshop was now my kitchen so it all made sense, he would have had easy access to the passage. Despite all of Guinevere James' denials. *She was probably trying to be kind,* I thought. Or maybe she wasn't.

I wondered if Ginny knew more than she said, it seemed likely, given her track record. The journalist who had written this report certainly did. I thought a little about what I'd learned. Marianne Parks discovered the body, her mother and father were also called Parks. And the dead woman's name was Mary-Ann Parks. It was definitely not a coincidence.

48

Now – Guinevere

Guinevere James placed the USB drive on the table between them. 'I hope you're satisfied now,' she said. She fixed her eyes on Martha, opposite. The day was mild, with a touch of spring and Ginny was sorry she couldn't enjoy it.

'I don't know if I'm happy or not, not having heard what you've got to say. You gave him the recording, like I suggested?'

'Yes,' said Ginny, 'and I'm sorry I did. I wish you hadn't involved me in this.'

'Nobody forced you to do it, Ginny. I'm surprised you're bothered, given what he is.'

'Yes,' said Ginny, 'I know what he is. It's just, he seems so pleasant and reasonable.'

'Lots of bad people are pleasant and reasonable. That's how they get away with their crimes. Please don't try to defend him to me. You hardly know the man, remember?'

And neither do you, thought Ginny, sadly, *despite all that's happened.* She dug around in her bag for the transcript then watched as Martha read the words, hearing the child through the printed page.

I want to see you. It's been so long.
But now you're gone.
It was all his fault. He took you away.
I want you back. And I want me back. And I want...
This awful time to be over.
But it can't be over. And I can't go back.

She watched as Martha raised her eyes and saw the terrible look on her face.

'I shouldn't have done it and asked you to do it. I wish I

hadn't.' Martha looked grim.

'Yes, and me but Cressida wouldn't have given her permission, not for this, and Aleph wouldn't have analysed the file without her agreement. Or Alice's either.'

'It's crying for God's sake,' Martha exclaimed. 'How did he get all of this out of that?'

Guinevere shrugged. 'He said it's possible, convinced me some more by saying he'd never done it himself. He works on analysing talking, normally. I think he was as shocked as we are.'

'But you told him the crying was ghosts, and he believed it?'

'He seemed to believe it and as you know he's heard them himself. Aleph Jones is somewhat damaged.'

'So he bloody should be. Don't expect any sympathy from me.'

'I'm not,' said Ginny, 'but it's easy to see the man's in pain.'

'That's too damn bad, he ran down a child, my child at that.'

'He was cleared of all blame, you know that Martha. The boy just ran out, there was nothing he could do, the witness said so.'

'The boy, the boy! That "boy" was my son, and don't you forget it. How dare you trivialise Daniel's death.'

'I'm not,' said Ginny, 'I promise, I'm not.' She leapt from her seat and hurried to her friend, putting her arms around her, gently. 'I know it's terrible, was and is, but years have gone by, and you need to heal. I'm sure the man's sorry for what he did.'

'But sorry won't bring my Daniel back.'

'Of course it won't, but I think for you, and also for Len and for the future, you ought to at least try to move on. Daniel would want that.'

'How dare you tell me what Daniel would want! He was a child, an innocent child, he'd barely had any life at all. And then that man came and took him away, gone in an instant. Leave me alone, you've no idea.' She struggled out of Ginny's embrace.

'Please, Martha, please, you'll make yourself ill.'

'And you think I'm not,' said Martha then, turning around and staring at Ginny. 'You think that every day of my life I'm not ill with pain and sick with loss and guilty as hell for not keeping him safe. And wondering how I'll survive my life. It never, ever gets any easier. Don't you forget that.'

'No,' said Ginny, backing away from Martha slowly. 'I know I can't comment, it's not my loss. I'm just worried, because you're my friend.'

'Yes,' said Martha, breathing deeply, 'and I'm glad you're my friend, because you got the file and that's what matters. Helping Cressida, because she's helping me.' She paused briefly. 'So what do you think the reversals mean?' Ginny considered.

'I think it means that Alice is troubled, deeply troubled, about losing Daniel. According to you, they'd always been close, despite the big age gap. Alice could have looked upon Daniel as a brother. The trauma of losing him must have shocked her, badly.'

'But she wasn't even there when we learnt what had happened.' She patted the nearby empty chair. 'Come and sit here.' Guinevere did.

'Cressida and Alice stayed overnight, like they often did when Len was away. The next morning, Alice went out to see a friend, but then we discovered she hadn't turned up when Annerley's mother gave us a call. So we both went out, looking for Alice, and because of the panic I left Danny alone, which was unforgivable. He must have got out of the garden somehow, even though I wasn't gone long.' She paused, thinking.

'I've wondered since, if Alice left the latch off. Daniel was in the garden playing, but he wouldn't have been able to lift that latch, all by himself. Alice could have done it, being that much older, but she wasn't there and I thought he was safe.' She choked back a sob. 'I asked her later if she'd left the latch off but Alice said no. It didn't seem like she was lying, to me.

'So when the police called round with their news, Cressida thought they were calling about Alice. We'd just got back from doing the rounds and were coming down the drive to the house when we saw them. I hadn't even realised Daniel was missing.'

'Perhaps Alice blames herself for dragging you away, so you weren't with Daniel, keeping him safe.' Martha flinched. 'Not that I'm saying...' Ginny trailed off.

'Maybe,' said Martha, 'or maybe she simply misses my son, but none of this explains why she won't talk to Cressida. She talks to the teachers, to me and her friends, so long as her mother isn't around. She uses her iPad for those she calls strangers, but once she gets to know them, she talks to them too. But she never, ever, talks to her mother. It doesn't make any sense to me. They used to get on well, before.'

'And now?' said Guinevere.

'Most of the time she tries to avoid her.'

49

Now – Aleph

I've always lived in the shadow of churches.

Well, perhaps not always, but lately it almost seems like always.

Where I grew up, my school and the church were almost next door. My parents didn't believe in God, but the vicar used to talk to me often, asking why we weren't there on Sundays. Then he would talk about Sunday School, and say I could go there by myself. 'Your parents can't stop you coming along.' But of course they could.

My parents hated the Church with a vengeance. Sundays were leisure time, mostly for fun, mostly with each other, and I was often left bored and alone. I survived my parents *and* the vicar, but I never went to Sunday School and can't say I'm sorry. Now, I think of all churches with dread. It didn't stop there.

Now, I live next door to a church. The abbey of course, with its rising spires and overarching splendour, but more significant, Curdizan Church, long since gone but not forgotten. People walk all over the gravestones, sit on the benches and smell the flowers. Pigeons walk in amongst the weeds, not that there are that many weeds. And Mary-Ann Parks, the vicar's dead daughter lives in my cellar.

Or lived, anyway.

When I killed the boy, Daniel, I remember seeing a church in the distance, just before the accident happened. Nothing special, just a spire, but it made me think of my childhood troubles and it stuck in my mind, was easily remembered, unlike the impact. People were quick to call me a murderer, a troubled man who was better off dead, unlike the victim, and although that hurt, it only affirmed what I already knew.

The police were compassionate, as was the man who saw it happen, but my neighbours weren't always and neither was Gerry. I lived the accident every day and, if by chance, I somehow forgot, there was always a 'friend' who'd help me remember, who'd assume I'd been blind or drunk or distracted. Perhaps I was. Distracted by toast.

So to learn that a woman had been murdered in my cellar seemed rather like justice, with me being a murderer myself, of a sort, and for her to be the vicar's daughter, and the church to have been next door to my house, seemed almost as if it was meant to be. Not that I liked it. I've always lived in the shadow of churches.

Part of me hoped that I was wrong, and Ginny was right and she hadn't been murdered in that passage, that her body had only been moved there afterwards. I trawled the rest of the month's papers, the ones of the time, and then the month after, hoping to find a little bit more about where she'd been killed, but I found nothing. I guess they didn't know where. I did learn where they'd buried her body, after removing it from the passage – Curdizan churchyard, no surprise there. So off I went to see her gravestone.

I went to see Daniel's grave, once. I was given an address, a c/o address and the parent's names, so I wrote a short letter saying I was sorry. I know it was inadequate, I couldn't find the words and even if I'd had some, none of those words would have been enough, to make up for what happened. But I owed them the letter, even though it scared me. No-one ever answered.

I decided not to go the funeral, it didn't feel like the right thing to do, not for the family, so a few days later I went to the churchyard and laid down some flowers. I don't know what I expected to see, my name and the words *Child Killer*, embossed on the grave, but I do remember thinking the grave seemed small.

When I stood in front of Mary-Ann's grave, I wondered

what kind of woman she was. And why her lover had chosen to kill her, even before they'd got to a church. Assuming they planned a church wedding. I'd have taken some flowers, I felt like I should, but although there were graves, they were flat on the ground, and set in the paving, since the improvements. Tourism ruled. Mary-Ann's grave made me feel quite angry, more than I'd ever felt about Daniel, I only felt grief and despair about him. And of course, the eternal guilt.

I wasn't in charge of my life anymore.

I thought of the cards I received every year on Daniel's death day, each in a black-edged envelope. I told Cressida, Gerry had sent them, but I knew it was a lie, the cards were too subtle, and Gerry was never, ever subtle. I thought they came from Daniel's parents. I'd only ever opened one.

Inside was a card, a rich cream colour, with a small black flower embossed on the right. Printed carefully was the word MURDERER. The word shocked me. The card reinforced what I thought I knew, but when I read it, it became real.

The line below had four long dashes, rather like the Hangman game, where you get to guess the correct letters but in this 'game' the dashes were words. The first word in the row was HE. I hadn't read the other cards, they were in the shoe box, waiting to be opened.

There were only four dashes, and the accident happened four years ago so I'm guessing the sentence is all played out. You can't imagine the hours I've spent, probably days, thinking and wondering what the words say.

HE WAS MUCH LOVED

HE IS NOW LOST

HE WON'T FORGIVE YOU

Sometimes, frequently, when I've been drinking, which I try to avoid, I almost forget I know the first word, and the possible statements expand even further, all of them awful, because let's face it, it's going to be awful. Whatever they've sent me, it won't be forgiveness.

WE HATE YOU ALWAYS

WE WON'T FORGIVE YOU
YOU WILL DIE SOON
YOU HAVE NO FUTURE
So it goes on.

If my supervisor, Terence Lyle, was here with me now, if I'd even told him, which of course I haven't, as I can't bear anyone else to see them, he'd tell me to open the envelopes now. I know he's right.

I should just open all three of them quickly, read the three words and deal with the sentence. Whatever the final sentence says, it can't be worse than I can imagine, day after day, in this waking nightmare.

Can it?

50

Then – Miranda

Miranda opened the shop door slowly, and as she did the bell tinkled. Percy Thomas looked up from the counter where he was showing some shoes to a woman. Miranda watched as he charmed her adeptly, wrapped up the shoes, and took her payment, far too much in her opinion. The satisfied customer left the shop. Miranda went over.

'I've come to tell you about some stock. It's stock that belonged to Matt McCarthy and it should be in here, now that he's dead.' She watched him carefully for a reaction.

'Right,' said the boy, but that was all, his face was giving nothing away.

'Thomas Islip, I believe you know him?' Percy nodded.

'Aye, I do. He's a mate, is Tom.'

'Well, Tom will be bringing this stock to you, a batch at a time. There's quite a lot, it's all brand new, ladies and gents, in various sizes. Mr McCarthy would have wanted it sold, like the rest, if he'd been here.' She looked around, checking that they were still on their own. 'Does that make sense?'

Something made sense, she could see the intelligence there in his eyes. As well as a feeling that looked like pity. She gritted her teeth.

'The shoes were found in McCarthy's home, after his funeral, when it was cleared. As you know, he kept orders there, special deliveries he'd requested.' *None of it like the stock in the trunks.* But what could she do?

'I think your boss must have been confused, it's not the sort he normally stores, or so I've been told. I'd hate it to look like he wasn't quite there, now that he's dead, if you see what I mean.' Percy nodded. Miranda paused.

'I hear you're good at keeping secrets?'

Percy nodded, looking sombre. Miranda turned towards the door.

'I can trust you then, to keep it to yourself? Talk to Tom, if you need to, he'll tell me and I'll come and see you. I guess you can smooth the accounting over?'

Percy nodded a second time and Miranda breathed a sigh of relief. Getting the records to match the stock was vital, essential, no-one must know where the shoes had come from.

And if she had tarnished McCarthy's name, just a little, in saving her mother, well, so be it.

'Say hello to Hannah from me. She's always kind, whenever I see her.' Percy spoke and Miranda nodded. *And now I mean to return the favour.* That's what he meant.

She smiled, satisfied and left quickly.

Miranda was still feeling vaguely unsettled by the time she arrived at Curdizan churchyard. She weaved her way through the graves, quickly, heading for the vicarage, a modest-sized house at the back of the church. She came to a halt when she saw Mary-Ann.

'I was looking for you,' she said to her friend, who was still wearing the blue necklace. Mary-Ann smiled and waited, patiently.

'I hear you're engaged?' Miranda went on and Mary-Ann nodded, her hands playing with the beads on the necklace. She couldn't hold back a smile as she did so.

'And is it true you're marrying Eisen?'

'Wetherby, yes, he asked me last month. I'm so happy, you can't imagine. But you don't look pleased, aren't you happy for me?'

'Not when you're marrying Wetherby Eisen. You know there are children going missing from the schoolhouse?'

'I didn't, no. But what has that to do with me?'

'Some folk are saying that Eisen's behind it.'

'That's spite and you know it, those people are jealous and all because he's a self-made man. Wetherby is a friend of my father's and my father wouldn't be involved in that. He is the vicar.'

'Maybe he doesn't know what's happening.'

'Maybe the stories are only rumours. A lot of those children are brought up rough. Their parents force them to go on errands, begging or stealing, you know how it is. Maybe they've got into something bad or maybe they were fed up and ran away. Wetherby isn't involved in this.'

'But he works at the school, he could be involved. And as for the kids at the school being rough, Curdizan Low where I live is rough, and you're not that far from the gutters yourself. Getting to be such a lady, are you? Too high and mighty to mix with us. Despite being only yards from the tenements.'

'How dare you accuse me of being stuck up. You know that's not true!'

'Thomas, a boy who helps in our pub, he goes to the school, but he's not like that, he's decent, hard-working and a credit to himself. You shouldn't believe all your father tells you, or Wetherby Eisen, for that matter.' Miranda pointed at Mary-Ann's throat. 'That necklace you're wearing, where did you get it?'

'I've told you before, the necklace was a present.'

'Did Wetherby Eisen give you that piece?'

'No, yes. It was meant as a keepsake, a tiny token, just something for the moment.'

'So why didn't you say that when I asked you before?'

'Because it was just a little trinket, nothing special, not like a ring.' Mary-Ann blushed.

'Can I look at it?'

'No, you can't! What's this interest in my necklace?' She placed her hands around her neck, as if to hide the necklace from Miranda.

'It's not like the stuff you normally wear. Those beads look cheap.'

'What do you mean?'

'Eisen's fobbed you off with that necklace. I bet he took it from somebody else. And maybe you know he stole it, too.' Somebody shouted for Mary-Ann, who looked around.

'That'll be my mother, we're meant to be visiting the sick today. About the necklace, that's not what happened, I'll tell you what happened, just not right now.' She turned away. 'I have to be go.'

'How very convenient, Mary-Ann. I'll expect your call *and* your explanation, whenever you've got the time to see me, just make it soon.'

'You want me to call at the pub to see you?'

'Well yes, why not?'

'My father's the vicar of Curdizan Church. I can't be seen in a pub in the Low, unless I'm delivering alms or something.' She drew herself up to her fullest height.

'And yet you'd marry Wetherby Eisen, a man with rumours circling around him. And maybe you'd sell your soul as well, rather than act in a way that's right.' Mary-Ann looked pale and bit her lip. Miranda went on.

'That, my friend, is a great deal worse than going in a pub. Even if it seems like a brothel to you.'

Miranda stalked off, leaving her friend silent behind her. She knew she'd won a token victory, the sort that made her want to cry. Her friend was not the person she knew, she'd changed because she'd become engaged.

Miranda sighed and hurried home. Some kids had vanished from a nearby school, and her friend was engaged to a dodgy man, who might be a thief but could be much worse. She longed for comfort, someone to tell, but who could she trust, apart from Tom and he was a boy.

And then she thought of Ben Tencell.

51

Now – Aleph

Next, I went to Cloud House Properties. Marianne Parks was in a meeting.

'Is it anything I can help you with?' Gemma said, smiling and looking inviting.

'No thanks, Gemma, I'll wait for Ms Parks.' The younger assistant looked at me oddly, nodding agreement and leaving me all alone and guilty. I remembered the day I'd first met her, right by my house; how we'd laughed, how the sun had been shining, how I'd had hopes, been innocence itself. Like before the accident happened. The sun went in.

After a while, Marianne Parks turned up. 'You wanted to see me, Mr Jones?' She looked tired, no, she looked old, her hair was dark, it was dyed almost black and her face was lined and covered in powder. She'd clearly suffered, well, so had I.

'Is there anywhere we can talk, please, Ms Parks? Preferably in private?' Her eyes narrowed.

'I hope this isn't a complaint,' she said.

If only it was, I thought, sourly. If only the problem was faulty plumbing or central heating that didn't work. Some practical thing that was easily sorted. 'Not in the way you mean,' I said. We went to a tiny, windowless room. I put the transcript down on the table.

'Guinevere James came to see me. She gave me a recording of a child crying and told me you had found a body, when you were five. This is the transcript from the recording.' I pushed the paper across towards her. 'Go on, read, it. It doesn't help, but you wanted to know what the crying meant. Here it is.'

Marianne Parks looked vaguely troubled. Her eyes flickered to the door, briefly, wondering, maybe, if she could escape. I could almost see the cogs in her mind, trying to decide what she should tell me. *The truth,* I thought, *just give me the truth.* Ms Parks looked cagey.

'Guinevere – James is a journalist. She sometimes writes pieces for us in her paper. About trends in the market and the rental sector. She's obviously told you about the body, and I wish she hadn't involved you at all. But I don't understand about the recording.'

'It was *you* who mentioned the ghosts, Ms Parks, *you* asked if they were laughing or crying. Don't you remember?'

'Of course, Mr Jones, but I also remember saying it was a rumour.'

I leant across the desk towards her. 'But the body you found wasn't just a rumour, was it, Ms Parks? And the crying I've heard is more than a rumour. This is a transcript of a child crying. Why did you ask her to give me the file and tell me the crying was the School Lane ghosts?'

'I didn't, Mr Jones, I would never do such a foolhardy thing, and certainly not to one of our tenants. It's more than my reputation's worth. I value my job at Cloud House Properties. I think dear Ginny has been stringing you along, which wouldn't surprise me one little bit. What you heard on the recording wouldn't have been ghosts, but a real, live child.'

After our meeting, I went back to the library, this time trying a different tack. I decided to research the School Lane ghosts. The member of staff I'd seen had vanished but his older colleague was just as helpful.

'All of the locals and most of the tourists know about the ghosts, they love that story. Some children went missing from a local school, a long time ago, and according to rumour, they never reappeared. Alive or dead. As to what happened, there are plenty of theories, some say the kids were sold into slavery.'

'Really?' I said, sounding scornful.

'It's not as stupid as it sounds, believe me. These were kids from the poorest families, their parents would send them begging for money or scavenging for goods which they sold on for cash, or even more likely, to get booze or fags, these people were desperate. The kids who were luckier got to go to school, but were easily tempted back to the streets or dragged away by troubled parents.'

'Sounds pretty grim,' I said, thinking of Tom.

'It wasn't all bad,' the man insisted. 'The brighter kids had jobs as well to make ends meet, rather than going out begging on the streets. But one of the rumours is about a bloke who worked at the school and according to folklore he sent the kids out to earn some cash, which he then pocketed, so neither they nor their parents saw it.'

'That doesn't explain why they vanished.' The man shrugged, shaking his head.

'Maybe they died of cold or hunger. Or maybe their family wouldn't let them go back, because they'd been giving their spoils to the bloke. Or maybe, and remember, this is only a rumour, they died of ill treatment and overwork, and the man from the schoolhouse hid them in the cellar.' He grinned, lazily.

'And what cellar would this be, exactly?' I didn't know why I bothered asking. I already knew what the answer would be.

'The cellar in the Old Schoolhouse, of course.'

'The one where the vicar's daughter was found?' The archivist laughed.

'I know, you're right, it doesn't sound likely, I did say the story was only a rumour. But you have to remember these kids disappeared, if indeed they did vanish, decades before that body was found.'

But according to the rumours, they all disappeared, both the kids and woman, around the same time. That's what matters.'

The archivist gave me a searching look. 'That's certainly true. But I thought this stuff was all new to you, that you didn't know anything about the ghosts?'

'No,' I told him, wondering if I was telling a lie. 'That's right, I don't.'

52

Then – Miranda

Time went by and Miranda was serving alone in the parlour. It was getting late when the door was pushed open and Tanya Curtis walked into the room. She slowly strolled across to Miranda.

'What a lovely evening,' she said. 'I'll have some light ale, when you've a moment.'

'I'll see the colour of your money first.'

The woman nodded and looked around. 'It's as well there's just you and me in here. It'll make it easier to conduct our business.'

'I've no business with you, Tanya Curtis,' Miranda told her, standing up straighter.

'I'm sure you recall our discussion last week.'

'Of course I remember, and I'm telling you now, as I told you back then, we've no money, and certainly not for paying blackmail.'

The woman smiled, but it seemed to Miranda that the smile was thin.

'There's still the matter of the shoe you have.' She raised her eyes to the shelf above them. 'Or should I say shoes?'

'I don't know what you're talking about. That boot up there was found by a tradesman a long time ago. There are shoes on my feet, but surely business isn't so bad you'd want to take those. But then again,' she gave the young woman a long, hard stare, 'perhaps it is.'

An indrawn hiss meant she'd hit her target. 'I might have to talk to your ma about this.'

'Talk all you like,' said Miranda, coolly, 'but I'm telling you now, it won't change a thing. There aren't any shoes, apart from the ones you can see in this room.' She reached across and poured out some ale. 'But do have a drink on us, *sweetheart.*'

The woman looked angry, really angry. 'You haven't heard the last of this.'

Miranda shrugged.

A few minutes later some men came in and the woman strolled out and Miranda thought that was all for the evening. At twenty to ten, she slipped out herself, as Cath was around and she needed the air. Not that the air was very fresh. She made her way round to the back of the pub, hurrying down the passage to the yard. She was almost there when Curtis stepped out and blocked her path. Unfortunately, she was much worse for wear. Miranda stepped back but Curtis grabbed her arm and held it.

'Let go of me now,' Miranda insisted. She was scared as hell but she wasn't going to show it.

Curtis laughed and instead moved her face closer to Miranda's. 'You implied before I was some sort of slut. Well, you're a fine one to talk, sweetheart, with your ma like she is, and you being pals with Ben Tencell. The one who buries the bodies, darling. You make a fine pair, you and him. Perhaps you let him have it on the cheap?'

'I'd say the pot was calling the kettle.'

'Like mother, like daughter, that's what *I'd* say. I hope you've learnt the facts of life. You don't want to end up having a child, not like some of the people I know.' Curtis laughed, a raucous laugh that ricocheted down the length of the passage. Miranda gasped.

'Mind your own business, you miserable cow. Ben and I are friends, that's all.' Which was totally true, although that didn't mean she didn't want more. She swallowed hard.

'You're always spreading vicious rumours. As for my ma, that's more of your lies. I know my ma and she's not like that.' Curtis laughed.

'Well, you're not very well informed. I pride myself on telling the truth.'

'So put your money where your mouth is, Curtis. If you've something to say, then say it now. Or run away, like the coward you are.'

Curtis smiled and looked at Miranda. 'Some weeks before Matt McCarthy died, not once, but twice, and the week before too, I saw a woman go into his house. She didn't knock, she went straight in, and before you say she was taking the laundry, it was in the evening, after seven.

'I didn't see her face, she slipped in the side way, but I saw her coat as she walked down the path, it was thick and long, a rich red and grey. I knew that coat, it used to be mine, before Matt McCarthy bought me another. I bet your ma's got a coat like that.'

53

Now – Aleph

I wasn't keen to go back to the house. I was tired and stressed and not about to go down to the cellar. I was glad I'd moved the fridge-freezer back. Now I knew why someone had done it, to keep the trapdoor firmly closed, *and* to keep out thoughts of the body, or maybe bodies, children's bodies. I couldn't bear thinking about that scenario.

I made myself tea and took a huge mugful into the lounge, stood by the window and watched life passing, people on bikes, tourists gathering and pigeons swooping down from the trees. It made a pleasant, distracting sight. I sighed, heavily. So many deaths.

Mary-Ann Parks and the boy I ran down, and possibly some others, the ghost children, whoever they once were. And there on top of the cupboard, waiting, was the old shoebox with its four envelopes, four words, and three of them still a mystery to me. My hand was on the lid of the box. I couldn't do it. I didn't want to know what the words would say.

Daniel was dead and words or threats, whatever they were, wouldn't bring him back, however much I wished it. Mary-Ann Parks was dead as well and I didn't know what had happened to the children. But I could do something for Alice Sewell. First I played the sound files again.

The files, supposedly of ghosts crying. The more I listened the more I was sure. The child I could hear was Alice Sewell. I'd have to have words with that damned journalist, Guinevere James, but first I'd speak to Alice's mother. I picked up the phone.

Cressida Sewell walked into the house on a bright morning

looking wary. And so she might. After our recent venture into strange territory with imaginary boys I wasn't quite sure what to expect. But she still looked as lovely as ever.

'I'm sorry I haven't been in touch. That business with Tom, it threw me a bit.'

'Have you spoken to Alice about him?'

'I don't talk to Alice, remember?'

'I only meant, oh never mind.' *Now for more trouble.*

'I was given a recording by Guinevere James. Here's a transcript.'

Cressida frowned and took the transcript. She looked puzzled. *Whatever she is, she's a good actress.*

'Who's Guinevere James?'

'She's a local reporter and possibly the cousin of Marianne Parks from my estate agent's. Posing as wanting help with a murder.' Cressida raised her eyebrows and stared.

'Wanting help to solve a murder. Go on, read it.' I passed her the transcript.

She glanced at it quickly and looked confused.

'So she's missing someone, possibly a him but maybe not, I'm not clear there. And she blames this someone, who's probably a man, for taking them away, the him or the her. And she's scared of the man or was scared then, and the person she's missing is dead and gone.'

'That's about it,' I said to Cressida.

'So are you thinking this is a murder?' So I filled her in on Mary-Ann Parks, just for the hell of it.

'Marianne Parks is the one who works in Cloud House Properties? And she might be this James woman's cousin? I know Ms Parks, we often do business with her company.' Cressida's firm was rather upmarket, it only dealt with exclusive clients. *Why hadn't one of them taken my house?*

Maybe because it's run down and haunted.

'But this is the voice of a child,' said Cressida. She looked worried, very worried. Now came the crunch.

'Mary-Ann's murder is not why you're here. The journalist,

James, said the voice on the file was the voice of a child. One of the School Lane ghosts, crying. I know, I know, it sounds very far-fetched. But, remember, Cressida, I've heard these children, or some kids anyway. Guinevere James is very convincing.'

'I'll bet she is,' said Cressida, curtly. She looked at me with something like pity. That would soon change.

'After I'd played the sound file a few times, I recognised the sound of the child who was on it, even though all I'd heard was crying. It's Alice, Cressida, and I think you knew that all along. Why did you send Ms James to me, *and* with such a far-fetched story?'

'I didn't,' said Cressida, getting to her feet. 'I'm sorry Aleph, I've got to go.'

'You can't go now, you've only just got here' I said, jumping up and hurrying after her into the hall. 'I think I deserve an explanation.' Cressida gave me a scathing look.

'Don't you worry, you'll get your explanation. And thanks for having such faith in me.' She opened the door and slipped outside. 'I didn't send James with the recording, Aleph.' And then she looked a little ashamed.

'But I'm almost certain I know who did.

54

Then – Miranda

Miranda walked into her ma's bedroom, and stared at the wardrobe over in the corner. It was large and dark with a huge bottom drawer which her mother kept sheets in. Miranda knew what she'd find in the wardrobe. Fortunately for her, her mother was out.

Her ma had said she was going to see Carol, Thomas's ma, but given that both of them worked in the laundry, that didn't make sense. Miranda was becoming exasperated.

She opened the door to the wardrobe warily. The coat was there in all its glory, thick and long, and a faded rich red with deep grey cuffs. Almost the same as Curtis had described it.

How dare he give that coat to her ma when he'd gone and bought Curtis a brand new coat? Miranda sat on the bed thinking. The answer was obvious, even though it hurt, Matt McCarthy hadn't valued her ma, not as much as he'd valued Tanya. Curtis was younger and prettier too. *Damn the man,* Miranda thought.

She no longer doubted Curtis's story. She was far too smug and all the facts fitted. How long had her ma been seeing McCarthy, and had it begun when her da was alive? Miranda ached with the pain of it all. And then there was that stupid boot. Her ma had admitted to having the boot for many years, but why keep a boot? It seemed such a silly thing for a keepsake, just one boot, and too small to wear. Her mother didn't seem the superstitious sort, but maybe she was. Maybe McCarthy had made her like that, frightened of losing the love that she'd found. Miranda sighed, it had to be done.

Slowly, she went through the rest of the things, first the coat, and then her ma's other, then some jackets and two old bags. She didn't know what she was looking for. Then, at the end, she found the old bag, hidden away behind the clothes, at the back of the wardrobe. She opened it up. There, inside, was the other boot.

Miranda emerged from the wardrobe, carefully, holding the boot aloft in her hand. Not just one, but a pair of boots, one downstairs and the other up here. How very odd. She suddenly heard a noise from below, the sound of footsteps, climbing the stairs. Miranda shoved the bag in the wardrobe, closing the door and standing up straight. The boot in her hand she shoved up her shirt and fastened her cardy loosely around it. She took a deep breath. Her mother walked in.

'Miranda, dear, what are you doing?'

'Looking for you, I thought you'd come back.'

'Since when have I spent my time up here?' Her ma looked cross, and disbelieving. She scanned the room, not a thing out of place. She gave Miranda a cool, hard stare.

'I think you'd better go back downstairs. Tom's turned up and he's asking for you.'

Miranda hurried downstairs, quickly. It was far too late for Tom to be here. 'What's the matter?' she said to him, anxious.

'It's about the shoes. I was talking to Jake, my mate in the workshop. The boy who forgot the key, remember?'

'Yes, I remember.' Miranda frowned. Jake was also Curtis's nephew, although Tom hadn't said he knew about that.

'Pike wants the shed in the churchyard cleared. Apparently there's a right fuss about it, because Eisen's against it, that's where he keeps his wood for the workshop, and it's where...'

'We hid the trunks.' Miranda groaned and swore, loudly. Would this nightmare never end?

'I thought I'd better come round at once. I'm sorry it's late, I've only just finished some extra deliveries.'

Of course, thought Miranda, *Tom's new job*. If Tom left the pub because of that job, she didn't think she could cope anymore. He might be a boy, but the lad was sharp and fun to be with, almost a mate. She'd never see Ben if Tom left the pub. *Stop!* she thought. *Forget about Ben and think about the shoes.* Tom carried on.

'We'll have to take them up to the shop. Percy will take them as soon as we say.'

'We can't take all of the shoes at once. Someone would see us and know it was odd. No, Thomas, that's what I wanted to avoid, remember? We'll have to leave them in the tunnel. That's what I wanted to do in the first place.'

'Ben won't like it,' Tom said, slowly.

'That's too bad, I'll have to persuade him, you see if I don't.' Miranda smiled briefly, sounding more confident than she felt.

But Tom didn't return the smile.

55

Now – Cressida

Cressida watched her friend closely. Martha was icing a chocolate cake. She swirled the frosting around on her knife, making patterns out of the sugar. It looked beautiful. Martha always made wonderful cakes, she even sold the best for a profit. She didn't remember Martha baking, before the accident. Before her world had fallen apart. Despite all that, Cressida was angry.

'Why did you go and give Aleph this?' She dropped the USB drive onto the table. Followed by the transcript.

'I didn't,' said Martha, licking her finger, 'Guinevere did.'

'It was your idea, and you took the drive from my home that night. And you edited out the words, so all he heard was Alice crying.'

'Yes,' said Martha, 'I wanted to help.'

'By going behind my back to others, including a man you say you hate.'

'I do,' said Martha, washing her hands, 'but I did what I did, for you, not me.'

'You had no business interfering, giving that recording to Aleph, or anyone.' Martha shrugged.

'Piece of cake?' she said mildly.

'Damn the cake, I'm not hungry.' Cressida paused.

'The worst thing of all is you gave this stranger, Guinevere James, someone who I haven't even met, something of Alice's and you told James all about our business. What exactly did you tell her?' Martha shrugged.

'That Alice was troubled and had problems speaking and I wanted to help her get over it.'

'By lying to Aleph and going behind my back to do it. And

making up stupid stories about ghosts.'

'That was Ginny,' said Martha mildly. 'The School Lane ghosts were her idea.'

'And a bad one too. You do know James is a journalist?'

'Of course I do, Ginny's my friend, we go way back.'

'I'd never trust a journalist.'

'I'd trust Ginny James with my life,' said Martha.

'Well, bully for you,' said Cressida bitterly. 'I don't think we can be friends after this. How can I trust you ever again? How dare you share my life with strangers!'

'I thought you wanted to help Alice?'

'I do,' said Cressida, 'but in my own way and in my own time. And furthermore...' Martha waited.

'Don't ask me to deal with Aleph again, do it yourself, or get your journalist gofer to do it. I've had enough of being your sidekick.' Martha said nothing.

'The thing with Aleph was all about you, about getting revenge. I don't know where you're going with that. He feels so bad, I know he does, even though he wasn't to blame. I saw him throw that card in the bin, the one you sent, he's not going to read it, or the rest, you're wasting your time. If you want him to hear what you've got to say, why don't you tell him, face to face? That's what you should have done in the first place.'

'According to you,' said Martha, sourly. She pushed the transcript across the table.

'You ought to think about what this means. It's clear Alice is really unhappy and you're not hearing what she's saying. Alice is obviously missing someone, I think it's Daniel.'

'Do you?' said Cressida, suddenly uncertain.

'And there's more,' said Martha, slowly. She looked nervous.

'Alice knows we both went out looking, trying to find her when she went missing and I left Daniel on his own. She might feel guilty and blame herself because we weren't there and Daniel got out.'

'She's not to blame,' said Cressida sharply.

'I know she's not, but she might not. I asked her once if she'd left the latch off, because that's how Daniel got out of the garden. She said she hadn't and I believed her, but that's not the point. The point is, Danny died not far from home. What if Alice did go to the park, just like she told us, but *after* she'd seen the accident happen? She might have been hanging around and saw it. Something like that could have caused the trauma, made her stop speaking. It seems obvious.'

Yes, thought Cressida, lost for words.

56

Then – Miranda

Miranda had worked extra hours at Chaucer's so she didn't arrive at Ben's until afterwards. She was hoping that Tom hadn't said to expect her. Clearly he hadn't as Ben seemed surprised.

She stood in the doorway and watched him work, smiled at how he was totally focused, using the plane with concentration. He turned around, surprise on his face. Miranda smiled.

'I wasn't expecting to see you now.' Her smile faded, the words were rather less than welcoming. It was too bad, they needed to talk. Her heart hardened.

'Are you busy? Because we've got a problem.'

'Right,' said Ben, with a bit more concern as he pulled her inside and closed the front door. It was dark in the room but a lamp changed that.

'Here, have a seat. Would you like some tea?'

'After you've heard what I've come to say. It's bad news.' Ben leant against his workbench and waited.

'Tom has discovered they're clearing the shed, the one in the churchyard, where we stored the trunks. We need to move the shoes, and soon. According to Tom, we've a week, at most.' Miranda went on.

'Why don't we store them in the tunnel? We could use the side passage that leads to the school from the tunnel proper, I'm sure the trunks would fit in there. Then they wouldn't be in your way. The tunnel proper would still be clear.'

Ben was shaking his head, looking pensive. 'It's not possible Miranda, sorry.'

'But this is a crisis, we need to get going and move them

now. Don't you understand?'

Ben laughed and grinned at Miranda. 'Now, this minute? You and I, and maybe young Thomas? Just like before, it was really easy. I'm sure you remember.' Miranda's eyes flashed.

'Fine, don't help me, I'll do it on my own, I don't need you, or anybody like you. It's all very well, you laughing at me, but the shoes still have to be moved from the shed. Imagine if somebody found them in there.'

'Oh, I am,' said Ben, 'I'm imagining everything, more than you would ever believe.' He stopped smiling and stared at Miranda. Miranda felt her face go red. Ben grinned, broadly.

'The shoes aren't the issue that's standing between us and you and I know it. But it can't go anywhere, you're far too young for me, Miranda.' Miranda stared at Ben disbelieving.

'How dare you say that I'm too young! I've been running our pub for years on my own, while Ma's been out doing God knows what. When I first started work in the bar, I had to stand on a crate to serve, I couldn't even reach the counter without it. If it wasn't for all the work I put in, we'd have lost our pub when Da keeled over, and might do yet, which is why I have to move those shoes. With or without your help, Ben Tencell.' She glared at Ben. 'That tart came into the pub again, Tanya Curtis, you know who I mean.'

'Yes,' said Ben. 'She's been spreading some rumours about your ma. I'm not going to ask if they're true or not.'

'My ma's bereaved,' Miranda said, and wished she hadn't. She sounded defensive.

'She was bereaved,' said Ben gently. 'Time has moved on and so should she. I should know, doing what I do.' He glanced around at the coffin lids.

'You don't understand.'

'I understand more than you think,' said Ben. He reached across and grabbed her hand, brushed her cheek with his lips softly. 'We'll move those shoes, like we did before. We'll find a way, I promise you that. But, we still can't move them into the passage.'

'So tell me why not?' It seemed the perfect place to Miranda. But Ben turned away, he seemed to be having some sort of struggle. Then he turned back.

'Because we need the passage for access. Wetherby likes to use that route to get to the tunnel, and also the church. He and I are in partnership.'

'The church?' said Miranda. 'I don't understand. And you and he are in partnership? In the business, you mean?' She looked around.

'In business, yes, but not my business, in the antiques business. Here, I'll show you.'

He opened a cupboard under the bench and pulled out a sack, then lifted it carefully onto the workbench, moving a coffin lid out of the way. She watched him open the sack with ease and pull something out, something quite heavy. Miranda gasped.

'You mustn't tell a soul Miranda. Promise me now, you'll not tell anyone. Just like I did with the shoes, remember?'

Miranda barely heard him speak. All she could do was stare at the object. There in his hand was a silver chalice. It was clear to her it had come from a church.

57

Now – Aleph

I was sitting at home, waiting for Alice. After our last, rather fraught meeting, something had shifted, with Cressida anyway. Now she was hoping I'd talk to Alice, to try to find out what was wrong.

'Remember what happened the last time she visited.'

'Can't you just send the ghosts away, at least for a while?' We were on the phone, so she couldn't see what I thought of her comment. I didn't bother answering.

'I'll assume that's a no then, shall I, Aleph?'

'Send her round whenever you like. But if she won't stay, you know I can't make her.'

'Fine,' said Cressida. 'I'll send her round, as soon as she's home.'

The rest of the day dragged on, relentless. Guinevere James had rung me twice; I'd left the phone to ring both times. I was up to my ears in a tedious transcript, a rather predictable business analysis. I toyed with the thought of giving up counselling, or any kind of paid work, and taking myself round the world for a year. It didn't appeal. Then the door bell rang.

'Alice,' I said and smiled at the girl. Why don't you come in?

Alice waltzed in, looking older and even more self-assured than before. She wandered ahead of me into the kitchen.

'There's nobody here, apart from us.'

'Good,' I said. 'I'm glad about that.' I offered her tea.

'I'd rather have coffee, if you don't mind.' Her new adult voice was quite like her mother's.

'Just like your mum,' I told her, smiling.

'It's about the only thing we have in common.'

'Apart from being female.'

'Huh!' said Alice. We sat at the table, me with my notes.

'Where's your iPad?' I asked her, smiling.

'I don't need it.'

'I'd noticed,' I told her. Perhaps she thought she could trust me now.

'Your name's Aleph,' she said to me then, stating the obvious.

'Always has been,' I told her, smiling.

'Some people change their names,' she said. She didn't much like me humouring her.

'True,' I said, 'but not in my case. I've always been Aleph.'

'It's an odd sort of name. What does it mean?'

'Ox, I believe. It's also the first letter of the Hebrew word *emet*, and that means truth.'

'Are you truthful?'

'Sometimes,' I said. 'I try to be.' *But would a reversal say something different?*

'Isn't it better to keep quiet, sometimes, if telling the truth can cause people pain?'

'It all depends on the case in question. Some things are better not said, that's true.' *Or done*, I thought.

She leaned towards me looking pensive. 'I was there that day, when you hit – the boy. I saw it happen.'

'Were you?' I said, my blood running cold. While the heart inside me beat faster than ever.

'I saw him run from between the parked cars. He ran into the road and I saw what happened.'

'Right,' I said, but my mind was racing, zoning out. I got to my feet and walked to the window, stared at the courtyard, once a graveyard. I was scared, frozen. Behind me, Alice still sat at the table, silent as the graves I looked at.

'Did you see anyone apart from us? Me and the boy?'

'I saw an old man but he didn't see me. At least, I don't

think so, but he did see what happened. I noticed him staring.'

So she *had* been there, she was telling the truth. That might be the reason for some of her behaviour. 'Have you told your mother what you saw?'

'No,' said Alice, smiling suddenly. The smile seemed wrong, and somehow shocking. 'She only knows what I want her to know. It's our secret, yours and mine. And you won't tell her, will you Aleph, you know it will only make me worse. I'll talk even less, if you tell her. Now would you mind if we talked about Tom?'

I didn't have much experience of kids but I still thought Alice's behaviour was odd. She'd been so serious when we talked about Daniel but talking about Tom was a different matter. It was hard to focus on what she was saying, I was still reeling from what she'd imparted and wondering what to say to her mother.

'You know Tom's dead?' she said to me then.

'What?' I said.

'He's a boy from the past, he's not alive now. But I guess you know that already, Aleph, if you've heard me talking on the recording. The one I did with Alison Clipper.' She smiled, slyly.

'Yes,' I said, 'I've heard the recording, and in reverse you said he was dead, but you weren't going to say so, not to Alison.'

Alice nodded and looked rather cross. 'I never thought all that stuff would work, playing the sound files in reverse. I'm not having anything else recorded.'

I smiled at that. 'That's fine by me. I'd have to have your permission, anyway.'

'That's alright, then, I won't give it.' Suddenly, Alice the child was back.

'How can you talk to Tom, Alice, if he's dead?'

'I don't know. I made him use the iPad at first, because that's what I do with everyone to begin with, but then, if I

221

want to, we can talk, like you and I are. He took me back to see his house.'

'Did you like it there?' I nearly said, *On Haversham Road?*

'I did and I didn't. It was dark and grim, and the factory towered over most of the houses and the gutters were flooded and overflowing. It smelt awful.'

'And the good things?' I said. Alice grinned.

'It was fun, and exciting to go somewhere different, *and* in the past. Tom said the next time, I can meet Norah, she's Ben's horse; Ben's his friend, and Tom said he'd show me a secret tunnel.'

'I don't think going in a tunnel is wise. It might collapse and land on your head.'

Alice's look said, *I'm not a baby,* but she didn't argue, just nodded agreement. 'Fine, I won't go.' I didn't believe her.

'I think you ought to talk to your mum. Before you go on any trips with Tom. Tunnel or not.'

But Alice was shaking her head, firmly.

'No,' she said. 'I can't do that. I never talk to my mother now.'

58

Then – Miranda

The next evening, when it was dusk, Miranda walked up to Curdizan High, heading up Croston and then Convent Court, slipping through the alley to Curdizan Church. She was praying she wouldn't see Mary-Ann. She passed through the gate into the churchyard, and made for the shed.

Jake had given Tom the key, under sufferance, so he'd said. 'You'll get me shot for this, Thomas Islip.'

'No-one will ever know, I promise. It's just for a mate.'

Miranda knew she had to be careful. The wood in the shed was stacked how they'd left it and in the right place to hide the trunks, although getting up close to the trunks was hard. *It wouldn't be such a problem for Tom,* Miranda considered, *when he takes the first stock to Percy. But, as for the rest, where could they put it?* She went outside and up to the door.

The key turned easily in the lock and Miranda stood at the top of the steps. She used her lamp to light her way and made her way down to the basement, carefully. Wishing today was a soup-kitchen-Sunday. Thankfully, the place was deserted. She swung her lamp around as she walked. She needed to find a storage space.

The basement wasn't designed for storage. There was one huge cupboard and plenty of space underneath several benches. All of the space was clearly visible and quite unsuitable for hiding trunks. Then she saw the small door to the right, with the key still in it. *Jake must have left it there for me.*

It was so tempting. She didn't know why she wanted to look. The door led into the narrow passage, the one that led to the wider tunnel, the tunnel she'd walked with Ben and Thomas. And although the passage was narrow and dark, she had the light and the courage to face it. *I'm looking for stock if anybody finds me.* Nobody did.

It didn't take long to reach the tunnel. She slipped through the door, was suddenly wary. What if there were some rats about? There, to the right, were the steps which led to the crypt of the church, Mary-Ann's church. Miranda wondered if she should climb them. Because of what she'd learnt last night.

'Undertaking's a badly paid business. And joinery too, when you're working for Pike. Teaching young lads to use a saw, for very little pay and far less thanks.'

So when Ben had heard some news from a mate, that the mate had some stock which needed selling, and better still, would be getting some more, he'd struck a deal, to take the goods off him. The job was big, too big for Wetherby, he needed a bloke who could store the goods and polish them up, even transport them and then sell them on.

'And that was you,' said Miranda, bitterly. *First my mother and now Ben, why am I surrounded by thieves?* Her heart contracted.

'Yes, that was me, and no, I'm not sorry, it's made me much richer, which means I can offer some funerals more cheaply and help the poor bury their dead. Because I can afford to. So it's not all bad, whatever you think.' His eyes twinkled. 'But don't go sharing this story around. Others might want a cut of my earnings.'

'Or they might want to shop you,' Miranda snapped. 'So where does all of this 'stock' come from?'

'Mostly old buildings, deconsecrated churches, that sort of thing. The vicar has left, the owner has died, and there's no-one around to claim the goods. If it's a church, the money could be useful for the person who gets it, for improvement work or alms for the poor.'

And you think I'll believe all that? Miranda felt bitter. 'Was there stuff from McCarthy's house?' Ben looked startled.

'No, of course not. I told you, Miranda, these are goods from older buildings like churches and manors and some unwanted haunts of the rich. Not from blokes like Matt McCarthy.'

'He might not have lived in a stately home, but to people like me, McCarthy *was* rich,' Miranda said, grimly.

'Yeah, right,' Ben agreed, looking rather sheepish. 'But you must see now why we can't use the tunnel for storing your shoes? The tunnel is how we shift the goods. And Wetherby needs to have access from the school.'

'They're not my shoes! But I do understand. You can't be seen to be moving them in daylight.'

'No,' said Ben and looked embarrassed, uncomfortable almost. Miranda felt bitter. How quickly the dreams of passion were tarnished.

And so, a night later, there she was, standing in the passage and staring at the steps that led to the crypt.

Remembering talking to Tom and Ben, suggesting they store the shoes in the crypt. And Ben saying no. She wondered why.

She gritted her teeth and made for the steps. As Tom had discovered, the door wasn't locked. The crypt was cool and dark as the night and the smell of old churches rose up to greet her. She drifted around, examining the space, swinging her lamp which flickered a lot. *I wonder what I'm looking for?*

She headed towards the steps upstairs, the ones that led to the nave of the church but her exit was barred by a wrought iron gate. Miranda stopped at the top of the steps. The gate was more or less shoulder height and far too high for her to climb over, wearing a dress. The gaps in the railing were also too narrow for her to squeeze through. *Tom must have climbed the gate,* she thought. She shook it again, it was definitely locked.

Miranda walked back down to the crypt, heading for the door that led to the tunnel, when she noticed some crates piled high in the corner. The sort that were used for fruit and veg but why would such boxes be sitting here? Miranda walked towards the crates, stretched out a hand and felt in the top, pushing aside some sacking to do so. What emerged, with a bit of a struggle, was a silver cup and further rifling produced jugs and a plate. Miranda was stunned. This didn't look like discarded stock, but rather like treasure to kit out a palace. She stepped back quickly. She didn't much like the smell of all this, and she liked it being stored in a church even less. She shoved the goods back into the boxes then hurried away as fast as she could. Once she'd descended the steps to the tunnel, she closed the door with a bang, and fast. Not hearing the high-pitched clang that followed as a jug bounced onto the floor from a crate.

Miranda hurried along the passage and back to the basement as fast as she could. She went back outside, shocked by what the crypt had revealed and no further forward regarding the shoes. She stood in the churchyard, silent, thinking. Then she remembered the second boot, the one her mother had stored in her bag. *Damn*, she thought, *I should have dealt with the boot first of all.* But where had she left it?

She found the boot by the workshop door and carried it carefully back to the shed. Once inside, she squeezed her way through the wood to the trunks and gingerly opened the first one she saw. Then she shoved the boot down the side of the trunk, where it lay half-crushed in amongst the rest. Miranda sighed and dusted her hands.

Having a boot in the bar for luck was fair enough and a good thing to do, but why her ma had kept the second, the other half, was a mystery to her. If someone found the second boot, it wouldn't do much for the old legend and people might gossip about Matt McCarthy's link to her mother. And a bigger pile of *brand new* shoes.

Which needed a new hiding place.

Miranda was feeling more than dejected. Apart from removing a single boot, all she'd done was discover more problems, big problems. The thought of the jugs and the cup bothered her.

59

Then – Thomas

I was feeling harassed, and tired. I'd been up at dawn to do the deliveries, fruit and veg all over the place, and then there was school, doing sums and prayers and other daft rubbish. Now, I was meant to be at the pub. I couldn't be late for my shift yet again.

I waited for Pike to turn his back; since he'd been talking about clearing the shed, I'd gone right off him. Not that I'd been that smitten before. But when I thought of the effort we'd made, and all for nothing, I felt really peeved.

A few minutes later, I slipped the leash, dashed out of the room and hurried downstairs. The front door was locked while school was on so I made my way out through the joinery workshop. I nodded to Jake as I hurried through the back door, stepped into the churchyard and stopped abruptly. Wasn't that Eisen by the woodshed? Talking to a lad who looked like Carson, Conrad Carson, who was meant to be missing.

'Jake!' I hissed and my mate came running. 'Who's that Eisen's talking to?'

Jake peered out of the workshop doorway, but Eisen was standing in front of the lad and all I could see, now that he'd moved, was a scrap of ginger, the lad's curly hair. I was sure it was Carson. I wondered if I dared get any closer?

'Mr Eisen, sir,' I called, sharply, regretting the words as soon as I'd said them. Jake swore, loudly and hurried back in. *The little wimp*, I thought and grinned. I stood my ground.

Eisen turned around and gestured. The boy had vanished, he'd sent him away. *Damn!* I thought.

'I wondered if that was Carson, sir?'

'And what's it to you, if it was, Islip?'

'Nothing, sir, but Carson's a mate. And I haven't seen him for quite some time.'

'Asking questions leads to trouble. Did nobody ever tell you that?' I shook my head.

'So what are you doing out here, Islip?'

'Running an errand for Mr Pike. I'm going to see Percy Thomas, sir; you know, at the shop. To ask if he can help with the gala.' This tripped off my tongue as easy as pie, but I wondered how I'd square it all later. I wasn't supposed to know about the gala, it was still under wraps, as far as I knew. Ben had told me the other day. When Eisen spoke I thought he was psychic.

'I've seen you talking to Ben Tencell, I suppose he told you about the gala.' I said nothing.

'I believe he lives not far from you, Islip?' *What was coming now?* I wondered.

'Not that far, sir,' I said slowly, shifting my weight from foot to foot.

'I'd like you to give him a message, lad. Seeing as you seem to like running errands.' Eisen paused.

'Tell him the vicar's had a disturbance, some things overturned, but nothing's gone missing. Tell him he doesn't have to worry about it. Think you can do that?'

'I reckon so, yes, I'm sure I can.'

His hand came out and clipped my ear, which burned with surprise and the shame of the slap. 'Less of your cheek in future, lad and step to it, now. And don't forget the sir, next time.'

'No, Mr Eisen, I won't,' I said. 'Sir, I mean.'

I was glad to escape from Eisen's clutches and rather bewildered by what had gone on, so I wandered around the town for a bit, thinking hard about what had happened. I found myself in Narrowboat Lane. I nearly went into Percy's shop, to ask if he would help with the gala, then I remembered I'd made that up. Just in time.

I stood outside the shop, thinking, wondering what the disturbance in the church was about and more crucially, why Ben had to know. My mind felt feeble, I was weak with hunger. I needed to get some bread, or something.

'How about a piece of chocolate?' There was Alice, complete with her iPad, whatever that was.

'That would be great, I'm starving, thanks.' I took a huge chunk.

'You remembered my name,' she said, smiling and gave me more chocolate.

'You're speaking!' I said, as I gobbled it down, I couldn't think where she got chocolate like this. It was better than Chaucer's any day. 'I thought you told me you couldn't talk.'

'That was what *you* thought,' Alice informed me. 'I can talk when I want, but I don't always want to.'

'Well, I'm glad you are, it was slow using that.' I pointed at the iPad.

'I still might use it,' she said, thoughtfully, looking as if she really was deciding.

'Don't, not today, please, Alice,' I told her, quickly. The day had been tough but had just improved. I didn't want to waste our time typing.

'Why are you standing outside this shop?'

'A mate of mine called Percy works here. We met when we were at school together.'

'Is that at the school that's really a house?' I thought about that.

'I know it looks like a house from outside, but it's definitely a school,' I said, firmly.

'It'll be a house again, in the future,' Alice informed me, 'after all the kids have gone. Or maybe not all, we'll have to see.' I didn't know what she was talking about. She dragged me under the arch by the elbow, taking me down towards Scriveners Road and passing my school. What if one of the lads saw me?

Alice laughed and let me go, once she saw how uneasy I was. 'I want to ask you a favour, Tom. You know you told me about the tunnel, that goes from the Low to Curdizan Church?'

'Yes,' I said, somewhat reluctantly. I really regretted mentioning the tunnel. I thought as she went to a different school and lived in Ebbenheart Green it wouldn't matter. I thought she'd forget but I'd thought wrong.

'I'd like you to take me along the tunnel, to show me exactly where it leads to.'

'You know where it leads to, Alice,' I said.

'But I want to go along it myself. Because I'm a girl, I get left behind, I don't get to do the fun things like you.'

'It wasn't much fun,' I told her, sharply, thinking of climbing through the window and creeping around in the dark in the basement. Dragging the trunks along the tunnel, watching for rats, and God knows what else. 'Trust me, Alice, it wasn't much fun.'

'I still want to do it,' she said, stubbornly, her eyes narrowing, becoming focused. '*You* got to go, with two of your friends.'

'Yes,' I said. 'But I can't say who, I promised I wouldn't.'

'I bet one was Ben,' said Alice, grinning. We'd stopped by the church and were sitting on the wall.

'You what?' I said, wondering how she knew it was him. I hadn't told her, I knew I hadn't.

'You mentioned Ben the last time we met,' she said, as if she'd guessed my thoughts. 'You told me the tunnel went from the coach house and Ben's the person who ran that place. Runs it, I mean.' She paused, briefly. 'That's right, isn't it? I bet Ben's your friend. You even told me his pony was called Norah.'

'Yes,' I agreed. 'I remember saying you could meet Norah.' But I hadn't mentioned Ben by name. She must have been asking around or something. I stared at Alice, the girl was sharp.

'So can I see this pony sometime, even if I can't go down the tunnel?'

'Yes, I suppose so,' I told her, abruptly, heading for the passage. I had to get back, Miranda would be waiting.

'And the tunnel comes up in Curdizan Church? That's right isn't it?'

'Yes,' I said, 'but you know I can't take you.'

'That's too bad, but fine, if you say so. Go on then, Tom,' she smiled at me, 'I thought you were in a hurry to get off.'

I stared at Alice, disbelieving. She seemed so mild and willing to agree, when moments before she'd been so insistent. I couldn't understand it. But I didn't have time to puzzle it out, I had to get to the Keepsake Arms. I raced down the alley, heading for the pub.

I liked Alice because she was bright; I also liked her because she was different, those were the things that made her my friend. Sometimes, the things she said bothered me, but what worried me most was her steely smile.

60

Now – Aleph

I wasn't having the best of days. I'd spent the morning in Leverhulme, seeing my supervisor, Terence Lyle. The man was someone I'd known before, in my previous life, by which I mean before the boy died.

'You're not coming to terms with things, Aleph.'

'I thought we were talking about this new therapy.'

'We're here to talk about any issues which affect your work, and the accident does.' Lyle looked sombre.

'I really don't want to talk about that. Is it obligatory?'

'No, of course it's not. But all the same, I think you should.'

'But I don't want to, at the moment. So about this new therapy...'

Terence Lyle sighed. After that, it all went downhill.

I emerged from the building feeling angry, *and* guilty, Lyle was right, I should have moved on, or at least achieved some kind of acceptance. That thought made me pause. When I got home, I opened the shoe box. There were still four envelopes inside.

Just open one, I said to myself, the second one. *Alright,* I thought. *But only the one.*

It was easy to tell which was the second, they were all numbered, in the top right hand corner. I opened the envelope and pulled out the card. It was just like the first one, and like the first, the word MURDERER, was printed at the top. I had to sit down.

It didn't take long to read the rest. The word HE I'd seen before. But the second word told me even less.

HE WAS... what?

I hadn't a clue. I put the card back inside the envelope, and threw it in the box along with the others. Read me, why don't you, the other cards begged.

Not a chance, I thought, as I slammed the lid on the shoebox, hard. The corner crumpled, damaging the box, but at least a box could be replaced, unlike a life. I felt like smashing the place to pieces. The telephone rang.

'How did it go?' said Cressida, softly. It took me a minute to understand.

'You mean with Alice?'

'Of course, with Alice, what else would I mean? Was she alright, she didn't run away?'

'Haven't you asked her?' I said, incredulous. That was last night.

'She didn't want to talk, not even on her iPad. It happens sometimes, when she's upset. I leave her alone at times like that, or at least, I do now. I didn't always.'

How hard it must be, I thought, with insight, *to admit all this to a relative stranger. And for her daughter to behave like this.* My heart went out to her.

'Alice was fine,' I told Cressida. 'But there are some things you need to know. Can you come round?'

'I'll be there by three.' And so she was. We sat in the kitchen.

The ghosts were more or less absent today, there was a slight chill, but that was all. Putting the freezer back had helped. I looked at the boot, which was still on the shelf, and wondered whether it mattered, and how?

Cressida was stirring her coffee vigorously. God knows why, she drank it black, *and* without sugar.

'Alice likes coffee,' I said mildly. 'That's odd, for a child.'

'Aleph,' said Cressida, tapping the table, 'sod the coffee and tell me... whatever.'

'Sorry,' I said, 'I've had a rough day.' *And bound to get worse.*

'Alice believes Tom is dead. She didn't expect me to find

that out, by playing her recording back, in reverse.'

'The one she did with Alison Clipper?'

'Yes,' I told her, 'and there's more. She likes Tom a lot, and he's promised to show her a pony called Norah. As well as a tunnel, that leads from the Low to Curdizan Church.'

'But Curdizan Church doesn't exist.'

'Not anymore, but it did back then, and although I told Alice to talk to you before going on trips with Tom, *anywhere*, I very much doubt, she'll do as I said. You'll have to have a chat with her.'

'I think you're forgetting one crucial thing. Alice talks to me when *she* feels like it, not when I want to, and by *talking*, I mean on her iPad. This would be a one-way chat, and I doubt she'd listen.'

'You're going to have to find a way, because Alice is determined to go down the tunnel, and as the church isn't there anymore, she could end up – well – God knows where.' Cressida was getting up from the table.

'I'm sorry, Aleph, I've got to go.'

'Cressida, wait, you've only just got here!'

Cressida paused and I continued. 'We need to pool our resources, you know, work together to help Alice. What do you say?'

'I don't think I can trust you, Aleph,' Cressida told me, opening the door and stepping outside into the daylight. Her eyes, however, were as dark as ever. 'She talked to you, didn't she, without the iPad?' I nodded, pensive.

'When were you going to mention that?'

'I'd have told you sometime, you just didn't give me the chance, that's all.'

'You're a terrible liar, Aleph Jones. I wish I'd never got involved in this or introduced my daughter to you. It's true what she said, you're nothing but trouble.'

'Alice said that?' I said, puzzled. Cressida frowned and shook her head.

'No, not Alice, it doesn't matter, forget I said it, it was

a slip of the tongue. I must go now, Alice needs me, even if she doesn't know it.'

I watched her hurry down the steps to the street and around the corner to Scriveners Road, imagined her wandering about the courtyard, looking in vain for the tunnel's entrance, for something which no longer existed. I sighed heavily and went inside.

I knew all about that kind of search.

61

Then – Miranda

She'd barely got back from Curdizan High when Tom turned up, looking rather sheepish.

'Get those glasses washed,' she insisted, and the lad nodded quickly, got on with the job.

Strange, she considered, *that's most unlike Tom.* She wandered through to the parlour at the back, where her ma was having a music night. The racket was terrible, what a surprise. Some men were standing in front of a table, clapping and shouting and then she saw why. A woman was dancing *on* the table, her skirts lifted up and showing her ankles. Nobody took any notice of Miranda. She looked around wildly, spotting a couple of men who she knew, including Tom's da, but God be praised, no sign of Ben.

He's far too busy thieving for that. She went upstairs to find her mother.

'What's going on in the parlour downstairs?'

'It's just the regular music night. To mark the start of the end of the week.' Her ma was putting some clothes away.

'There's a woman dancing on the table in there, and one of the men who's watching is Scotty, Thomas's da. He's often in here, and always drunk, and I'm the one who has to deal with it. Me and Steve, if he's around. You're never here.'

'I'm here, now,' her mother insisted.

'But you weren't back then, you were off and away with your fancy man.'

The hand came out and slapped her cheek.

'Oh!' said Miranda, and felt embarrassed, she was far too old to be slapped like that. She said as much.

'So act your age, instead of like the child you once were. I

237

loved your da, I've told you before, and I don't have to tell you anything, girl, so bear that in mind. Matt was not my fancy man, I liked him yes, and maybe I loved him, but not in that way. You ought to show me some respect. I am your ma.'

'I try,' said Miranda, holding her cheek, 'but it isn't that easy, not with those shoes and no explanation, and all the rabble downstairs in the parlour. You don't seem much like the mother I knew.'

'Well, shame on you, if you'd blame your ma for trying to make us some sort of living, even if how I do it doesn't suit you. Matt would have understood about the shoes, the man was a gem, he knew that living round here was hard. Besides, you don't know the full story.'

'So, tell me then, I'd like to know.'

'I can't, Miranda, it's not mine to tell.'

'Well, isn't that just convenient, Ma? And what about the rabble downstairs? Do you want this place to look like a brothel?'

'It's just a bit of a laugh, that's all. And as for Scotty, if he's in here, that makes it better for Carol at home.'

'But not for Thomas,' Miranda said, 'he's always giving the lad a clip. Perhaps that's why you have him around. You and him have got something in common, thumping your kids.' She gave her mother a pointed look then hurried downstairs.

It hadn't improved in the time she'd been gone. The bar was full, almost heaving, and even more men had piled in the back, were singing along with the woman dancing. *At least the takings will be high, tonight.*

She and Tom worked together in silence, along with Steve, an older lad, who helped them out sometimes, when they were busy. By the end of the night all three were shattered and Miranda knew her evening wasn't over. Now she had to go to see Ben.

Her heart started thumping, but she kept her cool with thoughts of the treasure and criminal acts and yet more worry about the shoes. *But all the same I'll wear that dress, the red satin dream and make myself nice, then maybe then I'll learn a little bit more.* Forgetting, as she planned, that the dress was torn.

She staggered upstairs, her feet aching sorely from a day at Chaucer's, a visit to the crypt, then an evening in the pub, serving ale and never sitting down. *But at least I haven't been dancing,* she thought. She opened the wardrobe. The dress wasn't there. Miranda blinked.

She didn't have much in the way of clothes and she loved that dress with its rich, vibrant hue, even despite the tear in the hem, a dress that was torn could be easily mended. Thanks to her father's practical ways.

He'd bribed a local headmaster with drink and managed to get her some free schooling, being too poor to pay the fees. My girl's a beautiful seamstress, he'd said. But not tonight.

Miranda checked the rest of her things then went downstairs to look in the laundry, but try as she might she couldn't find it. 'Damn,' she said and went back upstairs.

To hell with her ma, the shoes and Ben. None of these problems were her doing. She'd worked like a slave and done her best, and if things went wrong, it wasn't her fault. Hers or Thomas's.

She stripped off her things, pulled off her boots, climbed into bed and fell asleep.

62

Now – Cressida

When she arrived, she tried to look sorry. Cressida knew she'd failed by his look.

'Come in,' said Aleph, and held the door open.

'Thanks,' she said, and followed him slowly into the lounge.

'I thought it would make a change from the kitchen.'

'Fine by me.' She sipped her wine. 'This is good.' She took a deep breath.

'I was angry that Alice would talk to you, and yet not to me. She's done this before, with her friends and teachers, even the guy who delivers the post, but with you it was worse, because you and she were virtual strangers. It didn't seem right.' She paused and sipped a little more wine. 'I know she's angry at me for something, but she won't say what, she won't even admit she's angry at all.' Aleph said nothing.

'*You* could ask her what it's about, if you would.'

'I would,' he said, 'but only if you're really sure.'

'Of course I'm sure, I've asked you, haven't I?' She paused, looked guilty. 'Alright, I'm sorry, I didn't mean to snap, I guess I'm still angry about what's happened. But not at you, it's not your fault. Let me explain.'

'After we met, I went back home and spoke to Alice, and asked her about the tunnel and Tom. She denied it all, said there wasn't any Tom, or a tunnel or a horse, that she'd made it all up to amuse herself. Then she said I wasn't to hear the recording, because that was private, between her and Alison, and also you, because of the reversals. But she said I wasn't to believe what you say.' Cressida leaned forward.

'But, the thing is, Aleph, I do believe that Tom exists, or

did exist, even though it's madness, because I've seen him too, and Alice denying it must be significant, don't you think? But I don't know what I ought to do next.'

'And you'd like me to help if I can?'

'I would,' she said, 'because no-one else would believe this story, and you've been involved from the very beginning.' *Which is truer than you know,* thought Cressida, grimly.

She watched as Aleph got up from the sofa and poured them more wine. He sat back down.

I ought to tell Aleph who I am, especially if Alice saw Daniel's accident. That would explain an awful lot, why she's so traumatised and maybe even why she thinks she hears ghosts. But Alice hasn't mentioned Aleph, or the accident, so perhaps she doesn't even remember. Or maybe she didn't see it at all. And I don't know why she's angry with me. And if Tom is a ghost, why have I seen him? Oh God, I'm confused.

'I could always do some more research,' Aleph was saying. Cressida waited.

'We're both assuming Tom existed, possibly quite a long time ago. If we can prove it, show her he's real *and* that he's dead, these facts might chase his ghost away.'

'So you're assuming I'm crazy too?' Aleph looked blank.

'You said if we proved he was real *and* dead, Alice could face it, then she'd move on. But I saw Tom as well, remember. So are you saying, *I* have to move on?'

'Assuming you've something to move on from.' Cressida didn't answer.

'You might have seen a ghost,' said Aleph, 'but I've heard them crying and so has Alice. And that wasn't prompted by anything else.'

'The School Lane ghosts,' said Cressida, slowly.

'Exactly,' said Aleph. 'I've done some research on those already. And then there's the matter of Mary-Ann Parks.'

'I'd forgotten about her, said Cressida, thinking. How are she and Tom connected?'

'They might have lived around the same time. But I'd need to check if Tom existed. It shouldn't be hard to find

Haversham Road.'

'You're willing to do this for us?' asked Cressida.

'I'm also doing it for me,' said Aleph. 'I want the ghosts to leave, like you do.'

Cressida bit her lip and said nothing. There were other ghosts she could share with Aleph, but she knew that wasn't her story to tell. It was Martha's story but she, unwittingly, had become involved, and now, with hindsight, she wished she hadn't. And, what if Alice had been there when Daniel was killed? She hadn't dared ask, but she'd have to soon. They couldn't live in silence forever.

'I'll go to the library first thing tomorrow. Check out the census and the trade directories.' Aleph was writing some notes on a pad.

'I'm really glad you're helping us out.' Cressida smiled as she got to her feet.

'I'm always happy to help,' said Aleph. He moved a bit closer, smiling warmly.

You haven't a chance in hell, thought Cressida, and slipped past him quickly, into the hall. 'Ring me, if you learn something new.' She opened the door and went outside.

But not if it's bad, she said to herself, as she walked down the steps.

63

Then – Thomas

The morning was bright and I felt chirpy, like I used to do in the good old days, before Louise vanished and Miranda looked troubled and snapped all the time. I'd delivered the fruit and veg for Mason and was making my way up the stairs at school when I stopped with a jolt, half-way up.

The skull was sitting where it always was, perched on a shelf at the top of the landing. Its eyes were hooded, as if it was watching, keeping a beady eye on me. I saw this skull almost every day, except when Carson had used it as a football – a piece of the jaw had been missing since then – but *Mister* Pike still kept it on a shelf, a higher shelf that we couldn't reach, not that this stopped us from trying, hard. Mostly we failed.

Carson, I thought. I'd seen him once, I could see him again. I needed to find out why he'd vanished and what he'd been doing talking to Eisen. If only I'd seen him on his own. I glanced across at the landing window, which overlooked the church and the graves, and couldn't believe it when I saw him. Carson, I thought, don't you dare move!

I ran downstairs and right through the workshop, not even thinking to check for Eisen. Fortunately for me, the back door was open. I dashed outside and ran past the woodshed and hurried towards the back of the church. The path led out to Scrivener's Road. There was Carson, slipping through the gate. *Yes!* I thought. *You won't get away.*

'Carson,' I yelled and Carson paused, glancing behind him and seeing me there. He ran even faster, as fast as he could. *Hell*, I thought.

I followed him quickly across the road and then through

245

the alley and onto the street, Convent Court. Carson was slight and quick as a flash *and* a bit younger, but I had stamina, going out on the bike as I did. Before very long I could hear him gasping, noticed his legs were slowing down, so I stretched out a hand and reached for his sleeve. The damn thing tore.

'You bastard!' he said as he ground to a halt and glared at me. 'My ma'll go mad when she sees what you've done.'

'You shouldn't have run away then, should you?' I stood my ground and the lad stood his.

'What do you want from me, Thomas Islip?'

'A number of kids have vanished from school and you're one of them, and so is Mimson, and then there's a mate of mine called Louise. Any idea where she's gone?'

'No,' said Carson, rubbing his nose on his jacket sleeve and sniffing, loudly, to show his contempt. 'I've been too busy to notice girls.'

'Some folk are saying that Eisen's involved, and maybe that the kids are all dead. And then I saw you talking to him, and you're not dead, so what's going on?'

'Why should I bother talking to you?'

'Because I'm older and tougher than you, and some of the kids have family who care.'

'I don't know nothing about the others, so it's no good asking.' He shuffled his feet. 'Pike's been sending me out boot blacking, and polishing as well, they come up a treat.'

'You mean on the streets?'

'Where else?' he said. 'A lot of the toffs are happy to pay. Especially when I say I'm an orphan.'

'But you're not,' I said, amazed at his cheek.

'I know that stupid, but *they* don't know. They think I'm in need, and I am, of cash.' He reached in his pocket and showed me some notes. Coppers spilled out and fell on the ground.

'Christ!' I said, and reached for the wad, but Carson was quicker and whipped it away.

'Keep your hands off, Islip, you earn it yourself, if you

want some of this.'

'I bet you don't get to keep it,' I said.

'No, I don't,' said Carson, 'more's the pity, or at least not much. First Pike takes his cut, then my da has some, but I always manage to keep a bit back.'

'Pike takes a cut?' I said, with surprise.

'It was his idea. I'm working the streets, just like I did before I started at the school, but it's better than begging, because *we* do a job, and if I mention the school to the punters first, then that makes it right. I get more dosh, then Pike takes his cut.'

'I'm sure he shouldn't,' I told him, slowly.

'Why not?' said Carson, 'it was his idea. And he's got the contacts, well mostly, anyway.'

'What else do you do?' I asked, warily.

'Sometimes I sweep chimneys, but not very often, I can't say I like it, it's filthy work. Pike says I'm good cos I'm not that big, but my ma's not happy, although Da doesn't care, not so long as there's dosh at the end. I get well paid for doing chimneys.'

'And Pike takes some?'

'Yes, just the same as he does with the polishing. He knows the people who want it done, so obviously, it's down to him. It's easing off now, because of the weather and I can't say I'm sorry. With any luck I'll have grown too much to work by the winter.'

'But you don't know anything about Louise or Alec Mimson?'

'I've never even heard them mentioned. But I'll keep my ear to the ground, if you like, so long as you keep all this to yourself. It's meant to be private, unofficial, or so Pike said.'

'I'll bet he did,' I said, bitterly. As long as us kids were at the school, Pike got a bonus for every one. I remembered my ma once telling me that. He was claiming the bonus for all of us kids and putting a few of them out to work. The cheeky sod. 'That's wily behaviour,' I told Carson.

'You'd better not tell,' said Carson sharply. 'I mean it, Islip, keep your trap shut. Or, it might be you who goes missing next.'

'As if you could,' I said, laughing.

'No,' said Carson, 'I reckon I couldn't. But I do know folk who can make it happen, and I'm not joking.' He ran his finger across his throat. Then he grinned. 'There's one thing you should be pleased about.'

'What's that?' I asked him, curious.

'That I'm not dead, otherwise you wouldn't know what happened.'

64

Now – Cressida

Cressida was walking home from work, feeling the warmth of the sun on her back and seeing it shine on Ebbenheart Green. The actual Green, it still existed. Maybe that means it will all work out, she thought, wistfully, thinking about her daughter, Alice. She knew she needed to talk to her. She wasn't looking forward to the evening at all. She turned the key and went into the house. 'Alice?' she called. Alice didn't answer. Cressida felt at once relieved and then ashamed.

In the thick silence, she could hear Ron Mappen, her next door neighbour, mowing his lawn, the first of the season. She wondered if Alice was off with her friends or down in Curdizan Low with Tom. She shivered suddenly.

Damn Aleph Jones, for stirring things up. She'd rather not have known about that tunnel. Assuming it still existed, that is. It probably did. The telephone rang.

'Cressida, it's me, I've found Thomas! He's there in the census.' Aleph paused.

'Right,' said Cressida, pulling up a chair and sinking into it. God, she was tired.

'He lived on Haversham Road, with his parents, his father is down as a mill worker. I bet it's the one that backed onto the street, the enormous one that went down to the Blue.' Cressida sighed.

Aleph was really pleased, she could tell, but it pleased her less, knowing Tom was real and Alice had lied. 'I don't suppose there are photos?' she said.

'I only searched the census,' said Aleph, 'but there might be some in the local paper. I could try that next, although the chances of Tom being in it are slight.' He paused for a moment.

'I could try looking for the man called Ben, the one with the horse called Norah, remember? It doesn't seem much to go on, frankly, but I know he was based at the old coaching inn. I'll give it a try.'

'Have you tried looking for Mary-Ann?'

'The one who was murdered? No, not properly. Only in the papers, not elsewhere.'

'You told me she was a vicar's daughter. You know where the church was, it shouldn't be hard.'

'But we already know Mary-Ann existed.'

'You might find some people connected to her, in the streets near the church, and also in your house, the Old Schoolhouse.'

'Like Wetherby Eisen? He won't have lived there.'

'No,' she said, 'but he might have lived in a street nearby. There might be other material too, apart from the census.' Cressida heard the door opening. 'Alice is here, I'll have to go, now. Keep me informed on what you find out.' She followed her daughter into the kitchen.

Alice had eaten, and finished her homework and Cressida still hadn't broached the subject. Tom and the tunnel, and all the rest. She kept on thinking, *I'll do it now*, and then she backed off.

'Go on, just say it,' Alice typed quickly.

'What?' said Cressida, twisting her ring around her finger.

'Whatever it is you want to say. I don't want to wait all night to hear it.'

'Tom exists,' Cressida said, choosing the lesser of two evils.

'And did I ever say he didn't?'

'You told me you'd made him up, for fun. You also said you'd made up the horse and the tunnel, but I've since discovered Tom existed, and I'm assuming the tunnel did too. Maybe still does. You lied to me, Alice.'

'I bet it was Aleph who learnt all that, not you at all.' She typed furiously.

'You're right, he did, he found him in the census. And before you deny it, it is Tom, if he's the one on Haversham Road.'

'Did Alison say it was Haversham Road?'

'It's *Mrs Clipper*, and no she didn't. I got that from the sound recording.'

'The recording was mine and meant to be private, between me and her.'

'You once told me that Aleph could hear it.'

'Yes, but not you. You never let me have any secrets.'

Cressida studied her daughter carefully. *Alice acts like she hates me sometimes. What have I done?* She paused, thinking.

'Now we know that Tom existed, if you saw him, perhaps he's a ghost, and that's alright, but maybe we could talk about that?' She nodded at the iPad. Alice got up.

'I already knew that Tom existed, I didn't need you and Aleph to prove it. I don't want to talk about anything with you, even with that.' She glanced at the iPad. 'So what does it matter, if I lied? Have you never lied? I bet you're lying to Aleph right now.' She glared at her mother. Cressida felt shaken.

'Alice, wait. I haven't finished. There're still some things I need to say, about Daniel's death.' Cressida looked at her daughter intently. Alice stopped walking.

'What about Danny?' she typed slowly.

'You saw him, didn't you, on the street? Maybe you even saw what happened? Is that why you won't talk to me?'

'No, you're wrong! I didn't see him, I never saw him after I left. Why won't you leave me alone for once?' Alice stopped typing and shoved the iPad onto the table, hurrying down the hall to the door. She opened the door and slammed it after her. Alice had gone.

'Alice, wait!'

Cressida peered out of the door. Alice had vanished from sight completely. Right in front of the house was the Green, and in front of the Green were a few stray cars, circling the island, not very fast. There were shops to the left and enormous trees which lined her street and the edge of the green. It looked surreal in the artificial light. Alice could be anywhere.

Cressida went back inside the house and slumped on the stairs, pulling her boots on and lacing them up. Yes, it was true, she'd lied to Aleph. Or rather, she'd lied to him by omission. But Alice was lying as well, she thought. She'd seen something when Daniel died, maybe even the accident, and that was why she'd never been the same. And now, Alice had vanished again.

Cressida grabbed her coat and bag and hurried out into the street after Alice. It was getting late and Alice was alone, without any money, or even her iPad.

Which just went to show how upset she was.

65

Then – Miranda

Ben looked up as Miranda came in, squeezing through the gap in the door. He nodded briefly.

The room looked much as it had the last time, dark and chilly and uninviting, with assorted coffin lids dangling from the walls. Miranda shivered.

'I don't like it much in here,' she said.

'Well, don't come again, if that's how you feel.' Ben smiled and seemed amused, but he didn't stop working because she was there. 'Were you just passing, or did you have something you wanted to say?'

'Yes,' said Miranda, 'but I haven't got long. I've got to be back at the pub by six.'

'Better spit it out then,' he told her, briskly, putting down his hammer and staring at Miranda. She looked at the floor.

'This thieving you're doing, it's got to stop.'

'And who's saying that?' said Ben, coolly, pulling out a stool and perching on it. He stretched out his legs, taking up space. Miranda stepped back and blushed, unseen.

'I know you're in this with Wetherby Eisen, that it's not just you, but it still isn't right. Thieving, then storing the goods in a church. The crypt of a church.'

'And how the hell do you know where we store them?' Ben sounded grim.

'I discovered the goods the other evening. I was looking for somewhere to store the shoes, until we could move them up to the shop.'

'And you ended up in the crypt of the church?'

'Well, yes, more or less, but I didn't expect to see your – stock.'

'I'll bet you didn't,' said Ben softly.

'But what if the vicar found them there?'

At that Ben laughed, a rollicking laugh, that seemed to echo up to the rooftops. Miranda glanced out through the gap at the street, worried that someone would hear them and come. Ben leant across and nudged the door shut.

'Why do you think we use the church?'

'Because the crypt's dark and rarely visited?'

'No, silly girl. We use it because the vicar lets us.'

'What do you mean?'

'I can't just decide to stop when I want to, it's not just me and Wetherby involved. There's the vicar to think of, not to mention his family, do you know how little a vicar earns? *And* he's got a wife and daughters to feed.'

'Does Mary-Ann know the vicar's involved?' She was, after all, engaged to Eisen.

'No,' said Ben, 'and you're not going to tell her, do you hear me, Miranda? Mary-Ann Parks worships her father. Think what the news might do to her. It wouldn't be right.'

'But thieving's not right,' Miranda said. 'Nothing that's good ever came from stealing.'

'And what business is it of yours, exactly?'

'I'm your friend,' Miranda said, 'and Mary-Ann's too, and that's what friends are meant to do, help and advise each other in life. Even if that means saying tough things.'

'You're a darling girl, and pretty as hell, but nobody tells me what to do. Even you, Miranda, sweetheart. My life's my business and nobody else's. Is that clear?'

'Oh, yes,' said Miranda, 'it certainly is. I'm sorry I seem to have wasted your time.' She turned away and made for the door, trying in vain to pull it open. The handle was loose and came off in her hand. The door was still closed.

'Here, let me,' said Ben, amused.

'No! I'll do it,' Miranda snapped and grabbed the edge of the metal lock. She tugged on it hard and the door swung open, revealing a damp and chilly evening.

'Goodbye Ben,' she said to him, softly, turning right and hurrying away.

'Miranda, wait!' yelled Ben, getting up, but Miranda had no intention of waiting. By the time she had reached the junction with Croston, her heart was burning and her eyes were swimming with unshed tears. She blinked them away, annoyed with herself. She could hear her mother's voice in her head. *You got involved with the wrong man, it's sad but it happens. Now, get over it.*

'Ha!' thought Miranda, turning right, then hurrying quickly, away from her pub and Dogleg Lane. She headed up Croston towards the abbey. Who was her mother to talk, after all? Her ma had been sweet on Matt McCarthy, even assuming nothing had happened.

She kept on walking, right through the alley to Scriveners Road, and was just about to turn right for the abbey, but instead she paused briefly, and leant against the wall of the church, Curdizan Church, and burst into tears. *What a fool I am*, she said to herself..

Her tears subsided to feeble sniffles, which were brought up short when she felt the touch of a hand on her arm.

Ben! she thought, but was soon disappointed, for the person the hand belonged to was female, and much younger.

'I hardly ever find crying helps. Here, have this.'

The girl was tall, but still a child and she smiled at Miranda, handing her some paper, it was light and flimsy and soft to the touch. 'This is a tissue, for blowing your nose.'

'Right,' said Miranda, feeling puzzled.

'I bet you're Miranda, Thomas's friend. The one who works at the Keepsake Arms. Am I right?' Miranda nodded.

'Tom said he would show me the tunnel. The one that runs from beneath Ben's place to the Old Schoolhouse and Curdizan Church.' She nodded behind her. 'Tom's isn't here, but you are, instead. Will you take me down the tunnel?'

Miranda studied the girl, closely. She had long blonde hair, which wasn't tied back, and a healthy face and some very strange clothes. Why had she called it the *Old* Schoolhouse? She obviously didn't live round here. She watched as the stranger held out her hand.

'I'm sorry, Miranda,' she said, smiling. 'My mother would say I'm being very rude. My name's Alice, pleased to meet you.'

66

Now – Guinevere

Guinevere crossed the market square. She was heading down the street, making for the courtyard and Old School Lane and dreading the visit, she knew she wasn't the most popular of people. But Martha's call had been a shock.

'Alice is missing and Cressida is frantic. We're looking for volunteers to find her.'

'Right,' said Guinevere, 'I'll get my coat.'

'I'll send you a photo from my phone. I think you'd better start searching in Curdizan, instead of in Ebbenheart Green where she lives. Cressida has found out you gave that file of Alice crying to Aleph Jones. She's not very happy.'

'It was at your request,' said Guinevere, mildly.

'Yes, I know and I now wish I hadn't, but at the moment, we've got to find Alice. Cressida has contacted the police already, and Len and his mates are searching Leverhulme, but I think she could be in Curdizan. Try that first.'

'I'll do whatever you think will help. But what makes you think Alice could be here?' Ginny could have sworn she heard Martha laugh.

'I thought reporters were meant to be bright? If I was looking for Alice Sewell, Curdizan High's the first place I'd choose. Can't you think why?'

'Of course,' said Guinevere, smiling broadly. 'That's where Aleph Jones is based.'

And where Alice heard the School Lane ghosts. Apparently.

Guinevere hurried down Old School Lane. It was dry, thank God, but freezing cold, so she'd wrapped up warmly and pulled the collar of her coat up high. So much for spring. She hurried up the steps to Aleph's door and rang the bell, then waited a while but nothing happened. She tried again and saw a flicker at one of the curtains. Then Aleph appeared.

'You ought to get that bell fixed, Aleph.'

'Hello, Ginny, good to see you. Did you want me to solve a murder? Or maybe track down a couple of bodies? In my cellar.'

'Don't be like that. Can I come in?' She stared at the hall, just behind Aleph, invitingly warm and frowned with envy. 'Alice is missing and people are searching all over right now. In Leverhulme and Curdizan. I don't suppose she's come round here?'

'No,' said Aleph, looking troubled. 'I'm sorry, she hasn't. Why did she vanish?'

'She had a row with her mother, again.' Aleph frowned.

'I told Cressida I'd found Tom, and also some things I'd heard from Alice. I bet she told Alice everything I'd said. So now, not surprisingly, Alice doesn't trust us. What a mess!'

'Who's Thomas?' Ginny asked him.

'Never mind that, I'll tell you later. Wait here a minute.' He was back in a flash, wearing a coat. His eyes narrowed.

'I shouldn't really be talking to you. The way you lied about that recording.'

'I know and I'm sorry. But Alice is troubled and I wanted to help. All I've done is make things worse.'

'One of us has,' said Aleph, grimly. He closed the door and followed her slowly down to the road. They walked along it and round the corner.

'Blasted churchyard,' Guinevere said. 'I always seem to be hanging round here.'

'But it's not a churchyard, not anymore.'

'You know what I mean.' Guinevere laughed. Then she felt guilty, laughing with Aleph while Alice was missing. She grabbed Aleph's arm. 'Look, over there! Could that be Alice, talking to someone?'

'Don't you know her?' Aleph asked, peering to see and

sounding puzzled.

'No, I don't, all I've got is this phone photo. I'm not Cressida's friend, I'm – hell, Aleph, they're walking away. Let's go after them.'

'I can't tell if it's Alice or not, it's far too dark. And the woman she's with looks more like a girl. But her clothes are all wrong, they're too old-fashioned.'

'They're crossing the road, quick, let's follow them.'

Ginny and Aleph hurried ahead, trying to catch the others up.

'Why don't you call her?' Guinevere said.

'No,' said Aleph, 'we'd only scare her. If she sees us, she'll walk even faster, maybe even run and then we'd never catch her up. We have to be careful.'

'I think they're going down that alley, on the right.'

Aleph swore and stopped abruptly, looking anxious. 'I think you'd better go back to the house.'

'What do you mean go back to the house? That could be Alice, in there with that woman and now you're suggesting we should go back. Come on, let's hurry.' Aleph didn't move.

'I'm not suggesting we should go back, but I can't be sure that the girl is Alice. Somebody needs to stay at my house, in case she turns up.'

'Fine, you do it, it is your house. I'm going on.' They stood together at the entrance to the passage. Aleph looked thoughtful.

'You don't know Curdizan Low, do you?'

'No, so what?'

'It's a building site, and a hazard in the dark. The woman with Alice, if she's Alice, might have an accomplice and if I'm with you, I'm much more likely to be spotted, than alone. You said Alice doesn't even know you and if she sees us, she might not trust you. I'm better off on my own, on this. I can hide if I have to, and on my own I can deal with surprises. With you beside me, I'd only worry. Please, Ginny, do as I ask.'

Ginny was almost seething with rage. She hated the

thought of being left behind, but she knew she had to think of Alice.

'Very well, Aleph, I'll do as you ask, but only because I know it makes sense. But you really must hurry, you'll have lost them soon, if you don't go now.' Aleph threw her his door key.

'Don't you worry, I'll catch them up. I'll find them again, if it's the last thing I do.'

67

Then – Miranda

Miranda studied the girl Alice. There was something about her that seemed familiar.

I know what it is. She reminds me of those people I saw, the day I helped out at the soup kitchen. Not in her looks, but more in the way she carries herself, and the clothes she's wearing.

'Where are you from?' she said to the girl. Alice was leading her back down the alley.

'Ebbenheart Green, although we used to live in Leverhulme. I don't suppose you know where that is.'

Cheeky madam, Miranda thought, and scowled at the girl, but of course she was right. She had heard of Ebbenheart Green, though, that was lovely. It was where they held their summer picnic, a legacy from her father's day. Cath and Reg and sometimes her ma took a handful of kids from the worst tenements out for the day. Her eyes filled up with thoughts of her da. She shook them off.

'Shouldn't you be at home young lady? It is rather late.'

'I often stay out late in the evening, Mum doesn't mind. I thought I'd explore the tunnel tonight. Do say we can.'

Just like a little princess, thought Miranda. She wondered what she should do with the girl. They strolled past the turnoff to Dogleg Lane and she thought about taking her into the pub, finding her ma and looking for Thomas. But her ma would be out and Tom would be busy, and Miranda needed some space from all that. *I could call round at Ben's and see if he's in.* And then she cursed her stupid thoughts.

You're a fool, Miranda Collenge, she thought. *Soft on a bloke who doesn't give a damn. Haven't you got the message yet?*

It seemed she hadn't for she crossed the road and turned down Blackberry Close with the girl.

'Where are we going?' Alice asked her. 'This is such an amazing place! I love coming here.'

'Good for you,' said Miranda, sourly. 'Personally, I think it's a dump.'

'It's a lot more fun than Ebbenheart Green. That's so boring. All those trees and nothing to do.'

Spoilt little brat, Miranda thought. She was tempted to put her to work in the pub. That would teach her a lesson or two. *Maybe the next time.* Miranda smiled. They were nearing Ben's workshop.

'I'm taking you to see a friend, his name's Ben, he's a friend of Thomas's. This is his workshop.'

'Ben who owns the horse, Norah.'

'Yes, that's right. Norah pulls the cart with his coffins on.' If Miranda had hoped to shock Alice, she was disappointed.

'That's so cool. I've wanted to see the pony for ages. Is this where the tunnel starts from, as well as where the coffins are made?'

'It is,' said Miranda, somewhat amused. She pushed on the door, which creaked open.

'What a horrible smell,' said Alice, slowly.

'It's probably due to the dead bodies,' Miranda told her, knowing the smell was caused by the midden and the faulty drain which was always blocked.

'Poor Ben,' said Alice, frowning, 'having to work with this smell all day. There's nobody here.' She was right there wasn't. Miranda looked around.

Ben must have stopped in the middle of a job, his tools were still on the workbench waiting. *He won't be searching the streets for me,* she thought bitterly. She looked at Alice.

'Do you want to see this tunnel?'

'Yes,' said Alice, sounding excited. She also looked a little bit nervous.

I ought to take her back to the pub, Miranda thought, *that would be what my ma would do.* Taking her down the tunnel would be stupid, the girl would probably be terrified and cry. *And if Ben finds out, he'll kill me for sure.* That clinched it. Miranda picked up a nearby lamp. She turned to Alice.

'Now's the time, if you mean what you say.' Alice looked a little bit hesitant.

'I already said I wanted to, didn't I?'

'Fine, so let's do it. Remember to keep yourself well wrapped up, there are rats down there and spiders and cobwebs.'

'Rats?' said Alice, 'real, live rats? Are they big?' She paused, considering. 'I think I'd rather wait for Tom, if you don't mind.' Her voice quivered.

'Well, I'm ready now, so it's up to you. But if you're a baby and want to wait, we'll go back outside and wait for Tom. You could be waiting a while, you know.' Miranda's smile was less than friendly. Alice sighed.

'No, it's alright, I'm not a wimp. We'll go down the tunnel, now like you said.'

'You were the one who wanted to go.' Miranda bent down and shifted the bricks, then turned to the girl and smiled more warmly. She waved her arm towards the entrance.

'Ladies first.'

68

Then – Aleph

If I hadn't seen what I saw that night, I wouldn't have believed it. I hurried after the woman and Alice, knowing as I followed them into the alley, that I could be walking into the past. I glanced behind me, hoping to see Ginny or even just the world I knew, but all I saw was the curve of the wall.

I hadn't time to look and linger. Alice had vanished, and I had to hurry if I was to catch them. I rushed around the last of the bends, emerged from the alley and into the night. A different night. I paused, briefly.

I watched them walk down Convent Court, past the church hall, which looked a bit better. The streets were cobbled and the smell from the drains was unbelievable. I followed them right along Pasenheuse Road, which being historic hadn't much changed. I wanted to stop and take a look but we weren't that far from Curdizan Low.

Once they'd turned left onto Croston, I started considering what I should do. I didn't dare risk getting nearer to Alice, she and the woman seemed pretty pally, talking and nodding, as if they were friends. Maybe they were, Alice was a child, but the woman beside her seemed more like a girl. Her skirt, and the shawl she draped around her made her look older, but her jaunty walk and manner were youthful. I thought myself in some sort of dream. *Just like when the accident happened.*

No, I corrected, *that was a nightmare.*

Alice and I and the unknown woman wandered down Croston, I could hardly believe what I saw before me. Gone were the piles of builders rubble, the disused crane and the metal gates to fence off danger. Gone was the light and the open space, the remnants of cobbles and narrow paving. Now there were street signs and tight little corners, clusters of shops, most of them tiny and row upon row of grim terraces, drab little buildings, blocking out light. Croston was the best of the bunch, being wider than most. There were even some people peering through windows, or walking along, smoking a pipe, or chatting together. I was suddenly aware I was out of place, weirdly dressed and probably at risk. Strangers wouldn't be welcome here. I wished I was broader, rougher and tougher and wearing something a little less smart. Then, I realised the girls had vanished. I saw the Keepsake Arms on the right, all lit up, with the same shabby sign I'd seen before, swinging overhead, and I wondered if they'd gone in there. But I couldn't be sure.

I glanced across the road briefly, and noticed a street called Blackberry Close and two figures, fading in the distance. *Damn*, I thought and dashed across the road to the Close. It was hard to see in the limited light, but I thought if I hurried I might catch them up. I came across a long shabby hedge which bordered the road, and swore when I noticed what was behind it. *Another bloody church!* This evening was proving a real revelation. I paused briefly.

I'd often wondered, since the accident happened, if at the time, I'd suffered concussion. Not just the shock of killing the boy, but my head actually hitting the steering wheel, which might have explained the memory loss. The doctors didn't think so, they said I was fine. But it would have explained such moments as this, when life seemed unreal.

I knew all the same that this world was real. I could smell it, feel it, the sharpness of twigs on the hedge as I passed, the cool of the brick of the terraced streets and the unpleasant odours that rose from the road. Abattoirs, middens and open sewers. I smelt it all. Everything about me was real and solid. But where was Alice?

I scanned the street in the black velvet night and thought I could see them, just up ahead. I passed the church and spotted them vanishing into a building. A building I knew.

But how did I know it?

I held back a little, not wanting to be seen, and waited to see if they came back out and while I was waiting, I studied the building, a coaching inn door, painted bright black, and beyond the door, off to the right, some sort of yard. This was the place Alice had mentioned in the reversals. The place that Tom had told her about, and Cressida had seen, although by that time, the paintwork was faded and had mostly peeled off. I wished then I'd brought my phone with me, what a mistake to leave it behind. I could have used it to take a photo. Would the photo have come out, I wondered? It was all academic. Here I was in the depths of time, and Daniel hadn't even been born. I tried to shake such thoughts from my head.

Alice had mentioned the coaching inn door and a woman outside the pub called Miranda. Maybe the woman with Alice was Miranda. I'd seen the pub, the Keepsake Arms, a typical, lively, working class place but I still wasn't sure if the girl was Alice. I'd have to go into the building after them. It didn't look like they were coming out. The building looked like a funeral parlour, as well as a workshop. A funeral parlour next to a church? A building with a tunnel to Curdizan Church? Was that why Alice and the girl had gone there? The girl, Miranda, was showing her the tunnel. *Hell and damnation.*

Then a shadow caught my eye and the grip of an arm came round my neck, an arm and a body which was fuelled by drink. I could breathe the very strength of it. Then, suddenly, I was flung against the wall.

The next few minutes were slightly fuzzy. The man was broad and very well built, he had curly hair and enormous dark eyes. The hair didn't fit with his threatening look, he had meant to knock me flat to the ground. I tried to fight back.

I finally managed to free myself and stood my ground, thinking I'd given as good as I got. But the man seemed fine, protected by drink and a burly constitution, while I was feeling rather fragile. I held up my hand.

'I'm a stranger here, I mean you no harm.'

'You were following them, that kid and Miranda, I watched you mate, I reckon you're a pervert.'

'No,' I insisted, thinking fast, 'Miranda's mum is a friend of mine and I wanted to ask her where she was.' I prayed to God as I said the words that Miranda's mum was still alive, not lying in a coffin, or living in Australia. The man snorted.

'Well, if that's the case, and I'm not sure, seeing as how I reckon you look mighty shifty, you ought to be going to the pub to see her, not following girls in the dark like that.'

'I'll be on my way to the pub right now,' I told him, mildly.

'You said you're a stranger, and that's the truth, you talk very different, you're not like us. Perhaps you're a toff or maybe you're one of those loony types, they've let out from the workhouse. I've never heard of a ma being a mum.'

'My people live up by Curdizan Abbey, you know, where all the Irish are.' I held my breath and waited to see what the man would say. He still looked doubtful.

'You don't sound Irish, that's for sure. But you look the part, I'll give you that.'

By which he meant my hair was black and long for a bloke. I also had the grey-green eyes, but I wasn't going to let him get close to see.

'Happen I'll take you to the pub. I'm going that way myself,' he said. My heart sank, I needed to get away from the man. Not to mention, inside the house.

'Look, mate...'

'Scotty,' he said.

'Look, Scotty, I'll have to level with you. The girl with Miranda, she's my kid and she's always running away from home. I couldn't let her see I was following her, she'd only have vanished and her ma's worried sick. You can imagine.'

Scotty nodded but said nothing. I could almost hear the words in his head. *If she'd have been mine, I'd have given her a slap.* I held my breath.

'I guess I'll have to trust you mate, you can get off now

and find your girl. But I'll see you in the Keepsake Arms later, after it's sorted, I reckon you'll want to buy me a pint.' He looked me coolly in the eye. 'I know some folk who live in the High, it's best they know you and I are mates.'

I didn't dare speak, I knew what he meant, if I'd lied to him, he'd find me out. And I had, of course, and he probably knew it. I smiled at Scotty, a very thin smile, which wasn't returned, but he did turn around and wander off, back towards Croston.

I slumped against the nearest wall, my heart thumping, ten to the dozen. When I'd said, earlier, that the place was a hazard, I hadn't known then how true that was. Still, at least I'd managed some sort of reprieve. Now to find Alice.

I emerged from the shadows and hurried towards the coaching inn door, but before I could get there, a woman went in, she was dressed rather smartly, with her hair tucked under a rather trim hat. Despite her appearance, I was certain, convinced she was up to no good. As soon as she'd vanished, I rushed to the door, the time for stealth and silence had passed. My hand had barely touched the door frame, when I heard a clunk and felt a jar, I knew what it was.

Sure enough when I tugged on the handle, turned it even, nothing happened, the gap had vanished and the door was closed. That woman I'd seen had closed it behind her, and she was in there with Miranda and Alice, while I was outside.

I swore, loudly.

69

Then – Thomas

When I walked up the stairs at school, I noticed at once the skull had vanished. It was always there, at the top of the landing, on the shelf, but not today. What a surprise!

Nothing was safe from a bunch of lads, I knew that now. I might have stolen the thing myself, just for a laugh, playing a prank, but since Carson had used it as a football, it had a huge crack and was too well known. But someone must have stolen the thing. I blinked, tired.

When I'd got to the pub last night I'd found it in chaos, Miranda was missing and so was her ma. Reg was holding the fort by himself, it was Steve's night off and Cath was out somewhere, God knows where. I'd spent the evening serving ale, as well as washing the glasses like normal, and had to use Miranda's crate, the one she'd used when she was small, and couldn't reach the bar by herself. I didn't say much but I was worried. Miranda can flounce and she has a temper, but she never misses her evening shift.

There wasn't a lot I could do right then so I carried on serving and tried to look chipper, then Ben turned up and told me he'd had a row with Miranda, something and nothing, but that was probably why she was missing. But all the same, it didn't feel right.

I gave him a pint, then a few more after, and the night rolled on, then Ben went home.

Minutes later, Ben was back, cursing and swearing, as bad as I've heard. 'My damn door's locked and I can't get in.'

'At least you know it wasn't a thief,' said Reg, grinning. He wouldn't have bothered to have locked the door. He softened Ben up with a few more pints and offered the man a space on the couch and Ben being more than pleasantly drunk was happy to accept, and wait for the morning to call the locksmith, rather than break the door down now. *Thank God for that,* I thought, relieved.

When I got home, my da was dead to the world on our couch, snoring like hell and well past drunk, and filling the room with a terrible noise. Ma was, no doubt, trying to sleep. The factory hooter would wake us up early. I crept outside and slept in the yard, it wasn't as bad as you'd think it would be, I made up a bed with some crates and some straw, with cushions for a pillow and my jacket as a sheet. I didn't risk bringing a blanket outside, I'd have had to climb over my da to get that and I didn't dare risk disturbing the man. I slept in my vest with a shirt on top, I'd done it before.

So when, the next morning, I climbed the school stairs and noticed the skull had been stolen again, it felt like that was the final straw. Then I saw Eisen.

Eisen rarely came upstairs, he hardly ever left the joinery workshop, except when he went outside for a fag. Upstairs was safe, or so I believed, but not today. I stared at Eisen, slowly climbing the stairs towards me.

'Just the lad I'm looking for, Islip. I'd like a word with you, now, please.'

'Yes, Mr Eisen, sir,' I said. I wasn't looking for trouble today.

'Did you give Ben Tencell that message I asked you to? The one about the church disturbance?'

Hell, no I hadn't, I'd forgotten to, hadn't I, what with Carson, then Ben and Miranda. 'I'm sorry,' I said. 'I'm really sorry.' *Never mind sorry, I'm for it now.*

'Forget about that,' said Eisen dismissive, waving a hand, to my surprise. 'It's a lot more serious now, I'm afraid. Go and tell Ben, there's been a break in. Someone has stolen some things from the church.'

'I didn't think there was anything to steal, apart from a few old candlesticks.' *Thank God we didn't put the trunks in there.*

Eisen gave me a very strange look.

'Just do as I've said, and do it now. Right this minute, there's no time to waste.'

'But I'm supposed to be in class,' I said.

'I expect Ben's told you I'm not to be crossed. Forget about school and do as you're told.'

'Yes, Mr Eisen, sir,' I said. And hated myself for being a creep. I hurried on past him as fast as I could.

I wasn't happy at leaving school. I knew I wouldn't go back that day, which meant I'd miss my school dinner. I'd already missed the morning porridge and sometimes those meals were all I had. If I went home, there was always a risk my da would be there, would've skipped off work and would give me grief. And I was worried about Miranda. My stomach was in knots.

I hurried outside and round the corner, and then I saw Alice. I stopped, surprised.

I didn't know much about Alice's life but I wasn't expecting to see her then, at this time of day. She didn't look like the Alice I knew. She looked tired and grubby and much more like us. And, for once she wasn't holding her iPad. Despite Eisen's words, I had to stop.

'Are you alright?' I said, anxious, walking up to the wall, where she sat.

'Yeah, I suppose,' she said, vaguely, twisting her hair around one finger. She wasn't her usual confident self. I didn't know what to say to her.

'We could go and see the horse, today,' I said, smiling. 'I've got to go over to Ben Tencell's.' She shrank back a little.

'No, it's alright, I've already been down that way, recently. And I met your friend, the girl, Miranda. Miranda and I went down the tunnel. Yesterday evening.'

'You what?' I shouted, glaring at Alice. So that was why the door had been closed. I knew I shouldn't have mentioned the tunnel. I cursed, silently.

'You shouldn't have asked Miranda to take you. We were

273

going to go together.'

'No we weren't,' she told me, sharply. 'I'd already said I wanted to go, but you put me off, you know you did. Miranda was happy to take me instead. It was horrible, down there.'

'How far did you go along the tunnel' A nagging thought was bothering me.

'As far as the passage that leads to the cellar. I mean, to where they hold the soup kitchen.'

'You didn't go up to Curdizan Church?'

'I've been wandering around the graveyard, this morning, reading the slabs, because I was bored.'

'I meant last night, from within the tunnel. There's a way to the crypt of the church from the tunnel, it's very easy.'

'Yes, I remember, you told me once, and no we didn't, Miranda refused to go that way. What is this?'

'Nothing,' I said, 'forget it, Alice, it really isn't anything important. Are you sure you don't want to come and see Norah?'

Alice paused. 'Well, yes, alright, I didn't have time to see Norah last night. We were too busy going down the tunnel.'

'I'll bet you were,' I said, slowly. I couldn't help grinning, in spite of myself. I sauntered along and Alice followed. I wasn't sure I liked the new Alice. But I hoped she had the knowledge I needed.

'When you'd finally left the tunnel, where did Miranda go after that?'

'Home to the pub, I suppose,' said Alice. 'She said she'd been at work all day. In the sweet factory.'

'And what about you?' I asked her, puzzled. 'Did you go home?' Alice looked shifty.

'Of course I did. But then, this morning, the school bus was late, so I decided to skip school and come here instead. It's much more fun.'

'So how come you haven't got your iPad with you? And, what's a bus?'

'Too many questions,' said Alice, sharply. She was starting

to get that look again. The one that told me she was the boss.

'What do you mean, *too many questions?*'

'It's what we say to each other at school, if we don't want to answer questions.'

'I bet your ma doesn't like it much, when you say that to her,' I said.

'My mum would be glad if I talked at all. And no, don't ask, I'm not going to say.'

Fine, so I wouldn't. I'd have to remember that phrase for school, practise saying it to people in the pub, I could just see their faces when I did. I grinned, suddenly.

We were fast approaching the alley to the Low. Alice looked hesitant and I smiled broadly. 'There's no need to worry,' I said confidently, 'I'll keep you safe.' She must have heard of the alley's reputation.

'I'm not,' she said and followed me in. We walked its length, to Convent Court. Then Alice stopped and looked behind.

'I'm sorry, Tom, I'll have to go back, I think I dropped my iPod before. You go ahead, I'll catch you up.'

'Fine,' I replied, and carried on walking, thinking about the words she'd said. *What was an iPod, was it like an iPad?* Then I remembered an obvious point, Alice was all alone back there, it wasn't a good place for girls to be. I hurried back, as fast as I could. I'd never get Eisen's message to Ben, the way I was going.

I couldn't find Alice in the alley, she'd obviously walked a lot faster than me. I peered out onto Scriveners Road and saw the back of my school in the distance. I spotted some people walking towards me, all of them wearing very strange clothes. I had this disturbing, uneasy feeling as I looked around at my surroundings, the weather was the same, and so was the paving beneath my feet, but the church and Alice had vanished completely.

70

Then – Aleph

I hadn't meant to fall asleep. I'd rattled at the door, and shouted a little, but not too loudly, I didn't want Scotty coming back. But the door stayed closed and the woman I'd seen hadn't reappeared, and I hadn't a clue where Alice was. *If it was Alice.* But I guessed the tunnel must start from here, and lead to the church, Curdizan Church, and here, in this time, the church still existed, so if I was quick I could make it back, get into the church and so find Alice.

I rubbed my head where Scotty had bashed it against the wall, I knew I could be chasing a dream, I wasn't sure where the tunnel came out. *Was it inside the church,* I thought, *or even outside? Or if inside, the church might be locked.* But I had to try, and time was short. I ran like hell.

I turned onto Croston, passing the pub on Dogleg Lane, but I didn't look back and after a while, I turned off right onto Pasenheuse Road and before very long I was back at the alley. I hurried on through it and out to the church. I stopped, intrigued. I'd never seen this church before, only in pictures. It wasn't that special, just plain grey stone with some stained glass windows and a tired old rose that trailed up the walls, but the churchyard was pleasant, I liked it much better than our current courtyard. The grass went up to the back of my house, the Old Schoolhouse, fading out to a worn patch of gravel in front of the door. I blinked, surprised. I hadn't even known there was a door. Thinking back then to my own kitchen, all I could recall were the three scruffy windows. *Later,* I thought, and focused on Alice. I tried the church door but I couldn't get in.

I walked around the church's perimeter, looking in vain for

another entrance or maybe even an open window, but, of course, I found neither. There was nothing to do but sit and wait, and hope that Alice and Miranda would emerge. After almost two hours of sitting in the dark, I had to face it, they weren't coming. They'd probably gone back the very same way, through the tunnel and out of the door. I couldn't be in two places at once. I decided to go back.

Despite it being late, I could still hear people laughing and talking and drinking, probably, enjoying themselves. I wandered out onto Scriveners Road and turned the corner, looked at my house, the Old Schoolhouse. It looked just the same, if smarter and newer, well it was newer, but it wasn't that different from when I knew it. If only I could go inside and see it. Then I had a terrible thought.

I'd been through the alley and round the corner, back to my house on Old School Lane, but it wasn't my house and it wasn't my time, I was still in the past, Thomas's past. A past I didn't much like the look of. *Oh God,* I thought. *I'll never get out.* I nearly lost it there and then.

It was like when I killed the boy, Daniel, once I'd realised what I'd done. I'd felt like there was no escape, no way I could get out from it all, and of course I couldn't, then and now. I was living a life I hadn't chosen, in a terrible place, I couldn't move on from. All I could do was keep on going, so I headed back down to Blackberry Close. And then I reached the coaching inn door.

The door was still shut, still just as silent, as if it was guarding the people inside. Alice and Miranda, but also the female stranger in a hat, she seemed significant. I felt out of place, and then I saw Scotty, or I thought I did, he was staggering up the road towards me. I couldn't face that man again. I backed away and ended up in the yard next door, a grim place with a horse in a shed and a tap nearby. The tap was dripping.

The horse didn't mind, he lapped from the puddle on the ground at his feet and watched me lazily, barely blinking.

'Hello, Norah,' I said, softly. The horse said nothing.

I felt dizzy, my head was hurting so I sat down, quickly, on a patch of straw and leant against the wall with the tap. It was dark in the yard, much darker than the street, but softer somehow, a horse and the straw and something else, not quite so pleasant. I drifted off. When I woke up, morning had come.

The street was alive with a brand new day, people shouting hello to each other, the slip-slop of water carried in buckets and the sound of wheels on the rough cobbled road. I eased myself onto my feet slowly and emerged from the yard, looking around. I noticed some people heading this way, so I waited until they'd all walked past, wondering if I should try the door. But despite my efforts, after they'd gone, the coach house door remained firmly shut.

After one last attempt, I hurried away, keeping my head down and heading for Croston. The street to the north and hopefully home. I'd given up hope of finding Alice.

Until I saw the Keepsake Arms. This was where Miranda's mum lived, or worked or both, according to Scotty. I hurried towards it. The streets were now alive with people, it was well past nine, according to my watch, but for all I knew the watch might be wrong. The place was heaving.

I narrowly missed being hit by a cart, and some of the passers by stared and laughed. I doubted my clothes or my hairstyle helped. I stopped abruptly outside the pub and wasn't surprised to find it closed. But then I heard voices, coming from the passage next door to the pub and one of them sounded just like a girl's. I hurried along it, right to the end, peering carefully around the corner. There was the girl from yesterday evening, talking to a woman, her mother, I guessed. I couldn't see any sign of Alice.

'What have you done with my dress, Mother?'

'Which one do you mean, you've got so many?' The mother was pegging out clothes on the line.

'You know the one, it's red and satin, I love that dress and now I can't find it.'

'You mean the one that's ripped up the side.'

'I was going to repair it, sew up the tear, that's all the dress needed.'

'I thought it was rags and fit for the bin.'

'You're joking, Mother! That dress was the best I'd ever had, and you threw it out because of a tear! A tiny tear. I can't believe you'd do such a thing.'

'More than a tiny tear, Miranda. And as it happens, I didn't throw it out. I gave it to Curdizan Church for the sale, or maybe I gave it to the rag and bone man, I can't remember. I don't know why you're making such a fuss, it was only a dress, your blue one's better.'

'My blue one's plain, and boring, as hell. Thank you Ma, for nothing, as usual.' Miranda dropped the clothes on the ground and ignoring her mother's scream of rage, she hurried along the passage past me. I pressed myself into a nook, quickly, but she didn't even glance my way. When she'd passed I breathed out with a sigh, but knew I had to follow the girl.

I chased Miranda to Curdizan High, calling her name a couple of times, I needed to know where Alice had gone. But she was fast, much faster than me, and she knew her way around this place, at a time when the streets were full of people, and carts and washing, all blocking the way. It took far too long.

I caught her up as we reached the alley, she'd just disappeared, and I followed behind her, feeling that sense of déjà vu. When I finally reached the end of the passage, I saw the shadow of Miranda ahead. *I've done it at last,* I said to myself, *now I'll get to know where Alice is.* I left the passage and stepped out into the morning light, the light that fell on the road and the church, but there was no church, the church had gone. I stopped, frozen.

I looked about me, puzzled, tentative. All I could see was Scriveners Road and a smartly-paved courtyard, dotted with seats. Slabs of gravestone, flat in the ground. People who were wearing clothes like mine. I sighed with relief.

The world looked better than it had for ages. I'd lost Miranda and I hadn't found Alice, and little Daniel was still dead, but at least I was here, alive, in my time.

71

Then – Carol

Carol Islip, Thomas's mother, liked early mornings better than most. Her husband Scotty worked at the mill, and when he did earlies, he left the house sooner. Not that it made much difference to his drinking, he still drank every evening, and went on drinking half the night. Like the night before, a terrible night, when he'd come home even more worse for wear, raving about Miranda Collenge, a kid and a man with an Irish look.

'You need to lay off the booze,' she'd said, and she'd wondered if she'd gone too far, when she saw his face and the look in his eyes, when she put his breakfast down before him. But Scotty drunk and as mean as they come, was less so sober, or almost sober, a bit of a lout, but not with his fists, so he gobbled his food up and said nothing.

Carol watched him finish the bacon, a bit of a treat, though he didn't deserve it, mopping it up with a crust of bread, the last in the house. She felt a glow of pride inside, of work well done and a breakfast served and a man of her own, up and ready for the working day, and if Thomas was staring at his da, wanting a slice of bacon too, well, that was too bad, he'd get his own share up at the school, they fed him up there.

She frowned, thinking that Thomas wasn't like her, if she'd been Scotty, she'd have asked more questions, checked that the boy was really his. The lad was quick and as sharp as a needle, but sometimes too soft, despite her clouts and the surly looks and clips from his da. He's young, she thought, he'll grow out of that soon, as soon as he lands a job with men.

She didn't much rate the jobs he had, riding a bike and

washing up glasses, girls' jobs they were. She turned away to the sink quickly, pushing away the thoughts in her mind, the thoughts of the other, the one who was lost, who would have been hers. A single tear slid down her cheek.

'I'm off now Ma,' yelled Tom, as he went, and Carol didn't even look up from the bowl, just raised a hand and went on with the dishes, on Haversham Road and those much like it, the dirt and the dishes went on forever. Her husband left, and for a few moments, glorious, golden, precious moments, she had the place to herself, for once. The space to breathe. Before the bustle of the day began.

Carol didn't much like laundry work, it was physical work, hard and steamy and not for the feeble, lifting up heavy sheets from the tubs, feeling the cloth weighted down with water, the sweat and the soap and the slippery floors. But it paid the bills, thank God it did, and Carol didn't know anything else. She sighed heavily.

Now Tanya Curtis was at her door.

'Hello Tanya,' Carol said, frowning, wiping her hands on her morning pinny. 'I'm just off out, was there something you wanted?'

'I thought we'd have that cup of tea,' Tanya said, smiling, squeezing past Carol and into her house. 'The one you promised the other week. I'm sure you remember?'

Carol wished she didn't remember, but either way it didn't matter, the woman had made her way in, already. *Girl, really,* Carol thought, *she was only young, and not bad looking.* Grudgingly.

'I can spare five minutes, there's tea in the pot.' Like many of those who lived nearby, she kept well away from Tanya Curtis. The woman *looked* smart, she'd give her that, but everyone knew just what she was. A well-dressed tart. And not just for feeding a family, either. Tanya enjoyed it.

'I want to tell you a little story,' Curtis informed her, plumping herself on the chair quickly. 'Seeing as how I think we're friends.'

Friends? thought Carol, *Not in my book.* But she couldn't help feeling sad for the woman, apart from her so-called nephew, Jake, she was all on her own, and likely to stay so. Men liked Tanya, but not for keeps. It couldn't hurt Carol to sit for a while. Tanya smiled and sipped her tea.

'I know about the shoes,' she said. 'The ones you took from Matt McCarthy.'

'What?' said Carol, disbelieving. 'I don't know what you're talking about.'

'I think you do, said Tanya, slyly. You and that slut from the Keepsake Arms, Hannah Collenge, stole them from him. Not that I blame you, not like her, the uppity cow.' She stopped for a minute to gulp back tea.

'Hannah's my friend, you leave her alone.'

'You'd do much better with a friend like me, what has she ever done for you? Matt always had his eye on me, until *she* came along, smiling her smile and winning him round with her talk of beer. Then all of a sudden I'm on the street. Not literally,' she added, hastily. Carol said nothing and Tanya sniffed. 'But I didn't come here to talk about her. Although it does rankle, her being older.'

'So what did you come here to talk about?'

'I came to say, as a friend, Carol, that I understand you've faced tough times, that Scotty isn't always working full-time, that he's often laid off, especially when he's been on the booze.'

'Now, wait a minute,' Carol said, sharply, jumping up to defend her man, but Tanya laughed and waved her back down. Carol sat.

'So, as I say, I know you're hard up, and as you're a friend I'd like to help, and I will if you'll let me. I thought you might have a use for this.' She reached down into her shopping bag, and put the candlestick on the table. Carol gasped.

'Where did you get that? Is it silver?'

Tanya smiled and shook her head. 'You don't need to know, believe me, Carol, it's better that way, but it is silver and it's yours if you want it. It'll fetch a good price in the marketplace.'

'I take it, it's stolen?' Carol said, wary.

'As far as I know it's proper stock. Or it was before it came into my hands. Stock that was being disposed of elsewhere, if you get my drift.' She grinned at Carol, and Carol smiled back, a little uncertain. 'Most of the profit would be yours, you know. You and Scotty are the ones with the contacts.'

Carol nodded and picked it up, she'd never tried flogging silver before, but the piece was nice, and if there was more... She turned it around and put it back down. 'Where did you say it came from, Tanya?'

Tanya grinned and shook her head. 'It's better that you don't ask me, Carol. All I'm doing is testing the water, and if you're keen, that's a lot more stuff where that one came from.'

'Really?' said Carol, studying every tiny detail.

'There's a whole lot more,' said Tanya softly, 'and don't try saying it isn't worth much. I know enough, it's better than nice. So why don't we talk about my commission, assuming you manage to sell the piece? And maybe a bonus for regular stock.' Her eyes met Carol's.

Carol paused. She glanced at the walls which were always damp and covered with faded, peeling paper. She thought about how they shared the loo and how Thomas needed a few more clothes. How Scotty's arms ached from carrying sacks and how breathing was often a struggle these days. That factory job was killing him. She smiled at Tanya.

'I'm sure we can find a fee that suits, and there *might* be a bonus for regular stock, assuming, of course, we can sell this one. It's a specialist market, you know Tanya, not everyone wants this sort of thing.' *Like hell they don't,* said Carol to herself. 'I'll have to be careful how I do it. It didn't come from the Low, I hope?'

'No, not to begin with,' Tanya said, 'but it might be best sold out of town. If you get my drift, Carol, my love.' Carol did. She nodded, thinking.

'It's best to be careful.' She went to a drawer and pulled out a towel, wrapped the thing in it and put it away. 'I'll do what I can, as fast as I can, but I can't promise anything.'

Tanya nodded and smiled slightly, and just for a moment, she looked like a lass, instead of a hard case.

'Come back again in a couple of days, and I'll let you know then if I've had any luck. I can't rush it, Tanya, it'll spoil the price.'

'Fine,' said Tanya, standing up, 'but I've bills to pay, and Jake needs clothes. I'd be grateful for an answer as soon as you can.'

But not for money for Jake, thought Carol. *For drinks and clothes and chatting up men and also because you want it shifting. Before the 'owner' sees it's missing.* She smiled, knowingly.

'It's good to have friends,' said Tanya, coyly, as Carol then led her towards the door. 'I know you're a mate, I've always said so.'

Have you indeed? thought Carol, sourly, waving her off down Haversham Road and knowing she'd be late for work. She wondered amused, if Tanya would think she was such a mate, if she knew about her and Matt McCarthy.

72

Now – Aleph

I was tired out from my night in the past and besieged by messages on my phone from clients I hadn't had the time to contact. I couldn't get hold of Cressida either, not a good start to the day, all round. I stood in the kitchen, slightly bemused and made myself coffee, strong coffee, just for a change. The telephone rang.

'It's me, Guinevere. Did you get my note?'

'No, what note?' I told her, puzzled. I looked around the kitchen, quickly.

'It's in the hall, on the newel post. Go and have a look.'

Alice is safe and I'm going home. I'll call later. Hope you're alright.

Damn Alice, I said to myself. *What a waste of time, but at least she's safe.*

'So when did Alice get back?' I said.

'Six in the morning, or thereabouts. Cressida said she looked a mess. Or so I've been told.'

And I know why, I thought grimly. 'I bet Cressida was pleased about that.'

'She was glad to have her home and safe. She hadn't been out all night, apparently.'

'So where had she been instead? I asked. Did Cressida say?'

'She did,' said Ginny, her voice changing. 'According to Alice, she stayed with you.'

Later that day the doorbell rang. I'd made some appointments, drank more coffee and done some accounting, rather reluctantly. I'd still not managed to get hold of Cressida. I didn't know what I was going to tell her. Should I say what had happened or not?

I opened the door, and there was Alice, not looking that much better than me.

'You ought to get your bell fixed, Aleph. Can I come in?' I moved to the side and let her waltz past, a frown on her usually solemn face. I saw she wasn't carrying her iPad. I smiled warmly, a bit of an effort.

'Coffee?' I said. 'Or water or fruit juice?'

'Nothing,' she said. 'But thanks, all the same.' We both sat down at the kitchen table.

'I saw you last night, with Miranda, wasn't it? I followed you down to Curdizan Low.' Alice nodded, not sounding surprised.

'I thought you'd follow us into the tunnel. But you didn't, why not?'

'The door to the coachhouse was closed,' I told her. 'I couldn't get in.' I wasn't going to mention the woman I'd seen, I didn't want to frighten Alice unnecessarily. Although, maybe I should, if it stopped her doing such stupid things.

'It was awful,' said Alice, 'I wish I hadn't persuaded her to take me. The tunnel was dark, and it smelt horrible, and the ground was uneven, I kept tripping up, and then I fell over. We didn't come up in the church, either, Miranda refused to take me that way but she wouldn't say why. We were going to go through the basement instead, that's your cellar, but the door was locked and we couldn't get in. Talk about a right fiasco.'

'So then you had to walk back to the coach house?'

'Yeah, that's right and that was even worse than before. Miranda had brought a lamp with her, but the lamp was rubbish and she kept on trying to scare me stupid. Telling me tales of rats and spiders. What a cow!'

'I'll bet you weren't scared, all the same.' I smiled at Alice. 'You were the one who wanted to go.'

'Ha!' said Alice looking at me as if to say, *I know what you're up to. Humouring me. It won't work.*

'Didn't you think your mum would be worried?' I asked,

softly. I didn't want to alienate her.

'I never thought it would take all night! It wouldn't have done, if we'd done what I wanted and gone through the church. When we couldn't get out through the basement, I thought we'd be able to use the church. But no, Miranda insisted we couldn't. I was so annoyed you can't imagine. Besides, she shouldn't have agreed to take me, I'm only a child.'

That made me smile. 'It wasn't that good for me, either, sleeping outside, with the horse for company.'

'You've met Norah?' Alice perked up.

'I have,' I said, *and a man called Scotty.* I didn't think Alice would have liked Scotty much. 'Why did you run away, in the first place?'

'Mother upset me, just for a change. She asked if I'd seen... that boy you killed, after I'd left them, to go to Annerley's. She asked if that's why I wouldn't talk, to her anyway. '

'What did you say?'

'I told her, no, that I hadn't seen the accident. I know it's a lie, but you have to lie sometimes.' Her eyes were firmly fixed on the table.

'You should have told your mother the truth. She'd understand, you know she would. She'd even help you deal with the pain.'

'I can't,' said Alice, 'and you mustn't say I've got to tell her. Please don't, Aleph.'

My mind was running around in circles. 'How did your mother know what happened?'

'Probably from reading the local paper. I guess she remembered because of the date, it happened to be the day that I went missing.'

They couldn't have put my name in the paper, or Cressida would have known it was me. But odd to remember a stranger's death after all that time, except, perhaps because Daniel was a child, and it happened the day her daughter vanished, as Alice had just said. Maybe Cressida realised she was lucky, because her child, Alice came back alive.

'I guess you haven't told her then,' Alice was saying, sounding edgy. 'You haven't said it was you who caused it?' I shook my head.

'No,' I said, 'that's right, I haven't.' Alice looked angry.

'You told me once your name means truth. So isn't it time you said it was you?'

73

Then – Miranda

Tom wasn't his usual self, far from it, but Miranda didn't care. She stacked the glasses high on the shelf and dried her hands.

'I wondered when you were going to turn up. If doing that job, delivering veg, is making you late, you'd better decide which job you want. Because we need someone who turns up on time.'

'I'm not that late, and I'm here, aren't I, I'm always here. And I haven't been delivering veg this evening.'

'So where have you been instead?' asked Miranda.

'At home, mostly, hanging around. You're not so bright and chipper yourself. Could it be something to do with the tunnel?'

'So you've heard about that.'

'I have yes, Alice informed me, and Ben was here too, late last night, he'd been trying to get back into his workshop, but apparently someone had locked the door.'

'It wasn't me or Alice either. We left it open, like we found it.'

'Somebody dropped the latch on the door, Ben couldn't get in and neither could anyone else he asked, so he ended up sleeping on the couch in the parlour.'

'I didn't see him,' Miranda insisted.

'Maybe because you got back so late. I bet you didn't even look in the parlour.'

Miranda hadn't, but she wasn't going to say so. She leant across and snatched up a rag. 'I saw Ben this morning and he did look angry, but more than he should have done for being locked out. He would have got into his workshop by then.'

'He's angry about the thieving,' said Tom, arranging the

ashtrays on top of the bar.

'And what thieving's that?' Miranda asked. She was dusting the back of the chairs but she stopped.

'Someone's been stealing some stuff from the church, don't ask me what, Ben wouldn't tell me and Wetherby Eisen didn't say either.'

Miranda managed to stifle a gasp. 'Could it have been some silver or pewter?'

'All I know is that Eisen's not happy and neither is Ben, from what I can tell.'

'Haven't you been to school today?'

'Just for a while, until I saw Eisen. Ben now knows you went down the tunnel, taking Alice with you, and he also knows that Alice is my friend.'

'So what if she is?'

'I shouldn't have told her about the tunnel, and now Ben's angry with both of us. I don't know why he's bothered, anyway. There's nothing to steal in his workshop but coffins.'

But the tunnel leads from the workshop to the crypt, and silver and pewter and God knows what. Dodgy stock that Ben's involved with. And now someone has stolen the stock.

'It wasn't us,' she said to Thomas. 'I kept my eye on Alice always. We didn't go as far as the crypt, despite the princess wanting to.'

'Is that what you call her ?' Tom asked, grinning. 'You know I never thought it was you.'

'Then who the hell was it?' Miranda said, frowning, flinging her rag back onto the bar. *I'd better go back to the church tomorrow.*

Her previous visit, the one to find her red dress, hadn't been successful. The vicar was out and so was his wife, and she hadn't been able to find Mary-Ann.

'She'll probably be visiting the sick, dearie,' said old Margie Mace, who was often around.

'Do you know if they're having a jumble sale, in aid of the church?'

'Very probably, dear, they usually are. But not today, if that's what you mean.' Miranda sighed.

'Look, Mrs Mace, I know this sounds odd, but would you mind showing me the clothes for the jumble? My mother gave something away by mistake.'

'Of course, my dear, just come this way.'

Miranda followed Mrs Mace to the scullery. She'd seen the look in the woman's eyes, she was thinking, no doubt, they were having it hard and hoping to get some items for free. Miranda blushed with the shame of it all.

'It's a red satin dress,' she told Mrs Mace when they finally got there. 'It's torn at the bottom and I'd like it back, my ma wasn't meant to give it away.'

'I'm sure there aren't any dresses in here,' Mrs Mace told Miranda, scrabbling around in the box of donations. She was right, there weren't. No dresses, no shoes, in fact nothing of interest, just a few repaired sheets and some bits of old jewellery, falling apart.

'I'll come back tomorrow,' Miranda insisted. 'Just in case.'

The next day, when she got to the gate, she saw Mary-Ann. 'Mrs Mace told me you were missing a dress.'

'I am,' said Miranda, 'it's my best, red satin, and it's got a huge tear but it's still pretty good and my ma thinks she might have left it with you. I searched the box for the sale yesterday, but it wasn't in there, we looked all through it. I don't suppose you've some stuff elsewhere?'

'Not that I know of. Are you sure your mother gave it to us?'

'She left you a bundle in the porch outside. But the dress might have gone to the rag and bone man and if that's the case, I've lost it forever.'

'That's a shame,' said Mary-Ann, vaguely, looking as if she didn't much care. She didn't seem very keen to talk.

'Well, thanks for your help,' said Miranda, shortly, thinking, *not much help and a waste of time.* She wandered through the rectory garden, heading for Scriveners Road and the alley, and thinking about the box of scraps. *Sheets and socks and bits of old jewellery. Jewellery, damn!*

She almost turned round and went back to the church. But the sun had gone in, it was starting to rain and she knew her mother needed her help. And then she was down for the late shift at Chaucer's, more's the pity. She couldn't go back to the church, right now. But she would do soon, this time for Tom. She'd ask Mary-Ann about the necklace, the long thin string of turquoise beads, where Eisen had got it, and whether he'd stolen the thing from someone. Like Tom's friend Louise. Miranda shivered. She was seriously troubled.

All around her people were involved in dodgy dealings, stealing goods or keeping secrets, Mary-Ann, her ma and Wetherby Eisen and even Ben was reluctant to talk. But she'd find out the truth of that necklace, for sure.

Even if she never regained her dress.

74

Now – Aleph

Alice had seen Daniel die and Cressida needed to know about that. If I didn't tell her, someone else would, and then she'd discover I was involved. It was better coming from me to begin with. I dreaded Cressida hearing the story.

Once she knew, her manner would change, she'd start being polite, or even pitying and everything we'd shared would be lost forever. I wanted to be like I was before, an ordinary person instead of a monster, or an object of pity that people looked down on. I knew I hadn't a hope in hell.

I stared at Alice, feeling guilty. She shouldn't have to carry the burden, alone. I'd have to tell Cressida sooner or later. My heart sank.

'I don't know when I'm going to tell her,' I said, helpless.

'If you think she'll sleep with you if you don't, you're wrong about that.' I blinked, surprised, and stared at Alice.

'What?' I said.

'She's gay, you know. You can't have kissed her, or you'd know.'

I burst out laughing, despite my despair. 'Kissing isn't different, if you're gay.'

'How would you know?' said Alice, boldly. 'But all I meant was, if she'd rebuffed you, then you'd know.'

'Unless she just didn't like me much.'

'Yeah, there's that,' said Alice, nodding, managing to make it sound quite possible.

'So, your mother's gay,' I said, amused, but also somewhat sad and regretful.

'She wasn't always,' Alice insisted. 'When she was young, she liked men a lot.'

'Right,' I said. 'But if we're talking about the accident, I haven't told her because I'm afraid she'll change if she knows.'

'I haven't changed,' said Alice, stoutly, 'and I won't either.'

'Good,' I said, 'I'm glad about that.' I owed it to Alice to tell Cressida, but that didn't make my task any easier. Then the doorbell rang, it was Guinevere James. I'd never been quite so pleased to see her.

'Alice is here, we're just talking. Can I get you a cup of tea?'

'That would be great,' said Ginny, smiling and sauntering past me, into the kitchen. 'Your bell's no better.'

'I haven't exactly had time to fix it.'

'No,' said Ginny, glancing at Alice. 'Hello,' she said. 'I've heard about you. I'm glad you're safe.'

'I've always been safe,' Alice insisted. 'I was here all night.'

'Right,' said Ginny, looking at me. I poured more water into the pot.

'It was good that Alice turned up,' I said. 'I didn't want to have to search all night.' I smiled at the girl who frowned a little. But she said nothing.

Guinevere grinned and glanced at the shelf. 'There's a shoe up there,' she said, mildly.

'It's a boot,' said Alice, jumping up. 'A woman's boot, and very old.' She carried the boot to the table, carefully. We all stared at it.

'It's also small,' said Ginny, pensive, turning the boot around in her hand. 'I don't think it's a woman's boot, even though people were smaller back then. I think it's a girl's.'

'I'll try it on,' said Alice, eagerly. She pushed back her chair back and stretched out her foot.

'If the shoe fits,' said Ginny, mildly. We both watched Alice try on the boot. It was far too small.

Alice was clearly disappointed. 'She must have been even younger than me.'

'She'd be older, actually,' Ginny insisted. 'It's a very old boot, the girl's probably dead, whatever her shoe size.' Alice gave Ginny a filthy look.

'She could have been older than we think,' I said. 'In the past, people were smaller. The Brontës were known to have tiny feet, and if the person who wore the boots was malnourished, her bones might not even have formed properly. Then, most likely, she would be smaller.'

'That's true,' said Ginny, looking at me. I was sure we were both on the same track. Had the boot been Mary-Ann Parks'?

'But it is very small,' said Alice, determined. She was right, it was.

'Then it must be a child or a girl,' said Ginny.

And not the dead woman's boot, I thought, briefly relieved, and then I felt cold. *A missing child,* I said to myself, *and probably dead. A School Lane ghost, which was worse, even worse.*

I waited to hear a child crying. Nothing happened.

'I wonder what happened to the matching boot?' Ginny said then.

'Or the girl who owned it,' Alice continued.

'Let's hope she's not in the cellar,' said Ginny.

75

Then – Thomas

I'd barely been at school, yesterday, but today, I didn't even bother to go. My mind was transfixed by what I'd seen, a missing church and the flat gravestones. And Ben needed a helping hand.

To retrieve the shoes from Eisen's woodshed.

'Don't tell Miranda,' Ben insisted, 'she'd only make a huge amount of fuss.' It was true, she would, but more than that, I was glad to be working alone with Ben. It made me feel like one of the lads. A man, almost.

'Where are we moving the trunks to, Ben?'

'Near the school basement, despite what she says, and then over time, to McCarthy's shop on Narrowboat Lane. I've explained to Wetherby, he's going to help.'

'You've told Mr Eisen about the trunks!'

'I had to tell him, they're clearing the woodshed, tomorrow at the latest. He wasn't very pleased, on top of the news about the thieving, so I said we'd move the trunks to the basement, but only for a while, no longer than a month, I promised him that.'

'But the basement's used as a soup kitchen. Miranda said they'd be seen in there.'

'The trunks won't actually be in the kitchen. We'll be storing them in the narrow passage, the one between the tunnel and the basement, just for a while.'

'The place you didn't want them stored last time?' Ben sighed and looked disgruntled.

'I don't have to answer to you, Thomas. But as you're a mate, I'll do it this once.' I waited, patiently.

'Before, we needed to access the tunnel, using the passage that ran from the basement. But at the moment, for various reasons, we don't need to do that. So it's fine to store the shoes in the passage.'

Because of the thefts, I said to myself. *Something's changed, or stopped, because of them.* I stayed silent.

'So are you free this afternoon?'

'Today?' I squeaked, surprised and dismayed. Ben gave a hoot.

'Of course today, there's no point delaying.'

'Right,' I said. *No point at all.*

Getting down to the basement was easy, Ben had squared it with Wetherby Eisen. I just had to convince Jake.

'Tell him Wetherby says it's alright.' Ben had given me a pile of coppers.

'He'll believe that?' I said, sceptical.

'He will when you give him some of these.' My eyes widened. 'They're all for him?' I said, sourly.

'And you, as well, if we get the job done. I'll leave it to you to divvy them up. So long as you make sure Jake gets us in.'

'Right,' I told him, grinning broadly. I was definitely feeling a little taller.

We opened the door and trundled downstairs, into the basement. We then used Jake's key to get into the passage, the narrow passage that led to the tunnel. Then came the hard part.

Bringing the trunks down to the passage, one at a time. I was scared as hell that someone would see us, Pike or a mate, and ask us what on earth we were doing. Nobody did. Eisen and Jake must have fixed it between them, Jake for the dosh and Wetherby Eisen, because Ben asked him. *Why would Wetherby Eisen bother?* Then I remembered, they were meant to be mates. *Odd,* I thought, *Ben hanging round with a bloke like Eisen.*

We eased each trunk into the passage, first the one, then the second, lifting the second to put it on top. Then we opened the third trunk.

'Hand me that sack,' Ben insisted and I passed it across and Ben grabbed it, filling it up with the shoes from the trunk.

'Not too full,' I warned him, sharply. 'I've got to take that up to the street, and then along to McCarthy's shop.'

'You feeble thing!' said Ben, laughing. 'It won't be heavy, trust me, Thomas.'

'But it shouldn't look like stolen goods.' Ben stopped laughing.

He lifted the lid of the second trunk, shoving the unwanted shoes inside. 'Got to make sure I get them in pairs. Hold up the lamp.'

I lifted it up and Ben gave a grunt as he peered inside the neck of the sack. Then the light went out and Ben swore at the almost-dark as he dropped a boot from inside on the floor. 'We don't need this.'

I watched as Ben twisted the sack, knotting it, tightly, then handing the stock in the sack to me and getting to his feet. 'I reckon that's it, at least for now.' Ben shoved the passage door shut with a kick before locking it firmly, leaving the other two trunks inside. It was hard to see without the light.

Then I saw him pick something up off the floor and put it on a shelf, right at the top.

'It wasn't one of a matching pair,' Ben explained as we climbed the stairs to the joinery workshop. 'It was made for a girl, and didn't look new. I doubt she'll even miss the thing.'

How sad, I thought as we went outside, Ben holding on to the empty trunk. I wondered who the shoe had belonged to.

76

Now – Aleph

Not long after Ginny arrived, Alice departed. A little reluctant but knowing she had to go home to her mother. 'I really don't want to go,' she said.

'But Aleph will let you come back tomorrow. Won't you Aleph?'

'Yes,' I said, 'but that's not the point. She just doesn't want to talk to her mother.'

'She only wants what's best for you.'

'I know,' said Alice, looking at Ginny. 'And I do too.' Then she left.

After she'd left, Ginny and I sat there in silence, neither of us knowing quite what to say. Guinevere broke the silence first. 'We think she saw what happened that day, when the little boy died. Do you think that's likely?'

'You'd have to ask Alice,' I said, frowning. I couldn't break a client's confidence, and Alice was a kind of client. 'Talk to her mother, not to me. Except, I've remembered, you don't know Cressida, or Alice either. And yet you knew about Alice going missing. How did you get the sound file you gave me, with Alice on it?'

'I heard about Alice from a friend of Cressida's.'

'She was the one who gave you the sound file? And without Cressida's permission?'

'Yes,' said Guinevere, 'I know it was wrong.'

'You lied to me about your business, and the possible takeover, it was all made-up. That didn't stop you doing it again, when it came to Alice.'

'No,' she said. And had the grace to look embarrassed.

'So all that stuff about Mary-Ann Parks and her body in

the cellar was just a diversion? You haven't a scrap of interest in the woman.'

'You've got it all wrong, Mr Jones,' said Ginny. She was clearly relieved we'd changed the subject. 'I'm very interested in Mary-Ann Parks. Do you want to know why?'

'I expect you'll tell me,' I said, sighing.

'I'll have to confess to another lie,' said Guinevere, softly. She didn't seem sorry.

'Get on with it then.'

'You'll have noticed, I'm sure, that my cousin, Marianne, and the dead Mary-Ann are both called Parks. Well, that's because they're from the same family.'

'Well, what a surprise,' I said, sourly.

'After Mary-Ann Parks eloped, along with her lover, Wetherby Eisen, or so it was thought, the parents moved and nobody wanted the church's living. Clara went with them, she was Mary-Ann's sister, her younger sister. She later had a child of her own.

'The child was a boy and he carried on the name of Parks because Clara Parks had never been married and she wouldn't say who the father was. That boy was Marianne Parks' father.'

I slowly carried the mugs to the sink. 'How odd,' I said, 'that Mary-Ann's nephew should buy this house.'

'It wasn't,' said Ginny, 'it was planned from the start. Clara Parks was living abroad and she'd told her son about Mary-Ann. Reg, the son, was always intrigued, and when, later, he was discharged from the army, after the war, he came to England and met his wife and they decided to buy the house. When it came on the market, of course. Your house.' She looked at Aleph.

'He thought it might help to be on the spot. Curdizan Church had gone by then, no-one had wanted the church's living, like I just said, and Mary-Ann running away was a scandal, way back then. And it did help too, because Marianne Parks, Reg's daughter, discovered the body.'

'Weird,' I said, 'but I guess he didn't plan for that.'

'No,' said Ginny, looking sombre. 'But Mary-Ann's nephew was rather eccentric and very determined.'

'Well, you'd know,' I told her, thinking. 'As you're meant to be Marianne's cousin. And so presumably, part of the family.' My head was going round in circles.

'Well, here's the thing,' said Ginny sadly. 'That was another lie, I'm afraid. I'm not Marianne Parks' cousin. But I do have a vested interest though.' I waited, patiently. What was coming?

'I'm actually Marianne Parks' sister.'

77

Then – Thomas

I wandered into McCarthy's shop, leaving the sack of shoes in the doorway. Percy was buffing up glass with a rag.

'Where's your boss?' I asked him, warily.

'Gone for his tea,' said Percy, grinning. 'What's in the sack? I bet it's for me.'

'Shoes,' I told him, grabbing the sack and tipping them onto the high glass counter. Percy was always polishing that counter. 'You'll wear it away,' I told him, often.

I saw him start, then his eyes widened as the shoes spilled out, some of them bouncing onto the floor. He picked a shoe up and studied it carefully. 'Is this the stock Miranda mentioned?'

'It might be,' I said. 'There are two sacks to follow, after this one. You know we found them in his house?'

'I wonder why he kept them there?' Percy was staring at me, waiting.

'He was ill and tired, and now he's dead. He probably just forgot about them.'

I felt a twinge about adding a slur to McCarthy's name, now he was dead, but I hoped he wouldn't mind too much, because of my ma and Miranda's mother. I understood they'd been friends of his. And Percy was a mate of mine. I helped my mate to stack the shoes.

'I'll be back in a couple of days with some more. That'll give you time to get these moved. You won't tell him?' I said softly, glancing out back and meaning the bloke who ran the place. He was ugly as hell and as thick as they come, which was lucky for me, Miranda and Percy. Percy nodded.

'You told me you'd get me a few more fags.'

'You expect too much,' I said to him, grinning. 'Maybe you think I'm made of fags?'

'Maybe I know you've got two jobs, and a nice little sideline selling on shoes.'

'Oh, no,' I said. 'I've told you straight. These shoes are nothing to do with me.'

'And I'm the heir to the throne,' he said. But he grinned and nodded all the same. 'I won't say a word, you have *my* word, so long as you keep me sweet with these.' He waved a packet of fags in my face.

'You're sure you wouldn't like veg instead? Mason gives me a discount sometimes, and then there's the stuff that's almost rotten, that comes free.' Percy's face was his only answer.

I sauntered out of the shop, content, thinking I'd go the long way home, via the market's empty stalls. I didn't feel like facing the alley.

I couldn't help thinking about it, though, how I'd stared out at Scriveners Road, looking for Alice and Curdizan Church, and seeing instead another world.

I remembered the school looked just the same, just a bit more shabby, a little run down. But even now the school was shabby, I was used to that, and hardly noticed. But the church had vanished, gone completely, and how could a church disappear like that?

Thinking about it, the trees looked bigger, the churchyard was different, with a lot less grass and a lot more paving and even some seats, it wasn't a churchyard anymore. Then there was Alice.

Alice had always seemed different to me but I thought that was because she was posh. She always told me she wasn't well off, but she looked it to me, with her clothes and her shoes and that lovely clean smell. But now I saw it was more than that, it was something about the way she acted, older and smarter, and I thought I was bright as they come. Alice was so very different from Louise, and Louise was like me, she was bright and tough. *No*, I thought, *Alice is different because she belongs in a different world. A future world.*

There, I'd said it, a crazy assumption and yet, somehow, I knew it was true. I moved to the side to avoid some people, Narrowboat Lane was always crowded. I stared at them briefly, as they passed by, I was always looking, studying outlines, looking for someone who looked like Louise. Was she even alive anymore? Then I saw Alice.

She knows, I thought, *she's known for a while, that she crosses time's boundaries, and comes to visit us.* That was why she was with Miranda, she'd gone exploring.

We stood together in the middle of the road, as the horses and carts and the rest went past, the drivers yelling to 'get the out of the way, or else you'll be dead,' but I didn't care, I just fixed my eyes on this special stranger, now that I knew she was even more special and had come from a place where I couldn't go.

'But you can,' said Alice, 'you almost did.' She was talking about when we'd been in the alley. It scared me to hell when she read my mind. I said nothing.

'It's there in your face, you stupid boy,' said Alice, laughing, 'and I saw how you looked when I left you alone and you followed me back. I hid behind a tree and watched you, on Scriveners Road. Your face was a picture, total shock.'

'I was,' I said, 'and I'm still shocked now. I couldn't believe the church was gone.'

'Try walking around to Old School Lane. There aren't any tenements, not anymore.'

'And no Louise,' I told her, sadly. 'Not even in the present time.'

'Louise is your friend?'

'She is,' I said, 'Louise has gone missing, and I think Pike, he's the man who runs the school, might have sent her away. Or maybe Wetherby Eisen has harmed her, I don't really know. I don't even know if Louise is alive. All I know is, she said she'd tell me if she left, but then she didn't and that makes me worried. Yet Pike was the one who asked me to find her, he wouldn't do that if he was involved. Surely he wouldn't?'

'The School Lane ghosts,' said Alice, thoughtful, twisting her hair and swinging her legs. We were sitting on the wall right next to the church. At least by the church I knew where I was. And when I was.

'What?' I said.

'That's what we call them, the School Lane ghosts.' She looked at me, and her eyes shifted. 'I don't know if I should tell you this.'

'Tell me what?'

'Why we call them the School Lane ghosts.'

'You might as well,' I said, calmly, but my heart was thumping, as loud as could be. 'It's better to know, that's what I believe.'

'But is it?' said Alice. 'Sometimes knowing the truth can be hard. But yes, okay, you wanted to know. Some children went missing, years ago, no, now, in *this* time. Several kids, who knows how many? But ever since then, there's been crying and screaming, and sometimes laughter, around about here.'

Well, I thought, and stared at the darkening shadows of the street. They felt threatening.

'We say it's because the children were murdered and what we hear are their fearful screams or sometimes their laughter before they were taken. But you have to remember one thing, Tom.' Alice looked sombre. 'It's only a rumour and probably not true.'

'Who do they say was to blame for the deaths?' I said slowly, not looking at Alice.

'I can't remember, and nobody found any children's bodies.' She paused, thinking. 'I've heard the children crying, though. In *your* school, where Aleph lives now. He's a friend of mine.'

'You're friends with a boy in your own time?' I asked her, jealous. Alice laughed.

'I'm friends with dozens, we're all on Facebook. But Aleph's a man, not a boy. He's my mum's friend really, rather than mine. Well, maybe not friends, but she knows him, anyhow.'

I hadn't a clue what she meant about Facebook but I let that pass. 'Maybe the kids you heard were real.'

'It's a house, now, stupid, not a school. And Aleph doesn't have kids of his own.'

'I'm not surprised with a name like Aleph.' I was smarting a little, her calling me stupid.

Alice ignored me. 'When I visit his house, which was once your school, sometimes I hear this terrible crying and sometimes screaming and sometimes I hear those sounds in the street. Around the corner, outside the school. It's only a couple of children, probably, but it's terribly sad and really quite creepy. I don't like it.'

'Boys or girls?' I asked her, quickly, wishing and praying she'd say a boy. Let the crying not be Louise.

'Both, I think, but I don't really know, sometimes a boy can sound like a girl especially if he's upset or in pain. All I know is I hate hearing them, especially if Wetherby Eisen killed them.' She clapped her hand over her mouth, quickly.

'Wetherby Eisen killed those kids?'

'I don't know for sure, it's only a rumour, I didn't want to tell you, it might not be true. You know this man, then Wetherby Eisen?'

'I certainly do,' I said, grimly.

78

Now – Aleph

So Guinevere James was Marianne's sister. And both descended from Mary-Ann Parks, the murder victim. Which finally explained Ginny's interest. But why did she think I could solve the murder?

'Ghosts on audio files, Mr Jones.'

'I think we've been down that route already.'

'But I know you've heard them, haven't you Aleph? The crying children.'

'Yes,' I said, 'but I don't think I'm a reliable witness.'

'Because of the accident?'

'Because I can't prove I heard them cry, or if I did, that the children are ghosts.' I sighed heavily. The crash had made me doubt my mind.

'You don't have to prove it,' Guinevere insisted. 'The next time you hear them, just record them, then do a reversal, like you did with Alice's crying. If you record them, then play the file back, in reverse, we might find out what happened to my great-aunt. My sister and I both need to know.'

'I might not be able to record the crying, or even hear it again, ever. What do you want to know, exactly?'

'The name of the person who killed my great-aunt.'

'That's rather a lot to ask, Ginny.'

'But you can do it, Aleph,' she said. It didn't look like I had much choice.

The next evening, Cressida rang. Sounding more than a little desperate. 'Alice won't talk,' she said, grimly.

'I'm not sure what you want me to do.'

'Get her to talk, ask her what's up. She won't even 'talk' to me online.' She paused, briefly.

'I take it she wasn't at yours last night? It's not as if I hadn't checked.'

'No, of course she wasn't. She walked around Curdizan Low with Miranda. The girl from the Keepsake Arms, remember? Alice mentioned her on the recording, the one she did with Alison Clipper.'

'But the pub's closed down,' said Cressida, puzzled.

'The whole of Curdizan Low's closed down. Think, Cressida! You went there.'

'So that's where she went,' said Cressida, slowly. 'If only I'd known, I'd have got myself down to the Low straight away. My daughter alone on a building site, in the middle of the night!'

'But she wasn't alone,' I said patiently, 'and it wasn't a building site at all. She was with Miranda, who lived in the past and Alice went back to the past with her. And I did too.'

The phone went silent, I thought she'd hung up. 'Cressida?' I said. 'Are you still there?'

'You want me to believe all this?'

'Look Cressida, I was there, and I saw the streets *and* the pub, the place was alive, and the very next morning, I heard Miranda arguing with her mother.'

'But what about Alice?'

'She and Miranda went down a tunnel, the one that led to Curdizan Church.'

'Just like you were afraid she would.'

'But I didn't know she would go with Miranda. I couldn't follow her through the tunnel, the door was locked and I couldn't get in and Alice got back to the present before me, but she has been with me for part of the day. Guinevere Jones left me a note.'

'The journalist,' said Cressida, coldly. 'I'm finding this hard to believe, Aleph.'

'I followed them into the alley, Cressida, I thought the child with Miranda was Alice. I was right, she was. And as for believing, you were the one who first saw Tom.'

'Tom, yes, the boy from the census. Was he there?'

'Not that I saw. But I did met Norah, she's the horse and a bloke called Scotty, you wouldn't want to meet him, late at night. Or anytime, really.'

'We have to talk, I'm coming over.'

'No,' I said, 'send Alice instead. I'll try to discover what's the matter. But don't get your hopes up, Alice is stubborn.' *Just like her mother.*

When Alice turned up. It was barely light.

'I thought you'd be here much sooner than this. I was starting to worry. You shouldn't be wandering around in the dark.'

'I didn't want to come here, that's why I'm late.'

'I guessed,' I said. 'Now, look, Alice, it's time you grew up. Cressida might not be the perfect mum but she is your mum, and if you've got a problem, about her or the boy, the one who died, you owe it to your mother to sort things out. Just tell her the truth, or if you can't do that, tell someone else, a teacher, or a friend's mum, or even me. Before it destroys both of you.' Alice got up.

She wandered over to the kitchen window and peered outside at the darkening day. I knew she was thinking of Curdizan churchyard, the way she'd seen it, instead of how it was right now, a modern courtyard with all the trappings. She sighed heavily.

'It's not that I don't care,' she said. 'It's not that she's done anything wrong, well nothing she intended to do. I don't blame her, could I possibly blame my mum? If only she knew.' She turned away from the window to face me. Her face was all pain.

'The thing is Aleph, if she knew the truth, if it all came out, our lives would never be the same again, and she'd grow to hate me for letting her know. And I know if I speak, it will all come out in a row or something, even if I don't mean it to.

The moment I'm angry I'll blurt it out. So, it's best not to talk and then it won't happen.'

'You have to tell someone, Alice, believe me. And I really do think that now is the time. Don't you agree?' I waited, patiently.

But Alice didn't answer, she just stood there, staring, a big fat tear rolling down one cheek.

79

Then – Miranda

'Someone to see you Miranda,' said Cath. Miranda pushed the hair back from her face.

The bar was heaving, crawling with folk, gearing up for a rowdy night of singing in the parlour, and on top of all that, Tom was late. On nights like this, she hated her mother for what she'd done. Miranda had been at the factory all day. She raised her eyes to see Mary-Ann.

'I didn't think *you* believed in pubs. Especially the pubs that hold music nights.'

'Well, you thought wrong,' Mary-Ann insisted. She was dressed in her finest outdoor clothes, as if she was going to visit the sick. Miranda smiled.

'I thought you and I were friends, Mary-Ann, until you started telling me lies.'

'I've told you no lies,' said Mary-Ann, sharply, 'well perhaps just a few, but none that matter. Maybe you're jealous, because I'm getting married.'

'Not when you're marrying Wetherby Eisen, no, I'm not. If anything, I feel sorry for you. I notice, you're still waiting for a ring. Instead, he's given you a cheap necklace.'

'That's a horrible thing to say, Miranda, it's the thought that counts, not the value of the gift. I don't know why I bother with you.'

'Because we help you out at the church. With the soup on Sundays and the jumble sales, and that reminds me, where's my dress?'

'We don't have it. Mrs Mace told you that.'

'That's not what I was told by Ma. She shouldn't have given the dress to you, but now that you've got it, I want it back.'

'I've already told you, we don't have it. I only came round to give you this. I'd like you to give it to Thomas, from me.' She unfastened the beads from around her neck.

'Wetherby Eisen's engagement gift? You're giving it to Tom? He won't be pleased.'

'It wasn't from Wetherby, that wasn't true. I only told you that to save face. I didn't want you to think I was soft, saying yes to marriage, without as much as a ring or a token.'

'So you do lie then,' said Miranda, slyly.

'I've said so, haven't I? This was a white one, totally harmless. The necklace was given to me by Louise.'

'To you, not to Eisen? So Louise might not be dead after all?'

'Why should she be dead? The last time I saw her, she was leaving Curdizan and needed some clothes, but she had no money so I bought the necklace off her, to give her some cash. It wasn't worth anything at all, of course, but I never said, Louise is so proud. I offered her some things from the jumble box, but she said they weren't the type she needed. I don't know what she meant by that.'

'But wasn't the necklace meant for Thomas?'

'Yes, and he was going to get it, but I needed something I could say was from Wetherby, until he managed to buy me a ring. He's always so busy.'

I'll say he's busy, Miranda thought, *stocking up silver in the crypt.*

'Thomas was always going to get it, eventually. I just needed something to wear for a while, but I've changed my mind, now, it doesn't feel right.' She passed the beads across to Miranda. 'Here, have it, it's Thomas's now.' Miranda took the necklace, reluctantly.

'Did Louise tell you where she was going?'

'No, she just said she was going away and needed some clothes and the money to buy them. It was obvious she didn't want to part with the necklace, she said she'd meant to give it to Thomas. She asked if I'd tell him she was alright and not to worry, and I meant to do it, I really did.' She frowned, looked down.

'I just forgot, we were so busy, with the jumble sales and the soup kitchen and visiting the sick almost every day.'

'While Tom's been worried sick in the meantime, knowing she's vanished and thinking she's dead.'

'Why would Thomas think Louise was dead?'

'Because of the missing kids, Mary-Ann. Tom thought she might have been one of those, everyone thinks that Eisen's behind it. I've told you before.'

'But he's not that sort of man, Miranda.'

'So you've told me, but you don't know very much about him, like what he's been up to with Ben Tencell, not to mention your father.'

'What do you mean, "what he's been up to with Ben Tencell"?'

'Wetherby Eisen and Ben Tencell, and your da, have been shifting church goods and selling them off.'

'You're joking,' said Mary-Ann, looking pale. 'Why would you say such a terrible thing?'

'Because it's true,' Miranda told her. 'I'm a friend of Ben's, and he told me.'

80

Then – Thomas

So Eisen might be the one behind it, all those kids going missing from school, including Louise. Assuming what Alice had said was true. Just thinking about it made me feel grim. *But what about the lad, Conrad Carson?* He hadn't disappeared, like we thought he had, he'd just been working for Pike on the sly. I wondered if Pike would hire a girl. There was always cleaning and laundry work. My brain was buzzing with all the effort.

When I woke up the next morning, I felt really ill, a lot more than tired, hot and feverish, dizzy with nerves. I did my morning round as usual, but I couldn't face going to school afterwards, or even working at the pub that night. And as for going home in the evening, facing Da's wrath and Ma's nagging, *not on your life*. So, later that day, I crept around and grabbed some food, choosing a time when I knew they'd be out and slept out under the stars again, it was getting quite mild and the fields were free. I'd done it before, I could do it again, it wasn't that bad in good weather.

This carried on for several days. I left a note at the pub of course, and also at home, I didn't want Ma worrying about me, Da wouldn't care, but I knew I needed to be on my own. After a break, I felt much better, but I still had to sort out the Eisen thing, discover what really happened to Louise. I'd have to talk to Alice, again. I went back home and wished I hadn't. The house was piled to the sky with stuff.

'What's going on?' I said, horrified.

'We're packing, my lad, what does it look like?' My father looked happy, for once in his life.

'For a holiday, maybe, or a trip to the seaside?' He could

have knocked me down with a feather. We'd never, ever been on holiday, or at least not one that I could remember.

My da started laughing and couldn't stop, he was sitting by the fire and reading the paper. The fire wasn't lit and the paper was last week's but Da didn't care, at least he could read. A lot of the men round here couldn't. I suppose I was lucky, having a da who knew how to spell, but I didn't feel lucky.

'You're a hoot, Tommy lad, you should go on the stage. Since when have we had the money for trips?'

'I've told you, Scotty, his name's Thomas. Don't call him Tommy, that sounds wrong.'

'Your ma's going all la-di-da on me, just because we've come into some money.'

'Money?' I said. 'What money is that?' I noticed my da was in a good mood.

'Let's just say we've come into some cash, a bit of cash, with more to follow, if we like. And I do like, Tommy, I like it a lot. So, your ma's convinced me it's time to move on, to somewhere bigger and in a better street. Nothing fancy, much like this, but not so rough and more room to spare. I'm not sure, but your ma's the boss, I reckon she knows what's right for us.' I stared in amazement.

Since when had Da ever called her the boss? I reckoned it must be a *lot* of money.

'But what about your job at the laundry?' I looked at Ma.

'I'll probably keep that on for a while, but your da's giving up his job right now. It's never been any good for his health and he's planning to start his own business, now.'

I doubted the drinking helped his health, but I wasn't going to say so, not to his face. 'So what's this business?' I said, curious. 'I thought you only knew about flour.' And stepped back quickly to avoid a clip.

'It was when you got that job with Mason's that put me onto it, as it happens. People will always need to eat veg and I can be my own boss for a change, instead of working for somebody else. You can join me, Tommy, we'll have our own little family business, Islip and Son, that's what we'll be. I'm not talking about the future, you can start straight away.'

You've got to be joking, I thought, grimly. I couldn't think of a suitable answer.

'Cat got your tongue?' said my da, grinning.

'I don't want to live on another street. I like it round here, with all my mates.'

'You'll do what you're told, Tommy, lad,' said Da. 'You can start by helping your mother to pack.'

'I'm going to work,' I told him, quickly. 'Miranda's expecting me down the pub.'

'And that's going to stop as well, when we leave. You can stick with the fruit and veg if you like, at least for a while, having an inside source will be useful, but the pub can go and the schooling too. You're getting too old for school, I reckon.'

'But it's free,' I said, with a catch in my throat, I could see the world as I knew it dissolving. 'They feed me too and that saves money.'

'You'll be making plenty, once you're with me, don't worry about that and you'll be far too busy to go to school. It's time to grow up at last, Tommy lad.'

'I've got to go,' I said abruptly and ran for the door, as fast as I could. My throat was full, I could barely breathe, I'd been anxious before, but now I was scared. The thought of leaving the Low was terrible, Ben and Miranda, people I'd known and probably Alice, it was all too much for me to bear. And never knowing about Louise. I almost howled.

As I made my way to the pub, my brain was working as fast as my legs. I knew I'd have to run away, but tonight, I'd do my job like a man. I wished I could stay a boy forever.

81

Now – Aleph

Sometimes, when things are really difficult, almost impossible, the only thing is to do is the next thing. Whatever that might be. I switched off the light and walked down the steps into the street.

It was cold, no, sharp, it was one of those times when it feels like spring when the sun still shines but when night comes down there's an icy chill and a cloudless sky. I turned up my collar and hunched myself deep as I could in my jacket. Walking around to the site of the church, I could almost see it, no longer there, but there in my head as sharp as could be, like it had been for real when I went to the past. I set the equipment on to record.

I let the file run on for a couple of minutes, checked it was playing and sat on a bench and waited to see. Nothing happened. I heard an owl, or maybe some tourists and one or two people passed by and stared but I didn't hear ghosts, I didn't hear anything, not even a laugh. No doubt I seemed like a ghost to the tourists, a faded outline sitting on a bench, hidden in the shadows, or maybe they thought I was drunk or crazy. Or maybe, possibly, someone in shock. I still remembered Alice's words.

'The Sunday it happened, I was meant to be going round to Annerley's house. That's in Leverhulme, where we once lived. We were staying at a friend of mum's, near Annerley's.

'I didn't want to go round to Annerley's. I thought she was boring and I wanted to have some time to myself. I had to pretend I was going, though, they wouldn't have let me out go out on my own, not for so long. I should have told Annerley not to expect me, then they wouldn't have caught me out. It was such a stupid mistake to make.' Alice sighed.

'I walked around the streets for a while, and then I met up with some kids from my school and stayed out longer than I'd meant to do, and when I realised what the time was, I thought I'd go home and make some excuse. It still wasn't lunchtime but I was hungry, Mum always makes me get up early, even on a Sunday. I was walking home when the accident happened.

'When I got back, still in shock, because of seeing the accident happen, the nightmare just got even worse. I'd known the boy who was killed, Daniel, he was my friend, and he should have been back at the house that I'd left, but he'd had been outside in the garden, playing, and they'd all gone out, looking for me. They'd left him there, free to escape. I felt so guilty.

'By the time I got back, I'd been gone for hours, because after I saw the accident happen, I went to the park and sat and cried, I never guessed they'd been looking for me, I assumed they'd think I was still at Annerley's. I couldn't tell them what I saw, there was just no way. They asked me if I'd left the gate open, or maybe not put the latch back properly because that was how Danny got onto the street. But I said I hadn't, I knew I hadn't, and I think they believed me, they had to believe me, it was true, wasn't it?' She paused, then sighed and bit her lip.

'Nobody knew just how he'd got out, and neither did I, because I knew I'd been very careful. But a few days later, my mum was saying she'd got in a panic when she'd learnt I was missing and had used the garden gate to go out. Instead of using the front as normal.

'That was when I think it happened. Maybe she closed the gate behind her, but forgot to check that the latch was connected. It's easy to do, I've done it myself, but I know I didn't do it that day. She would have been in a hurry that day, thinking I was missing.' Alice sighed.

'What's more, Aleph, I know I'm right, because when I came back, after seeing the accident, the latch wasn't down, the way I'd left it. And the only person who'd gone that way, as far as I know, apart from me, and of course Daniel, was Mum.'

'You never told her?' I said to Alice.

'How could I say? I put the latch back and closed the gate properly, without even thinking, I was too much in shock, and it was only later that I saw what it meant. So when she asked me if I'd shut it after I'd left, I told her, yes, and over again. I never told her, she was the one.'

'That was brave,' I said, softly, finding it hard to even speak.

'It wasn't brave,' said Alice, defiant, 'I had to do it, I had no choice. If Mum had known what she'd done that day, that she was the one who'd left the latch off, then she'd think she was a killer too.'

82

Then – Thomas

As I walked to the pub that night, my head was spinning with questions, decisions. I wasn't going to leave my home, Curdizan Low was where I belonged. And how had my parents, always struggling, managed to find the money to move? And suddenly too, as if by a windfall. Maybe my da had been putting on bets, but no, the season had barely started. And drinking not gambling was his vice. It had to be something different from that. *But what?* I wondered.

'You look fed up,' Miranda told me. 'And you're late.'

'Lots on my mind,' I said to her, shortly.

'A trouble shared...'

'My parents are leaving Curdizan Low. They've come into money.' *Yes, don't laugh.*

'What?' said Miranda. *Not very likely,* is what she'd be thinking.

'That's what they said and they're taking me with them. We're going to live in a better street. Ma has already started packing.'

'No,' said Miranda, disbelieving.

'Go round yourself, you'll see it's the truth.'

'No, I believe you. Well, that's odd.'

'Odd's not the word I'd use to describe it. How about tragic? I don't want to go.'

Miranda wiped the bar casually. 'How did they manage to find the money?'

'I wish I knew, I was thinking the same myself, before.'

'The thing is, Tom,' Miranda looked thoughtful, 'you know those shoes, the ones in the trunks?'

'As if I was ever likely to forget them.'

331

'Well, you know they were going to sell the shoes on, your mother and mine? And Eisen told you some stuff had gone missing from the church, lately? Well, I was thinking, if the things that went missing, valuables mostly, were then passed on to a helpful person willing to sell them, and at the right price, wouldn't that person have extra money?'

'You mean like my parents?'

'It's possible, Tom, it could explain things.'

'It's just what my Da would do,' I agreed. I knew I should be defending the man, or at least my ma, if I couldn't defend him, but I couldn't be bothered, not anymore. 'What sort of goods are we talking about?'

'Silver, cups and bowls mostly and a little bit of pewter, an assortment of things. The kind of goods that come from a church and would fetch a nice price, unlike the shoes.'

'You've got to tell me who was involved, I won't breathe a word, I promise I won't. I need to know if my ma's involved.'

'Ben and Eisen and probably the vicar. No, scrap the probably, definitely the vicar. He gets it all from disused churches, or so Ben told me. The stock is stored in the crypt of the church. That bit's right, I saw it in there. There's masses of the stuff, you wouldn't believe.'

'Oh yes, I would, I'd believe anything, of Wetherby Eisen. But Ben and the vicar? Surely not. And passing the stuff to my ma and da? No, that's wrong, they don't even know them.'

'Eisen said some goods had been stolen. Maybe they didn't pass it to your parents, maybe your parents just took it, Thomas.'

'Why would my mother go to the crypt? She's never been in a church in her life, except perhaps when her parents died and she went to the funerals. And maybe not then, I couldn't guarantee it.'

Miranda polished the bar a bit more, and served a quick pint, chatted a little. I willed the customers away, quickly. She turned back to me.

'Maybe she followed me into the tunnel.' I must have

looked blank.

'When Alice and I went down the tunnel, you said Ben couldn't get into his workshop. But I didn't lock it and neither did Alice, I looked behind to check and make sure. Maybe your ma came along afterwards, locked it behind her and followed us all the way to the crypt.'

'That doesn't sound much like Ma to me,' I said, doubtful.

'People aren't always what they seem.'

83

Now – Aleph

I had to tell Cressida what Alice had said. I didn't want to do it, of course I didn't. So I delayed telling her until the next day. Hoping, I suppose, that Alice would tell her. Alice didn't.

'I know why Alice won't talk,' I said.

'I'll be round as soon as I can,' said Cressida. Soon as she could was incredibly fast.

'What's that doing on the table?' she said. Giving the recorder a filthy look, as if I was going to record her thoughts.

'I've been trying to record the ghosts crying, with not much success so far,' I explained. 'I stayed in the courtyard until one in the morning, but I didn't hear a single thing.'

Cressida looked at me as if I was mad. *You were the one who first saw Tom,* I wanted to say. I poured out her coffee, she was going to need it. Out in the street, the rain poured down. Cressida looked more fragile than normal, if that was possible. *God*, I thought. *Get on with it man.*

'Alice saw the accident happen, when the boy died. She told me she saw it.' Cressida nodded and I rattled on.

'She also told me, the child, Daniel, was playing in the garden, and she shut the gate when she left the house. But when she came back the latch was off, someone had used the gate since then, giving

Cressida's face had turned grey as the rain, had sunk into shadows. 'Alice must hate me, think I'm a killer, if that's what she believes happened.'

'No,' I told her, 'actually, Alice wants to protect you, wanted to stop you from blaming yourself. She thought if she spoke it would all spill out, and it almost did, a number of times, when she was angry. But it's harder to blurt things out on a screen.'

'But she couldn't go on like that forever.'

'No,' I said, 'and I think she's finally realised that. She needs your help and support, Cressida. I know it's terrible, what you're hearing, but leaving the latch off, if you did, was just a mistake, a tragic error.' *Rather like mine,* I thought, sadly.

'A mistake which caused a child to die. And you think I shouldn't care about that? Well, I guess you would.'

'What do you mean by that?' I said. I already knew.

'Nothing,' she said, standing up, 'I didn't mean anything, or perhaps I meant you're weak and a coward. With the cards, for example.' She headed into the other room and picked up the shoebox. I hurried after her.

'These old cards from your girlfriend, Jenny?'

'Gerry,' I said and stood and watched her, mesmerised. She waved the box in front of my face.

'All of these envelopes, how many are there, one, two or three? No, there are four. I see you've opened the first one already, but when are you going to open the rest? And if you're not, just throw them away. Why don't we do it right now, Aleph. Or, maybe I could open them for you?' She picked out one of the sealed envelopes.

'No!' I told her, almost shouting, 'they're mine, those cards, they're nothing whatever to do with you. Give that to me.'

'How do you know,' said Cressida, slowly, 'if you haven't opened the envelope?'

'Just give it to me,' I said sharply, 'and the box. Now, Cressida.'

Cressida sighed and dropped the box on the nearest chair. An envelope fluttered onto the floor.

'Sorry,' she said, 'I shouldn't have done that. I think I'm in shock with what I did, or didn't do. I'm sorry Aleph.' She sat on the sofa.

'You mustn't blame yourself,' I said. 'The person who drove the car was to blame.' I couldn't look her in the face.

'The way I heard it, Daniel rushed out. Which makes me much more to blame than... the driver.'

The air was thick with things unsaid. I knew I needed to ask some questions, and hear her replies and deal with all that. I already thought I knew what she'd say. I looked at Cressida and thought about asking. I couldn't do it.

84

Then – Miranda

When, later that evening, Tom went home, Miranda's thoughts were all of a turmoil. Should she have let Tom into the secret? What would she do if Thomas left? He was only a boy, but she'd really miss him, and his work. Could his mother have stolen the silver? It didn't seem likely. Shoes, yes, with the help of another. But trundling down a dark, dirty tunnel? It certainly wasn't the work of Scotty. He'd barely have found his way along it, full to the brim, as he'd be with ale. She wiped her hands on an old towel and wandered along to her ma in the parlour.

'Carol and Scotty Islip are leaving. Packing their bags, as we speak.' She watched her ma, for a reaction.

'You're having me on, Miranda, surely.' Her mother cleaned a tray with a cloth.

'No, I'm not, it was Tom who told me. He said his da had come into money, with possibly more of the same to follow. You wouldn't know where the money's come from, would you, Ma? Seeing as Carol and you had that sideline. The one with the shoes.'

Her mother sighed and sat down on a chair. 'Matt McCarthy was our friend. He'd have laughed if he'd heard what we'd done with the shoes. Well, maybe not laughed, but forgiven us, anyway. I don't know anything about Scotty's windfall.' She pulled out a fag and lit it up.

'I wish you wouldn't smoke, ma, please.'

'I'm not on this earth to please you, Miranda. But, as for Scotty, it's news to me. And after all I've done for that woman.' Hannah Collenge shook her head.

'You've been a good friend to her, Ma, that's true.'

'I've been a lot more than that, Miranda, I've stuck to that woman through thick and thin. And all through the time with Matt McCarthy.'

'I don't know what you're talking about.'

'I mean her fling, you stupid girl. Well, more of a love thing, it lasted for years. I shouldn't have said, and I shouldn't be smoking. It's not very classy.' She took a quick drag and nipped the ends of the fag together. 'Remember, Miranda, I've told you nothing.'

'Are you sure you haven't been drinking, Ma? I thought it was *you* and Matt McCarthy.'

'Of course it wasn't, I told you that. It was always Carol and she was so scared that Scotty would find out. So I would go round to Matt's house in the evenings and act as lookout, or make out that Carol and I were together, having a gossip. All to keep Scotty Islip happy. You know that man's got a hell of a temper, when he's been drinking? And no man likes to be made a fool of.'

'Yet you encouraged him to come to this pub.'

'That was all part of the plan, Miranda. When Matt died, Carol was gutted, heartbroken, really. So I did what I could by bringing Scotty here, filling him up with booze and fags, to stop him going home to be with Carol. So she could cry to her heart's content.'

'You did all this for Carol Islip?'

'She's a friend, Miranda. She'd do the same for me, I'm sure.'

Miranda wasn't quite so sure. 'I never knew you were such a saint. How long had this been going on?'

'Years, Miranda, a very long time. It proved a bit of a problem sometimes, especially with Scotty being like he is.'

'You mean, jealous and drunk and lazy as hell. Well, I'll tell you Ma, I'm glad they're going, I can't stand the man, but I will miss Thomas, he's a hard-working lad.'

'Yes, at least she's got Thomas, that's something I guess.' Miranda said nothing. She hadn't much pity for Carol Islip.

Grabbing a broom, she walked back down the passage to the bar. The passage was chilly, as if the door to the bar had been open, but the door was closed, just like she'd left it. She peered back down the passage to the end and noticed the back door was slightly ajar, enough to cause a bit of a draught. *I'm sure I closed that door earlier.*

Had someone come in the back way? she wondered, after she'd closed it to keep out the cold. Cath and Reg and Steve had long gone. Miranda paused and felt apprehensive.

She hoped no-one had heard what they'd said.

85

Now – Aleph

Cressida didn't want to talk so she left as soon as she could after that. Leaving me with my thoughts, unsaid.

I'd never faced up to the part I'd played in Daniel's death, all I'd done was run away, but now the past was coming back, in spite of all my efforts to keep it away. Daniel was known to Alice and Cressida, they'd been staying at Cressida's friend's house; that friend was probably Daniel's mother. Daniel's mother would have known my name, I'd written to her and her husband afterwards. So Cressida must have known all along.

I doubted Alice had told them anything. Alice liked secrets, and Cressida had always kept her own counsel. But she'd hinted at something that time with the shoebox, why had she never told me the truth?

Later that day, the doorbell rang.

'You've fixed it, I see,' said Guinevere James.

If only everything else was so easy. I invited Ginny in.

'How are the ghosts, Mr Jones?' she said.

'They're not playing. You can make the tea, today, you know where it is.' Guinevere followed me into the kitchen.

'I sat around in the freezing cold for half of the night and didn't hear a single sound. I even tried in the house as well, and checked the recording, in case it was me. I got absolutely nothing. I didn't try the cellar, though, I've no intention of going down there. I've never heard the ghosts in the cellar.'

'I think you're scared, Mr Jones,' said Ginny, and passed me the tea, which was better than mine. 'We've run out of biscuits.' She put the empty tin on the table.

'I'll try again before too long,' I said, thinking, 'and then, perhaps, I'll go down the cellar, if you'll join me.' I looked at Ginny.

'You know how to make a girl feel special,' said Ginny. 'I've got some news, as it happens.' She paused, for effect.

'I went along to the library yesterday, checked the census and guess what I found? A number of people who might be of interest. Not just Eisen and Mary-Ann Parks, but someone called Miranda Collenge who lived at a pub called the Keepsake Arms, and a man, Ben Tencell who worked at the coach house. He was an undertaker.'

I wondered where this story was going.

'The reason I've latched onto these four people is that ten years later they'd all disappeared, every one of these people had vanished. Not just Mary-Ann Parks and Eisen, which is what we'd expect, she would be dead and he would have scarpered, but the other two as well, and three of the people were similar in age. Miranda Collenge was slightly younger, she was just eighteen.'

'So the three still alive had vanished from the census ten years later, what does that mean? They could have moved on for jobs or marriage.'

'Maybe,' said Guinevere, looking thoughtful. 'But these were traditional working class areas around Curdizan Church and Curdizan Low. Sure, the itinerants came and went, usually the Irish or casual workers, but most of the families stayed for years, even the young people. It was rough and tough, but solid, substantial.'

'It certainly was,' I said thinking back. 'Exceedingly tough.'

'You sound like you know.'

'I do,' I said. 'You might as well hear it, you know all the rest.' So out it all came, Miranda and Alice, and the boy Tom.

'So that's who Tom was,' Guinevere said. 'And the woman we saw was the girl, Miranda?'

'Yes,' I told her, regretting sharing the story already. 'And don't go telling this story to the tabloids, or anybody else, for that matter. They'd think I was crazy or made it all up.'

'Or troubled,' said Ginny, 'which is hardly surprising, given what happened.'

'You can ask Cressida, if you don't believe me. She found Tom, and I've checked the census and Tom is dead.'

'I don't know Cressida.'

'But you do have a mutual friend,' I said. 'And I think I can guess just who she is.' Suddenly Ginny wouldn't meet my eyes. I took a deep breath.

'I had to give Cressida some very bad news about Daniel's death. Alice thinks Cressida is partly responsible and that's why she won't talk to her mother.'

'Have you told Cressida you were the driver?'

'I'm almost certain she knows already. Doesn't she Ginny?' Ginny said nothing so I hurried on.

'This friend of Cressida's, the one whose house they were at that day, when Alice went missing and Daniel died, I'm guessing she's probably Daniel's mother? And your friend too?'

Ginny didn't answer, instead she stood up. 'I have to go, I've copy to write, I'm on a deadline.' She looked quite concerned, and not about the deadline. She still wouldn't look me in the eye.

'I think you owe it to me to tell me.' But the friend I thought I had shook her head.

'You need to talk to Cressida, Aleph. About Daniel, and about what happened, it's not my story. But from what you've just said, Cressida will probably blame herself for what happened to Daniel, even if you and Alice don't. And I know you don't want that, Aleph.'

86

Then – Tanya

Tanya Curtis picked up her broom and pretended to sweep in the farthest corners. She hated her job cleaning the church. Today was one of the typical bad days, there were people all over, Mrs Mace, adjusting the flowers and Mary-Ann Parks, who kept popping in and out. She normally left such work to her mother. She watched the girl bend over a box and put something in it, some kind of cloth, or a shawl maybe, she couldn't tell what. *More for the jumble,* thought Tanya bitterly. As if *she*, Tanya Curtis, didn't need clothes, she'd worn this skirt to rags, she had. And then she perked up, recalling the silver she'd sold to Carol.

I won't be wearing old clothes much longer, she said to herself, *now that we're on to a winning streak. But I'll wander over to the box later. There might be something for Jake in there.*

She worked her way down the church, carefully. The vicar was strict and liked the church to be clean and polished and Tanya was good at such surface work, hiding the dust under pews and in corners where no-one would ever find it for ages. She approached the steps that led to the crypt. *Time to go down,* she said to herself.

She hadn't enjoyed her tunnel walk. Alone in the dark, risking the rats and God knew what, she needed to find an easier way to get to the goods, via the church. The door to the crypt was locked, unfortunately, but that didn't bother Tanya much, she knew where the vicar kept the key. She opened the door.

Tanya walked down the stairs, slowly, gripping the rail, it was dark down here, as black as pitch. She hadn't thought to bring a lamp. *My eyes will adjust,* she told herself.

The steps were narrow and very uneven but Tanya finally reached the bottom. The crypt, she knew, ran the length of the building and when lit up was rather attractive. *Unlike now, but at least it's wider than the tunnel,* she thought. She'd have to get a system in place.

She made her way to the corner, quickly, to the place she thought the treasure would be. She knew she hadn't a lot of time, if she was caught, she might get the sack, and then it would be the tunnel or nothing.

As she walked over, Tanya's eyes adjusted slightly, she identified shadows and shapes and stone. She almost fell over a chair at one point, but did a quick turn and managed to avoid it, twisting her foot, and cursing loudly. Then she saw crates, piled up in the corner. She hurried towards them.

Reaching inside she yelled with surprise, the boxes were empty, there was no stock in them, no silver or pewter or anything else. All her lovely treasure had gone. Tanya moaned.

Later that day, she called on Carol, knocking sharply on the door, instead of going in, like most people did. Carol was funny, she didn't like people going in her house, without her permission. It gave her a name for being stuck up. Tanya shivered, the day was cold, and she pulled her thick shawl around her shoulders. She wanted to feel the warmth of the fire. *After the crypt,* she thought, bitterly. Then she saw Carol's face at the door, the face of a woman not pleased to see her. She felt even worse.

But I'm the one who brings you the stock. Not anymore.

She tried to stand taller, as Carol emerged and followed her into the tiny back room. It was warm and dry, unlike Tanya's rooms, and the fire was hot and glowing with coal. She felt a sudden burst of envy.

'That broth smells good,' said Tanya, hungry. She hadn't eaten since eight in the morning.

'It's only a bone and some veg Thomas got me. You know he's working at Mason's at the moment?' Carol gestured to a pile of boxes, all ready for packing. 'I need to get on. What did you want?'

Why do I have to want anything? Can't I just come round for a chat?
'Moving, are you?' Tanya asked.

'Yes,' said Carol, looking defensive. 'Now our little agreement's begun, Scotty and I have decided to move. Scotty's always wanted to start his own business and Thomas can quit the pub and join him.'

Tanya laughed, she couldn't help it. 'And Thomas is alright with that, is he?'

'Not at the moment,' Carol frowned, 'but he'll soon come round, in a better house, with likely more money, working for his da. He doesn't know what's good for him, yet.'

'And how have you managed to find the money?' Tanya could feel the bitterness rising, the sense of betrayal, an anger brewing but she managed to contain it, there'd be time enough for anger later.

Carol smiled. 'Well, we've made quite a bit, and we're very grateful. We couldn't have done it without you, Tanya. Scotty has contacts, good contacts, and they've been happy with what you've supplied.'

'You mean you've made a killing, Carol.'

'No, not a killing, of course we haven't, but Scotty's contacts know what they like, they knew which goods had value and worth, and paid accordingly and that's thanks to you.' Carol paused briefly.

'Then, when you give us more to sell, they'll do the same, and that'll help too, help all of us, you and me and Scotty and Thomas.' Her voice tailed off.

They've ripped me off, thought Tanya, bitterly. *I thought the treasure was just old stock, silver and pewter, but nothing special, but those two have made good money out of it, and on my back. How dare they do that! All I've been given is the crumbs from the table. Well, I'll show them.*

'Assuming there's anything left to sell,' she said to Carol.

'What do you mean?' said Carol, slowly. Tanya smiled, a

cold, cruel smile.

'Today I was meant to be cleaning the church. Sweeping and dusting, that sort of thing. So I went downstairs to check in the crypt, to see the goods for sale were still there.' Tanya watched Carol. She'd never said where the stock had been stored, but what did it matter, now it had gone? No-one could prove she'd taken the things, not even Carol. She watched the woman she'd thought was her friend. *What did he see in you?* she thought.

'The stock has all gone, all of it Carol, there are just empty boxes, piled up high, with nothing inside them, not even dust. I know because I checked them all. I'm sure I don't have to spell things out. Your little dream of a life elsewhere is simply that, a sad little dream, unless, of course, you've enough already.'

Carol hadn't, Tanya knew, it was easy to read that much in her face. Tanya smiled as Carol went white, and thought that watching her friend's dreams crumble, almost made the loss worthwhile.

87

Then – Miranda

Her head was buzzing with loads of things, like what Ma had said about Carol Islip. Carol and McCarthy, who'd have believed it? After finishing work at Chaucer's one evening, she went round to Ben's.

'I knew you'd come back,' said Ben, grinning. He was holding a hammer and nails in one hand.

'Only because I need information.'

'Really?' said Ben, his smile vanishing. 'Maybe you also need some tea? The water's still hot.'

'Who do you sell the stuff to, Ben?'

'What did you say?' said Ben sharply. He'd dropped the hammer and picked up a mug but now he put the mug on the bench. And stared at Miranda.

'You told me about the goods you sell. But Tom said some of the goods have gone missing, been stolen, apparently. Isn't that right?'

'Yes, as it happens, but I don't see why I should answer your questions.'

'That's the wrong answer,' Miranda told him, coming up closer and shaking her head. 'You should have denied that things had gone missing, or told me the truth for once, Ben Tencell.'

'There's no such thing as the truth,' said Ben, 'it's all about your point of view. Do want this tea I've made, or not?'

'Yes,' said Miranda, trying to grab it, but Ben swung the mug right out of her reach. Most of the tea went over the floor.

'Damn you, Ben Tencell, why won't you give me a straight answer?'

'I will if you tell me why you're asking. And if I think that's good enough.'

Miranda frowned and gave him a look. 'Scotty and Carol are moving away. We don't know where they got the money. All I know is it happened suddenly, very suddenly, for a bloke like Scotty. That man's been here since the start of time.'

'Really?' said Ben, moving in closer. 'For that I think you deserve a kiss.' He grabbed her quickly and kissed her lightly, then a bit harder. She pushed him away.

'You told me once I was far too young.'

'Well, maybe you're a bit older now. And I've missed you, though only a little.'

'Ha!' said Miranda, stepping well back. 'I've told you my reason for wanting to know. It's time you kept your part of the bargain.'

'Fine,' said Ben, 'I'm a man of my word. I sell the goods to a bloke out of town. Certainly not to Scotty Islip, or to his wife. But that doesn't mean they didn't take them. You're right that some of the stock has been stolen.'

'Well, I can't see it, Miranda said, thinking. Following me down the tunnel to the crypt doesn't seem much like Carol Islip. And Scotty would be far too drunk to manage it. I'm sure I'd have heard him.'

'Maybe they had a go-between.'

She didn't tell Tom she'd been to see Ben. He wouldn't want to know her suspicions, that Carol and Scotty had sold on the goods. No-one wants to think badly of family. *But it fitted alright,* Miranda, thought. And went with Carol deceiving her husband. 'A rum sort of woman,' Miranda said, scrubbing the counter as hard as she could. She was only eighteen.

'I presume you're talking about Carol,' said Hannah. She was cleaning out ashtrays, a thankless task.

'They were married, Ma,' Miranda said. She twisted a wet rag around in her hands.

'You try marrying Scotty Islip and see if you like it.'

Hannah paused, briefly. 'Matt was her life and he wasn't married so she wasn't breaking anyone's heart. It's not as if Scotty had a heart to break.'

'Carol still betrayed him, and that's what matters, even if the bloke is a man like Scotty.' *And you don't know about the thefts, Mother dear. Carol's not exactly whiter than white.*

Hannah reached up and wiped the mirror clean with her cloth. 'I know you're only young, Miranda, but Carol's had a terrible life. Scotty gets angry and violent when drunk, but it's more than that, and almost worse. If I tell you something, will you keep it to yourself?'

'Of course I will,' Miranda said, wondering if she really meant it. What if she needed to tell Ben or Thomas? What the hell, she'd wait and see. She perched on the arm of the nearest chair.

'Go on, Ma, I'm ready and waiting.'

'Less of your lip,' her mother laughed. 'And open that door, it's boiling in here. But only a bit.'

Miranda got up and opened the door that led to the passage. She looked up and down to check it was clear. It was quiet at last, for the first time that evening. Then she left the tiniest gap for air. Miranda smiled at her mother, invitingly. Her ma looked nervous.

'Years ago, when you were younger, Carol had a child with Matt McCarthy. Scotty doesn't know, I helped keep it secret, took her away until the child was born. And now Carol's leaving and that means leaving the child as well, who also lives around these parts. Or so I believe.'

'She gave a child of her own away, a child like Thomas? I can't believe it.'

'She had to, Miranda, because of Scotty. He'd have beaten her, half-killed her maybe, if he'd found out the truth.'

'So why not leave him and move in with Matt?'

'That's what I told her, but Carol said no. She loved Matt much more than Scotty, but Scotty was her husband and she had Thomas, he was only a baby, not even two. Scotty would never have allowed him to leave.'

'Why didn't she pass the child off as his?'

'I told her that too, but Scotty and Matt – they looked so different, Matt was fair, if you remember. She was scared the child would grow up like him and Scotty would guess and separate them. She really needed to keep seeing Matt.'

'The selfish cow,' Miranda said. 'Nobody thought what the child might need.'

'I did,' said Hannah, smiling at her daughter. 'Carol was walking a very fine tightrope and both of us knew it. She couldn't have done it alone, you know. People always gossip in places like this. Even now, I think they all know.'

'So how *did* you do it? What did you do?'

'They thought it was mine, the child, I mean. I told them all, including your da, we were going away for better air. You won't remember, being so young.'

'And Da believed it, thought you'd given his child to strangers?'

'No, silly girl, we told your da, and everyone else, the child had died. Carol came with me to help my spirits. I was fragile, you know, when I was younger, I had a weak chest, and often caught colds.'

'Did you, really?' Miranda said. Her ma didn't strike her as fragile now.

'It must have been the smoking, I think.' Her mother laughed. 'We gave the baby to somebody local, a woman I knew, poor of course, but she seemed good hearted, I knew the couple would be kind to the child. We gave them money as well, of course, as much as we could.'

Miranda shivered. 'Of course you did. Do you think we could close the door now, Ma?' Her mother nodded. Miranda went on.

'So the child was settled with a new family?'

'That was the plan, but the da ran off, or so I was told, and the mother died, unfortunately, and then the child just disappeared. I'd lost track, with your father dying, and Carol never wanted to know. I think she felt guilty.' Miranda frowned.

'So Carol's child is out there somewhere, without any parents and maybe a home. That's brilliant, I must say. Well done, Ma.'

'We don't know that for sure, Miranda.'

'I think you do, if you're honest, Ma. I'd like to think that the kid is alive and well and happy, and also well-fed, but I very much doubt it, from what you've just said.' She heard a door slam.

'What was that?' said Hannah sharply, both of them hurrying to the door. Miranda peered out, into the corridor. Someone had left the pub quickly. The door to the yard was closed, she could see that, but she went outside to the yard, just to check. Someone had been there, she knew that at once, the door to the street was wide open.

Miranda stood still, her heart racing, her thoughts buzzing. Someone had been there, that was for sure, in the passage and outside their door. Probably hearing Carol's story, although how much they'd heard was anyone's guess. Miranda sighed. She ought to have known, from the last time it happened.

She hugged herself to keep herself warm and went back inside to find her ma. What would her mother say when she knew? It was bad enough with Matt McCarthy but now the stakes were even higher. A secret child who could be anywhere.

88

Now – Cressida

Cressida and Martha were sitting in a coffee shop. It was Narrowboat Lane's best offering, huge glass windows filled with cakes and pink linen tablecloths. Cressida and Martha didn't notice.

'So, Alice is talking now, you said? Well, that's great news.'

'But I almost wish she wasn't, sometimes. Isn't that awful? I feel so guilty.'

'Because of what she thinks you did? There's no need, Cressida, I don't blame you, you know I don't. Even if you did leave the latch off.' Martha paused. 'Naturally, you were thinking about Alice, she was the one we were worried about.' She sipped her tea, her favourite, chamomile.

'If only Alice had gone to Annerley's...'

'So now we're blaming Alice instead? No, Cressida, blaming each other gets us nowhere. I want to focus on who's responsible, Aleph Jones. He was the one who killed a child.' Martha took out a cigarette. 'Or maybe I should blame myself? I was his mother, I shouldn't have left him alone in the garden.' Martha's face darkened. Cressida frowned.

'You know you can't smoke in here, Martha. Put it away, until later, please.' She looked around the café quickly, but the mostly Italian staff hadn't noticed. 'I can't go on with this anymore, the Aleph Jones thing. 'I think it's time we stopped it for good.'

'Because Alice is speaking again? Or because you feel grateful and think that you owe him? You think he's done you some sort of favour?' Martha leant back in her chair and smiled.

'No, you're wrong, you don't understand.' Cressida's voice

was low but urgent. 'I just think we should call it a day. For everyone's sake, yours especially.'

'I thought you meant what you said, Cressida.' Martha's voice grew loud and angry. Cressida looked around in alarm. The café was becoming increasingly busier and people were starting to look their way. 'You said you'd stay until he knew the truth. He's still in blissful ignorance, isn't he? Unless there's something you haven't told me.

'He's got all the cards together in a box. He can find out the truth whenever he wants.'

'But he's not going to read them, according to you. You told me he threw that last one away.' Martha bent down and picked up her bag.

'He took it out later, and put it away. He'll read them eventually, just give him time.'

'But I don't have time, we're leaving the area.' Martha dumped some change on the table. 'And as you know, there's a new baby coming. I hope he has more time than Daniel. I want Aleph Jones to know the truth.'

'You want him to suffer, that's what you mean. But I think he has, and more than enough. I won't be a part of this anymore.' Cressida rose and made for the door, but stopped, abruptly and turned around.

'If you want Aleph to know the truth, then I suggest you tell him yourself.'

89

Then – Miranda

The sun shone brightly on Dogleg Lane and the Keepsake Arms, but not for Miranda, she was feeling fed up, as well as bitter at having to work in the pub, yet again. On her one day off.

I need to get a different life, she said to herself, as she thought about Ben. Thinking about Ben made her feel better, despite him being a bit of a crook. Her ma walked in and Miranda smiled.

Knowing the truth about Carol Islip had made such a difference, knowing the things her ma had done, to help her friend. Even if her ma had made mistakes, at least she'd tried, and that made a difference, a big difference. Miranda felt proud. She polished the mirror a little harder.

'I wiped that mirror the other day, it's a waste of time you doing it again. Especially when there are glasses to stack.' Hannah Collenge frowned at her daughter. 'We've got a few in, regulars mostly, even though it's still quite early.' She peered at Miranda. 'You look tired.'

It's hardly surprising, Ma, thought Miranda. Keeping secrets was tiring work. She hadn't told Hannah that someone had heard them talking last night. That someone might know about Carol and the child. *Please don't let it be Scotty,* she thought.

Thinking about it, she doubted it was. He'd be far too drunk to stand still and listen, it was probably a woman, or maybe a child. But it had been late. Then a thought struck her.

She turned around and stared at the wall and the shelf on it. The boot was still there. She reached up and took it down, then looked at her mother.

'This wasn't one of McCarthy's shoes, was it, Ma?' Her mother went pale. She looked around.

'No,' she said, 'it wasn't Matt's, it belonged to the girl, Carol's child, the one she gave up.'

'So it was a girl,' Miranda said. 'I wondered if I was right about that. Because, if she'd had another boy, well she had Tom already, but being a girl, she couldn't forget.'

'She wouldn't have forgotten whatever it was. Every child is different, Miranda.'

'But I still thought it was a girl,' said Miranda. 'Yet the boot's not the boot of a *little* girl.'

'No,' said her mother,' looking embarrassed. 'I only went to where she lived twice. I waited until the family were out, then crept inside and took the boots. I know it was wrong, but Carol wanted some sort of keepsake. A pair of boots was the best I could do.'

'So where exactly did they live?'

'It was only a room, shabby and dark, it made our place look like a palace. I felt really awful.'

'But where was it?'

'I'm sorry Miranda, I can't tell you that. I shouldn't have told you anything at all. But the girl doesn't live in that place anymore, or so I believe. So it hardly matters where she lived once.'

'You took the boots and brought them here?'

'I put one in the wardrobe and one on the shelf, so Carol could see it, each time she came in. She didn't dare keep them at home with Scotty, she'd have had no reason to have such a thing.' She paused, looked sad.

'I've no idea where the other one went. It wasn't in my carpet bag, the last time I looked.'

It's in a trunk, Miranda thought, *or maybe it's now on Percy's shelf. Or, much more likely, in the bin.* She looked at her ma and frowned, thinking.

'You said the room was really grim, that means they were poor, very poor. But you stole a pair of boots from the girl, maybe the only boots she had. How could you do that, even for Carol?'

'I replaced the girl's boots with a brand new pair, that's why I went back to the room again. I took the replacements from Matt's stock.'

And so the theft of the shoes was born.

'You shouldn't have done it, Ma,' said Miranda. 'They would have noticed the boots were different.'

'So what if they were, they were still brand new. They were much better made than the ones I'd taken.'

'But Ma, for God's sake, don't you see? Her parents would probably have sold those boots and spent the money on drink, most likely. That's what a lot of the families do, around here, anyway. You should have known that.'

'I only wanted to help Carol.'

'By doing her daughter out of boots.' Miranda dropped the boot on a stool. She could hardly bear to look at it now.

Miranda was finding it hard to settle, her mind was reeling with revelations. Reg and Cath weren't working for once, which was why she was here, in the middle of the day; the pub was quiet which made it seem pointless. Until Ben turned up around half past one.

'Well what a surprise,' Miranda told him. 'I don't suppose you've come to see me?'

'I have in a way.' He looked embarrassed. 'How does a man get a pint around here?'

'Try asking,' she said, 'it often works.' She quickly drew him a pint of ale.

'I've been thinking about the other business.' Ben gave her a look, while knocking back ale. 'My, that's a good pint.'

'We aim to please in the Keepsake Arms. The other business, *literally?*'

'That's right,' said Ben. 'I've been thinking it's time I gave it up.'

'Really?' she said, not daring to hope. She doubted he'd

mean it this time tomorrow. 'So what have you got up your sleeve instead?'

'Not a lot, that's the trouble. I knew it was wrong, but the profits were far too good to refuse. But when the stock started going missing, I realised that this was a wake up call. And then we moved the goods from the church, but I'm still concerned that someone might talk. Not that I've said as much to Wetherby, I don't think he would want me to quit.'

'Of course he wouldn't,' Miranda said. 'He likes to have someone to share the risk. The vicar's not going to do that for him. Especially now the church isn't used.' She leant across the bar towards him. 'You know you're making the right decision.' She gave his arm a friendly squeeze.

'Squeeze me again and I'll know for sure.'

'Maybe, later,' Miranda told him. 'I ought to thank you properly for this. But now I've got to work, more's the pity.' She turned away, to serve a pint. but also to hide a beaming smile. The day was getting better at last.

By early evening, Miranda was shattered.

'I think you'd better skip tonight,' her mother insisted when she came down later. 'Thomas and Steve and I can manage. You look as if you could do with the rest.'

'Fine,' said Miranda, 'I'm not going to argue, especially as I'm on earlies tomorrow. But I need to have a word with Thomas. Alone, if I may.' Her mother nodded and left the room. She heard her walking towards the bar. Thank God, for once, she hadn't asked why.

'Tom,' she said, 'I've something to give you.' She felt in her pocket and brought out the beads. 'This should be yours, it belonged to Louise.'

Tom blinked and stared at the necklace. 'This is the one she said she'd give me. Where did you get it? How did you get it?'

'Never you mind, it's not important. All I know is, she needed the money for going away and sold the necklace, to buy some new clothes. Now I've got it, and it's yours to keep. I know she meant you to have it, Tom.'

Tom took the necklace and stared at the beads, his dark eyes glowing, his face a big grin. 'Yes, this is hers, I can't believe it. So, do you know where Louise is now?'

'No, I don't, and the person who gave me the beads doesn't either. I've already asked, you can trust me on that.'

'And you really can't tell me who that is?'

'No,' said Miranda, 'but believe me, Tom, they don't know anything, nothing at all.' *And I hope to God that's really true.*

'Here, have it back,' said Tom, sadly.

'What?' said Miranda, pushing it away. 'It's yours, you fool, she wanted you to have it. That's why I went to the trouble of getting it.'

'Yes, I know, and I'm glad you did, but it's best you keep it, on loan if you like. I can't take it home, not at the moment, not with the move and our stuff all over. Such as we have.' He made a face and Miranda sighed. She took the necklace.

'Don't you fret about that, Tom, something might change, who knows what might happen. But of course I'll keep it, I'll wear it for you.' She slipped the beads around her neck.

'Thanks, Miranda,' Tom said grinning. 'You're a mate, and a good one, and I'm really grateful.'

'I know,' said Miranda, smiling at Thomas. But inside, the anxiety ate at her heart.

90

Now – Aleph

'Have you talked to Cressida yet?' Guinevere asked me, the next time we met. We were taking a break from moving the freezer.

'I'm just waiting to find the right moment.'

'Sometimes that moment never arrives. Sometimes you have to make it yourself. That's quite a substantial trapdoor, Aleph.'

'But easy to open, all the same.' I looked at Ginny. 'I don't think this is a good idea.'

'You're just scared,' Guinevere said. She was right, I was. Of telling Cressida.

I stared at Ginny, who stared right back; two immovable, stubborn objects. Along with a third, the upright freezer, which was already standing against the wall. I lifted the trapdoor and peered down.

On my last visit, I hadn't been worried, the cellar had been just a cellar back then. But that was before I knew about the body. 'Be my guest,' I said to Ginny who grinned and grabbed the torch and went down.

Intrepid journalist strikes again, I said to myself. I thought, vaguely, about closing the trapdoor and shutting her down there, but dismissed the idea almost at once. The plan had a certain symmetry to it.

Dead woman's great niece trapped in cellar where body was found.

I followed her down the rickety steps.

'There's not a lot to see down here,' Guinevere commented.

'And even less than the first time I visited. At least there was a boot, back then.' I pointed up at the empty shelf.

Guinevere nodded.

'Did you bring the recorder with you?'

'I thought we should have a look round first. Didn't want to scare them all away.'

Guinevere frowned in the eerie light. She thought I wasn't being suitably serious. I was trying to lighten the mood. I was dreading opening the cupboard door. And going beyond it.

'You know I barely lived in this house, unlike my sister?'

'Was that because of the body?' I asked.

'Presumably,' said Ginny, shrugging. 'I know we moved out fairly soon after, and we two kids were sent off to school. I went later, because of my age. My parents rented the Old Schoolhouse out. But when we'd grown up and Father had died, my mother came back, she liked this house best, and always had done, despite what had happened. The ghosts didn't bother her, real or imagined.'

'Why did she leave the house to your sister?'

'She left a house to each of us and Marianne always liked this place, just like my mother had. Not that she came to visit her much and neither did I; we should have done more.' Ginny looked sad. We stared at the cupboard I'd opened previously.

'Mother implied that the tunnel began behind that cupboard. That's where they found her, not in the cellar.'

'It's still too close to home for me.'

'Ha!' said Ginny, grinning broadly. I bit the bullet and opened the cupboard.

'Clara insisted it wasn't her sister,' Guinevere told me, dunking her biscuit in her tea. She poured us both another mug. We were back upstairs and having a break, finding the courage to get on with the job.

'I thought it was fairly conclusive,' I said.

'Not by today's standards it wasn't. There was no DNA and the parents were dead and the body had rotted down to the bones and a few scraps of clothing. Some of the characteristics fitted, the gender for one. But nobody proved it was Mary-Ann. Not to Clara.'

'So Clara Parks was still alive?'

'Oh yes,' said Ginny, 'she was seventy-eight. Clara was bright, or so I was told. After her sister, Mary-Ann vanished and the parents died, Clara went abroad to work, and then she became a single mum. Later, her son came over to England, met his wife and bought the house. But Clara never came back, ever.'

'Not even when Mary-Ann's body was found?'

'She was far too old, or so she said. The details were passed across to the States, to see if she thought the woman was her sister. But she swore till she died that it wasn't Mary-Ann.'

'Why was that?' I said, curious.

'Because of the necklace they found with the body.' Ginny stared at the biscuits, wistfully.

'For God's sake, Guinevere, just have another,' I said, exasperated.

'I can't, I'm afraid, I'm on a diet.' Guinevere looked like she'd lost a fortune.

'So that explains why you're so grumpy.' Guinevere gave me a filthy look.

'The police showed Clara a photo of the necklace, but she said she'd never seen it before. She said Mary-Ann wouldn't wear such a thing.'

'I presume they didn't believe her, though?'

'You're right, they didn't. They'd found some people who'd known Mary-Ann and two of those people remembered the necklace. They also remembered Mary-Ann wearing it, not long before she disappeared. The police thought Clara wouldn't face the truth, that her sister was dead and not coming back.'

'Did Clara ever change her mind?'

'No,' said Guinevere, 'she never did.' She paused, considering. 'My great-aunt thought the beads were too cheap.

"Common," she'd said, "as cheap as muck. My sister would never have worn such a thing.

"'The beads of a child,'" were the words she used.'

91

Then – Ben

Ben was putting the lid on a coffin, this one was empty. He tested the joints, they seemed to work. Then he heard a noise and looked around. Tanya Curtis was standing behind him, right by the door. Ben swore, but under his breath, and cursed himself for leaving it open. But that was how it normally was. He glanced at Tanya. 'Need some help?'

'I've come to make you a little proposal.' Tanya smiled and edged a bit closer and Ben stepped backwards, banging his thigh on the table leg. *Damn, that hurt.*

'If you want to sit down, there's a chair over there, I've not got long, I've got to go out.' He wiped his dusty hands on a cloth, he could hardly tell her to leave, right now, not before he'd heard her out. And saw if her words posed any threat. *I'll be damned if they will*, he said to himself. He smiled at the woman, she was a looker, right enough.

'I'll stand, thanks,' said Tanya, shortly, eyeing the coffin and moving away. 'About my proposal, it concerns your business.'

'The funeral business?' said Ben, slowly. He'd already guessed what Tanya meant.

'The removal business, shall we call it? I've learnt that you and a man called Eisen ply a trade in removing stock and selling it on. Valuable stock, or so I've been told.' She paused for a moment and Ben smiled.

'Wood,' he said, 'we've a trade in wood, and it isn't a secret, everybody knows it. There's a bloke I know who gets it cheap and Wetherby uses it in his workshop, not for the good stuff, but for training the lads. Some of it's spare and we sell that on, it's all above board and the school benefits.' He smiled at Tanya, feeling more confident.

'I'm not talking about the wood, this is what I'd call valuable stock, antiques, shall we say. You know what I mean, I've seen them, Ben.'

'Have you?' said Ben. 'Well, all *I'll* say is wherever you look you won't find any stock of mine, apart from the wood and that's legit. And also the bodies, but you know about those.' He stroked a coffin. Tanya paled.

'You've moved them out of the crypt, right enough. And into the tunnel, or so I'd imagine.'

Ben shook his head and sighed, heavily. 'So, you were the one who followed Miranda into the tunnel, locking me out of my own workshop. Breaking and entering, that's what *I'd* call it. Not to mention, probable theft. And now *you're* trying to threaten *me*.'

'No, not threaten, you've got it all wrong. I'm just suggesting a business arrangement, for keeping an eye out, for a small fee. I'd squash any rumours I hear about treasure, put people off, that sort of thing.' She smiled at Ben, a radiant smile that made her look lovely. Ben barely noticed.

'Go away Tanya, I haven't the time. The rumours you talk of would only be rumours started by you. I'm up to my eyes in dead bodies, I haven't got time for this sort of thing. Besides,' he paused, 'you've got no proof.'

'Ah, that's where you're wrong, I do have proof. Solid and shiny, that's my proof.' Tanya paused. 'I'm only after a little assistance, a regular fee to feed my nephew. A business expense, that's all it is. It's peanuts to you.' Ben leapt to his feet.

'There's *nothing* to link such goods to me. Get out of my workshop, now,' he said, 'and don't come back, if you know what's good for you.' He moved towards her and Tanya, alarmed, stepped out of the way.

'You haven't heard the last of this. I could go to the police with what I know.' Ben laughed, loudly.

'That's a joke if ever I heard one. We've only two men for

the whole of the Low, and one's an old soak, and the other's just old.' He grabbed Tanya's arm and shoved her carelessly out of the door.

'Nobody likes a snitch around here. Whatever you've got could have come from anywhere; you'll never prove I knew anything about it. So don't come back, I don't want to see you.' He slammed the door as she hurried away, barely noticing Carol Islip who'd just walked past on the other side.

Later that day, he was taking a drink at The Tavern with Miranda. She toyed with her glass and looked around.

'I feel disloyal sitting in here, instead of us drinking at home in the Keepsake. I shouldn't be propping up others' profits.'

'You wouldn't relax if you were back there. Besides, Miranda, *we* need to talk.' Ben gulped at his pint.

'Why, what's happened?'

'Curtis, that's what, she only tried to threaten me, she said she wanted a cut of the profits. From the church takings.' Miranda went pale.

'No, you're joking!'

'I wouldn't joke about something like that. Curtis followed you down the tunnel, that's what I reckon, and found the goods and thought she was onto a real winner, probably passing them on to a mate. Then we moved them, which must have annoyed her and now she thinks I owe her for that. A business arrangement, that's what she called it. So she can get rich, while all I get is to stay out of prison. I'll see her dead and in hell first.'

'Ben! Shh! You mustn't say that, at least not in here.' Miranda looked worried. 'She can't know much, it's all speculation, just ignore her. You didn't agree to pay her, I hope.'

'Of course I didn't, you stupid girl. But she does have some of the stock, she told me. It must have been Tanya who stole the goods.'

'And that's my fault, because I took Alice down the tunnel. Tanya must have followed us right to the end.' Ben shook his head.

'Never mind that, it's far too late for saying *I wish*. We just have to make sure nothing comes of it.'

'And how are we going to manage that?'

Ben looked thoughtful and leaned in closer. 'You know I said earlier we'd moved all the goods? Well, I've also told Wetherby I want out of the business, and he's not very happy, but I reckon I can live without his approval. So, I've been thinking, it's time I left Curdizan, time I moved on to someplace better. The Low isn't great, it's a dump, really, especially in summer, when the river and the middens stink to high heaven.'

Miranda said nothing and Ben carried on.

'I know I'm still young but I'm set in my trade and there'll always be somebody dying somewhere, but if I'm to leave, I could go on my own but I'd much rather take a good friend with me. A friend I can trust, who'll be loyal and true and who might someday be more than a friend. What do you say?' Miranda looked stunned.

'You mean me?'

'Who else would I mean? I'm certainly not talking about Tanya Curtis.' Miranda giggled.

'I'm only eighteen.'

'You told me once you'd be nineteen soon and you're already tied to a pub and a factory. Always someone else's skivvy, is that what you want for the rest of your life?'

'Of course not,' Miranda said, sounding sombre. Ben sat back.

'Well, I'm going to go, I've made up my mind and you can come too, if you want to join me, that's up to you. I know there are people you care about here, your ma and Tom and Mary-Ann Parks, but people move on, like Thomas will do, eventually, even if Carol and Scotty stay.' He paused grimly.

'You ought to get going while you can, Miranda. And I'm

the best offer you're going to get.'

'Ha!' said Miranda, standing up.

'Where are you going?' said Ben, alarmed.

'I'm going for a walk to think things through. I'd like to say yes to you right this minute, but you're asking a lot and I need to give it some serious thought. You're not going to leave before I've decided?'

'Not if you make your decision quickly. I want to go soon, now that I've made my mind up to leave.' Miranda nodded.

'I'll let you know soon, and that's a promise, but don't you dare leave the Low without me.' She smiled at Ben and he grinned at Miranda, watching her weave her way through the drinkers.

His smile soon faded, what he'd told Miranda wasn't the truth. He hadn't even talked to Wetherby yet, let alone told his mate he was leaving. He didn't like to think what Wetherby would say, when he finally found the courage.

92

Now – Aleph

Back in the cellar, inside the cupboard, the first thing we did was take out the shelves. The lighting was poor but we did have a torch, if not a very good one, the last one had died.

'Anyone would think you'd done this before.'

'I always wanted to be a ghost hunter, I grew up on things like Borley Rectory. I was only three when they found the body, I don't remember anything about it. But it grew over time like stories do and became a part of our family history. I wished I'd been the one to find her.'

'No, you don't,' I told her, firmly.

'Maybe not now, but I did back then, you know how kids are, they like ghoulish things. I always meant to follow it up, but life and work took over as usual.'

'So long as this isn't a quest for a story,' I said sharply.

'You're so untrusting, Mr Jones,' said Guinevere, smiling. 'Pass me the screwdriver.'

It didn't long to remove the shelves. I could see at a glance that the boarding behind was very flimsy, badly put up and of poor quality. Guinevere poked around for a gap. 'The best bet's here,' she said from the floor. 'There's a definite space, but I need to get a grip on this wood.'

The space was where I'd once noticed a draught, I remembered that now. It almost seemed like a different lifetime.

'There wouldn't have been this cupboard, then,' Ginny informed me. 'The door we came through would have led to the passage, but someone back then must have blocked the space off with a couple of planks, and then with boarding, and after that, shelves.'

How easy it was to disguise the past. And how easily undone.

'Got it!' said Guinevere, tugging hard and backing away from the wall, quickly. I stepped back too, to give her more room and suddenly there was a rending sound, like paper tearing, but ten times worse, the crumble of plaster, the clatter of nails, and a huge piece of boarding collapsed on the floor. Dust exploded into the room.

'Hell,' said Guinevere, gasping for breath. 'Hand me the torch again, please, Aleph.'

I did as she asked and stared at the gap she'd just uncovered. Sure enough, there was a passage, with a very low ceiling and smelling of mould. It looked uninviting.

'Time to put the kettle on,' I said, mildly.

'Time to investigate further,' said Ginny. We ventured slowly into the space.

Guinevere shone the torch down the passage, as far as it went, which wasn't that far. We investigated further, stumbling down the narrow tunnel until Guinevere spotted what looked like a door. 'This will lead to the tunnel proper.'

I had no reason to doubt her words. Surprisingly, the door was unlocked.

'This won't have been opened in sixty years,' she told me, triumphant.

'And maybe not now,' I said, hopefully. The door was proving a little resistant. We saw a gap at the top by the ceiling and lifted it over a pile of rubble. The air beyond was even more dank.

'I've had enough for the present,' I said.

'Curdizan Low's to the right,' said Ginny. She shone the torch on some steps to the left. 'These probably once went to Curdizan Church. Now, they go nowhere, the church is long gone. And the route to the abbey too, I suppose. Now, right is the only way out of the tunnel.'

'Or back,' I said, 'to the Old Schoolhouse. Where exactly was Mary-Ann found?'

'In the passage we've come through, probably right behind

the cupboard.'

I thought about that and it did make sense. People could use the school basement *and* the tunnel and no-one would know the body was there, just yards away. I shivered, suddenly. 'Do you want to go back to the house?'

We wandered back along the passage, even the cellar was preferable to this, a low-ceilinged space with a really dank smell. I couldn't wait to get back to the kitchen. Then, I stood on something.

'I hope that's not a bone I've stood on.'

'Ha!' said Ginny, and shone the beam of the torch on the culprit. She picked something up.

'What have you got?' I said, not bothered, already dreaming of cups of tea.

'It looks like Mary-Ann Parks' necklace.'

93

Then – Miranda

Miranda couldn't concentrate. She spilt two drinks and then short-changed the punter afterwards.

'Since when was this pub a posh hotel? I think you've charged me a bit too much.' Miranda sighed and gave him the cash.

Since she'd considered leaving the Low, the pub and its occupants seemed much nicer. The bar looked warm, instead of just tatty, her mother kind, instead of unfocused, and Tom the best worker they'd ever had.

I'll have to tell Tom, Miranda considered, *but no, that's no good, he'll have to come with us. He doesn't want to move elsewhere with his parents; and what about Ma?*

'How's the packing?' she'd asked Tom earlier.

'Oddly, enough, they've stopped for the moment,' Tom said, grinning. 'I didn't ask why, in case it reminded them to start up again.'

They've most likely lost their supply, thought Miranda, *now the stock's been moved somewhere else.* She smiled to herself. Then, later on, her ma came to see her.

'I'd like you to help in the parlour, Miranda. They're wanting somebody to play the piano.'

'You know how I hate them singing in there.' Miranda scowled and glared at her mother.

'Just do as you're told, for once, Miranda.' Her mother stopped as she turned away. 'What's that you're wearing round your neck?'

'It's a necklace, Ma, it belonged to Louise, she used to go to Thomas's school. It's Tom's necklace now, but I'm keeping it for him, just for the moment.'

'Louise used to go to Thomas's school?'

'That's what I said. She and Tom were once good friends, until she went away and never came back. A lovely girl, or so I've been told. But then, Tom's biased.'

'He would be,' said Hannah, 'though he won't know why.' She leant against the bar for strength. 'Louise is Carol's daughter, Miranda.'

94

Now – Aleph

I was sitting, holding the dirty necklace. It was old and broken, but despite all that I could see the beads were once turquoise, probably vibrant, now very scratched and mostly grey, but still, I thought, the very same. The one that Mary-Ann Parks had been wearing.

'I thought she'd had it around her neck, when she was found?'

'I believe she did.' Guinevere sipped her tea quietly.

'So, how did it end up in the passage? It should have been with the police records, or if not there, with the family.'

'We were the family, Aleph,' said Ginny. 'Her parents were dead, Clara was abroad, and she didn't believe the necklace was her sister's. She never believed it was Mary-Ann's.'

I'm going start drinking coffee, I thought. I needed the caffeine to keep me on track. Ginny went on.

'My guess is, Mother and Father kept it, and when they moved out, they left it there, in the passage, probably where the body was found. Like a kind of memorial.'

'Shouldn't they have left it in the grave?'

'That was the grave for many years, and no-one was sure the necklace was hers. Maybe my father believed his mother, or maybe he thought the necklace was jinxed, I've no idea.'

I swung the beads back and forth, slowly. 'I wonder if we dare move it now?'

'We already have,' said Ginny, wryly, 'like you removed the boot from the cellar.' Both of us stared at the shelf and the boot.

'I'll put the boot and the beads together,' I said, getting up. 'Clara called it a child's necklace.'

Guinevere watched as I draped the beads around the boot and I shivered suddenly, looking at Ginny to see if she felt it, the deepening chill that covered us up. As if a ghost had walked into the room. Her face was like stone. The telephone rang.

'Who could it be? It's very late.' Guinevere watched me pick up the phone.

'Cressida, what's happened? Is Alice okay?'

'Alice is fine. I just need to talk. There's something I need to tell you, now.'

'Right now, this minute?'

'Yes, just listen. All that stuff about coming to see you, so you could help Alice, that was a lie. Alice wouldn't talk, and I needed help, that was certainly true, but it wasn't the reason I came to see you. That was about Martha, she asked if I would tell you the truth, but even now, I still can't do it, even though she's leaving Leverhulme.' Cressida gave a strangled sob.

'Martha wants you to tell me what?' I could feel the pulse of sudden anxiety, I'd only ever known one Martha and that was back in the distant past, when I'd been happy, innocent, almost.

'It's about the accident, Daniel's death.'

So, I thought, *Cressida and Alice had both known Daniel, and Cressida, like Alice, had known who I was.* Why had she not said as much to me? Martha, I guessed, was the boy's mother. I'd only known them as Mr and Mrs. The room felt cold.

'I don't know a Martha,' I told Cressida.

'But you did do once.' She was right, I had.

So Daniel's mother *was* the Martha, I'd known back then. When Daniel had died I'd only been told the family name: Mr and Mrs L. Peters. Martha Peters could be the wife and the woman I'd known, now with a husband. And now I'd learnt I'd killed her son. The nightmare had turned into something worse. Then I saw Ginny standing beside me.

'Cressida, listen, you're not making sense. Please, just say it, just tell me the truth.'

'Open the envelopes, Aleph,' she said. 'Read the cards that Martha sent you, and then you'll know. I'm really sorry, believe me, I am, especially for my part in it all.' Then the phone went dead.

I toyed with the thought of ringing her back.

'Don't,' said Ginny, grabbing my arm, almost as if she'd read my mind. 'Put the phone down and do what she said. It's time you opened your post at last.'

95

Then – Carol

Carol wasn't pleased to see Tanya Curtis. Tanya's news that the stock had vanished had tarnished her dreams of a golden future. A move would be hard with no more proceeds, nothing to live on but two lousy jobs. One, uncertain. Carol sighed.

She'd been happy enough with what she'd got, until Tanya had shown her a little bit more, well maybe not happy, but almost content, when Matt was alive, but now he was dead and her dream was gone and life seemed drab, no, worse, almost dire. With no more cash, from shoes or silver. Somehow the future seemed even more grim. Then Tanya turned up on her doorstep again. Carol frowned.

'I hoped you wouldn't be at work just yet. Any chance of a cuppa, my love?'

'Sure,' said Carol, rather reluctant, knowing she owed the woman something. A lot, probably, the goods had brought in quite a bit of money, pity that most of that money had gone. If only she'd kept a little more back. She ushered Tanya into the house.

'That's a nice frock you're wearing, Tanya,' Carol observed, as she gestured the woman over to the table. 'I've always liked that very bright red.'

'I got it in the jumble,' Tanya said, grinning. 'It's satin too, and had a big tear, but I soon fixed that, and now it's fine, almost good enough for best. A bit posh for everyday, but what the hell, I wear what I like.' She knocked back her tea.

'Is there anymore news on the missing stock?' Tanya shook her head, slowly.

'I asked a few questions, but nobody's telling me where it's gone, in fact the source denied all knowledge. I reckon we've come to the end of that windfall.'

'A pretty short windfall,' Carol said, sadly.

'I take it you've used up most of the profits?'

'All of the profits,' Carol informed her. 'You know what Scotty's like with his cash, it's here today and gone tomorrow. He's spent it all on his new business. A cart and some stock and then renting a shed. And now we can't afford to move.'

'Surely there must be something left?'

'No there isn't,' said Carol bristling, 'and even if there was, what's it to you? We made a deal, and I kept my part of the bargain, Tanya and paid what I owed.'

'But that was based on there being more stock, and more cash coming up right behind. I reckon I gave you the stuff too cheap, I reckon you probably owe me something.'

'Now wait a minute,' said Carol, sharply, getting to her feet and folding her arms. 'We made an arrangement fair and square. It's not my fault that you've lost your stock, ahead of your plan, Tanya Curtis.' She paused, thinking. 'You said the goods were gone from the church. I bet you went to see your source, and I'll bet you tried to twist the knife. And he's called your bluff, whoever he is, and now you're stuck, without any left.'

'You're wrong,' said Tanya, getting up. 'I've still got some stock and that means proof. I'll see that man in jail, I will, if he doesn't come up with a little more cash.'

'You're *so* stupid,' Carol laughed. 'You might have some stock, but it only proves *you* took the goods, and not that the bloke was involved at all. You silly cow.'

Tanya went as red as her dress, her face was like thunder, she was seething with rage. She leant forward and pushed Carol.

'You're talking rubbish. I've enough on you to ruin your life. And don't you forget it.'

'Oh, you have, have you Miss? Well, I'll tell you, you don't push me, *nobody* pushes Carol Islip.' Carol stepped forward and shoved Tanya, not very hard, but enough to make her stumble backwards, towards the fireplace. Tanya looked livid.

'Why don't we start with Matt McCarthy and then we'll move on to his trunk of shoes. Or should I say, trunks? I reckon that's quite enough trouble to begin with, especially when Scotty hears the news.'

'How dare you come into my home and threaten me! After I've fenced your dirty goods for you, given you cash and tea as well. You're an evil cow, that's what you are.' She jabbed Tanya hard in the chest and Tanya stepped back, getting closer to the fire.

'Matt's gone now and so have the shoes, so you try proving anything, lady. Scotty can be trouble like any bloke, but he'll stick with me in the end, you'll see, and you'll be dust underneath my feet. You might even end up in the river, if you're not careful, Scotty knows a bloke who isn't that nice. And, at least *I've* got a man of my own.'

'You call that worm of a bloke a man? But even a worm will turn in the end, he might put up with all your whoring but he won't put up with a bastard child. I guess that's why you gave her away.'

'You what?' said Carol, feeling the colour leave her face.

'I'm talking about your precious daughter, dumped and abandoned to save your marriage. A marriage that wasn't worth saving anyway. I know all about it, and so will Scotty, before I'm finished with you, Missus. Unless you'd like to come to terms.'

'You know all about my little girl? You're going to tell Scotty what I did? Like hell you will, I'll kill you first.' Carol put her hands around Tanya's neck. The women were right by the fireplace.

'Let go, you fool,' croaked Tanya, angry, beating at Carol's arms with her own, but Carol held on, she was all fired up and meant to be tough and teach Tanya a lesson.

'You won't be coming back here again.'

Tanya would have answered Carol, but the effort of

speaking was now beyond her. She struggled as hard as she could to get free, eventually shoving Carol away. As Carol released her, thinking she'd made her point at last, Tanya's foot twisted, slipped on the hearth and she fell to the floor with a noisy yell, banging her head on the fireplace. Carol watched, in slow motion, it was only seconds but it felt like minutes as the fight that had started as lively banter ended in death. She stared at Tanya's lifeless form. Carol screamed.

'No,' she said, and knelt on the ground.

Tanya's face was contorted with something, maybe surprise, or maybe just shock. The look was permanent.

Carol reached out and touched Tanya's face. Her face was still warm, but the body felt slack and drained of life, a check of her pulse proved it was so. Carol tensed and turned her over, finding the courage from deep within her, probably from working at Pickart's Grove, in the distant past. She'd started in the laundry at just fourteen. Pickart's was the local lunatic asylum.

'No,' she said, for the final time as a trickle of blood from Tanya's head dripped onto the hearth and pooled by the edge. 'You can't be dead, I won't believe it.' For probably the very first time in her life, Carol wanted Scotty.

Scotty and Carol stared at Tanya.

'So this is where it happened, is it?' Scotty had just got home from work.

'No, I've just dragged her over to the fire, because she was cold.' Carol had lived a long few hours, waiting for Scotty, unable to leave the house for a moment, just in case a neighbour dropped by. Nobody locked their doors around here. 'What are we going to do, now, Scotty?'

'Get rid of the body, that's what we'll do. And good riddance too, that's what I'm thinking.'

'You've changed your tune in a week,' said Carol, who was doing her best not to break down, she hadn't meant to kill Tanya, whatever she'd said to the woman at the time. 'You thought she was great when she brought us the goods.'

'Well, now she's just a source of trouble, this is all your fault, yours and hers, we were fine before you both got greedy.'

Oh no we weren't, said Carol to herself. *You've always drank our money away, and you were the one who spent our profits on a brand new business.* She said nothing, she hated Scotty in moods like this. And this was before he'd taken a drop. She wondered if Scotty had slept with Tanya, he might have done, he looked distressed and she wouldn't put such behaviour past him. But, even if he had, he'd stick by her. Just like she'd always stuck by him.

'I know the perfect place to put her, if you'll give me a hand with the body Carol, later today, when it gets dark. I'll need to bring home some tools from work.' Carol nodded, she wouldn't tell him the whole story, about her daughter, there was no point stirring up trouble now, now that Tanya was dead and gone.

She glanced at Tanya's body again, feeling relief that the woman was silenced, sorry yes, but still relieved. Carol listened to Scotty's words.

'When this is all sorted, we'll pack up our stuff, the stuff that's not done, and leave straight away, as soon as we can. I've still got some cash put by from the sale, and even some stock, though not very much. I knew it would come in useful sometime, and not just for drink.' He grinned at his wife who blinked in surprise.

For once Scotty Islip had managed to surprise her.

96

Now – Aleph

The next morning, I opened the door and Cressida was there, standing on the doorstep. She looked terrible. I ushered her in and watched her wander into the kitchen, joining Guinevere at the table. Neither woman looked happy at that.

'I gather you haven't met before?'

'Not as such,' said Cressida stiffly. 'But I guess she knows the whole story.'

'I certainly do,' said Guinevere gamely. *I'm not leaving,* is what she meant. Cressida ignored her.

'I'm sorry about last night,' she said. 'I thought I ought to be here in person. In case you decide to open your post.'

I shook my head and smiled sadly. 'I'm afraid you've left it too late for that. You should have come round yesterday evening.' There, on the table, were the opened envelopes.

Late last night, Ginny and I had sat at the table, staring at the unopened envelopes, the two I had opened sitting there mocking. I picked up the third.

'Just open it, Aleph,' Guinevere said. I tore at the paper.

More cream card and another small flower embossed on the right. The same familiar word, MURDERER. It still had the power to shock and stun me, make me believe it couldn't be me. Even despite expecting to see it. *The power of the printed word,* I thought.

The third word didn't make sense on its own. It left me just as unenlightened. Ginny and I stared at the card.

HE WAS YOUR

what?

Nemesis, fate, victim, sentence. All of those probably. And

I still didn't understand the message.

From a distance, far away, I knew that Ginny was holding my arm, patting my hand, putting her arm around my shoulder. It felt like nothing, the world was nothing, all of my life had shrunk into this. Darkness and fear.

'Open the envelope, Aleph,' she whispered. So, I did what she said.

Cressida wasn't making much sense. She was blathering on about her and Martha, about how our meetings, hers and mine, had all been planned, all of it planned, apart from Alice not wanting to talk, but how, now, finally, she'd seen the light, refused to cooperate, told Martha no. Since she'd discovered she'd played a part too.

'It wasn't your fault,' I said, coolly.

'That's not how it feels,' Cressida said. 'I understand now, that by lying and stringing you along like I did, I was being very cruel, thoughtlessly cruel, and I'm sorry for that.'

Now you know how I feel, I thought. But I envied her position, nevertheless. 'At least you weren't driving the car,' I said.

'Daniel's death was an accident. Martha is angry and rightly so, but it wasn't your fault, it was one of those terrible things that happen. I'm sorry she dragged me into this. I shouldn't have done it.'

I looked across the table at Cressida. Where was the woman I thought I'd known, a woman I'd laughed with, eaten with, talked to, a woman whose daughter I'd grown to love? A woman whose unknown act I'd uncovered. I felt nothing.

She wants absolution, I thought, sadly, *she wants forgiveness and I can't give it, because that would mean the words don't count.* The four little words on Martha's cards. They did count, terribly.

The words she sent which ripped out my heart.

For once, Ginny had sat there silent, the intrepid reporter without any words. I'd traced my finger around each card, seeing the letters, spelling the words and taking them in.

Knowing I'd never feel the same. Remembering thinking, ages ago, that nothing was worse than killing a child, that whatever they said, it couldn't be worse. I had been wrong. Four little words that meant everything.

HE WAS YOUR SON

97

Then – Miranda

She'd given the suggestion considerable thought and time had passed, but not too much, so when she woke up, she'd skipped her job along with her breakfast and hurried down Blackberry Close to see Ben. But his door was shut and the place had a silent, empty air which wasn't typical. *Hell,* thought Miranda, *perhaps I'm too late.* She felt gutted.

'Ben,' she hollered, banging on the door. 'Are you in there?'

Cath walked past on her way to the pub and nodded to Miranda. 'You'll have to shout a bit louder, love. He's as deaf as a post when's he's making those things, I sometimes think he climbs inside them and has a quick kip.' She winked at Miranda who smiled back, feebly, feeling guilty. Reg and Cath were related to Ben but she doubted he'd told them about his plans. She was just deciding whether to leave, when the door opened, slightly and Ben peered out.

'Quick! Inside, and don't argue.'

Miranda, puzzled, did as he said and was soon standing inside the workshop. The room was pitch black, there were no windows. Her eyes adjusted, very slowly.

'I'm going to put the lamp on now, but you mustn't scream, promise you won't.'

'Alright,' said Miranda. 'But why should I scream?'

The lamp flickered on, and with it came light, shapes emerged, familiar sights, the stacks of wood and the coffin lids, the long worn workbench and the door to the room which led to the tunnel. Ben reached out and gripped her arm. What was the matter?

'Now through here.' He led her slowly through the door,

to the room beyond, gripping the lamp with his other hand. 'Look at the floor.'

She did as he said, and would have screamed but he'd covered her mouth, almost stopped her breathing properly. Ben let go. 'Oh my God.'

'It's Tanya Curtis.'

'I can see that, Ben. Is she dead?'

'Yes,' said Ben, 'and from what I've been able to see of her head, she's had some kind of fracture, probably from a fall, or perhaps from being hit on the head very hard.' He looked at Miranda.

'It wasn't you?' said Miranda, faintly. The room retreated out of focus.

'Of course it wasn't, you stupid girl. I arrived this morning, a short while ago, and found her here, dead on my floor. God knows how he got her in here.'

'He?' said Miranda. 'Who's this he?'

'The man who killed her or moved her body, I doubt a woman could have done it alone. Are you sure you're feeling alright, Miranda?'

'It's just the shock of seeing her there. And she's wearing my best red dress. My mother told me she'd given it to the jumble.'

'I thought it looked a little familiar. Curtis worked for the church as a cleaner. She probably nicked the dress from the box, along with my silver, the thieving cow.' Miranda said nothing. 'You do believe I didn't do it?'

'Of course I do.' Her voice was strong and as clear as a bell. *But was she telling the truth?* she wondered. He had a good motive, right enough. 'How did the killer get in here?'

'I've no idea. But whoever did it had a key, or knew a bit about picking locks. Of course, the spares are hanging up there. Whoever broke in before might have had them. I never heard a single thing. I was sleeping upstairs the whole damn night.'

'Good God,' said Miranda, feeling quite ill. Ben just sighed.

'I need your help to move the body.'

'Aren't we going to tell the police?'

'I'd have to explain I moved her in here. I found her in the main workroom. Then after that, the questions would start, it would all come out, the thefts, the shoes, your mother and Carol. Do you want that?'

'No, of course I don't. But that's the price of doing bad things, you sometimes get caught. And now it's gone and led to this.'

'We don't know that, we don't why she ended up here. I know that selling that stuff wasn't right, but it's over now, for good, I promise. I've talked to Wetherby, he's agreed, we're all leaving, him and me and Mary-Ann, and you as well, if you want to come with us. You will, won't you?'

'Mary-Ann too?' said Miranda, speechless. 'The vicar's daughter is running away?'

'She's going to marry Wetherby, Miranda. It's what she wants, not a snow-white life as the vicar's daughter, sorting the jumble and giving out soup in the school basement.'

'It's a kitchen,' Miranda said, rather primly.

'It's a basement,' said Ben, 'or rather, a cellar, and Mary-Ann wants something better than that. A life that's a little bit more exciting. She'll certainly get that with Wetherby Eisen. So what's it to be?'

Moving the body took quite some time. Ben had acquired an old hand cart which Eisen had used for shifting wood. He'd already carried it into the tunnel. Getting Tanya herself down the steps to the tunnel proved a little bit harder.

'I think I can carry her down myself, if you can help me balance her first. Manoeuvre her onto my right shoulder.'

'If I must,' said Miranda, gritting her teeth, her hands were shaking, she was sick with nerves. 'But I can't be sure I won't throw up.'

'You'll be fine,' said Ben and he smiled with approval.

'If you'd like to take her head for now. Yeah, great, that's good, now just let go.' Miranda did.

Miranda stared in horror at her hands. 'Oh, God,' she said, 'I'm covered in blood.'

'That's down to me, I'm afraid,' said Ben. 'The wound had dried, but dragging her along the floor must have opened it.' He put Tanya's body on the ground again, ripping a piece off the hem of the dress. Miranda's old dress. It tore easily.

'Here, wipe your hands on this for now.' He tore off some more and wiped the back of Tanya's skull. 'There, that should do it.' Then he took the bloodied cloth off Miranda and dropped both pieces on the floor, kicking them over to the corner of the room. 'I'll make it up to you, later, Miranda. We weren't the ones who did this, remember.'

But it all began because of the thefts. And can I be sure you're telling the truth? She followed him carefully down the steps, once he was carrying Tanya again. For such a young woman, and as thin as she was, she seemed very heavy.

Miranda was trying not to burst into tears. They pushed the cart along the tunnel, Ben at the front, and Miranda behind, making their way towards the church. She thought about when they'd done this before, the time with Tom and the trunks of shoes, and it seemed so innocent, how had they got to where they were now?

Ben stopped when they finally reached the church.

'We're going to leave her in the passage, the one between the school and this tunnel. And before you ask, I've moved the shoes. I had to dump the rest, I'm afraid. The trunks are in the basement now, no-one will care, they're completely empty. And I'll fix the door from each of the exits so no-one will know that Tanya's in there.'

'But the door from the basement leads straight to the passage.'

'Not by the end of this evening it won't. Wetherby's going to put a false wall in, even some shelves to make it authentic. No-one will know there's anything there. Or at least, not until we're all long gone.'

'You've told Eisen about the body!'

'I had to, Miranda, I had to be sure nobody would find her. That way we know we'll be safe for a while.'

'How do you know he didn't kill her?'

'I don't Miranda, I took it on trust. That's what you do for friends, I reckon.' Miranda said nothing.

The next few minutes were spent in silence, easing the body into the passage. The narrowness made it even more difficult and the lamp kept flickering and almost went out. Miranda swallowed and bit her lip. She thought how much lighter the shoes had been.

'I think that's as good as it gets, right now.' Ben got to his feet, as much as he could in the very low tunnel. 'This throw I've brought will do to cover her.' Miranda said nothing and Ben frowned.

'Don't start losing your nerve, now, Miranda. You know I'd bring her back if I could.'

But would you, I wonder? Miranda considered. She unfastened the necklace from around her neck.

'What are you doing?' said Ben, curious.

'I'm giving her a gift, it just feels right.' She slipped the beads around Tanya's neck. 'We might not be able to bury her properly but at least we've shown her some respect. Louise won't miss it.'

'Who's Louise?' asked Ben, puzzled, but Miranda shook her head and sighed.

'Never mind, that, I'll tell you sometime. Now, can we go?'

They walked back up the tunnel slowly, each of them thinking separate thoughts. Then Ben spoke.

'We're meeting on Blackberry Close tonight, at the church near mine, around about midnight. You can come over after your shift, if you're coming. But if you are, don't bring much with you.'

'Won't you collect me?' Miranda faltered.

'I can't, it's too risky.' He pulled her towards him. 'I hope you'll come with us, I want you beside me. Especially now you've proved your worth.' He grinned at Miranda in the flickering light. 'But a choice like this, it has to be yours, you're giving up all the things you know, your home, your life, for a different future. But, in exchange,' he paused and grinned, 'you'd be getting an adventure.'

And I'd get you, Miranda thought. *But what about her mother and Thomas?* 'What about Thomas?' she said to Ben.

'You know we can't take him,' Ben insisted, 'much as I like him. He's only a lad, and taking a boy would be too much trouble. We need to be free to do as we please, not always looking over our shoulder.'

'We might be doing that anyway,' Miranda told him, thinking of Tanya.

'We're not taking Tom,' Ben repeated.

'Where are we going?' Miranda asked, not understanding she'd made up her mind.

'I'm not that sure that it matters, to be honest, so long as we're well away from here. Wetherby might have thought of somewhere.'

I know somewhere, Miranda thought, smiling inside as she thought it through. *I know a place where we'll never be found.*

98

Now – Aleph

'I want Martha's address,' I said. 'I need to talk this over with her.'

'Martha and Len are leaving Leverhulme. Len's the man she married, afterwards. I doubt they'd be there, even if I was to give you the address. It's only rented, a temporary place.'

'I suppose you won't tell me where they're going?' I couldn't help the bitter tone.

'I asked Martha not to tell me. Just in case you asked me that.' Cressida sounded rather regretful.

'I still need her previous address.'

'I thought you'd already written to her once.'

'I did, just after Daniel died. But that was to a c/o address and according to you they've moved since then. And, I didn't recognise the name.'

'No, you wouldn't have, Martha was married to Len by then.'

'I'll give you the address,' said Ginny, suddenly. I watched her writing it down carefully.

'Did you know who he was?' I said. 'Did you know that Daniel was mine?'

'No,' said Ginny. 'I swear I didn't.' She looked unhappy. Cressida sat there, stony-faced.

'I'm sorry,' she said. 'I really am.'

'Sure,' I said. 'Now that you know what it's like to feel guilty.' The time for saying sorry had passed. I grabbed my jacket and made for the hall.

'Where are you going?' said Cressida, sharply.

'I'm going to find my son's mother. Remember to close the door when you leave.'

She was right of course, the house was empty, almost abandoned. I walked right up to it, knocked on the door, but no-one was there, the house didn't speak. Martha and I barely knew each other, we'd had a brief fling, years ago, before I met Gerry. A one night stand that had turned into a week's celebration and then, after that, there was nothing but death. A lifetime's tragedy for all concerned. I kicked at a stone.

I'd liked Martha, she was warm, effervescent, the life and soul, wherever she went, but I always felt she was holding back, and now I knew that was just how she was. After our week of love and fun, she announced one night she'd met someone else, someone more suitable, more *appropriate*. I guess that was Len. She never wrote later and said she was pregnant, how did I even know he was mine? But somehow, I did.

What a terrible thing.

The bungalow was modern and smart, it was just like all the others in the street and exactly the right kind of house for Martha, superficial and easy to care for. I wondered, briefly, if Len was like that. The neighbours next door couldn't say where she'd gone, or even if she'd gone for good. I made my way down the path to the back and saw a low gate, it was through such a gate that the boy had escaped, my son, Daniel. It was still so hard to believe it was true.

If only Cressida hadn't left the latch off. But I was the one who had driven the car.

By the time I got home, it was early evening and the house was empty, the guests had all gone. I sat alone at the kitchen table and stared at the shoe on the mantelpiece. A mystery solved and one more to go. Who was Mary-Ann Park's killer? I couldn't have cared less.

Then I heard the doorbell ring. I'd finally managed to fix the chime, and Alice, it seemed, intended to use it. My heart sank as I ushered her in, gesturing towards the living room, just for a change. Alice went in and straight to the window, peering out into the street beyond.

'I'm not stopping,' Alice told me. 'I've come to tell you goodbye, actually.' Her voice wobbled.

'Goodbye?' I questioned, disbelieving. I'd only just got to know Alice, got to like her, thought of her as a kind of daughter. *A replacement for my missing boy.* And now Cressida was taking her away. Well that was only to be expected.

'Mum insisted I wasn't to visit you, but that's not the reason I'm saying goodbye.' She left the window and came to sit down. I sat down too, in a chair facing her.

'It's because of what I did, you see. I never realised Danny was yours.'

'Neither did I,' I said, sadly.

'Danny and I used to play together, I liked him a lot, even though he was so much younger. I thought of him as a younger brother, that's why, when it happened, I just couldn't speak.'

I nodded, slowly, trying to smile. She didn't smile back.

'On that Sunday, when I skipped Annerley's, I wasn't that far from Martha's house when I spotted Danny across the road.' She faltered, stopped and I nodded, encouraging. 'Before I saw you.

'I waved to Danny, surprised he was out and gestured to him to cross the street. I thought we could walk back to Martha's together. Danny always did what I told him to do, I wish now he hadn't. I wish I had crossed the road to him.

'Then, well, you know what happened. He stepped off the pavement and into the road, between the parked cars where you couldn't see him. And then he started running towards me. There was nothing I could do, it was over before I'd realised what happened. I don't suppose you remember I screamed?'

'No,' I said. I didn't even remember the accident.

'I saw that man, the elderly one, but I'm almost certain he didn't see me. Then there was you, and him and the rest and the sirens started, they sounded like screaming, the screams in my head that just wouldn't stop, so I turned around and ran away from it all, leaving Danny alone in the road. I was a coward.' She looked at me.

'So I won't be coming to see you again. Now that I know who Danny was.' Her voice trembled.

Then Alice jumped up and ran for the door, brushing the tears from her face as she ran.

'Alice, please wait, it wasn't your fault, we need to sit down and talk this over. I was the one who was driving the car. Wait, Alice, please.'

I don't know if she didn't hear, or simply chose to ignore my words, but whichever it was she didn't stop. I chased her down the steps to the street and round the corner to Scriveners Road. The street was crowded with eager tourists, blocking my way at every turn. I knew I'd never find her now.

99

Then – Miranda

It was cold by the church, but Miranda was more than frozen inside, and that was what counted, the chill in her heart. She buried her face in Ben's jacket. That way she wouldn't have to look at his workshop. Miranda shivered.

'The others should be here about now, I reckon.'

'I couldn't care less,' Miranda told him. 'I don't think I care about anything now.'

'You will,' said Ben, 'in time, you'll forget. It'll dull, you'll see.' She shrugged, indifferent.

The church in Curdizan Low was bleak, it was hardly used, and so unlike the vibrant abbey or even solid Curdizan Church. Miranda wondered if they were coming.

'This is where we're supposed to be meeting?' Miranda felt very uncomfortable here, so close to what they'd recently done. She clutched her bag of clothes to her chest.

'It is,' said Ben. 'But about this place you say you've chosen, are you sure we'll never be found?'

'Oh yes,' said Miranda. 'But I'm not that sure, if they don't turn up.'

Ben flashed her a grin at her impatience, and Miranda's heart lifted. *There's hope,* she thought, *and maybe a future, so long as I know he didn't do it. I won't believe it.*

Then she saw Eisen emerge from the night.

What if it's Wetherby Eisen instead? All the doubts that besieged her came back with a vengeance. *Is this a murderer's friend I'm with?*

Mary-Ann, her own friend, appeared by the hedge, she was looking very thoughtful, but was well wrapped up. The two girls hugged and set off immediately, walking up Croston, arm in arm. They were careful to keep to the side of the road.

When they all finally reached the alley, Miranda guided them through from the front, with Wetherby Eisen walking at the back, keeping a look out. As the passageway neared its end, she stopped briefly, catching a glimpse of Curdizan courtyard. *Yes,* she thought, *the intent worked. This is the place.* Miranda smiled slowly. Then she saw Alice.

She leant back and gestured to Ben, getting her friend to bring them all closer. 'Have a quick look and see what you think.' She'd primed Ben, she knew she could trust him to do the right thing. While they were looking she gestured to Alice.

Alice came closer, into the passage. They huddled together in a tiny corner. Miranda struggled to open her bag.

'I'm so pleased to see you Alice. I didn't have time to talk to Tom. Would you be able to give him a message?'

'Yes,' said Alice, sounding fed up. Miranda looked at the girl more closely. Her face was swollen, with crying probably, and her hair was a mess, gone was the little princess she'd met. *She's sad,* thought Miranda, *we're all very sad.* She took the single boot from her bag.

'I'd like you to give this boot to Thomas. It's very important you do what I ask. I know I can trust you to do that, can't I?'

The girl didn't speak but she managed to nod and Miranda felt guilty for not asking questions. But she didn't have time to deal with the girl.

'Tell him the boot belongs to Louise. She's a friend like you, *and* also his sister although Tom doesn't know that, you'll have to tell him. Remind him she left of her own accord and that means she will probably come back, whenever she's ready.' Miranda didn't know if the last bit was true, but Tom needed hope, especially now that she and Ben were leaving. She paused, briefly.

'Tell him I'm sorry about the necklace, I felt I had to leave it for Tanya. I couldn't leave the woman with nothing. He might not understand that bit, but that doesn't matter, just tell him, anyway. And last of all, please tell him I'm safe and alive not dead, I've just gone away, to a different place. That he'll always be in my heart, forever. You will remember to tell him that, won't you?'

'Of course,' said Alice, 'I'm not stupid.' She took the boot. 'We've got a boot like this,' she said. 'Or Aleph has.' She looked downcast.

'I hid the other in a trunk off the tunnel. Maybe it's yours.' Alice smiled.

'Tom admired you, looked up to you, really. And he called you a friend; a mate's what he said, more than once.'

'We were,' said Miranda, 'and we always will be, like I told you. I have to go, now.'

She beckoned to the others and smiled at Alice, and then she walked past her, afraid she might cry, and indeed, a tear dripped down one cheek, but she brushed it away and emerged from the passage onto the street and into the start of a brand new life. A brand new, twenty-first century life. The others were standing together, amazed.

'You're sure they won't find us here?' said Wetherby.

Miranda shook her head and smiled. 'It's what you might call a new beginning.'

100

Then – Thomas

It wasn't until I arrived at the pub, the next evening, that I understood Miranda's behaviour. She had been restless the evening before and hadn't been amused by the things I'd said. She'd looked as if she wanted to cry, but she was a mate, and stoical with it, and you didn't ask mates that sort of thing. Ma and Da had been miserable too, even more so than normal, but I'd assumed they were fed up with packing. The packing seemed to have started again. So, today, I avoided all of that, and after school had finished for the day, I went round to the pub. Miranda's ma was sobbing her heart out.

'What's the matter with her?' I asked Cath and Reg, who were sitting in the parlour, drinking whisky.

'Miranda's packed her bags and gone,' Cath informed me, filling her glass to the brim with spirits. 'Perks of the job,' she said, winking.

'I don't think Hannah would want you to do that.'

'It's Mrs Collenge to you,' said Cath, 'and if I'm right, the woman won't care. Seeing as she's lost her only daughter.'

'What do you mean?' I said, fearful.

'Because Ben's gone and done the same. His workshop's shut and where's the sign? I bet he removed it before he left.' She eyed me keenly.

'No,' I said, 'I don't believe it.' Miranda and Ben as a couple, yes, I'd noticed something had finally happened. But running away together, no. Miranda wasn't that sort of girl. And how could they have left me behind?

I don't know how I got through the evening. The pub had a lot more trade than normal, people came round to soak up the gossip, then went home indignant when they'd learnt nothing new. Hannah Collenge stayed out of the way. Reg and Cath were serving in the bar, but as they'd been drinking whisky all day, they were worse than useless. Besides, Cath was only used to ale.

The moment the pub closed down for the night, I grabbed a couple of tools from out back and hurried across to Blackberry Close. Then I hid in the yard until it was quiet.

Ben's workshop was all locked up, but being at school with a load of rogues had taught me things, some of them sometimes more than useful. I took out a file and prised the door open, just enough to weaken the lock, then a twist and a turn with a couple of tools and I was inside. Holding a large lamp, nicked from the pub.

I reckoned if there were clues to them leaving, I'd find them in here.

The workshop was cold, dank and creepy and missing Ben's presence and so was I. I swallowed hard and tried not to run. Maybe this was the time to grow up. I didn't much want to.

I cast the lamp around the room, the tools were in place, and neatly stacked, Ben was a stickler for that sort of thing. The coffin lids hung on the walls proudly, some of them seemed to sway in the dark. I took a deep breath. The place smelt odd, but I put that down to the work he did, although I can't say I'd smelt it before. I felt the smallest prickle of unease.

Next, I shone my lamp on the floor. Everything looked the same as normal, apart from a mark, I thought it was paint. The paint was a dark reddish-brown colour. *That's new*, I thought and ran my finger across the smear, it was almost dry. But when I sniffed, the smell was familiar. I jumped back quickly.

That's blood on the floor! Then I heard a rustle, and froze suddenly.

It's probably rats, I told myself. But the blood on the floor was something else. I knew I ought to get a policeman. But what if that meant trouble for Ben? I had to look further.

I looked around the room carefully. I couldn't see any more blood anywhere. Maybe Ben had cut himself, on a tool or something. I didn't believe it.

Then I noticed the door to the room. The room that led to the tunnel and the church. I remembered that room, I needed to check it.

Don't, said a voice, *you'll only regret it.* But I had to look, whatever I found. By now my mind was racing ahead, imagining all the worst that could happen. *It'll be alright,* I told myself. *Sure it will.*

I tried the door but it wouldn't open. Relief was followed by more apprehension, what was in there that it had to be locked? So I did what I always do when I can, I picked the lock. The door opened, released suddenly, and I fell backwards onto the floor. Onto the smear of almost dried blood. *Shit,* I thought.

The room that led to the tunnel was small. I moved the lamp around carefully, there was nothing to see, just a mug and some fags and an empty floor. But the smell was stronger.

I wasn't prepared to go down the tunnel, I'd thought about that and dismissed the idea. But I had to be sure I'd checked in here. I shone the lamp in all the corners. Then I saw the rags on the floor.

I picked them up to examine them closely. A couple of pieces were doused in blood and I flinched at the sight, both the rags and the blood and dropped them at once. But then the lamp flickered and I saw in my hands I'd held the proof. There was too much blood and the dress was Miranda's, the red satin one she'd worn to tempt Ben. Miranda's blood, all over my hands. And Ben's betrayal of love and friendship. I couldn't believe it. I stood in the dark and howled like a kid.

When time had passed and I'd cried myself out, and feeling slightly ashamed of myself, I thought a bit more.

I wondered where her body was hidden. It had to be Ben

who'd hidden Miranda, this was his workshop, why else would her blood be on his floor? Even if somebody else had killed her, like Wetherby Eisen, Ben must have known for the blood to be here. *It had to have been a man,* I thought, I doubted a woman could move a body, not down to the tunnel and all by herself.

So was she in the tunnel? I wondered. I wasn't going to look.

I knew I ought to fetch the police, for Miranda's sake, but she was dead and Ben was alive, although God knows where, and I didn't want him to suffer either, in spite of what I believed he'd done. I couldn't turn him over to them. I stared at his bench, at the now cold tea, and then at his jacket, hanging from a hook behind the door, and touched it lightly, feeling the fabric. Then I turned around and left the room.

The next morning, very early, I returned with a lock and a huge bag of nails and secured the door to the tiny room, hammering hard until it was sealed, locked and nailed up, so no-one else would see what I'd seen. I left the scraps of Miranda's dress, but covered them up with some leaves from the yard and a flower I stole from behind the bar. Its white petals were already drooping, but the white of the plant went well with the red. My job was done.

I emerged carefully onto the street, feeling weak and weighed down with guilt for letting Miranda's killer go free, and then, out of nowhere, I thought of Louise and the whole damn thing was just too much. So I wandered up towards the school, despite there being no classes today, just for something normal to do. The sun was shining and dogs were barking and wherever I looked people were laughing, or making a joke or a deal or two. But I wasn't laughing.

After hanging around for several hours I made my way back to Curdizan Low, and as I approached the alley's dark shadows, I saw a tall figure walking towards me. I smiled, slightly, in spite of it all. 'Alice,' I said.

101

Then – Thomas

Alice and I sat by the tenements, not the ones Louise had lived in, this was a block off Convent Court, but far enough from the pub to be safe. I wanted to be away from people and prying eyes, so we moved to the courtyard, next to the privies, to talk in private. Alice, it seemed, had a lot to say.

'I saw your friend Miranda recently.'

'Yes, I know. When she took you along the tunnel,' I said. Even hearing her name was hard.

'No, more recently, yesterday morning, very early, after midnight. She was in the alley by Curdizan church, with three other people.'

'No,' I said, 'that can't be right, Miranda's dead. It was dark Alice, you couldn't have seen her.'

'Of course I saw her, why does everyone think I'm stupid? She gave me this, to give to you.' She handed me a small brown boot.

'It's the one from the pub,' I exclaimed, surprised.

'She said it belonged to a girl called Louise. Miranda said the girl was your sister.'

'You what?' I said. 'Louise, my sister? You've got that wrong.'

'That's what she told me,' Alice said, sharply, looking annoyed. She also said Louise would come back, but she didn't sound sure.'

'Miranda's dead, I know, I've seen – don't ask me how, just, trust me, I know.'

'Alright, I won't. But she looked like flesh and blood to me. She wasn't a ghost, if that's what you're thinking.'

'I wasn't,' I said. 'Was there anything else?'

'She said she was sorry about the necklace. She felt she had to leave it with Tanya. She said she couldn't leave her with nothing.'

'Really?' I said. I didn't dare hope or even wonder. Was the body Tanya's instead? Maybe Tanya had stolen the goods and they'd used the dress to mop up the blood. But if it was Tanya, why had she died and who had killed her? What I was thinking wasn't much better, Miranda alive but someone had still killed Tanya Curtis. It must have been Ben.

'Are you sure that's it?' I said to Alice.

'She said to tell you she wasn't dead, just gone away to a different place. I think they were coming to my time and place, if you know what I mean. She said to tell you, she'd never forget you.'

'And I won't, her,' I said, choked up. I was glad Miranda was alive and not dead, but she was still lost, to me at least, and Louise was still missing, and Ben might still be Curtis's killer. All of the people I'd cared for were gone. I stared at Alice.

'You could go too,' said Alice to me then, 'to my time and place, if you want to. I've got the gift to take people through. Miranda has too.'

'Maybe,' I said, thinking it could be better and brighter and alive, much more exciting than living my life in this dark, grubby, world, without all my mates. But what about Louise? I'd been waiting and hoping for news forever, and now I knew more, but Louise was still missing, might never come back and if she did, I wouldn't be here. The friend I'd not known as a sister was gone. Along with the rest. I thought my heart would break right then.

'I once had a friend,' said Alice, suddenly, 'apart from you. He was younger than me and his name was Danny.'

'That's a pretty cool name for a lad,' I said. Alice just smiled.

'Danny was killed, he was hit by a car, and the man who was driving the car was a friend. Although he wasn't a friend of mine when it happened.'

'That's very sad,' I said, confused.

'You know what cars are, Tom, don't you?'

'Of course,' I said. *How dare she ask!* I'd seen a few on Scriveners Road, an amazing sight, they were going so fast. We all got out of their way, sharpish. 'I'm very sorry,' I told her, softly. 'About your friend. That must have been bad, to have had that happen.'

'It was,' she said. 'And Aleph, the friend who drove the car, he blamed himself, and my mother, Cressida, blamed herself, and I, also, blame myself, because I waved to Danny and he crossed the road and got knocked down. I didn't even get to say goodbye.'

'That's terrible, Alice,' I said sadly, and patted her shyly on the arm. 'That's so terrible.'

'But now I see,' she said, thoughtfully, 'it was just what happened, the cycle of life and death goes on. We all do our best, and sometimes, often, things can go wrong, and that's just how it was with Daniel. I miss Danny loads, and you'll miss Louise, especially now you know she's your sister, but life goes on, it has to, Tom. Trust me, it will.'

'Alright,' I said. 'I'll come back with you.'

'No, Tom, no, it's not with me. You can go there yes, but only for yourself.'

'I'll need some things,' I told her, thinking. 'And I want to say goodbye to them all. Without them even knowing I'm saying it.' Alice nodded.

'I'll give you till mid-afternoon,' she said.

Going back home to Ma and Da seemed almost unreal. I passed the pub, but didn't go in, I didn't want to see all the regulars, people I'd known for several years but wouldn't know soon. I didn't want to sense Miranda, feel her presence and know she was gone. It would be too sad.

When I reached home Ma was still chattering.

'Mary-Ann Parks and Wetherby Eisen, would you believe

it, the vicar's daughter? Mary-Ann's ma is so upset, you wouldn't believe.'

I would, I thought. *I really would.* My ma didn't seem like herself today. She loved to hear gossip, would soak up the scandal and share it all too, but today her reactions seemed rather subdued. *Maybe they're not leaving, after all*, I thought. Their dreams have been shattered and plans cancelled while everybody else is leaving instead. And then I remembered Tanya Curtis. Did anyone know?

I grabbed some things and stuffed them into an old canvas bag, which I put out back so they wouldn't see it and went to fetch my boots from the fire. I hardly ever wore my boots, Da had told me I couldn't have them but Ma had gone soft and bought me some once.

'Only for Sundays,' she'd told me, sternly, 'and maybe at Christmas.'

I bent down, to pick up the boots, and noticed the streak of red-brown on the hearth, it was much the same as I'd seen at Ben's. I did the same as I'd done before and rubbed a finger across the colour, it came away smudged and smelt like blood. The blood was dry but some flakes of dust had come off on my skin. My mother came in.

'Tanya?' I said, and watched as her face went pale with shock. My mother looked ill. She sat down in a chair.

'Was it Da?' I said, slowly, and my ma shook her head and looked regretful.

'No, it was me, and, truly Thomas, it was an accident, I didn't mean it. We'd had a struggle and Tanya fell over, she slipped on the hearthstone and banged her head. Then your da came home and between us we moved her, before she was seen.' She paused, breathed deeply. 'You've no idea how sorry I am.' She burst into tears.

'I'll leave the boots,' I said to her then. 'You can sell them on, after I've left and no-one will ever find the body. You've no need to worry.'

My ma looked up and stopped snivelling. 'That's not why

I'm crying, Thomas. I'm crying because I shouldn't have done it.'

'Like Louise?' I said, and this time I thought she really would faint, but instead she drew herself up a little.

'I loved Louise and I wanted to do what was right for her. There's no way your da would have let her come here.'

'No,' I said, 'I suppose he wouldn't. Assuming she wasn't his flesh and blood.' My mother coloured.

'I'm sorry Ma, I've got to go.'

'Got to go where? Because of this, you're leaving us.'

'No,' I said, 'not really, Ma. I just have to make a new start that's all. Now that all of my friends have gone.'

'So that's what you meant about selling the boots. You're not coming back.'

'No,' I told her. 'Probably not.'

I never loved my ma more than then. She didn't beg, or ask me to stay.

'Will you come and see us Thomas? When you're older?'

'Probably not, if I'm honest, Ma. Where I'm going is far away. Far too far to come back for visits.'

'Are you going with them, then, Thomas? Mary-Ann Parks and Wetherby Eisen?'

'Probably not,' I said sighing. 'I'm more than likely to be on my own. But I'll never forget you Ma, I promise.' Then I gave her a hug and hurried away, half-wishing then I'd never gone back. But at least I knew about Tanya now. The poor cow, she'd had a raw deal. Stuck in poverty's web like us, and not like me, with a chance to get out. I felt a sudden jolt of fear.

What if Alice didn't come back?

102

Now – Aleph

I rang Ginny, I knew I needed someone to talk to. But first I rang Cressida, she needed to know what had happened with Alice. I told her I'd been to see Martha's house and then I told her what Alice had said. That Alice believed she'd caused Daniel's death. By calling the boy across the road.

'And after she'd told me, she left the house and disappeared in a throng of tourists. I knew I'd never be able to find her.'

'You stupid man,' said Cressida, sharply. 'I truly wish you'd never been born.' She slammed down the phone.

I stood there shocked and worried for Alice, I was still clutching the phone in my hand. I knew I was done with keeping secrets and trying to keep everybody else happy. A child had gone missing, a vulnerable girl.

'So where is she now?' Guinevere asked me, when she turned up later, looking harassed. I'd dragged her away from a pile of work.

'Nobody knows,' I said, with a frown. 'I rang Cressida back, she's called the police.'

'Why aren't you out there, searching for Alice?'

'Martha's out looking and so is her husband. I gather they don't want me anywhere near. So Cressida said.'

'You sound very bitter.'

'I am,' I told her. 'Cressida knew where Martha had moved to, despite pretending she hadn't been told.'

'Never mind that, just think about Alice. At least she's talking to her mother again, and that's an improvement, and all thanks to you. The feelings she has are better off said.' Guinevere passed me a mug of tea.

'But now she's gone missing again, and she's troubled. And I've no idea where she might be.'

'You know you once told me she visited the past? Went walking through that tunnel with Miranda? If I was Alice, that's where I'd go, to visit my friends in their make-believe world.' I sighed, exasperated.

'It wasn't a make-believe world, Guinevere. Curdizan Low was a place that existed, but I can't go back, not even for Alice. I tried it once, just took the same route, but I ended up in a pile of rubble. It's a demolition site that's never improved. I think you need a guide to take you, Miranda, perhaps, or maybe Alice, but I can't do it, I never could. I'll give it a go, but I doubt it will work.'

'So, why don't we try something else, instead? Let's listen to your recording of ghosts.'

I played back the file of that second cold night, when I'd sat on the bench and waited for death. It felt like that was another life.

'I can't hear anything,' Guinevere said. She sounded disappointed.

'I can,' I told her. 'It's faint but it's there, there's at least one child, unhappy and sobbing. They're sounds of despair, not screams of terror. Somehow I never got that before.'

'Is it a boy or a girl? Could it be Alice?'

'I'm not really sure, I think it's a boy. Whoever it is, it's not Alice; if you remember, I've heard her before.' Ginny and I looked at each other.

'You'll have to do a reversal, Aleph. Maybe that will tell you something.'

The next day, I did a reversal and later that day Ginny came round. I'd rung Cressida, who'd spoken to me briefly, Alice was tragically still missing. Not a sight or sound of the girl anywhere, despite huge efforts by all concerned. *Could Ginny be right?* I wondered, pensively. *Could Alice be wandering around in the past?* The audio file was a welcome diversion.

'It's a boy sobbing,' I told Ginny, 'maybe it's Tom. He's crying and saying, "I'll miss you, Miranda." And then he says that "no-one will ever know you're down here. No-one will ever discover this room, I'll nail it up tight. I'll leave the jacket and everything else, they're not important. You're the one who's important, now. And now you're dead."'

I paused the recording and looked at Ginny. 'I can't believe Miranda's dead. It wasn't that long since I watched her walking along the street, with Alice in tow. You saw her too.' Guinevere nodded.

'Of course,' I said, 'she'd be dead now anyway, given that this was a century ago, but all the same it's still shocking. When I saw her, she was just a young woman.' I stared at Guinevere. 'What's the matter?'

'Haven't you realised what this means? My great-aunt Clara was right after all. It can't have been Mary-Ann Parks in the cellar, it must have been the girl, Miranda. Marianne will be so pleased when I tell her.'

'I still wish it wasn't Miranda.'

'Where were you when you made the recording?'

'Scriveners Road, in the courtyard. I sat on a bench and waited for ages. Nothing happened.'

'So what did you do that made a difference?'

'I wandered down to Curdizan Low. There's not much there, but the coaching inn is. I stood outside and listened for noises. That was where I heard him sobbing.'

'Tom,' said Ginny, 'it must have been Tom who found her body. What a terrible thing for a boy to face. It all fits, Aleph. There's something else I haven't told you.'

'What a surprise,' I said sourly. Guinevere smiled.

'Years ago, when the demolition started, some builders found a hidden room, in an old house on Blackberry Close. I'm betting that house was the coaching inn. You know the tunnel started there, that's probably how they moved the body. Whoever they were. And then, Tom sealed up the entrance.'

'You can't be sure it's the same building, or the same body.'

'Yes, I can. The boy we've just heard mentions a jacket, the builders found one too, hanging up. And I bet he mentions a mug of tea. They also found a mug on the bench. The tea, of course, had long since gone.'

'Yes,' I said. 'He mentions the tea. So the woman who died was the girl Miranda. I really wish it hadn't been her.' Then we heard the doorbell ring.

Ginny and I both went to the door. Alice was standing outside with a boy. They both looked like they'd been sleeping rough.

'Your mother's tearing her hair out, Alice,' Ginny said sharply. Alice ignored her.

'This is Tom,' she said to me. 'He needs a new home, he's not from round here.' I stared at them both, almost disbelieving.

It was strange meeting the lad at last, after I'd learnt so much about him. Where he'd come from didn't seem to matter. 'I'm sorry about Miranda,' I said. 'I'm so sorry.'

'You think she's dead?' said Alice, then. 'She's not, she's alive. And Ben is too, and Mary-Ann Parks. Really alive, like here and now. And Wetherby Eisen, more's the pity.' She wrinkled her nose.

'So who did Tom find in the coach house?' We were still all standing on the doorstep.

'Tanya Curtis, she knew my mother.'

'The local tart.' Alice grinned.

'Alice!' said Ginny. 'That's not very kind.'

'She's not,' said Tom, and laughed, loudly. 'She called me a wimp, before, for crying. For Louise,' he said, and his eyes went dim.

I turned to Alice. 'Your mum's frantic and everyone's searching. You mustn't go off on your own like that. It's not very fair.' But Alice shook her head.

'I'm not coming back,' she said, insistent. 'I only came here to introduce Tom.' And before I could grab her and drag her inside, she was off down the steps and around the corner, presumably running for Curdizan Low.

Damn, I thought. *Hell and damnation.*

I glanced at Tom, who looked bemused and rather bedraggled. 'Welcome to the twenty-first century, Tom.' I ushered him in.

While Ginny rang Cressida to tell her the latest, I went into the kitchen and made some more tea. Tom dumped his old canvas bag on the floor.

'You'll need some boots, or at least some shoes,' I said severely, glancing at his feet while I passed him his tea and a packet of biscuits. He gobbled them up.

'There's a boot up there,' he said, watchful, staring at the boot on the shelf, up above us.

'I found that boot in the cellar downstairs. There's only the one.'

'But I've got the other,' he said, grinning, rooting in his bag and pulling out a boot. Sure enough, it matched my boot, though the one in his hand looked smarter and newer.

And so it would, I told myself, *his boot hadn't been in a cellar for a century. More even.*

'What's up there with the boot?' asked Tom.

'It's a necklace,' I told him, suddenly wary. 'We found it in the narrow passage, that leads from the cellar to the tunnel proper. We think it belonged to Mary-Ann Parks. Or rather, to Tanya.'

'It belongs to Louise, and I bet that boot is hers as well, just like mine.' His voice wobbled. Ginny reappeared.

'Who's Louise?'

'Louise is my sister and also my friend. But she went away and never came back and now I'm here, I'll never see her, ever again. By now she'll be dead and gone forever.' He stared at us both, his eyes welling up. We waited, patiently.

'That necklace up there was meant for me, but I didn't get it. Miranda left it with Tanya instead.' He leapt from his chair and grabbed the beads from the top of the shelf, clearly determined to have them this time.

'You think the boots belonged to her?' Guinevere asked.

Tom nodded, he couldn't speak.

'Why don't you put them on the step outside? Then if she comes looking, she'll know you're in here.'

'I'll do that,' said Guinevere, quickly, giving me a look which said, *you're crazy*. But she did it anyway, for which I was grateful. Tom glanced around the kitchen, curious.

'This used to be a joinery workshop,' he told me, frowning. 'It's different, now, from how it was then. There used to be a door right there. He wandered over to the back of the room. It led straight into...'

'Curdizan churchyard,' I finished, smiling.

103

Then – Louise

Louise had been walking for hours, it seemed. The trams didn't go as far as the Hall, it was out in the country, miles from anywhere, more's the pity. Louise sighed and stopped by the hedge for another quick rest, she knew she had quite a bit further to go. It was dark and cold in the country lane, and back in Curdizan, the air would be thick with mist and menace. Out here, the damp seeped into her bones. Louise felt sad.

She'd left her place and with it, her prospects, but she'd had no choice, she'd been lonely there. I didn't belong at the Hall, she thought. *I'm a town dweller's child, my place is in Curdizan.* The Low or the High, wherever she had a friend like Tom. Being in service had chipped away at her untamed heart, but how would she live without a job? She thought again of Tom, briefly, she knew he'd be wondering where she was.

I didn't dare tell him the truth, she thought, *not with Pike using kids as workers.* If Pike had even guessed at her plans he'd have stopped all that and had her out cleaning, as quick as a flash. *At least I had a proper place, with food in my belly and somewhere to sleep. And gave it all up for a town,* she thought.

A town that was just a tenement room and a mother who'd failed to stay alive.

She remembered seeing her mother jump, fall five flights down, be shaken and tossed and land in a heap, with barely a sound or a strangled cry. It hardly seemed violent, not like the blood on the slaughterhouse floor, or the fights in the bars on a Saturday night. But blood or not, or sound or not, her mother had died, eventually, and there'd been no reason to stay anymore. Apart from Tom.

I'll go and see Tom straight away, Louise affirmed, *the moment I'm back. No, first I'll go and see Mary-Ann, and maybe she'll let me buy back my beads. And, perhaps there'll be some work I can do.*

Her thoughts were all on her blue necklace, she didn't even hear the horse ride up. Then she heard the clip of the hooves on the track and saw the shadow of the man behind her, and heard herself gasp.

The next thing she knew she was falling through space, the blow came down as if from a distance, and then felt nothing, apart from the night. The eternal black, that swallowed her up.

When Louise woke up she was on the ground, chilled with the cold, and her bones ached. The beautiful sight of the dawn approaching didn't help cheer her aching heart. Had she been fed and warm and safe, Louise would have loved the sight of the day. The sun sparkled and the dew glittered, but all she could think was how cold she was. And how her head ached from where she'd been hit.

She dragged herself to her feet, carefully, saddened to see she'd lost her possessions, such as they were. Damn the scoundrel!

Slowly the night came back to her mind, the man who'd pushed her, knocked her so hard she'd fallen to the ground, then stolen her cloak, and her bag and vanished. Her bag had contained nothing but clothes, and a little loose change, but she'd miss that change; because of the theft she had no cash for tea. Or a soft spicy bun to fill her up. It was hours since she had departed the Hall. *But at least I'm alive,* she said to herself.

Louise sighed, weary, wondering what she would face at Curdizan. But at least she'd have Tom.

It was just gone ten when she first saw the abbey, standing so tall as it always did, reminding her then, that people lived lives which were more blessed than hers. She stood on the street by the steps to the school, wondering whether to go inside. Then she remembered the door would be locked, as it always was after school had started. *I'd better go round the back,* she thought. She wandered into the joinery workshop. Jake looked up.

'I don't suppose you remember me?' Jake looked worried.

'Maybe I've seen you somewhere before, but this is the workshop, it's only for boys. Not that it matters so much today.' He looked around. 'Nobody's bothered to come in but me. And I'm only here to pick up my things.'

'I'm looking for Tom, have you seen him?'

'No, not recently.' Jake looked wary. 'Why don't you go up and have a look?'

'I used to go to this school,' said Louise. 'But then, I walked out, without any warning. Pike will go mad if he sees me in here. I will go upstairs, if I have to, for Tom. But I'd rather you did it, then no-one will care. I'll give you something, for your trouble, a couple of coppers.' Then she remembered she'd nothing to give.

'I can't,' said Jake, looking regretful. 'I'm not even meant to be in the building. But I had to come back and get my things.' He grabbed some wood and what looked like a cloth.

'I don't understand why you're leaving at all. Have they chucked you out for something? Tom always said you were one of the keen ones.' Jake hung his head.

'My aunt's disappeared, and she used to give Pike some money for schooling, so he's thrown me out as there's no more dosh. I don't think he thinks I'm worth a free place. So now, I'll have to go begging again.'

'Tanya Curtis is missing?' said Louise.

'More than likely dead, I reckon. My aunt's not the sort to vanish at will, she liked her creature comforts too much. She never took anything with her either.' He paused, looked hesitant. 'That's not all that's happened around here.'

'What?' said Louise, feeling uneasy.

'Several others have scarpered as well. Miranda Collenge from the Keepsake Arms and Ben Tencell, the undertaker. That's no surprise, they were sweet on each other. But Mary-

Ann Parks and Wetherby Eisen, that was a shock, although somebody told me they were engaged. That's why none of the lads have turned up. Most folk are pleased that Eisen's missing, nobody liked him, not one bit. But I'm fed up, I liked it here, not that it matters, now my aunt has gone.'

'Miranda's vanished?' Louise said slowly.

'Yes, and Tom, I didn't like to tell you, though it's only a rumour that's going around. People are saying they haven't seen him, he certainly isn't at the Keepsake Arms. I expect he went with Miranda and Ben. He had no reason to leave, otherwise. I reckon you should ask his ma, Carol. She's the person most likely to know.'

'No,' said Louise. 'That can't be true.' She stood there, stunned, as still as a stone.

'I'll go upstairs and check, if you like. I reckon it's worth it, if you're upset. But I'm telling you now, he won't be here.' Louise nodded and Jake dashed off.

Louise sat down on the tired old floor, and burst into tears. The tears soon turned into racking sobs. She'd given up what she'd won for this, a world without Tom.

When Jake came back and shook his head she got to her feet and ran outside and around to School Lane, glancing up high at the schoolhouse windows, looking in vain for Tom, her friend. She knew he wouldn't be there, of course. Then she turned around and ran back down the road to the churchyard, crying as if there was no tomorrow. Her sobs resounded around the streets. *He must have felt like this*, she thought, *when I went missing, without any warning.* But at least he'd had a job and a home. Unlike her.

A few minutes later, she dried her tears. *I have to talk to Carol Islip.* She dragged herself through the gate to the alley and then past the church hall to Pasenheuse Road. As she approached it she noticed a girl, standing on the pavement. She went to walk past, but the girl grabbed her arm.

'I bet you're Louise.'

'So what if I am? Let go of my arm.' Louise shrugged her

off, the girl talked posh, but Pasenheuse Road was posh for round here. Yet she looked like a scruff. 'What's it to you? I'm in a hurry.'

'If you're going to the pub to look for Tom, you're wasting your time. Tom isn't there.'

'How do you know?' Louise said, sharply, her heart was thumping as if it would burst.

'My name's Alice, I'm a friend of Tom's.'

'Oh, are you?' Louise said, feeling resentful. 'I bet you don't know where he is, all the same.'

'Of course I do, and I'll take you to him, he's staying at the house of a friend of mine. But you'll have to promise me something first.'

'I'm not in the mood for playing games.'

'This isn't a game, I swear it isn't. Don't you want to see Tom again?' Louise frowned and stared at Alice.

'You'd better not waste my time, Alice. What have I got to agree to then?'

'Once you're there, in this place with Tom, you can't come back to the Low, ever.'

'I've never heard anything so ridiculous,' Louise said sharply, pushing the younger girl out of the way. 'Leave me alone, you silly cow.' She started walking towards Croston.

'If you don't come now, you'll never see Tom, ever again.' Louise couldn't help it, she stopped abruptly and turned back to Alice. Her head was throbbing, really stinging. 'Don't even think about threatening me. You're just a kid.' She turned away, started walking again.

'Do what you like, but you'll live to regret it.' Alice's words had the ring of truth. Louise paused and looked at the girl. She no longer cared about living in the city, all she wanted right now was Tom.

'Very well, Alice, I'll do what you want, but if there's no Tom, you'll be the one who lives to regret it.'

Alice grinned, broadly. 'Like brother, like sister.'

'What did you say?' Louise said, stunned.

The girls stood in the narrow alley, right by the exit, peering out onto Scriveners Road. Louise was amazed, she couldn't believe it.

'Where have the church and the graveyard gone?'

'It's all been demolished,' Alice said coolly. 'All that's left is the old brick wall. The graves are still there, with their now flat headstones, see over there, by those three benches. Round the corner is Aleph's house, you can see the back of it there, look.'

'That's the schoolhouse,' Louise insisted.

'Was the schoolhouse,' Alice informed her. 'Now it's Aleph's and that's where Tom is.'

'How do I know you're telling the truth?'

'You don't,' said Alice, 'but you've seen all this, how things have changed and the church has gone. Only Curdizan Abbey is left. Just go and find out.'

'But if I go, I can't ever come back?'

'No,' said Alice, 'I can't be taking you back and forth, I have to find somewhere new to settle. But what you have got to stay here for? There, there's Tom and a brand new start. Why would I lie?'

Louise swallowed and stared at Alice. She'd left before, she could leave again. Especially for Tom.

She took a deep breath and left the passage, sensing Alice was right behind her. She walked up the road, which was almost the same, except that the trees seemed larger and lush. The courtyard was posh, the door to the workshop no longer existed. She'd only seen Jake minutes before and now he was gone. Gone as in dead. She turned the corner.

The school seemed much the same as before, if somewhat shabbier with flaking paintwork. She stared at the steps and saw the pair of boots at the top.

'They look like mine,' she said, amazed, glancing at Alice. Alice just smiled.

'They're very small.'

'They were my boots, from years ago. I always wondered

where they'd got to. Now I know.' She glanced at Alice. *What to do now?*

'You're not going to stand there all day, waiting?'

'Aren't you coming with me, then?'

'No,' said Alice, 'not today. There's somewhere else I have to be.' Then she turned away and was lost in the crowd.

Louise sighed and shook her head. *What a very strange girl.* Then, slowly, she climbed the steps of the schoolhouse.

Alice weaved her way through the alley, along the streets and down Croston, coming to stop on Dogleg Lane. She pushed at the door of the Keepsake Arms.

It was still early and apart from a lad who was sweeping the floor and an older man who was putting out ashtrays, the place seemed empty, deserted, almost. She saw the woman standing in the corner. The woman looked tired and worn with care.

'I'm guessing you're Miranda's mother. My name's Alice, I'm a friend of Miranda's.'

'Miranda's not here, she's gone away.'

'And Tom as well,' Alice observed.

'Quite a few people, altogether,' the woman said, slowly, taking a drag on her cigarette. 'It's all very odd, I have to say. I'm missing Miranda sorely, Alice. So, what can I do for you, young lady?'

'I was thinking you'd need a new barmaid now,' Alice informed her. The woman laughed, loudly, in spite of herself.

'You're a little too young for that, sweetheart.'

'I'm sure I'll get better, as I get older. And didn't Miranda start very young? I heard she used to stand on a box, to serve the ale, because she was small.'

'That's right, she did. But how in the world did you know that? You're not from round here.'

'Miranda told me,' Alice explained. 'And I can tell you more, if you'd like, like where she's gone, and who she's with.'

The woman's eyes grew wide with longing. 'Can you

431

Alice?' she said to her, slowly. 'Can you really?'

'Yes,' said Alice, 'though I can't bring them back, they've gone for good. But I can stay and help you out. Tom used to wash the glasses, didn't he?'

'He did, yes, he was good at it, too. I expect you could learn to be just like him.'

'I expect I could,' said Alice, smiling. 'I was told I was good at washing up. Before I left home.'

Alice could see the woman considering. She could hear the sounds of the men laughing, as they came in and ordered their pints. She could hear all their jokes and smell all the ales and imagine the songs of the Keepsake's singing nights. She imagined it all and waited to see. Mrs Collenge smiled at Alice.

'I've given your offer some thought, my dear, and I think I'll accept, just for the moment.' She threw a large cloth across to Alice.

'You can start with all these.'

Epilogue

In the late 1980s, Curdizan Low was mostly demolished. They kept the pub and a couple of smarter, larger houses, one of which once belonged to a merchant.

'All of it built on shoes,' said Dave, nodding at Jim and kicking some rubble out of the way.

'Aye, but he died too young to enjoy it.' Jim was a local history bore, his wife had started her family tree and that was where it began for him. Now he read that stuff all the time. They walked across the rubble slowly, stopping outside another house.

'I know you'll tell me what this was.'

'It used to be the old coach house once, where people would set off on their journeys, and after that it became a workshop.' Jim gave a smile.

'Bit of a wreck inside, isn't it?' They looked around the remains of the room, the rotten wood stacked up against the wall, some chisels and other tools still hanging up.

'Kind of creepy,' Dave agreed. 'I reckon a carpenter worked in here.'

'Or something else,' said Jim, grinning. 'Some of those lids look coffin-shaped. This was the local funeral home.'

'No,' said Dave, but he knew Jim was right, although given its age and the limited daylight, it was hard to be sure.

'What's in here?' said Jim, musing. He pushed on a door which seemed to be locked.

'We haven't got time to be messing around,' Dave said, sharply.

'Sure,' said Jim, 'but I want to have a look and then we'll go. I know it's probably only a cupboard. But all the same...'

'You're only bothered because there's a lock. Here, have

the torch, you'll need it in there.'

Jim took the torch and messed around with the lock for a while. It finally gave way. Then he shoved on the door and went inside, with Dave following, vaguely curious. They studied the room in the flickering light.

'It is a room,' breathed Jim, slowly. 'Not just a cupboard.' The tiny space had a wooden bench and on the bench was an old grey mug. Next to the mug was an empty packet, Dave suspected it might have held fags.

'Well, I'll be damned,' he said, shortly, swivelling round towards the door. He noticed something hanging behind it and reached out a hand, to touch some cloth.

'It's a jacket,' he said to Jim, behind him, feeling the wool, all shabby and worn. 'A bloke's jacket.'

Jim nodded and grinned at his mate. 'You know what I reckon?'

'No,' said Dave, for once not amused, but caught up in the web of the past, there in the room.

'It's like a bloke stepped out of his life, just for a moment, and never came back. Maybe to go to war or something.' Dave considered.

'Yeah, perhaps, or maybe,' he said, feeling the sense of something other, something he didn't quite understand, 'maybe the bloke's still alive somewhere and living a very different life.'

'He'd be dead by now,' said Jim, laughing. 'Well dead, mate, for decades, I'm sure.'

'Maybe,' said Dave as they closed the door and went on their way up Blackberry Close. 'Or maybe he isn't.'

ACKNOWLEDGEMENTS

Thanks are due to Pat G Nightingale for her insightful information on the Inner Voice of Truth and Reverse Speech – a fascinating topic. I am also indebted to my marvellous readers and proofreaders, Jann Tracy and Sarah Davies, whose valuable comments and eagle eyes have helped me avoid numerous errors.

Thanks also to James Allwright, who yet again has provided an evocative cover.

I'd also like to add my thanks and appreciation to David Gaughran, Guido Henkel and Mark Coker whose works on publishing and formatting, I couldn't have managed without. Thanks guys!

Lastly, my appreciation goes to the City of York (UK), and its inhabitants, past and present. Curdizan, in which this novel is set, is a fictional city, but draws for its essence on historic York. Who's not to say that if you wander around York in the evening, you might not come across Alice and Thomas...

RESOURCES AND FURTHER READING

As part of the research for this novel, I read numerous books on historic York, especially those covering the late nineteenth and early twentieth centuries. Those listed below were amongst the most useful, and gave me a real flavour of life at the time.

- Hall, R (2004) Bedern Hall and the Vicars Choral of York Minster, York Archaeological Trust (Exploring York, 1).
- Knight, C B (1944) A History of the City of York, 2nd ed. Herald Printing Works.
- Rowntree, B Seebohm (1903) Poverty: a study of town life, new ed. Macmillan.
- Webster, A E (2006) Looking Back at Goodramgate & Kings Square York, Reeder Publications.
- Wilson, V (2007) Rich in All but Money: life in Hungate 1900-1938, rev. ed., York Archaeological Trust (Oral History Series, 1).

ABOUT THE AUTHOR

Ellie Stevenson is also the author of *Ship of Haunts: the other Titanic story*, where ghosts, ships and child migration intermingle and *Watching Charlotte Brontë Die*, a collection of surreal, scary and sometimes spooky short stories.

She has also written 70+ articles for magazines and websites on history, careers, travel and the arts.

Ellie is a member of the Alliance of Independent Authors and is currently working on her third novel, fuelled by inspiration, determination and plenty of coffee.

Visit her at:

Blog: http://elliestevenson.wordpress.com
Facebook: http://www.facebook.com/Stevensonauthor
Twitter: http://twitter.com/Stevensonauthor
Pinterest: http://www.pinterest.com/stevensonauthor

Want to read more of this author's work?

Read two extracts in the following pages.

Ship of Haunts: the other Titanic story (extract)

1

Carrin's Story – 2012

Not every girl gets stalked by a ghost. Or haunted by a ship.

The ghost was called Lily but the ship came first. It always did. The ship was Titanic. I drowned on that ship.

I was up on the deck, right at the top, running and running, as fast as I could, towards the stern. Away from the water, around my feet. I wasn't alone.

And though I ran fast, as fast as I could, the stern rose up, out of the water, and we rose with it, slipping and sliding on a frigid deck. Not everyone made it.

I grabbed for a railing and held on tight, feeling the steel dig into my skin. I knew it was hopeless. Many more people did just the same. And then the stern shifted, twisted and turned, a corkscrew ride, high in the air. We held our place, just for a second. Then down she fell, faster and faster, heading for the bottom, where no-one ever goes. And then I fell off.

My arms flailed and I let out a scream, one more voice, in amongst the rest.

'I'm going to die. I'm going to die.'

And die is exactly what I did.

But unlike the others, I had help.

I said there was a ghost and her name was Lily. Not that I knew she was called Lily to begin with, she was just a voice, driving me crazy.

I first met Lily in 1912, when I lived before. Now you know it. I *am* crazy.

Ellie Stevenson

Well maybe you're right, but why don't you ask me where we met?

We met on Titanic, which sank in the night on her maiden voyage, in 1912.

Such a beautiful ship, sailing the ocean, and then – nothing.

So many died – fifteen hundred people, it was tragedy, failure, on dozens of counts.

And the last sentence, very important.

I was there.

2

Lily's Story – 1911

I was proud to be called a Yorkshire girl, Yorkshire had made me what I was. I never wanted to leave the north. But since I had...

When Mother gave me the crumpled letter I knew it was bad. Give it to Maddy, is what she said. Maddy will help. I didn't care. I knew it was bad, without the letter, her white, pinched face and the constant cough. I opened the letter. Just as I thought.

Lucie and I had to go south. To a place called Southampton.

Three days later, my sister emerged from Mother's bedroom. Her face was pale, as pale as a ghost. 'Mother's gone,' she said to me sadly. 'What will we do?'

I pulled the letter out of my pocket. 'We're off to Southampton, to stay with our aunt, Madeleine Rawlins. Mother arranged it.' Lucie blinked.

Lucie was distant, dark and plump, not a bit like me, although we were sisters. I was tall and fair, with thin skinny bones and flyaway hair. Lucie was pretty, I had to protect her. I thought Southampton would keep us safe, keep the old wolf away from the door. How wrong can you be?

Aunt Maddy's house was a total shock. We'd lived in a farmhouse, out in the fields, in a place called Linsit. Linsit was vast, with moors and the cliffs, and the Bay below us, with us in between. We were renting a farm and managing somehow, then Mother died. Aunt Maddy's house was completely different, right in the town, it was tall and thin, just like her. She didn't seem all that pleased to see us.

'So you're Lucie?' she said to my sister, her cold eyes sharp.

Lucie just stood there, silent, as always. Maddy was dark, like Lucie was dark, but Madeleine Rawlins' face was cold. She was watchful and wary and didn't look like my mother at all. I didn't warm to this woman one bit. But I had to try.

'Good to meet you at last, Aunt Maddy,' I said to her, taking her hand. She didn't bother to look my way.

'I'm not your aunt,' she insisted sharply, looking at Lucie. 'I'm far too young to be anyone's aunt.' It was true she was, being barely thirty, and now expecting a child of her own. But she *was* my aunt, my mother's sister. I also thought she was Lucie's aunt. My mistake.

Her man, Joss Rawlins, who she called her husband, when he wasn't, had just got a job. He was a stoker by trade, he worked on the ships, shovelling coal. Or at least, he had, until the coal strike started. No-one had worked on the ships in months, because of the strike. For a place like Southampton, which lived by its docks, the strike was bad news. And it made Joss restless, hungry for change.

I knew how he felt, I was restless too, I wanted a life, a world full of colour, not grey, grimy streets and second-hand clothes. I had my adventures, stealing mostly, we needed the food, that was my excuse. The truth was, I loved the excitement. I also stole things I could pawn later.

But a new dawn was coming, a ship called Titanic, and Joss signed up, Aunt Maddy couldn't stop him. I could see it in his eyes, he was eager to leave, his woman expecting and two teenage girls who weren't his own. It was then I had my fatal idea.

I thought it would give us a much better future, Lucie and me. I also thought it would free up Mad.

That was my third and final mistake.

To be continued...

Want to read more of this novel?

Ship of Haunts: the other Titanic story is available both in print and as an ebook.

See Amazon for details. (authl.it/B007SPGR98)

Watching Charlotte Brontë Die: and other surreal stories

Extract from Watching Charlotte Brontë Die (the story)

We'd been in the flat a year when it happened.

The night had been cold, and extremely wet. I was sitting in my chair, over by the window.

My wife was out working, she usually was. It was then that I heard it, an enormous crash, a screech and a thud, followed by silence. Someone's life, played out on the pavement. It wasn't the first time our street had done that, claimed a victim, with its deadly camber, its rain-stroked curve. The road was treacherous, sometimes lethal.

I leapt from my chair and ran to the window. She was lying there, in the middle of the tarmac, broken, damaged, her head to one side. She was calm and quiet and didn't move, and the bike beside her was bent out of shape. My heart stopped beating. It was Charlotte Brontë.

And it looked to me as if she was dead.

I dressed quickly, with trembling fingers, opened the door and ran down the stairs. The street would be empty, it was access only, apart from the tourists. There were no tourists on the street that night. I opened the door that led to outside and looked to the right, I knew the woman would be just around the bend. I rounded it quickly, as fast as I could. There was nobody there.

I blinked sharply and looked again, in case I'd missed her. I saw the rain, it was heavier now, streaming down gutters, flooding the road. I saw the light on an empty can, a broken bottle, remains of a toy. But that was all. No bike wheels spinning high in the air, no ghastly corpse, or crumpled victim propped against a wall. The street was damp and devoid of life, but also of death. I watched the water running away. All I

445

could think was one small thought. I hadn't known Charlotte could ride a bike.

It wasn't the first time I'd seen her.

My wife has a job at the local uni, teaching English, she loves all things Brontë. That's how we met, at a Brontë conference, in West Yorkshire. I married my wife because I love her, but also because she looks like Charlotte. I should feel guilty, but I don't, not at all. I'm privately pleased and secretly proud, as if I've discovered a hidden treasure. Perhaps I have.

Charlotte Brontë, born again.

My skills and training are different from my wife's. *I'm* not a teacher, I'm a writer's researcher, but that's alright, I love my work. I study theology as well as the Brontës, ferret out the facts from the archives. And I love the place where I find those facts, a cathedral library, and that's the place where I first saw Charlotte. Not in one of the first editions, but there in person, right by the shelves.

I was up in the gallery, quietly working. Dozens of volumes piled up high. They were all so beautiful, all so original, it's a wonder I did any work at all. I was taking a tract from the nearest shelf when I heard a noise and looked right down to the room below and there she was, right beneath me, and all lit up from the stained glass windows. I caught my breath. She was just like the photos, quaint and homely with a small, shy smile and rosebud lips. But her eyes were different, cool and piercing and quite unlike the rest of her look. Even though we were far apart, and I was standing up in the gallery, I could see those eyes, staring right through me. I watched and waited, noticed her beckon. But she still didn't speak.

Forgetting where I was, I walked over to the railing. I forgot that the railing, normally solid and made of cast iron, had been replaced by a tape for repairs. Nobody ever came up here. All there was between me and a fall, a terrible drop,

CPSIA information can be obtained at www.ICGtesting.com
Printed in the USA
BVOW03s1410090215

386975BV00003B/78/P

maybe death, was a thin strip of tape, not even taut. I was seconds away from the worst that could happen. I stopped suddenly, looked down at the floor. Miss Brontë had gone. I was safe, for the moment.

But she always came back.

A few weeks later, I was in the library, just for a change. The rain poured down on an autumn day. It was normally dark, the building was old, but today felt different, colder somehow. I shivered in the chill, caught in the alcove by the spiral staircase. The room I was in was called the Cage, it was small and narrow with a strange metal door, which looked more like a gate. Somewhat reminiscent of an old-fashioned lift in a French hotel. I was looking for a book but couldn't find it, was thinking I'd have to go upstairs and visit the gallery once again. I wasn't keen. I peered up the staircase and there was Charlotte, sitting at the top.

Her dark brown dress looked very real and so did she, she was reading a book. I wanted to touch her, stretch out a hand, but I thought if I did, she'd vanish like mist. So I smiled instead.

She ignored me completely.

Unable to resist, I walked towards her, and as I moved closer, the book she was reading slid out of her hands and fell to the floor. A cloud of dust filled my vision. When I could see, Miss Brontë had gone. I picked up the book.

It wasn't like any I'd seen before.

To be continued...

Want to read more of this story or the others in ' collection of spooky and surreal tales?

Watching Charlotte Bronte Die: and other surreal stories is ava both in print and as an ebook.

See Amazon for details. (authl.it/B00AZYXASU)